LAST VOYAGE FIRST

a Novel by

Joseph Halsted

Note: All characters portrayed in this work are purely fictional creations of the author, except for noted historical figures, illustrated pursuant to published historical reference.

PROLOGUE

It was born 980 miles east of Caracas, a swirling vortex of wind-blown rain. Within 30 hours it reached tropical storm intensity and was named Carrie, the third named storm of the year. Three days later she had grown to a category 3 hurricane, and was churning through the Caribbean, wreaking havoc on the southern coast of Cuba. As she reached Cancun she had grown to a massive category 5, tearing into the resort hotels and obliterating the thatched-roof beach bars. A large low pressure front turned Carrie north, then north-east; residents of the Gulf Coast from Houston to Tampa were boarding-up windows and storing gasoline. The front turned her more to the east, bearing the enormous hurricane directly towards the sleepy retirement community of Naples, Florida.

The light gold Cessna Citation 414A with the blue logo of *Shaw Industries* approached Hilton Head Airport at noon. It flared and made a perfect touchdown on the hot tarmac, then taxied through the blazing sunshine to stop in front of the new full service terminal.

The captain, former Navy flyer Jim Cox, unfastened his safety belts and turned to his two passengers quipping, "Bloody hot out there. It's ninty-six degrees and the humidity is over ninety too. You two will find a cold drink inside while I the plane refueled."

He passed between his passengers and opened the door, dropping the aluminum steps.

He then watched David Saunders, a young man in this twenties, rise out of his seat and, stooping his slender six one inch foot height, crab back to the exit. Jim liked this guy with his clean features, deep brown eyes, and a mouth that seemed to always hold a secret smile.

David said, over his shoulder, "Come on Connie, we both can use a stretch."

Connie Shaw stood up from her seat to her full five foot two inch height, shook her short dark red hair and stretched her arms over her head. Jim had to work to keep himself from ogling at this beautiful young woman, his boss' daughter. She had a perfect firm shape with a narrow waist, slender hips and a small but perfectly proportioned chest topped with a heart-shaped face. Her eyes were bright blue under delicate auburn brows; yet the set of her chin and her direct mannerism didn't encourage approach.

She joined David, her fiance', at the bottom of the steps and the extremely hansome young pair walked hand-in-hand through the heat into the terminal. Jim had to focus away from viewing her small white shorts as she walked.

An hour later they were airborn again.

"Weather's terrible ahead," Jim spoke through the cabin speaker. "Hurricane is gonna cross Florida, leading bands probably getting to SheltAir just as we do. Commercial flights into Fort Lauderdale are being diverted. Perhaps we should drop down in Jacksonville and wait it out?"

Connie looked at David and shook her head.

"Jim," David spoke loudly enough to be heard, "if it dangerous, then we can divert if necessary, but if it's just bumpy and rough we really need to get there. Connie's Dad is expecting us and he may want to scoot ahead of the storm".

"Okay, we'll go for it. We've enough fuel to double back if we need to."

An hour later at 10,000 feet, with Florida's east coast white sandy beaches hidden in dark clouds under the Citation's whirling propellers, the bottom dropped out and the plane fell over 3,000 feet. It shuddered and dipped a wing nearly vertical.

Jake Shaw, dripping wet in his cut-off jeans and nothing else, strode to the front of the main salon of his ketch rigged sixty-eight foot yacht and flipped on the TV built into the bulkhead just in time to hear the talking head on the weather channel continue speaking with yet another report on Hurricane Carrie.

Jake had just turned 46, although he looked far younger. At over six feet, he was tall and lean with a sailor's ropy upper body. His brown hair over bright blue eyes was kept "military short" since he worked with Admirals in the Pentagon on a daily basis. His company, in his family for many generations, designed and built specialty boats and small ships for the Navy and Coast Guard.

The reporter was saying, "This massive category five storm has just made landfall on Naples. It packs winds in excess of 150 miles per hour at the eye-wall with hurricane-force winds extending over 200 miles from the center. It is moving at 18 miles per hour and is expected to cross south Florida in hours, exiting to the Atlantic"

He switched off the TV and ran his hands through his short hair. His fingers ran across a bruise where the heavy aluminum support for the dodger, the canvas covering over the cockpit (wheel station), had fallen on his head as he'd removed the material to keep it safe from the storm. He then looked ruefully at his hands. On his right hand there was a painful blood blister between his thumb and forefinger where the clew from the mainsail had pinched him badly when he'd removed and packed away that sail today. The fingernail on his left thumb was wrapped in a Band-Aid where a stubborn shackle on the tack of flying Genoa had resisted his efforts to break it loose., It had almost torn the nail completely off.

Jake smiled at his minor injuries knowing it would have gone better if he'd had a helper, or less wind to fight.

He had arrived at Pier 66 in Ft. Lauderdale the day before yesterday, returning with two Navy captains from a sea demonstration of his new assault craft. *Shaw Industries'* new fourteen foot semi-inflatable speedboat was designed to silently transport Navy SEAL Teams at over 40 knots. This first sample of the boat was painted to match the bottle-green of the hull of his yacht. It was hanging in the davits at the stern. The unique small boat, designed by *Shaw*, featured a four-cylinder inboard engine made of a special alloy which weighed less than forty pounds and was sealed in a sound box. Powered by a jet out-drive, the craft could carry up to an eight-man SEAL Team in almost total silence.

The Navy buyers had been impressed, and Jake looked forward to an order for hundreds of these boats.

After the Navy captains departed from Homestead Field in their Navy Lear, Jake spent the rest of the day re-provisioning his yacht for his next trip and topping off the fuel and water. He'd been looking forward to a day of rest when, yesterday morning, the hurricane had turned to the East.

Looking at his Weather Fax printout, his first instinct had been to cast off and sail north in the Gulf Stream turning into the Atlantic around Walker's Cay, where he could safely avoid the approaching storm. *Anne Marie,* his 68 foot ketch, was rigged for single-handed sailing even including electrically powered winches to trim the large sails.

No, he'd quickly decided that he couldn't run safely from the storm and sail happily north to his waterfront home in Deerford, Connecticut. He would instead have to wait here in Fort Lauderdale to pick up his daughter, Connie. She had just graduated with a degree in veterinary medicine, and was arriving in his corporate plane with her fiancé, David.

He thought hard about where in Florida's Inland Waterway his 22 ton ketch might be safe from a hurricane? Then he remembered his friends Dave and Shirley Sheppard, whose house had 200 feet of frontage on a deep but very narrow canal just north of downtown, close to Lighthouse Point. It would be perfect. He punched Dave's number up in his cell.

"Sure, Jake," Dave had quickly replied to Jakes query, "Place is yours. Shirley and I are anchored in Newport on our boat so the dock is empty. In fact, my neighbor across the canal is with us in his boat, so their dock is empty too. Let me know if the house is standing after the blow."

So, this morning Jake awoke with his boat tied in Dave's slip behind the house. But David's small floating dock would never hold *Anne Marie* in a category five.

Jake had spent the day preparing his ketch for the worst.

First he'd launched his new navy sample tender, the demo-inflatable, and with it had dragged one of the two heavy anchor chains across the canal, shackling it to a huge old palm tree. The other anchor chain was then dragged to cement piling at the corner of Dave's yard and shackled there. It had taken most of the morning to get the yacht properly centered in the middle of the small canal, tied off with eight large chains and ropes. And, after that, he had to remove all the sails and loose gear above decks.

The genoa jib came down first as the initial bands of wind and rain began to hit. It had to be unrolled from its self-furling, then dragged to the deck and folded. As it flapped in the growing wind, the clew smacked into Jake's hand, ripping his thumb nail; still he fought it into a tied-up roll and stuffed it below into the sail locker. After that came the staysail, which was easy. Next was the huge mainsail made of heavy, unyielding Dacron and weighing over 300 pounds; his hand had been caught in a sail slide as he yanked the huge sail from the mast. It was all his tired body could do to get that massive sail likewise stuffed below to the sail locker. The last sail to come off was the mizzen, thankfully smaller than the mainsail.

As he stood in the salon dripping on the deck and watching the storm approach Naples on his TV screen he was confident that his small ship would now be safe through the coming hurricane.

'Damn', he thought, *'where are the kids?'*

Connie and David had exactly the same hair and skin coloring. Both were fair-skinned and both were redheads. Neither could be comfortable in the tropical sunshine for long. Were David not so lean and tall while Connie was short and compact they could be taken for siblings. And, both of them loved ocean sailing on this, his hand-designed *Anne Marie*. Together they were really good at it too.

Jake was worried about them. His pilot should have called-in hours ago.

He thought for a moment about his soon-to-be son in law. David was an interesting young man from somewhat of a mysterious and reclusive family. He and Connie had met at the Edgartown Yacht Club in Martha's Vineyard seven years ago, and had been inseparable since. The Saunders family, David's parents, were also descended from a long line of Americans, and the family was apparently very wealthy. But they were also very conservative. Their ancestors, reaching to the early 1800's, had made a successive number of amazingly fortunate land and mineral rights acquisitions. Still, David had put himself through MIT on academic scholarship, earning a Doctorate in Engineering at only 24 years old.

Jake sucked on his sore blood blister. He dropped his wet cutoffs to the deck and yanked a fresh dry pair out of a drawer. Pulling them on followed by a dry t-shirt, he weaved forward in the yacht as the strengthening wind again heaved the boat over to one side.

"Damn," he muttered to himself again, "still no sign of them."

His cell phone chirped.

"Hi Dad, we're almost there", Connie said. "It was a scarey last ten minutes on the plane, but Jim's a terrific pilot. Couldn't get a cab at SheltAir so Jim borrowed a car. Are you at Pier 66?"

"Wphew, I was getting worried about you two." Jake replied into the phone. "No, I've moved ten miles up the ditch to Dave and Shirley's place, remember it?"

"Sure Dad. We'll be there soon", she rung off.

Another strong gust heeled the ketch again. Jake forgot his minor pains and dashed up the hatch to the center cockpit, now open to the weather with all the canvas coverings safely stowed below. Stepping out of the hatch he flinched as the battering raindrops stung his cheeks. The wind was already howling from the south, leaning the boat over at each gust. Jake walked carefully forward, stepping over two spring lines tied to the main mast, and inspecting the scope on the two anchor chains riding through the brass rollers in the bowsprit. He then darted back to the main mast, taking shelter in its lea for a moment before dashing along the deck to the raised center cockpit. In moments he was soaking wet again. Still, he had all the lines properly adjusted to ride out the storm safely in the center of the canal.

He had left only one final adjustment, one rope that pulled the stern of the small ship closely to Charlie's dock. It was there so the arriving couple could get aboard.

"Hey Dad," he heard tossed across the wind.

He saw his short redhead girl in a yellow rain-jacket lurch with the wind around the corner of Charlie's house. She was dragging a large duffle. Just behind her a tall slim young man with the same color hair was shouldering two more stuffed duffels.

They waved.

David dashed back to the stern pulpit, tied close to a piling. The youths hand-in-hand crabbed gingerly down the narrow finger pier. Jake grabbed Connie's duffle as she swung it to him, then he grabbed her arm and pulled her up to the deck. Moments later David tossed his two bags over the rail and pulled himself aboard.

Jake had to yell above the increasing wind to be heard, "toss your stuff below and help me get her back in the center of the ditch."

He then slacked off the one tight stern line until it matched the tension of it's twin while David and Connie took up matching slack on the other side. They then readjusted the spring lines and finally descended, soaking wet, to the dry warmth in the cabin below.

An hour later the full fury of the storm blasted upon them.

The ketch heeled over to almost to 45 degrees, pushed by the enormous south winds against her bare masts. The howling of the rigging made it hard to hear each other. The television flickered, dimmed, and the picture went to snow.

Jake laconically rose from his arm chair at the Nav Station, marked the page in his book and popped his head out of the main hatch. He wanted to check the mooring lines, but he could barely see ten feet in the flying spume. He ducked back inside and slammed the hatch closed.

Periodically they could hear thuds and crashing from the over their heads as branches and other debris carried by the wind smashed into the hull and blew across the deck.

"What happens if the lines break?" David shouted into Jake's ear.

"Worst case, we crash through the pilings into the cement canal walls. Let's hope that doesn't happen. I think we'll be okay though; all the lines are doubled and nothing has parted yet."

For another two hours both Connie and David huddled together on the couch in the salon watching the wind gage and listening to the local AM radio station as the storm crashed around them. Meanwhile, Jake was lying back on cushions buried in an old "Hornblower" novel. Occasionally they would hear the large bang of an electrical transformer ashore shorting out, throwing off sparks and blue flashes.

Suddenly, all the lights ashore went out.

Then the wind and rain sharply stopped.

The three of them opened the hatch and went up on deck. A moment later the setting sun came out. Everything became very quiet; they could hear only the muted thrum of the on-board generator.

"What?" queried David.

"Eye wall. Let's check for damage; we should have at least twenty minutes," replied Jake, tossing a slab of roofing shingle from a nearby house into the flotsam-filled water.

The ketch sat in the millpond-calm canal, which was totally covered in vegetation and driftwood from the neighboring yards. There were three or four palm trees upended ahead of them, the leafy tops hanging over the cement breakwaters of the canal. A large gas grille had gone through a french door at Dave's neighbors, and all the formerly perfect yards were covered in debris.

"Check all the lines and the chafe, especially on the starboard side", Jake instructed. "The back wall of the eye will hit from the north."

The three of them readjusted the heavy ropes holding *Anne Marie* in the center of the canal. Just as they were finishing they heard a roaring sound, similar to an approaching freight train.

"Down below! Here comes the back wall," shouted Jake.

Jake had just settled back with his book when, with a shriek, the wind and rain again blasted the yacht, again leaning her sharply over in the other direction.

"What does the anemometer say?" Jake asked Connie.

She dashed to the Navigation Station and peered at the wind speed gage.

"WOW, it's steady at 120 and, WOW, it just jumped to almost 145!" she exclaimed.

Minutes later the rear end of the large ketch slammed down towards the water, and the boat heeled past fifty degrees.

X

"What the hell!" Jake barked.

He jumped up from his book and slid open the hatch. The wind almost blew him back into the boat, crunching the side of his head against the varnished teak combing.

He shook his head, "Can't go out there."

And as he dashed to the aft cabin, his stateroom with windows on both sides, the boat rose to a level position. Soon the three of them were peering out the deckhouse windows in Jake's stateroom to see a white motorboat with two huge outboard motors piled up on the canal wall between them and Charlie's house.

"Damned thing must have blown right across our stern lines. Hope they'll hold now," Jake muttered.

An hour later the storm had almost completely passed. Connie and David, both excellent cooks, offered to make dinner while Jake checked the mooring lines to make sure they were secure for the night. As they were sitting down to a meal of roast duck a l'orange, the television came back on.

They ate in silence, looking at the reporting of the damage left ashore by Hurricane Carrie.

Jake's cellular rang. He looked at the number displayed and thumbed it on.

"Hi Martha," he said to his wife, "You don't need to ask. Of course we're all just fine."

He listened for long minutes, and then he replied, "Yes, dear, I'll tell Connie you called. We'll be sailing north first thing in the morning, so we'll be out of cell contact for a few days. I'll call soon as we get cell service in New York, should be four to five days."

Then they all went to bed. It had been a long day.

Early the next morning, long before the young couple stirred, Jake carefully looked over his boat finding nothing damaged save a minor scratch from the half-sunk fishing boat. He hauled in the mooring lines, started the big diesel and motored gently out of the canal. He truly appreciated the strength of the aluminum ketch he had designed and built.

Anne Marie was constructed with a reinforced aluminum hull, wide of beam and with a cutter rigged ketch sail plan. All halyards and sheets were designed to run aft to the cockpit, allowing a good sailor to handle her alone, assisted by several cleverly located electric powered self-tailing winches. Her hull below the waterline was a modified modern ocean racer's fin keel affording an unusual turn of speed under sail while maintaining good stability.

Below decks she had a large stateroom aft with its own skylight and ladder topside. Under the center cockpit was a spacious engine room, and amidships was a roomy salon which doubled as charthouse, galley, and living area under a partially raised deckhouse. Below the foremast she had two snug cabins with an adjoining head. The crew's quarters and the sail locker were in the forepeak.

On the port side of the engine room the yacht had a large locked equipment hold which held an impressive array of salvage equipment, two inflatable Zodiac boats, two outboard motors, and diving gear. Well hidden, under the deck, Jake had concealed a weapons locker "just in case." Bill, his cautious son, had given him a piece of his mind when Jake told him what he had down there, but Jake had simply made a great buy when the ban on automatic weapons went into effect.

In any marina, *Anne Marie* usually drew admiring glances with her dark green topsides, varnished spruce masts and scrubbed teak decks. She was indeed a capable world cruiser with excellent marine radar, bottom mapping sonar, computerized GPS system and other navigational aids normally used by far larger commercial vessels.

An hour after Jake had left the canal *Anne Marie* passed through the breakwater at Port Everglades. As the ketch rose to the first of the large remaining swells from the storm Connie's head popped up the hatch.

"As soon as you and David can get the canvas back on the masts we can sail. It'll be a lot faster. Smoother too," Jake said to her.

"Okay, Dad. Nothing changes. Work before breakfast, as usual, huh?"

He smiled, "Just give me a genoa and mainsail to start. We'll get the rest up later."

Later that morning, after all the sails were up and drawing, *Anne Marie* scooted northwards at over ten knots.

Jake quipped, "If the weather holds as National Weather Service advises we'll clear Sandy Hook in less than six days and have you home a week prior to your big event!"

On the evening of the third day though, as the sun was setting, the wind began to increase. It looked as if the sea, as it will, had other thoughts! Jake didn't like the look of the sky. He checked the Weather fax and the National Weather Service broadcast, and then appeared on deck with a more somber than usual expression.

"Another damned Hurricane is hooking up from the South; I should have checked the weather more closely last night. This one is already named for you, David. It was expected to pass into the Gulf but it's turned into a fish storm and veered north," he stated.

"We may be in for a blow. What say we bear west and run up the Inland Waterway from the Chesapeake?"

"Dad, aren't we well ahead of it? If it's just gonna get wet and a bit rough why not sail through the outer bands?" suggested Connie. "David and I don't want to be late for our own wedding, and we'll have to be able to handle rough weather anyway. Besides, David's mom would kill us all if we aren't there at least a few days before the Rehearsal."

"Really, Jake," quipped David, "GPS shows us only 566 miles from Sandy Hook; let's go for it. We can be at your stone pier by Saturday noon if we just go on."

Jake reluctantly agreed.

By the next morning he knew his instincts had been right, but it was too late.

The wind had veered more to the west and was gusting over forty knots. *Anne Marie* was slogging to windward into twenty foot swells under shortened sail and making barely six knots. While she was unable to hold a course directly for Sandy Hook, it was totally unrealistic to try now to beat directly into the rising gale towards the entrance to the Delaware Bay and the relative safety of the Inland Waterway. Still, the yacht was built to handle this type weather easily. Jake, Connie, and David all wore both safety harnesses and inflatable life vests with lights and EPIRB radio personnel locators attached when on deck, just in case someone should go overboard.

Hurricane David was catching up. They wouldn't reach Deerford by Saturday.

Conditions continued to worsen as Hurricane David sped northward at four times *Anne Marie*'s speed. At sundown, which was hardly noticed in the darkness and flying spume of the storm, they had to heave-to under a storm trysail on the mainmast and a sea anchor, drifting southeast with the fierce winds and seas.

The ketch rode all night in those wild conditions with Jake, Connie and David taking two hour watches at the helm, tied to the wheel post. And again the same continued on through the next day with no relief.

Still, *Anne Marie* was built to handle the weather. The galley offered plenty of microwavable and canned food, and all three of them were too experienced at sea to worry about seasickness. The ketch stayed dry and comfortable below decks, although she was tossed about quite a bit.

On the second night of the storm Connie had the 10:00 - 12:00 watch. She had come on deck at ten dressed in well-sealed foul weather gear with the life jacket, EPIRB radio unit and strobe flotation light attached; upon all of which Jake had insisted. In addition she wore a webbed safety harness with a strong wire lifeline which was always to be attached to a strong fixture on deck.

It was a truly wild night. The sky was totally black above decks with rain and salt spume flying horizontally through the air. *Anne Marie* was riding to a sea anchor with only a very small storm trysail on the main mast. She would ride up each huge swell to the wind-flattened top, stretching the sea anchor rode to its limits, then fall off the rear of each swell. The sail held her bow into the wind as the anchor rode slacked riding down each wave, only to bury her bowsprit in the next huge angry wave. The sea anchor jerked her nose back into the wind, and do it all again.

Connie made her way carefully through the screaming wind and water across the cockpit. She ducked behind the small windscreen and sat next to David clipping her harness to a stanchion. It was now her 'watch', to sit and hold on; watching the gyrations of *Anne Marie* for the next two hours while Jake and David tried to get some rest below. It was at least dry and reasonably comfortable in the cabin, notwithstanding the wild movements of the little ship. Jake would relieve her at midnight with David again back on deck at 2:00AM.

It was the essential job of the watch-keeper to keep an eye on the radar repeater to insure they wouldn't get run down by another ship, as well as to watch the small storm sail and the anchor rode; able to call the others if anything became amiss. Jake had shortened the usual four hour watches to two as it was so physically exhausting simply to hang on in the raging conditions on deck.

David gave her a hug. She giggled, thinking it was like two bears hugging at the zoo as they were both so bulky in their life jacketed storm gear. Talking was impossible. David had tried to say something; the words blowing away. He shrugged and smiled, gave her a brief kiss on the cheek, then crawled around the low wind screen to the main hatch, disappearing below for his four hours rest.

They didn't notice, but as David brushed past Connie the switch on his EPIRB (Emergency Personnel Locator) switched 'on'. Neither noticed the small glowing red light.

Connie settled in behind the large becketed wheel watching the hooded radar repeater circle around and around showing an empty ocean. She shined her powerful spotlight on the sail and on the anchor rode periodically to insure both were holding-up with no lines fraying.

Just before the end of her watch, a little after 11:30, the wind slacked off momentarily giving Connie a chance to re-snap her lifeline to a closer and more comfortable location. But before it was re-hooked, she paused hearing a roar like a huge jet plane! *Anne Marie* was instantly pushed over to her port side as if by a huge hand.

An unseen huge waterspout roared over the little ship spinning her around like a child's toy.

As it hit, Jake, who had just pulled himself from his bunk for his watch, was thrown sharply against the built-in dresser in his cabin. He hit his head with a resounding thud, and fell unconscious to the deck.

David was also thrown from his bunk to the deck of his cabin. He was instantly worried about Connie so he dragged himself through the inside of the wildly tossing yacht. He staggered to the main hatch remembering to strap his life line on as he pulled the heavy hatch open. He then snapped the life line to a heavy cleat. His life jacket was still clamped under his arm.

He dragged himself through the hatch into the wild maelstrom.

Pulling himself erect and looking towards the back of the boat he spotted Connie in a flash of lightening, hanging on to the large chrome wheel with her face contorted in fear. Just then the wind caught the main boom in a wild jibe. It smashed into his head and knocked him unconscious to the deck. As he fell the cord popped on his life jacket. It self-inflated, caught the wind, and skipped away across the wave tops.

Connie saw David fall. She sprang to her feet, unsnapped her lifeline, and ran forward to where he lay on his back secured to the deck by his lifeline. As she jumped up with her focus only on the fallen David the tossing yacht buried itself under a wave from bowsprit to stern rail. With nobody at the spinning wheel the ketch broached in the force of the waterspout.

Anne Marie was buried under tons of water. David was yanked by the wave to the end of his lifeline, attached to the railing under the hatch. He was dropped sharply back onto deck as *Anne Marie* recovered and came back upright.

Connie was not so lucky. She had unfastened her lifeline. The wave plucked her off the deck and tossed her over the side like a rag doll.

Her last sight of *Anne Marie*, before a wave pulled her under, was of David lashed unconscious to the deck as the big ketch righted herself from the broach and headed back to windward in another rippling flash of lightning.

Fear shot through her as she was dragged under the crashing waves. In mere seconds she had totally lost sight of the boat. She flailed her arms wildly as the waves rolled her over and over under water.

She fought back the panic and almost without thought she yanked the inflating cord on the life jacket. In seconds she popped to the surface and dragged a lung full of air. As she crested the top of a large wave she spun her back to the wind. The life jacket kept her face above water just far enough to draw another breath.

She calmed herself down. Yes, she was floating. She turned away from the wind; she could breathe. The life jacket held her head above the water, but *Anne Marie* was gone.

Remembering her many 'man overboard drills' she flipped the switch on her strobe light just in case anyone could see her, and switched-on the EPIRB. The red light glowed reassuringly. Yes, she could stay afloat, and yes the locater beacon would bring help as soon as the storm passed.

Yet she had no way of knowing that the antenna lead inside the locator beacon had parted when she had been smashed across the life rail. It was broadcasting nothing.

Connie rode the storm all night.

By the time dawn was lightening the sky to the east the sea quieted quickly. When the sun was up Connie found herself afloat all alone on an empty ocean.

She checked the EPIRB transmitter, noting the red 'operating' light, and relaxed in the life jacket as much as possible. She knew that her father on *Anne Marie* would tune to the same frequency and could easily locate her. Even if the equipment on *Anne Marie* didn't work, she knew that the U.S. Navy had satellites monitoring the EPIRB frequency that could also locate her quickly.

She hoped she would be rescued soon because she had swallowed a lot of salt water and was horribly thirsty.

It was Lt (jg) Sue Blackmore enroute back to NAS Bermuda from a Search and Rescue call from a Tanker with an injured crewman from the storm who first noticed it. Her EPIRB receiver began to beep. She plotted the position and confirmed the signal with the Base. Having enough fuel to reach the indicated position, and getting clearance, she pulled the collective to the right and veered away from Bermuda. She flew lower and lower across the empty and now smooth ocean below.

It was just a speck of orange on the azure sea. Keeping the orange speck in sight she pulled back on the collective, circling, and then hovering the 'copter over the orange life vest.

A moment later, Seaman Paul Rousseau was in the hoist lowering himself towards the water. He splashed into the ocean very close to the inflated orange life jacket. He discovered it was a just that, a nearly new inflatable life jacket with an operating strobe and EPIRB. There was no sign of its former occupant. He held his thumb up for the short hoist back to the deck of the helicopter.

The empty orange lifejacket was embossed with the name *Anne Marie*.

CHAPTER ONE

Jake was the first to stir aboard *Anne Marie* as a ray of sunshine found its way through a porthole and glinted in his eyes. It woke him to a splitting pain on his forehead. Not even sure where he was, Jake rose to his knees, slowly shaking his head trying to clear the waves of pain and nausea.

Full consciousness came to him. He remembered the storm and wondered why he was on the deck of his cabin? The ships clock rang three bells; it was five thirty. He didn't remember the fall against the drawer, but the three bells quickly focused his mind. He knew he was supposed to have been on watch over five hours ago.

Pulling himself to his feet he weakly called out, "Connie ? David?"

Getting no reply, he gathered his strength and pulled himself to his feet. He leaned against the varnished mizzenmast at the front of the cabin and tottered forward to the main hatch in the pilot house. He swung the door open and realized the sun was just rising out of a calm sea to the east.

Surprisingly, the vicious storm had vanished. *Anne Marie* lay becalmed on a glassy ocean with her storm sail still lashed to the main boom which Jake could hear slating idly back and forth over his head as the boat rocked.

He pulled himself up the steps to the main deck, squinting into the bright daylight and almost tripping over David who was sitting on the deck. David's lifeline was tangled around a cleat. He was staring vacantly towards the sea. There was a nasty cut at his temple, and a line of blood trickled down his cheek. He didn't seem to notice.

Jake saw no one was at the wheel. He briefly wondered where Connie was, then stepping clear of David untangled the lifeline from his legs and shook his shoulder. David stirred.

"Sit still," Jake urged gently, "are you okay?"

"She's gone," David said dully

"Where's Connie?" Jake flashed back, "Isn't she asleep forward?"

David replied, speaking faster now, "We took a knock-down last night. I saw her at the helm, but then I don't remember anything."

Jake sat down next to David questioning," You sure? She's not below in her bunk?"

Then Jake answered his own question, "Of course not, she'd never leave her watch without calling one of us."

He continued, shaking his head in dismay, "No, she can only have gone overboard. Somehow her lifeline must have come loose or broke."

David hung his head. Drops of blood mixed with several tears dropped on his wet and tattered jeans.

The realization that Connie had gone overboard in the storm left them both shocked. They sat and simply stared at one another for a long time, wordless. Both knew the worst had happened, and they were unable to voice their fears.

Finally Jake started, "I simply don't remember what happened last night. I remember waking up for my watch at about 11:30, and I think I lost my balance in a swell. Must have fallen into something and knocked myself out."

David replied softly, mouth quivering, "It was a waterspout. Woke me up. I saw Connie at the helm as I came up the hatch. I think we took a jibe in the spout. Broached. The main boom must have hit me in the head."

"EPIRB!" Jake exclaimed as he jolted up and dashed towards the nav station, "She swims like a fish and she'll have it on."

"We'll have her back." he stated with conviction, "She knows what to do if she's separated from the ship. We've had a lot of drills; she certainly can't be far away."

He yelled over his shoulder as he disappeared below towards the radios, "Check us out on deck, get the storm sail off and start the engine. With any luck at all I'll have a bearing on her in a minute or so."

David, full of fresh hope, allowed himself the luxury of three aspirin from the first aid kit and a fast bandage on his throbbing temple. He then made a quick but thorough inspection of *Anne Marie*'s standing and running rigging, impressed that there was no apparent damage from the storm except that the rode to the sea anchor had parted. He coiled the remaining section of the frayed line around the very substantial capstan on the bow and returned to the cockpit to start the big diesel. He needed to get the boat moving before he could furl the storm sail.

Jake was also busy. He first inspected the engine room to be sure nothing had torn loose. He then started the diesel generator and powered-up the EPIRB receiver, the VHF Radio and the GPS navigational system.

As David was reaching for the gear shift lever for the main diesel Jake called out to him, "David, something's strange here; come have a look."

David stepped down to the sophisticated navigation station to find Jake sitting at the chart table with all the navigational electronics very apparently 'on'; green lights glowing and gauges alive all over the electronics console. There was a very perplexed look on Jake's face.

"Can't receive a thing," Jake muttered.

"What do you mean, you can't receive a thing?" David replied.

"Look," Jake was explaining as if to himself, perplexed, "the GPS is doing everything it's supposed to, except it's not receiving a single satellite. It's searching like crazy but can't lock-on to anything."

He tapped another glass indicator saying, "Same with the LORAN. Look at that dial going crazy trying to auto-search for a frequency. Even the VHF isn't receiving, not even on the weather channel."

"And, worse ---," he continued, simply pointing at the silent EPIRB receiver.

"And, listen", he said, keying the mike of the radio, "Any Station, Any Station, MAYDAY, MAYDAY, MAYDAY, Yacht *Anne Marie*."

Clicking off the mike, he waited. The radio remained silent

David's heart plummeted like a stone. There was no signal from Connie's EBIRB.

Scanning the impressive array of gages, dials and repeaters on the console only the radar set was apparently functioning normally, sweeping twenty miles of empty ocean. And, the fathometer was showing 458 fathoms of water. All the other equipment was apparently operating, yet receiving nothing.

"David," Jake suggested, "I want to see if we're transmitting and receiving. I'm going to take the hand-held VHF to the bowsprit and try a test transmission on Channel 16. Sit here and see if you hear me."

"Okay," replied the younger man in a soft voice.

David's stomach was in knots of fear for Connie.

Several minutes later the VHF set above the chart table crackled to life, "*Anne Marie* to *Anne Marie*, this is a test."

David keyed the mike and replied, "Loud and clear."

Both men met in the cockpit and just sat for awhile, deep in thought, behind the big chrome wheel. Neither Jake nor David could imagine why none of the radio receiving equipment would function beyond the length of the vessel.

"I'd guess," Jake spoke up, "that the coax feeds to the antenna got shorted in that knockdown last night. Connie's likely somewhere close, and her EPIRIB is working fine. If we don't find her, someone else certainly will."

"Still"," he continued, "let's try to find her as best we can the old-fashioned way."

"How's that?" asked David, perking up at the thought of a recovery plan.

"Well, our DRT works fine. We'll just do it by visual search with one of us at the first spreaders while the other runs an expanding box pattern on the helm. She can't be far away. We can effectively search a two-mile path with one of us up the mast with binoculars while the other steers".

"You're up first," Jake said to David, "while I plot a search pattern."

David walked to the base of the main mast and thumbed-out the first set of small chrome steps that folded into the mast. As he climbed up he kept thumbed out more footsteps, pulling himself aloft. Reaching the first set of spreaders, thirty feet above the deck, he hooked a tool belt around the mast with his feet on the spruce spreader bar. His hands now free, he snapped the binoculars to his eyes.

Yes, it was difficult and uncomfortable to stand on a small slick varnished bar, tied to the mast, while searching a full circle carefully with binoculars. He didn't mind the discomfort at all.

Jake and David alternated watches at the masthead; one hour each to maintain maximum alertness. After several hours of searching a carefully plotted 'box' search pattern on the flat calm ocean, a breeze came from the south, yet they continued an exacting plot at slow speed using the motor.

They 'boxed' the ocean again and again, believing that they couldn't have moved more than perhaps ten miles from where Connie had gone adrift. Using the Inertial DRT system, which worked perfectly, Jake started with a one mile square box, extending to three miles the next swing, then five. As dusk fell they had completed nine search boxes, having sailed eighty-four miles in perfect squares in their search.

They found nothing.

"Should we keep looking in the dark?" David asked

"Let's keep it up. She'll have her strobe on. We'll simply have to cross and re-cross the box we worked today at dead slow watching the Inertial. We'll leave the deck lights on too. Connie may see us and yell."

He continued, "Go get some rest. I'll call you at midnight."

They were both dead tired, but neither could sleep for more than a few moments.

Jake's mind circled over and over the question of how Connie, such a well trained seaman, would have ever let her lifeline loose in a storm? She knew better. But, perhaps she saw David getting hurt.

David couldn't forget his last mental image of Connie, white-faced with terror, looking up at the huge wall of water as he stepped up from the hatch.

As the sun rose at 5:31 the next day Jake and David kept up their search, gritty-eyed from lack of sleep and bone sore from hanging on to the mast. They kept it up all day, but Jake's hope was fading.

By sunset David had barely eaten a thing in two days. He was more gaunt and thin than ever. Jake had become very quiet. Yet, in their growing realization of the tragedy, both had seemed to have become an integral part of *Anne Marie,* working the vessel's needs without conscious thought.

Both spent all their waking moments glued to their binoculars.

Jake, seated at the large wheel as the sun went down after 36 hours of searching, flipped the auto-pilot switch 'on' and slid around to where David was staring fixedly at the empty ocean. He put his arm around David's shoulders.

"Son," he started with a breaking voice, "she's just not here. I won't believe she's lost. Think of it, David, even if she drowned the life jacket would keep her up, and the EPIRB will work for seven days. Since we haven't found her or it, the Navy or Coast Guard must have gotten to her first. We've got to believe that. It's our only hope."

Jake just wouldn't accept that his beautiful daughter had been taken from him. 'No', he kept telling himself, 'life couldn't be that cruel.'

He was certain that her EPIRIB must have been heard, and someone else just had to have picked her up.

David nodded, not really convinced, but he allowed this ray of hope to buoy him up. He knew he had to believe Jake, and trust in Connie's recovery by someone else.

Moreover, Jake was still concerned that none of the electronic navigational gear or radios showed any signs of life away from *Anne Marie*.

"My watch got smashed in the storm," Jake said solemnly to David, "does yours keep better time than the ships clock?"

"Yeah, it's a Rolex Oyster."

David too knew it was time to give-up the search and find their way home with the holding to the hope of Connie's recovery by others. He wanted to believe that that had she been saved but he couldn't completely convince himself. He thought that she wouldn't have quit a quest to search were it he lost.

He knew too of Jake's deep religious convictions, which lead Jake to a quiet acceptance of those things which Jake perceived as beyond his control. This was clearly one of those circumstances, although Jake's quiet acceptance was not easy for David to emulate.

"Lots of folks have snickered at this old sextant the past few years," Jake commented, coming out of the hatch with a varnished box in his hands.

He continued, "we know every drop of water within fifty miles but we still have no good fix on our position."

He handed David a pad with several columns asking, "Please time my sights on these stars?"

He took his sights on the listed stars, and after a few calculations on the laptop Jake cursed, "Damn, this thing just isn't computing. I'll have to work these sights out longhand."

An hour later he emerged from the Nav Station with a perplexed look.

"I've got a good latitude, but the longitude calculations simply don't work. My best guess is that we're about 600 miles East South East of Sandy Hook.

With heavy hearts the two men raised the main, foresail and Genoa, They pointed *Anne Marie* west, on a course of 310 degrees. The little ship dutifully healed to the fresh breeze, and clipped along at 8 knots.

✵ ✵ ✵

By dusk of the second day from the search for Connie both men were getting more and more concerned about their total loss of any ability to transmit or receive anything on any radio, loran, e-mail, weather fax, or the GPS system. None of the celestial sights produced a correct longitude; they only had accurate latitude, so they ran due west towards New York Harbor. Even David's old trusty Walkman wouldn't receive a thing when they were but forty miles off the coast of New Jersey.

Both of them were trying to think of any way to contact any authorities to find out about Connie.

During their first night from the search area the Radar did pick up a faint 'blip', showing them to pass nineteen miles from a slow moving ship. They tried to contact that presumed ship by VHF radio on both Channel 16 and on Channel 9, with no response.

Still, navigating by advanced sun-lines during the day, Jake was certain of their position due east of Sandy Hook; he just didn't know how far east ther might be. He was expecting to see the Sandy Hook Light Tower any time.

They would get news soon.

The Tide Tables showed that the flood would start in the East River, through New York, at around noon that day. Jake planned to ride the flood quickly past Manhattan, where there was no place to dock *Anne Marie*, and to tie-up at City Island before dark. He could have the antenna wire harness in the mast checked by an electronics shop there, certain that the communications problem could only be there.

Meanwhile, he should shortly be able to get a cellular signal. He couldn't wait to call home and learn that Connie was safe. As soon as they arrived in City Island Martha would drive down to pick them up, leaving the boat to get repaired.

Martha would be frantic, both with worry for them and because the wedding had to have been delayed. Yes, in some ways he was almost relieved that he couldn't transmit Connie's loss to her by radio before he knew she was safe. Still, yes, he'd have to 'phone the instant the cellular would show a single 'bar'.

He and David had not mentioned Connie to each other since they'd left the search area. They both knew she was foremost in the other's thoughts.

At 4:40 AM the Radar picked-up the New Jersey coast 28 miles to their west, and by plotting the coastline against their chart Jake soon had re-verified the accurate 'fix' on their position. He dashed to David's cabin and shook him awake.

David came up on deck and took a quick look around. It was a beautiful clear summer night with the boat skipping through small whitecaps; the moon just setting on their port quarter.

"Good morning, David," Jake began, cellular phone in hand and a worried look on his face, "something must be terribly wrong ashore."

"Not only ashore," replied David thoughtfully, flipping the dials on his Walkman, "we're only thirty miles from New York City, in the middle of the busiest shipping lane in the World and we've not seen anything in days except that slow blip several days ago."

Jake replied, "Why don't you go back up the mast for a look?"

Jake understood that on a clear night like this, with the moon just setting, David should easily see lights ashore from the masthead. He should also see a bright glow from the west, from New York City on an early Friday morning. If nothing else, David should easily spot the light tower marking the approach to New York Harbor, now only twelve miles ahead of their position.

"Sandy Hook Light should be dead ahead, see it?" Jake called up to David.

"Nope, and dead black ashore," David called back. "Do you suppose it's a major power failure, you know, like the big one in, what was it, '84 or '85?"

He slid back down the mast.

Jake shook his head, confused, saying, "Tough to imagine a blackout this far, David. Even that one only affected half of Manhattan Island, not Jersey. And, our cell phones should be picking-up as far as Atlantic City from here."

"Look at that!" Jake started, looking at the radar repeater.

There was another small faint blip showing only eight miles ahead.

"Light Tower?" he asked.

Usually the radar would pick-up any ship at over twenty miles. Jake wondered how they had missed this one earlier. But, as they watched the screen, the 'blip' was moving. Jake knew that Light Towers don't move.

Then the 'blip' changed course and headed towards their position, but it was moving very slowly, only at about 6 knots.

Fifteen minutes later, with *Anne Marie* moving at close to ten knots reaching in a fifteen knot southeasterly, the 'blip' had closed to two miles. It was close enough to be able to see its navigational running lights.

There weren't any.

"This all is really strange," muttered David, glued to the radar repeater while looking in the direction of the'blip', which was still moving very slowly towards them.

"No lights ashore, no light tower, no radio signals, and no lights on him," David pointed in the direction of the oncoming vessel, now clearly something sizeable under sail in the faint moonlight.

Suddenly there was a bright yellow flash at the bow of the oncoming 'blip', followed a few seconds later by a loud 'CRUMP' and a large splash only 100 yards to their lee.

"What the Hell?" queried David.

"Christ," Jake hollered, "those assholes are shooting at us!"

Jake instantly reached for the navigational light switches and turned them off, plunging *Anne Marie* into total darkness except for the reflection of the fading moonlight on the smooth sails above.

He continued to react instantly, "Coming about," he said, while simultaneously putting the helm to leeward and releasing the genoa sheet. As the bow swung through the wind David pulled the lee Genoa sheet in with the electric Lewmar while the Main and Mizzen slatted over his head to the new tack. Jake fired-up the big diesel and within two minutes they were headed due south, hard on the wind, at almost twelve knots.

The other vessel likewise came around closer to the wind, but angled about four points to leeward of their heading. It didn't increase speed from its original six knots, and soon disappeared to leeward.

"David," Jake said thoughtfully, "I have no idea what's going on here, but I don't like it. We've been five days with no radio contacts whatever. Something real strange has to be going on ashore."

David shook his head as if to clear his thoughts and said in reply, "Wow, and I thought we were the ones in trouble. I mean, we only left Lauderdale ten days ago and we haven't had any world news since. But, the World has been real quiet this year. What could it be? Al Qaeda? A Chinese attack? Pretty unlikely, and I can't imagine any sort of local trouble. UFO's?"

"Don't get strange on me with that UFO crap," Jake replied lightly. "I can only deal with real stuff, and I do know that we're off the coast of New Jersey, and that there are no lights or radio signals from the mainland. We also just apparently just got shot at by something pretty small and slow with no lights and no radar."

"No radar, you're sure?"

"Look," Jake pointed at the repeater beside the wheel, "that guy has hasn't increased his speed above six knots since the shot, and he's tracking four points below our course. If he had radar and any kind of power, and if he was really looking for us, he'd be all over us."

"He simply doesn't know where we are, and they clearly can't catch us."

He continued, "Hate like hell to wait for news of Connie, but what say we pass on New York and bear off for Montauk Point? It's a bit longer getting home, but we won't have to deal with this."

"Besides," he added, "it'll be afternoon when we get there and we can at least see whatever is going on ashore in a more empty area."

"Yes," he finished, "whatever is going on here may not be so at the end of the Island."

David looked beaten. "I dunnow," he mumbled, sitting down, his head in his hands, "Connie's gone. Nothing's ashore. No radio. Something's very wrong."

He shook his head dejectedly.

"Go on back and try to get some sleep," Jake said gently, easing his helm up and bringing *Anne Marie* through a gentle jibe to her new course, north of east.

David simply nodded and disappeared below, very troubled and bewildered.

☆ ☆ ☆

Jake was determined to allow David sleep in that morning. The younger man was clearly worn out with worry. Jake felt that he could stay alert all day, knowing they would not possibly reach the end of Long Island until late that evening at best if the breeze held strongly. Still, although not a worrier by nature, he was deeply concerned about the events of the past five days.

No, he was not a bit bothered by anything on the *Anne Marie*. She was fully found and performing as well as ever. They were still fully provisioned, less a hundred gallons of water or so had been used, and most of the eight hundred gallons of diesel fuel was still in the tanks.

It was the events ashore that had his mind in turmoil. Jake didn't know what was happening that caused everything to go dark, and all transmissions to go silent. All he could envision was some sort of massive terrorist attack on the electrical grid? He could think of nothing else that could possibly obliterate all radio transmissions and navigational aids.

Further, he questioned who it was that shot at them?

Was it just some sort of hackers in a boat outside New York Harbor? That was inconceivable. Again, he considered perhaps some sort of terrorist's attack on New York? A 'dirty bomb'? That would perhaps fit the circumstance. He briefly worried that he and David might become contaminated by fallout, but he rejected that because it was an on-shore wind.

Still, his worry gnawed at him, if it was a localized New York area problem, why could he not get Boston or Philadelphia on the radio? Heck, he'd tried the short wave for days, and was not able to get anyone in the world from Moscow to Sydney.

He reassured himself that the fault had to be in the antenna.

And, no-matter his tough guy act to David, his heart ached with worry about Connie. Yes, he told himself that she's a very capable little lady, and yes, she could take care of herself, and yes again he was almost totally certain that she had been picked-up. Still, in twenty-two years this was the first time he didn't really know where his little girl was.

Jake decided he simply wouldn't have any answers until the next morning when they'd reach the eastern end of Long Island.

He was very tired.

He set the auto-pilot on his course, did a final trim on the sails, set the proximity alarm on the radar for 10 miles, and leaned back on the seat cushions allowing him to drift off to a light sleep. Having single-handed *Anne Marie* several times across the Atlantic, his body would sense any change in wind or trim, and the radar's alarm would give him ample notice of anything within ten miles.

Jake rested. David slept below in the starboard cabin. They left Connie's port-side cabin as she'd left it.

Sometime later Jake rose from his cushion and looked around at the seascape. The air was amazingly clear. The wind, still holding at about fifteen knots from the southeast was raising a few whitecaps on the deep green water. Jake couldn't remember the Atlantic this close to Long Island being so clear and clean. The air seemed to have a particular clarity.

Checking the radar he found himself still fifteen miles off the Long Island south shore, about at the Hamptons. He stretched and thought that with the day as clear as it was, he just might be able to see the Long Island from the mizzen.

He climbed up, stepping onto the single spreader. He hooked his arm around the mast and looked to leeward towards Long Island.

Jake was amazed to see such detail at such a long distance. He almost didn't need his binoculars to pick-out the individual trees on the deeply forested shoreline.

"Whoa," he said to himself, "if this is South Hampton, where are the houses?"

Looking behind him towards the open sea he saw a long line of low clouds approaching.

"Damn," he muttered under his breath, "fog".

He quickly descended to the deck, slid down the companionway to the salon and ducked into David's cabin. He lightly shook the young man's shoulder saying, "Rise and shine, you're the cook".

Forty minutes later, just as David brought up a hearty meal, the fog bank rolled over them rendering the bowsprit of the *Anne Marie* out of sight from the wheel. The wind died, and they spent an hour drifting with the out-bound tide while they ate. It got dark.

Finally, Jake stated, "Time we used the Iron Wind (as he called their diesel engine) to push us in. I can't wait for wind to learn what's happening ashore."

With that he started the engine and kicked her up to a fuel-saving seven knots. He set the auto-pilot towards Montauk and Long Island Sound ahead.

Four hours before dawn he again awoke David as Montauk came abeam on the radar repeater. Once on deck he briefed David on their position.

"Montauk Point dead abeam. Radar shows a contact three miles to the east, but she doesn't reply to the VHF, and she's dead in the water. I'm going below for a quick shower and nap. Wake me before we're through Plum Gut and into the Sound."

With that he went below, snapping on all the cabin lights as he took a shower. Then he turned all the lights off before his head hit his pillow. He was asleep quickly, leaving David with the calm misty early morning. In fact, he thought, it's already but just an hour before dawn.

David watched as the early morning mist slowly burned through, leaving the day bright and cloudless. As the sun appeared he could see the eastern shore of Gardner's Island as they motored slowly towards Plum Gut and the entrance to Long Island Sound. He knew that currents were dangerously fast here so radar or not, he didn't want to enter the Plum Gut alone.

He called below for Jake, and then he cut off the motor and raised the sails to take advantage of a freshening breeze.

Presently Jake's appeared at the companionway asking, "Coffee?"

He came on deck a bit later with two mugs in hand, and looked around at the approaching land.

"David," he said excitedly, "look there. It's a boat to port. We can get some news. Maybe they have a working cell phone? We can call and ask Martha about Connie."

As they sailed closer they saw that the boat looked very different from other small boats that either Jake or David had been familiar with.

It was a beautiful wooden dory, about sixteen feet long, propelled by two sets of oars manned by two boys, who looked to be in their mid-teens. A very grizzled-looking older man was at a tiller in the stern. The boat also had a short stumpy mast with a lateen-rigged sail slating back and forth, not doing much to help them at the moment.

Using their binoculars Jake and David could see the three in the boat were dressed in white cotton shirts with no collars, and brown rough woolen pants which were tucked into what looked like stiff leather boots. All three sported dark blue funny looking hats.

"Ahoy there." shouted Jake as they approached the small boat.

The older man immediately jumped to his feet, brandished a fierce old pistol and shouted, "Ye'll not get me fish 'thout a fight!"

Then he peered more closely as *Anne Marie* ghosted closer.

He hailed loudly, "Who be thee?"

By then *Anne Marie* had come up to several hundred yards from the smaller boat. The two boys ceased their rowing and stared open-mouthed at the yacht.

Stunned by the appearance of *Anne Marie,* the younger boy elbowed the elder whispering, "By God, look at 'er silver rigging. What kind of privateer be she?"

The older boy replied "Aye, and the silver wheel. Megads, those two gents are barely dressed. Why, they are in their undershorts and shifts! Look at the writing on that one's yellow shift. What does it say? *City Lights*? What's that?"

Jake had quickly noticed the appearance of the three in the small boat, and further noticed their wide-eyed stares at *Anne Marie*, David and himself. He ducked into the cockpit, grabbed the wheel from David and put the helm to lea, turning away from the questioning stares of the three in the fishing smack.

"Godspeed," he hollered at the small boat as *Anne Marie* sped away.

As *Anne Marie* turned from the wind, the fishermen could see the Stars and Bars in the Ensign flying from the luff of the mizzen.

"Aye," stated the old man, "that'll be the new Betsy Ross flag. She'll surely be a Baltimore blockade runner f'r New London. Say nothing of 'er, me boys, she'll be one o'ours. Still, she's mighty pretty."

With that he turned to his tiller, continuing, "Give way smartly now me lads, we've fish to catch."

Aboard *Anne Marie,* David was confused by Jake's hasty turn away from the first humans they had contacted in weeks. He wanted answers to the many unanswered questions plaguing his mind. And, he was quite curious about the strange appearance of the small almost hand-hewn appearance of the fishing craft, as well as the unusual dress and speech of its three occupants.

"Jake," he began.

"David," Jake cut him off, waving his hand as if he knew the question, "there's only one answer which could fit the patterns we've found. I'm almost embarrassed to say what's on my mind, but that small boat has almost proved the crazy thoughts I've had. Sit down and listen. Let's, put it all together."

"Okay," David agreed, sitting slowly.

"First, there are no radio transmissions of any kind. Second, there was no light tower at Sandy Hook. In fact, we've seen no navigation markers at all. Yet, we are certain of our position from radar, and we've both sailed here countless times. Third, we've seen no lights ashore and no buildings or houses at the Hamptons, or for that matter over there on Orient Point," pointing at the low, sandy strip of land which was now visible off the port bow.

"David, somehow it seems we're in the right place, but I can only conclude that we've gotten ourselves into the wrong time."

David's head was in his hands. He muttered, "You can't be right. It's just not possible; but still."

"What else would explain it?" Jake interrupted.

Continuing slowly, as if to convince himself, "Those slow blips, and the shooting at us. What's that about?"

He looked back at David saying, "Those fishermen back there clinched it for me. Did you notice the homespun clothes? The shoes with brass buckles? And, it's been over a hundred years since small boats used thole pins instead of oarlocks."

He went on, "What about the tri-corner hats on the all three of them, with the red, white and blue pins on them? This all is just not adding up."

"David," he continued more gently, placing his hand on the younger man's shoulder, "I wonder if Connie really disappeared? Perhaps we're lost, not her. Hell, she probably got picked-up by a 'copter when the first satellite picked-up her EPIRB signal."

"It almost seems that we simply vanished. It wouldn't be the first time a sailboat was lost at sea with no trace; it happened to Harvey Conover in '58."

"Harvey who?"

"In 1958 a great and well respected ocean sailor, Harvey Conover, was returning to Miami from Key West on a new and well found sloop with several other guys as crew. There was only a mild squall reported ashore, but Harvey and the boat simply vanished. There were no reports of any collisions at sea, no reports of extreme bad weather and no recovery of any part of the boat. Harvey and his crew simply vanished."

"Maybe we did too."

"You think Connie's okay?" David smiled.

"Yeah, most likely. But, perhaps we're not."

David looked up at Jake, "You mean, what?"

"Yeah, somehow, for whatever unknowable reason, in that storm I can only think that *Anne Marie* and all aboard got somehow thrown to a different time, if not place. What else would explain what we've seen? We know exactly where we are, almost no doubt about that, but perhaps we just don't know exactly when."

"Why would anyone be shooting at us?" David asked.

"Hmmm, I don't really know, David. I think we should get on up the Sound to Deerford and get some answers. We won't get them here."

Jake fell silent.

Both men grew very quiet in their own thoughts while Jake steered *Anne Marie* on a course parallel to Orient Point towards the entrance to Long Island Sound at Plum Gut. Neither spoke for an hour, until finally Jake broke the silence.

"Look, there's no lighthouse in the Gut,"

Indeed there was no lighthouse on the usual pile of rocks in the center of Plum Gut. Instead, as they drew closer, they could see the stubby masts of a shipwreck visible on a rocky shoal in the center of the narrow channel.

"Whoa, this looks dicey!" Jake said, "There are no markers, and we don't know where the channel goes. And, the current appears to be flooding, so it'll throw us onto the rocks in a minute."

With that he switched on the bottom mapping sonar and jammed the diesel throttle foreword.

"Here we go, David", he shouted.

They rode the current through the Gut, close to the western edge and away from the wreck on top of the rock pile in the center.

As they slipped into Long Island Sound it was evident that there was no activity ashore, indeed, there were no houses even on the Connecticut shoreline, and none of the usual summer houses on Fisher's Island. There weren't even any boats in this usually busy end of a normally crowded waterway in July.

David finally spoke-up as Jake slacked sheets, running almost due west along the deserted north shore of Long Island.

"Where to, Jake?"

Jake replied thoughtfully, "I've been thinking about it. If the breeze holds we ought to make the 120 miles to Deerford by midnight. Instead of sailing upriver to the yacht club, let's instead sneak behind Roank's Point and into William's Cove."

David and Jake both knew that William's Cove was a very small and almost totally landlocked harbor. It was almost entirely encircled by the large Williams Estate, and the land around it was deeply forested. David quickly recognized this as a safe destination since the channel into William's Cove was quite tricky and almost impossible without either channel markers or a good fathometer.

And, whatever was happening ashore, if the channel markers weren't there, *Anne Marie* had current charts on the laptop computer and a reliable bottom-mapper.

Once there, David and Jake knew they could certainly get themselves quietly ashore, and find out what was really happening.

CHAPTER TWO

Connie almost fell asleep. Her face fell forward into the sea. She gagged on a mouthful of salt water.

"Aaaaugh!"

She paddled her legs and arms around quickly to stop herself from shivering, and then she looked at her watch.

She'd been in the water nearly eight hours. It was just after sunrise, and the EBIRB indicator light was still glowing. That little glowing red light was telling her that it couldn't be much longer before help would appear.

She was thankful that the water was seasonably warm. Her 'sweat suit' under the jeans and flannel shirt, covered by the foul weather suit, was keeping her warm if well wrinkled. But, she was thirstier than she'd ever been.

Just then, from the top of a long lazy swell, she glimpsed a white spec on the horizon.

A sail! She thought it must be *Anne Marie.*!

"Oh Yes!" she shouted aloud.

A sail! She thought it must be *Anne Marie*!

But, as she floated to the top of the next gentle swell, straining her eyes, something didn't look just right. Pushing herself up in the water from the top of the next wave she realized the sails on the approaching vessel looked much too dark and gray for *Anne Marie*.

And, their shape was wrong.

She told herself it didn't matter at all that the approaching boat was not hers; it seemed to be heading right towards her anyway. She'd be saved. It was probably homing in on her EPIRIB right now.

She waved vigorously as the funny shaped sailing vessel grew closer, convinced that they'd soon see her. She knew that she was saved, and they'd be able to radio her rescue to *Anne Marie*.

Waving wildly, she was thrilled that she might still make her own wedding!

CHAPTER THREE

"Bong bong, bong bong, bong bong, bong."

The seaman on the helm struck the ship's bell seven strokes and flipped the glass. It was only a half hour until the Watch was over. He saw that the cook had fires lit in the galley. Breakfast would be more boiled salt pork and hard tack, but he was hungry and well used to the fare. Yet focusing his attention on food for a moment, he'd allowed the ship to drift a half point to windward, throwing a curl into the leading edge of the forecourse.

"Mind your Helm, Lubber!" shouted the 2nd lieutenant, standing at the windward rail.

Seaman Will Thompson hauled the huge wheel a half turn to port. He felt the Frigate curve back on course and heel back properly onto the wind.

Yes, it was a delicate business to hold a three masted ship balanced on course, even a small Frigate of only one hundred and two feet long, and with but thirty-two guns.

Will had transferred to this ship, *HMS Reliant*, only a fortnight ago when Captain. Aaron had assumed command. Before that, Will had been Lieutenant Aaron's boson for four years in the larboard watch of three decker, *Indomitable*.

In fact, Will enjoyed his duty on the smaller frigate. A sailor's life was much better here than on the huge ship of the line. For example, he could handle the helm of the *Reliant* by himself. He'd previously spent years working the double wheels of the ungainly three-decker, where there had to be always two men pushing together, and often it took four to keep that huge ship on course. Sometimes, whenever the *Indomitable* reefed sail, eight men were needed at that the helm of that huge and awkward sailing ship.

Reliant was indeed a pleasure to sail, and pleasures were few in the Kings Navy.

The seven bells woke Captain Aaron. He was still startled at his privacy in the Captain's cabin. He'd only had the luxury of this small cabin for four months, having been surprised by having being awarded Command of *Reliant* after her former Captain was promoted to the *Yardley*, a new 44 gun Frigate.

Aaron was certain that his promotion to Commander from Lieutenant had been due to his handling of a Yankee brig the *Indomitable* had taken as prize last winter. Given temporary command of the captured little ship, enroute back to New York as Prize Master, Aaron had taken two other Yankee prizes. He'd captured a well founded schooner and a snow using both cunning and stealth to lure the unsuspecting Yankee Captains under his guns.

The sale of those prizes made him a tidy sum and also fattened the purse of Post Captain Wembly.

He stretched for a moment, enjoying the feel of the frigate under him as it reached along in a moderate breeze. The ship was under orders from Hamilton, Bermuda to Montauk, having delivered dispatches for Admiral Howe.

He heard all the familiar sounds of a well-run ship at dawn. The pumps started to thump and he heard the scraping of holystones on the deck above his head. The little ship rolled to the ocean swell, and he could smell pork cooking through the open skylight.

All was well. It was June of 1777. The Crown Fleet was headquartered in New York with the *Indomitable* as Flagship under Post Captain Sir Wembly.

Lieutenant Aaron had arrived with *Indomitable* the previous fall as the ship's first lieutenant. He had spent most of the winter freezing in New York Harbor aboard the ship with the 740 other souls it took to keep a three decker fighting. The ship had been dispatched from the Channel Fleet to help control the insurrection in the Colonies, but neither the Army nor the Navy had moved out of New York since their arrival. Only the smaller frigates and sloops were sent to sea to, as they were now doing, blockade the other Yankee ports.

It was just a month ago that now Commander Aaron had been given command of this small frigate. Yes she was older than he, and small for today's standards. Still, she was a fine sailing ship and he'd trained his crew of over 200 men to work as a single unit.

Reliant had sailed from New York to Bermuda a fortnight ago with Orders to sail thence with dispatches and from there, and until relieved, to stay between Montauk Point and Block Island on blockade duty. They were to arrest all Yankee shipping.

Blockade Duty was said to be an almost impossible task, for each time the British blockade vessel got to the east of the patrol area the clever double-damned Yankees slipped under Montauk to the west. And, when they gave chase, others would sail 'round past Block Island to the East. That thirty mile stretch of ocean really needed two ships to properly close, but there were never enough sloops and frigates. They were the eyes, ears and the workhorses of the Fleet.

After the rigid dogma and ceremony of the Flagship, Aaron was delighted to have the freedom of action in his small and handy *Reliant*. He was thrilled with his small command, even if the duty was said to be frustrating and dull.

He pulled himself from his cot, yanked on his boots and his third best uniform; 'sea duty' blue breaches and coat. He stood up, just barely remembering to duck under the low beams overhead. As his feet hit the floor his steward, a cripple named Ian who'd had his left leg amputated in the French Wars, arrived with a steaming mug of tea.

"Ready for ye'r shave Sir? Lovely morning i'tis," quipped Ian as he lathered Aaron's face, careful of the scar that ran from Aaron's left eye to the corner of his mouth, a result of a close call with a Frenchman's cutlass.

Suddenly, the lookout was heard to cry from the mast head, "man in the water two points on the larboard bow."

Aaron heard Williamswright, the watch officer, order, "Helm down two points. Man the Braces. You, sailor, call the Captain to the deck."

Aaron was on deck with his glass under his arm before the scurrying seaman reached the scuttle. He leapt into the larboard fore shrouds and, halfway to the futtock, hooked his leg through a ratline. He peered through his long glass at the brightest speck of orange he'd ever seen on any ocean! Looking closer, the small orange blob was topped with a reddish mat of hair, and bright yellow clad arms were frantically waving.

'Orange? Yellow?' he was shocked, thinking to himself, 'what the deuces could be that color?'

He hollered down to the deck, "Heave To. Boson, man the gig."

By the time he'd slid down the ratlines and reached the leeward quarter his crack crew had the topsails backed and the twenty-two foot gig launched, bobbing along beside the ship. Eight oarsmen jumped into their places, with Will, his boson, at the tiller. Aaron leapt into the bow as the boat cast off and rowed towards the strange orange and yellow apparition a hundred yards under the lea of the hove-to frigate.

Connie was fully alert now. Her discomfort was forgotten as she incredulously saw a fully rigged three-masted ship pull smartly to a neat stop. A boat was instantly lowered and, instead of turning on a motor in the small boat, eight guys in striped shirts with their hair in pigtails started to row towards her.

Another guy was standing in the bow of the little boat, fully dressed in a blue and gold cutaway coat. He wore a fantastic swoopy hat and was brandishing what looked like a real sword in his right hand!

'What the hell was this?' she wondered. 'Hollywood?'

She was dumb-struck as this bizarre crew pulled-up next to her in their white rowboat.

The fancy dressed guy in the front simply barked, "Get 'em aboard lads, and cover 'em up with a boat cloak."

Connie was unceremoniously hauled over the side and dumped onto the chines at the feet of the guy who was apparently in charge. A smelly rough woolen cloth was thrown over her.

The tall lean man with a cruel looking scar on his face said kindly, "Keep ye covered with that cloth, boy. We'll hear ur tale once aboard."

Aaron pondered the startling appearance of the boy they'd found adrift, hundreds of miles from anywhere. Indeed, he initially appeared a very fat young boy when he was in the water. Yet, the bright orange 'body' around him was some funny sort of squishy stuff, which wasn't part of the boy's body at all. And, the shiny yellow shirt and ankle-length pantaloons were of a texture of cloth the likes he'd never seen.

'Damn,' he remarked to himself, 'but the small shoes were pure white!'

"WOSSSSSSSSH," sounded from the pile at his feet.

"Toss oars," commanded Aaron, "Whale!"

The boat crew stood their oars straight upward and they all looked nervously around at the slowly rolling ocean, expecting to see a sperm whale surface.

Hssssss –

Aaron heard the dying sound from his feet. He looking down at the form of the fat boy huddled in the bilge.

The fat was all gone! Instead, he saw a sheepish face and a small hand holding a leather tab which was attached to the orange thing. It was now all flat.

"What the Hell?" he thundered.

"My life jacket, uncomfortable –." Connie started to explain, then bit her lip.

After a moment's thought, while looking closely at Connie, Aaron ordered, "Boson, best keep this," pointing at Connie, "inside the boat till tiz in the chocks. Then ye get it to my cabin under wraps."

Continuing sternly after another pause, "And, if ur oarsmen have a word of it I'll see 'em under the cat."

The oarsmen dropped their long oars into the sea and resumed pulling. Soon the boat rounded under the stern of the ship. Within moments the eight man crew along with the guy in the blue coat seemed to fly up its side.

Before Connie could believe it, the boat was attached to ropes and hauled, with her inside, up over the tall side of the sailing ship. It was quickly blocked, high over the main deck. Connie was then lifted out of the boat by several rough hands and was carried like a sack of potatoes down a hatch.

She was dumped onto a hard bed in a small dark cabin. The door slammed shut.

As the cabin door was closed and bolted she jerked herself up on the bed. She was now thoroughly wet and cold, and still very very thirsty.

The smell in the cabin was horrible. It reeked like the inside of her brother's old sneakers after a hundred soccer games, or worse. On top of the thirst came a wave of nausea; she could hardly breathe this foul air.

She was wet. She was also cold and, yes, she was more than just a little bit worried.

She heard ropes squealing through blocks overhead, followed by the muted sounds of orders given. Feet were pounding above her head on the deck.

Shortly she felt the cabin lean over and she heard water moving past.

They were sailing again.

She stripped off her deflated life jacket, the foul weather gear, the wet sweat shirt and her wet jeans. She pulled off the soggy sneakers and even her socks. She huddled in a corner of the bunk wrapped in the dry rough woolen blanket wearing only her damp t-shirt and underwear.

She warmed slowly wondering what and who these people could be?

CRASH!

The door flew open, and the same tall guy in the funny formal clothes stood just outside.

"Ye're all right boy?" he demanded, offering a metal dipper of water.

Connie grabbed the dipper and took a huge swallow of the tepid water. On the second swallow she realized it was a brownish green color, with a noticeable odor not unlike swamp water.

"AGGGAGH," she gagged, thinking she was going to vomit.

"On yer feet, Lad" the guy was saying, "Thee seem no worse for the wear, and after a few answers we'll swear thee into the Kings Service."

With that he pulled off the blanket saying, "Come along now."

And then he stopped and stared again at Connie who, standing without the blanket over her wet t-shirt, was very clearly not a young lad at all. Her rounded pert breasts in her sports bra were very clearly outlined by the wet cotton.

"Aye," he said, tossing the blanket back over her shoulders.

He took her by the arm, leading her out through door saying, "Best ye come to the cabin with me."

Connie grabbed her bundle of wet clothing, forgetting the sweat shirt under the bunk. Following the strangely dressed man, wrapped in the itchy blanket over her still wet underwear, she was now really getting concerned. She wondered who these rough sailors might be.

Aaron led her to the right from the small cabin doorway and through a room with a table built around what was clearly a mast. Several blue coated men were sitting in chairs under an open skylight. Their conversation stopped as the tall guy pulled her through another door and shut it behind them.

'Aah, she said silently to herself, 'this is better'"

She found herself in a far larger cabin. This one was about 12 feet square with windows across the opposite end, which was very clearly the stern of the little ship. Connie could see their wake rolling smoothly behind them. The best part was the fresh air; the windows were open and the incoming breeze clean.

"Sit ye down madam," said the man, pointing at a cushioned settee under the open windows.

He took a seat at a chair bolted to the deck behind a table that had a chart tacked on to it with a dividers and parallel ruler laid on top. Connie noted no evidence of even a VHF radio, let alone a Loran or even a hand-held GPS unit. She was amazed at the apparent re-creation of a very antique sailing ship. It was all so very authentic looking!

Connie spoke first saying quietly, "Sir, thank you for rescuing me. I really admire your lovely replica ship. It looks very authentic. I think I saw one like it in Newport several years ago, the *HMS Rose.* Didn't Russell Crowe make a movie on it? Is this the same ship? Hmmm, what's it called now? Oh yes, the *Surprise.*"

She rattled on, continuing, "I was washed overboard from our ketch, the *Anne Marie* last night in the storm. I don't see your radio, but would you try to raise the *Anne Marie* on your VHS? They can't be far away. My fiancé, David, and my Dad will be frantic with worry. They're probably quite nearby; I know they're looking for me."

"Milady, there was no storm last night." the man quipped, "and, what be this 'radio' thing of which ye speak?"

Continuing, he said, "Maam, you're aboard His Majesty King George's Frigate *"HMS Reliant'*. I am Commander John Aaron. I've lookouts posted at the main top looking for any Yankee shipping. If we find yer Yankee *Anne Marie*, for surely ye be a Yankee lass, we'll neatly take her prize and yer fine fiance'll be sworn a Kings sailor, or feel the cat until he does.

"Now, what be these?" he asked sharply pointing at the pile of foul weather gear and kicking at the deflated orange life jacket. The EPRIB's transmission indicator wasn't flashing.

Connie, finally loosing her patience, shot back, "Hey buddy, cut the crap! I don't know what type of silly re-enactment you're all playing here, but I'm cold and tired and thirsty and hungry and wet. This isn't a joke to me. Would you please just dig out your goddamned little radio, wherever you hide it, and call up *Anne Marie!*"

"Madam," Aaron replied, standing up and pacing across the cabin and back, "I understood little of what ye've just said. What is 'buddy', and 'rein—what'?

"Maam, I am a Kings Commissioned Officer, and I don't know what ye be. We found thee drowning in the ocean and we just pulled ye aboard. Please just give me some simple facts. Ye'r name, if thee please?"

"Constance Anne Shaw, people call me Connie," she replied downcast.

"And the name of the ship that ye were on, *Anne Marie* i'twas?"

"Yes, an auxiliary ketch of sixty-eight feet. My Father's her owner and captain, and I know they're still in radio distance. Won't you please call?" she plead.

"Aye," replied Aaron, thinking she had become a bit addled by her being cast adrift, "Ye'll have to tell me what is this 'radio' later, but from where did ye sail, and where be ye bound?"

"Look," she replied, "we left Fort Lauderdale about, I guess, six days ago heading home to Deerford. We ran into Hurricane David. I was washed over by a wave last night. I know that David and my Dad are probably looking for that EPRIB beacon now, but it seems not working.

"You must know of my father?" she continued, "Jake Shaw of Shaw Industries? Most serious sailors do know of him."

"Oh please, cut the silly play acting and get on the radio. What the hell's the date anyway? I wonder how long we were in that storm," she finished.

"Miz Shaw, the date is July fifth in the year of our Lord seventeen hundred seventy-seven," replied Aaron, thinking her even more addled with her incoherent babbling of words he'd never heard interspersed with most impertinent speech habits. She spoke with a very strange accent to her English language.

Going on, as he'd at least learned there was a Yankee ketch in these waters, he added, "Now ye say ye'r washed overboard last night, and ye'r ship was bound for where?"

"Deerford, of course, in Connecticut," Connie replied.

Aaah, thought Aaron, with a day lead they'd never catch the Yankee ketch. Or, was it Yankee indeed? Pretty story, he thought, but the lass spoke a very strange English language. He knew that the Florida's were Spanish, allied, or at least not currently at war with, his King.

He thought deeply about this strange woman, tapping his lower lip with his finger. Just then there was a rap at the door

"Enter," thundered Aaron, startling Connie.

A short and grizzled man with a wooden leg limped in with a package of bundled cloth.

Aaron spoke to her, "Ye need rest. 'Ere's a dry shirt and pantaloons, indeed perhaps too big. If ye'll change into these my steward Ian'll dry your things. Please take a rest here, ye're safe enough, and we'll talk later".

With that he stood and walked out of the door. The little crippled man tossed the bundle of clothing on the table and left without a word.

Connie, totally bewildered, stripped off her wet things. She pulled-on the warm soft shirt and pants that had been offered. She left her wet t-shirt and underwear in the pile with the rest of her wet clothes before falling across the captain's bed, instantly asleep.

Eight bells struck.

Captain Aaron was on deck to watch his third Lieutenant, Kenneth James, a mere boy of seventeen, relieve his second Lieutenant, Roger Williamswright, whom everyone called 'Willright'. All hands were piped to midday dinner; the ship's routine continuing while Connie slept.

"No sight o'that Yankee ketch?" asked Aaron.

"Lookout reported a speck o'what coulda been a sail to windard 'bout four bells, but t'was gone before I could get a glass on her".

At six bells of the afternoon watch Aaron went below to find Ian. He had placed the passenger's clothing to dry in Lt. 'Willright's cabin, he being dispossessed of same until the mystery of the passenger could be answered.

"Cor, Sir" started Ian, "I never seen the likes o't. Lookee these!" holding up Connie's sports bra and bikini panties, now dry.

"And Sir," continued Ian, "wats this?" He was holding up the sweat pants, pulling on the elastic waistband and pointing at the red and white stylized print of a sloop on the t- shirt, reading 'DYC' there under.

"Ian, ye'll breathe nary a word o'this," said Aaron.

He scooped-up the now nearly dry heap of clothing and gear. He tromped into his cabin and laid it all out on his chart table. The girl was still sleeping across his bunk.

Aaron sat at his chart table puzzling over the plastic buttons and the shiny red plastic light on the EBRIB. The strobe light was in pieces. After puzzling over it all for a long time he left the cabin, knowing he could get answers from the girl when she awoke.

Connie awoke an hour later. Feeling warm and rested, she allowed her mind to dwell on this strange new environment. Slowly opening her eyes she saw her pile of now dry belongings piled on the table.

She stood and inspected the cabin. It was about twelve feet from front to back, and perhaps wider than that. On both sides of the cabin a huge brass cannon rested on a little cart pointed towards a hatch that would open; they must be gun ports she thought. There was a red and white checkered canvas rug on the floor, and the chart table was bolted to the deck in the center. At the back end, where the windows opened, the starboard side was partitioned off. Sneaking a peek she saw a narrow bed inside and a covered hole through the counter at the rear.

There was no electrical wiring. There were only four oil lamps. There were no electronics at all, and the 'head' was just a hole in the counter, opening to the sea.

Considering it all Connie was coming to the belief that the man, Aaron, was perhaps not lying. There seemed no doubt this ship was not made in the 20th century. More, all of the language she'd heard was truly archaic.

Nope, it seemed not a re-enactment. The simple void of any electrical lights, wiring or even a head attached to the cabin spoke of a true authentic. The smells and sounds confirmed her fears.

Incredibly, had she really ended-up over 240 years back from where she started?

The thought was terrifying. She bit her lip to keep from crying. An enormous feeling of loss enveloped her.

She sat for a moment, head in her hands, almost starting to weep.

But no!

She forced herself to keep in control.

She told herself that her Dad always did insist that crying never did anyone any good at all. And, like her Dad from whom she'd learned so much, she knew that she was a person who had been taught to accept that which life handed her, and that which she couldn't change.

Her father, Jake Shaw, while not a routine church-goer in any specific religion, was a deep Christian believer in God. He often stated that all organized religions on Earth simply seem to worship the same God and preach the same human behavior. They just do it in different ways. Her Dad had also claimed to have had his life miraculously saved as a far younger man, when he should have died in an 'almost' skiing accident. He claimed to the present day that the 'tree moved an instant before his impact'.

But, she considered, if she were truly displaced centuries back in time, how could she make the best of it? She knew nobody here, and almost nothing about this time.

Aah, the first thing she thought to do was to get rid of the damning evidence of her origins.

Dashing quickly to the chart-table she scooped-up the yellow foul weather gear, with strobe and EPRIB, along with all the clothing, and tossed it all out the open stern windows into the ship's boiling wake. She saved only the deflated life jacket, which might have some value if she could escape, and her underwear. She slipped it on under the sailor's shirt where it couldn't be seen.

Her heart pounding, she then reclined back on the cushioned settee in front of the open stern windows.

'Poor David!' she thought. He was sailing home with Dad in *Anne Marie* right now. They must think her drowned at sea.

Oh what was she to do?

She put her head in her hands and shook with sobs. This was a bizarre situation.

She wondered how she really could be moved in time. It just didn't seem really possible to her, outside the television fantasies of 'Star Trek' of course.

But, she then reasoned, if it had happened to her, then it quite probably also happened to *Anne Marie*? Indeed, it was more than possible that Dad and David were also in this time, and wouldn't they now be looking for her?

She thought of that damned EBRIB beacon. The red indicator had not been glowing; perhaps that's why *Anne Marie* hadn't shown up to save her?

'Cut it out, Connie,' she told herself. 'Dad said there's a reason for everything, and there's got to be one for this. Accept it.'

She'd resigned to herself to the simple fact that she was powerless to change anything at this time just as the door banged open and the Captain entered.

"Miz Shaw," the Captain began, "Ye're looking rested. I thought ye'd be back in ye're own clothing. D'ye feel better?"

"Yes sir," answered Connie, keeping her eyes downcast.

"Aye there!" he exclaimed with a startled glance at the empty chart table, "Where'd ye put ur own clothes and ye'r fancy yellow suit?"

Connie screwed-up her courage, rose, and walked to the chart table.

"There," she calmly said, pointing to the open window, waving at the wake.

He ran to the window and backhanded her onto the settee.

"Filthy bitch!" he swore at her, swinging a back-hand at her cheek, "damn but I should've kept it all. They'll never believe me now."

She instinctively wheeled, bounced off the settee, and using the kickboxing routines her Dad had insisted she learn, dealt him a swift blow to the gut with her left heel. Quickly, keeping her balance, she followed with a right heel to his groin, and a left jab to his chin.

He dropped to the deck.

She gasped; what had she done?

She knelt to his side.

He spluttered and slowly sat up, rubbing his jaw.

"Megods, woman. I've nary seen the like o'that," he mumbled weakly.

"Sorry, sir, but I was taught to defend myself."

Rising to his feet he shook his head and said, "Ye said ye hail from Fort Lauderdale in Spanish Florida?"

"Yes sir, that's where we sailed from."

"Then with ye'r strange tongue thee must be from the Spanish Colonies?"

Connie thought quickly.

Indeed, if this Captain were to think of her as Spanish, then perhaps he could explain her language. She thought to embellish this train of thinking.

"No, Sir, I am not pure Spanish," she retorted. "My family was from New England. I was captured by a Spanish frigate as a girl and was held for ransom. When pirates attacked the island where I was being held, I was taken into hiding by local slaves. My family learned of my location and rescued me just months ago. That might explain my strange language, and my knowledge of healing."

Connie was inventing all this very quickly. She really knew little about Spain and their relations with the English. She thought quickly that here may be a chance to keep her free.

"Aye, lass, ye'r a strange one indeed. Be ye'r father a Spanish noble?"

"No sir. He's been in the service of Spain for some years while trying to find and free me. My fiancée accompanies him. We were bound for Cadiz this voyage to bring my healing learnings to Madrid."

Aaron sat back, the ache in his groin almost recovered from her incredible attack.

Yes, he mused, she did speak the King's language with a very strange pronunciation, yet she spoke not a Spanish inflection; he had heard that. He wondered if her speech be an Indian influence?

The tale she told was perhaps credible, although still hard to believe. Had she not said earlier that she was bound for Connecticut? Still, it would not do to chance a situation with Spain. At least that was one Country not at War with England at the present.

He looked her over. She was standing there over him, her breath heaving. He could clearly see the shape of her small round breasts and even the tiny hard pointed nipples. She had a very flat and hard stomach below a tiny waist, and a well rounded bottom. His breath caught in his throat, and his groin stirred.

Momentarily he fought the urge to grab this beautiful young woman, drag her to his cot, rip the clothing off her and have his way.

But, reason prevailed.

Yet, in that moment she had caught his lingering stare, and was tensed for his further attack. The captain had an amazingly tough and wiry body; he was clearly a seasoned hand-to-hand warrior.

She prepared to fight him off.

"Mistress," he spoke, slowly rising and turning so she would not see the extent of his instant arousal, "ye'r on an English Man o'War in Colony waters. We're defending an insurgency of these Colonies. I can not have thee as a passenger."

"Did ye say thee have medical skills? Might ye assist this ship until we can get thee to my senior officers who might assist ye to regain yer'self to Cadiz?"

"Yes, Captain," returned Connie, realizing her veterinarian training for what it was, "I am the best doctor you may ever find. With the promise of good treatment and a private cabin I'll place myself at your service until you can release me ashore or return me to my family."

Connie had thought-out and accepted that her degree as a Veterinarian, although without a lot of experience, would make her better than any 'people doctor' in the eighteenth century. She'd certainly be better than anything on this smelly old boat.

And, with this Captain thinking she was protected by an ally of his Country, perhaps she might survive long enough to find David?

She had to believe she would find her Dad and her David.

"Aye" Aaron replied thoughtfully, recovering his composure.

"We're not rated a surgeon on this small frigate, although the sail maker does right well. I'm tempted to heave ye out yon port to follow ye're slop, but I am a Kings Officer and gentleman. Ye'r story about ye'r Court presence with King Phillip stays me hand."

"Still," he continued, rubbing his sore jaw, "methinks it best to sail into New York and report to Sir Wembly about ye'r disposition, and ye'r lost ketch *Anne Marie*, before we take station at Block Island."

Addressing her directly he said, "Miss, ye're to keep urself to the mate's cabin. Ian'll bring ur meals. Ye may come on deck, mind thee the quarterdeck only, and only during daylight in good weather. Lieutenant Williamswright'll show ye to the orlop and show ye t'the sail maker who's the actin' surgeon."

"Ye'll please him 'n I'll have a good word for thee with Sir Wembly."

"Sir," asked Connie, not wanting to be indelicate but feeling a need, "where is the head? And, may I take a bath?"

"Madam, there's no facility for women passengers on a frigate. Thee may use this head", sweeping aside the little curtain to reveal again what looked like an outhouse seat on a little bench.

"When I'm not in the cabin ye may enter, but mind ye to always knock on my door first. Ian'll also place a pot in ur cabin."

Then he snorted, "Bath, haah! We'll get thee a bucket o' seawater. If'n ye need to bathe it'll be in seawater."

Connie returned to the little smelly cabin. She sat on the little bunk. Then she felt a sharp cramp in her tummy.

"Oh damn," she wailed to herself, "it's my period, and I've nothing to use."

Casting about the little cabin she saw the red sweatshirt that she'd overlooked earlier. Using a sharp corner of the sea chest on the floor she ripped it into a dozen small pieces.

Then she cried herself to sleep.

The next morning, feeling better, she opened the door to a light knock. She found a tall blonde young man standing there in a blue officer's uniform.

"Lieutenant Williamswright at ye're service, Maam," he said softly while bowing formally, "if ye'r feeling better Captain's said ur to have a look at the surgery in the Orlop. Ee's also allowed that ye might take dinner with the officers in the cabin."

Connie nodded to the man and simply followed him out the door of the cabin and up a half-flight of narrow steps to the main deck of the ship.

The main deck stretched forward, open at the top with wooden sidewalls that rose above her head. Along both sides of the deck were row upon row of brass cannons on little wheeled carriages, just like the ones in the captain's cabin. She counted fourteen on each side.

She guessed that the ship was just over a hundred feet long, plus an enormous bowsprit. Looking up, she saw it was rigged with three masts with square sails on all three. The only fore and aft sails were the three jibs and a gaff rigged 'spanker' on the mizzen mast.

The ship was healing ponderously to port and sailing smoothly across the white-capped swells.

Connie's guide made a U-turn on the main deck and ran up a few more steps to the quarterdeck where a sailor was steering the ship, looking occasionally at a magnetic compass in a gimbaled stand. The railing here came to her waist, above which was netting filled with rolls of canvas cloths. There were two smaller cannons on each rail.

Men swarmed everywhere, all very busy.

"This be the Quarterdeck," stated the officer. "Ye'll please not be on deck elsewhere. Follow me."

He then turned and descended back below decks the way they had come. Instead of turning into the wardroom he descended another half-stairway into a long and gloomy room with barely enough headroom for Connie to stand.

The room was filled with knots of sailors, some sleeping in hammocks, some in groups playing cards, and some in solitary pursuits. Even though it was bright sunshine on deck, this 'tween decks' was illuminated from an open hatch somewhere in the middle and a couple of oil lamps. Before Connie could do more than take notice of the deck she was hustled down through yet another hatch and down another steep ladder to the very bilges of the ship.

To the right they passed through a tiny doorway. Connie found the smell down here was truly nauseating.

They entered a very little room with canvas covered pallets along one wall, a wooden table bolted to the deck in the center, and a large locked chest built into the bulwark. The only light was from several hanging oil lamps.

"This be the Orlop," the Lieutenant stated. "I'll meet ye to th' sail maker at dinner, four bells o'the dog watch."

"Please," she gagged from the truly awesome odors, "may we go back up on deck?"

✲ ✲ ✲

"Fog rolling in again," Roger 'Willright' stated to Captain Aaron after the watch had been changed.

Both were standing at the windward rail of the quarterdeck. This was the usual spot reserved for the Captain when he was on deck.

"Aye," agreed Aaron, "post double watches and heave a lead in a half hour. Come about when ye find ten fathoms. It shallows sharply hereabouts. Better shorten sail to main and forecourse, spanker and jib. Damned Yankees love this weather".

The *Reliant* was nearing the approaches to the Delaware Bay enroute to New York Harbor several days after finding Connie at sea.

"Beat to quarters?" asked Roger.

"Nay," replied the Captain, "as usual just keep a full crew at the forward 12's and keep 'em double shotted. Fire at anything ye see, and hail for 'em to 'eave-to."

Aaron noted that his first mate made a careful visual position fix just before the fog closed them in at two bells of the morning watch. *Reliant* was ten miles east of Cape May, crabbing to an ebb tide at four knots.

"Masthead." shouted Aaron.

"Aye Aye, Sir," came the reply from above.

"Any sail in sight?"

"Nay Sir."

"Lt. James," Aaron addressed the young officer with the watch, "as soon as the fog settles ye'll wear ship to northwest for New York., Perhaps we'll catch a damned Yankee napping by doubling back in this pea soup weather."

"Aye Aye, Sir."

Aaron went below knowing that it simply wouldn't do to have the Captain pacing about on deck.

He was total master of this little world including four officers, his sailing master, the surgeon (that woman, Connie), two hundred five seamen, a marine lieutenant and twelve marines. They were somehow all packed into the little hull of the thirty-two gun *Reliant,* now ghosting along under shortened sail towards Cape May, looking and listening for Yankee blockade runners as they tried to make it to open ocean.

Presently he heard familiar commands from the deck above to bring the ship about, followed by the bustle of seamen's bare feet running. *Reliant* came into the wind and fell off on her new tack, gliding to the east in the fog.

Aaron settled into his routine of checking the Ships Log from the day prior and reviewing the purser's report. He was increasingly disturbed that the ship's water casks were dangerously low after almost four months at sea, not having refilled them in New York. The salt pork was almost too rancid to eat and the hard tack was full of worms. *Reliant* might at least refresh her water casks while he made his non-ordered report to the Port Captain in New York. The salt meat and bread would likely just have to suffice.

"Sail Ho," a cry came from the masthead just after the watch changed at noon.

"Where away?" queried Lt. Willright.

"Two points to larboard, about four cables. I can see 'er tops'ls above the fog," came the reply from the lookout, who was in fact totally out of sight in the fog far above the deck.

Reliant's three masts disappeared upwards into the grey wisps.

Aaron heard the exchange from his cabin and was on deck in mere moments.

"Ee's wearing ship," a further report came from the mists above.

Aaron dashed to the chart table.

"Where are we?" he queried the Lieutenant.

Willright simply pointed at a small X on the chart.

"Aye, he'll be inbound, and having seen us 'ee'll try to run back t'sea. Bear off three points, Lieutenant, and shake-out ur courses," Aaron ordered.

He stepped to the windward ratlines with his telescope tucked under his belt.

Noticing Connie through the wisps of fog he yelled over his shoulder, "Ms Shaw, get urself below decks, now."

Aaron then ran up the rope ratlines to the maintop, disdaining the lubber's hole, swinging his body around the futtock shrouds and was, moments later, at the masthead. It was an amazing sight. The day was clear and sunny up here. The mast below simply disappeared into the cloud of low lying fog.

"Thereaway sir," said the sailor on lookout duty, pointing his arm just to the left of the ship's course.

And there she was.

The tops of the other ship's two masts were plainly visible a mile ahead. As Aaron watched he could see the angle on the brig's masts sharpen as they too were also bending on more sail in an attempt to flee.

"Willright," Aaron shouted down through the fog, "beat to quarters."

"Aye Aye Sir,"

The Captain heard the drummer begin to rap on his drum as the crew ran to their stations. The guns were hauled inboard across the wooden decks with loud rumbles. The tampions were removed and rammers were pulled from their racks on the bulkheads. Young boys ran up on deck with pre-measured bags of black gunpowder for each gun, which were pulled from their hands by the impatient gunner's mates. The powder was rammed down the barrels of all the cannons, followed by twelve pound round shot and wadding.

The Marines smartly climbed the ratlines to the main and mizzen tops, hauling large swivel guns and muskets up behind them. Still, one Marine was posted at each hatch to keep any frightened crew from hiding below decks.

Connie was roughly grabbed by a sailor and almost thrown down the hatch and further down the two ladders to the tiny stinking surgery in the orlop.

She was terrified at all the noise, huddling on a pile of rags in a corner in the dim light of a smoky lantern and breathing the incredibly foul air through the cuff of her shirt that she held tightly under her nose.

The drum stopped and Aaron checked his watch. The ship was at Quarters in six minutes twenty seconds.

He was pleased.

Reliant quivered and sharply healed over as the courses began to pull. Aaron could hear her twenty-thirty-two 12 pounders and four quarterdeck swivel guns being run out. Although he was blinded by the fog below him, he could picture in his mind the frantic but controlled action on the main deck eighty feet below.

He slid down the windward backstay to the deck. The slow matches were in their tubs, and the youngest seamen, boys of twelve, were spreading sand on the deck to insure good footing should the deck get too slippery with blood. The wooden screens on the main deck, walls to the cabins, had vanished. All the cabins and their personal gear had been struck below to the hold. The fighting main deck was now clear from stem to stern, and the gun crews stood at attention at their huge cannons, awaiting his orders.

"Nother point to larboard, sir," the cry was heard from the lookout.

Aaron had just reached the Quarter-deck.

"Willright," he shouted, "we'll not loose this one. Mast top with thee, and let me know when we can range him with a bow-chaser."

"Aye sir", the reply came as Williamswright leapt for the main shrouds.

It was indeed a strange feeling to be creaming through the sea at eight knots under full sail in a blinding fog, through which it was difficult to see even the foremast from the quarter-deck. Yet, at the main top, it was a clear and sunny day, and the Yankee Brig's masts were in plain sight.

Forty minutes later Willright called, "Deck thar, try a ranging shot. Maximum elevation, quarter point plus a half to the larboard bow."

Aaron ordered, "Helm up a half point. Gunner, fire your windward chaser at maximum elevation."

"Crash," the boom of the double shotted cannon thundered.

"His courses are furling and he's wearing to larboard," Willright shouted from the mists above.

A minute later Aaron simultaneously saw a large waterspout off *Reliant's* leeward side, and the longboat shattered in its chocks as a cannonball turned it into deadly flying splinters. A seaman screamed as a large splinter pierced his thigh.

"Not bad shooting," said Aaron to himself, "now it's our turn."

"Helm to weather. Stand by to wear ship. Starboard battery, fire on command. Mast top tell me when he's abeam," Aaron rattled off his commands.

As the *Reliant's* bow came to the left the fog lifted just enough to see the shadowy outline of the Brig.

"Gunners, Fire as ye bear," commanded Aaron, as loudly as he could.

The starboard side began to erupt in gunfire crashes as the gunners drew a range on the Brig.

Just as the fog closed-in again Aaron could see that his ragged broadside had had good effect! The Brig had lost her bowsprit and fore top mast. There was a fire started in her waist.

"KABOOM," an enormous explosion came from the brig, and a huge orange fireball appeared off the quarter where the brig had been just a moment before.

"What the devil, sir!" mouthed Will Thompson from the helm, his jaw agape.

"Damn. Gun powder," replied the Captain, "That's a damned valuable cargo that General Washington shan't get."

Reliant again wore ship and traversed the sea where the Brig had exploded, seeking survivors. They found nothing but charred bits of wood and cordage. Nobody survived from the smuggler.

Meanwhile, in the Orlop, as soon as the drums stopped above, old Macy, the sail maker and 'doctor', staggered through the small doorway. He saw Connie trembling in the corner and grabbed her hand, though not unkindly.

"Here be the surgery if'n were needed," he said, reclining on a coil of rope with a bottle in his hand, "safest place on a ship in action, 'less'n they get the magazine, or she's holed bad".

The ship had become very quiet here below decks.

Connie, a bit more used to the putrid odors of the bilges, rose from her seat and busied herself studying the various crude but very sharp surgical instruments.

Suddenly, without warning, she heard a tremendous crash in the ship. Connie went pale and started for the ladder up.

"Calm urself," uttered the half-drunken sail maker. "Tis only a bow chaser. Ye'll hear a full broadside soon."

And C R A S H ! Fourteen times over and again!

Connie thought her eardrums would pop! Or, perhaps the ship was hit? If they were to sink, she almost panicked; she'd never get out of this stinking black hole alive!

Then they felt and heard a deeper BOOM, and the ship shuddered.

"Tiz nothin, just a broadside. Calm urself", the old man spoke slowly, taking another swig.

"Hmmm sounds like something else was hit," he slurred.

"That was a broadside?" she asked of the near-drunk, "You mean all the guns fired?"

"Aye, but only on the one side. An somewat else too. Dunno wat."

A few moments later two dirty crewmen, covered in black gunpowder, soot, and some smears of blood slid down the ladder carrying a very bloody man between them.

" Tiz Corey," one of them said to the grizzled sail maker. 'E's got a splinter in e'es leg."

The old sail maker groaned to his feet and told them to hold the injured man down on the table bolted to the deck.

Corey, the young injured sailor, was thrashing around in their firm grip.

"No!" the young sailor wailed, "E'll kill me!"

He pushed away from the table with his good leg.

The old man then calmly grabbed each of the man's flailing arms, one at a time, from the struggling sailors. He methodically tied each down to a strap fixed to each corner of the table. Then he did the same with the uninjured leg. When he roughly grabbed the leg with the large bloody splinter sticking up from the thigh the young sailor screamed in pain.

The surgeon then dug in his pockets coming-up with a small dirty piece of wood. He jammed it into the man's mouth, between his teeth.

"Bite hard, ye" he mouthed.

"You two," he growled to the two dirty sailors, "back t'ye'r guns."

Pushing behind Connie, he dug both a stained and wicked-looking scalpel and a dirty bone saw from the chest. He approached the bleeding five inch round jagged wood splinter sticking out of the man's thigh.

"E'es off wid t'leg," said the sail maker, "'tiz none other fer it."

"Stop it!" screamed Connie, "You'll kill him."

"Likely so," calmly replied Mr. Oakes, the grizzled old goat. "Ees splinters mostly putrefy. We'll off with the leg and perhaps e'll live".

"NO!" shouted Connie again.

It was bedlam in the small orlop with Connie and Oaks yelling at each other, and young Corey writhing in pain, as the two sailors backed out and ran back to their guns.

Connie instantly understood why there was a wide bladed iron 'spatula' heating to red hot in a small charcoal brazier; it was to cauterize an amputated stump.

"I can save the leg," Connie stated firmly.

"Ye can huh? Then fine," snarled the geezer over the howls of the injured man. 'Ave at it, then."

He retired to his coil of rope and uncorked his bottle of brandy.

"Might as well be ye that kills 'em as me," he growled, taking a long pull from the bottle.

Connie picked-up the sharp knife, disregarding the bone saw, and placed it in the brazier. She next turned fast to the drunken sail maker and yanked the bottle of cheap brandy out of his hands.

"He needs this more than you," she said grimly, ignoring the man's grasping at the bottle.

Corey moaned again in pain. She looked at him and mopped his pale and sweaty face with a wet cloth. His eyes were wide with terror. Her heart went out to him, knowing the worse pain he would soon feel.

"I've got to do this," she told herself, stiffening to the ugly work.

"Corey," she said quietly, offering the half-filled flask of spirits, "this will hurt but I can have you walking again. Drink what you can of this quickly."

"Waste o' good brandy," quipped Oates.

The sailor chugged down several swallows. Then, he howled in pain as Connie dumped most of the bottle onto the bloody splinter; the strong spirit knifing into the wound.

Connie then focused on the leg, ignoring the man's writhing. Then she quickly pulled the now red-glowing scalpel out of the brazier, holding the handle in a rag and with a quick twirling motion cut the huge wood splinter free of the man's thigh. She then quickly filled the bleeding hole with the remainder of the bottle.

Her patient howled once, almost biting the wood plug in two, and then mercifully fainted.

The large splinter had come out cleanly with several bloody pieces of flesh still clinging to it. Still, it had apparently not broken a major artery, and she thought she'd gotten all of it. While Connie would have been happier were she then to have been able to stitch the gaping wound closed, the best she could do was to bind it tightly in the cleanest linen bandages she could find in the bottom of the medicine chest.

The sailor had passed out, but the wound was soon clean and bound.

The old sail maker, stirred awake by Corey's last howl, was now open-mouthed, gawking at the bound leg.

"Cor but 'ave ne'r seen the likes 'o that," he was rattling on as Connie finally turned her back on her now unconscious patient.

Her stomach heaved. She had to get out of the stinking orlop deck and into some fresh air! She felt filthy, bloody and smelly. She was exhausted.

"Get me some fresh boiled linen," she commanded the amazed Oates as she dashed for the ladder to the deck.

Connie stood on the main deck enjoying the fresh air while the crew reassembled the after cabins. When the partitions had been re-installed she entered hers. She threw her bloody shirt and sailor's trousers on the deck and fell on her bunk in her sweaty underwear. She only wanted to sleep, closing out the bloody horror, but she couldn't.

She felt another wave of nausea, and knew she would do anything to avoid more of the heathens on this nasty old ship, but she was stuck.

She began to softly sob again, and then finally she drifted to sleep.

"BANG BANG," Connie was awakened

"I'll not be serving thee, Miss," Connie heard the crippled servant's voice, "but the Mate said t' bring ye the last o'breakfast."

Thud; she heard a bowl drop by the door.

Opening it, she picked-up the usual portion of the same god-awful slop she'd been offered since arriving on this ship. Yes, it was the usual slimy gray greasy and salty boiled pig fat they called meat covered with brown pea paste, and with a rock-hard brown hunk of bread swimming on top. Bugs were climbing out of the bread. Thank goodness there was a strong mug of tea, which almost hid the swampy flavor of the water.

Still, Connie was ravenous. This time she held her nose and was able to force most of the mess down her throat without gagging; however the buggy bread was just too foul to stomach.

Now, having forced herself to eat, she had to relieve herself. That meant either trying to squat over the little bucket she had been given, or again asking the captain to use the little hole through the counter of the ship behind the curtain in his cabin. She hated the thought of crossing the gunroom in her bloody and smelly sailor clothes and with her hair tangled like a briar patch. She'd not even been able to even properly wash her face in days. She still had both dried blood on her hands and the taste of that greasy horrible food in her mouth.

'Oh,' she thought, 'what would I give for ten minutes in a hot shower?'

Aah, she spied the Lieutenant's trunk under the bunk. She considered that surely he'd not mind if she were to borrow a fresh shirt and pants? Maybe later she could wash out her other bloody clothes, although they'd certainly be stained forever.

She gave in, urinated in the bucket, and used another piece of the wadded sweatshirt.

She told herself that she'd better get moving. She knew that she had to get someone to boil more bandaging for that poor soul in the orlop. If nothing else, perhaps she'd saved his leg. She knew that she absolutely could not count on old Oakey to do anything.

With fresh dismay she wondered how soon she could get off this horrible little ship. She again had to force herself to believe that Dad and her David were somewhere nearby with *Anne Marie,* her own private head, her razor, her deodorant, her scented soap and her shampoo.

The next morning, some hours before dawn, while approaching Sandy Hook off New York in a faint moonlight, Captain Aaron was awakened by a sharp knock at the cabin door.

"Captain Aaron, sir, strange vessel on the larboard beam," a sailor said outside the door.

Minutes later Aaron was on deck, buckling his sword around his waist as he clambered up the scuttle.

"What 'av you got Willright?" he queried, noting that *Reliant* was sailing full and by at about six knots under just a glimmer of moonlight.

Willright simply pointed.

There on the beam several miles out a large white square light with a single green light was moving at good speed across the water.

"Glass please," said Aaron, holding his hand towards the helmsman for the telescope.

He was shocked!

Through the telescope he could see a lighted pair of oversized square portholes and the shadowy outline of a ketch with pointed sails. As the ketch was smaller than *Reliant*, she should be sailing at a slower speed than his Kings frigate; at best moving at a knot or so slower. No, that vessel was moving fast; well over six knots.

"What the hell?" he exclaimed.

Just then the light inside the mystery ship was extinguished, plunging it again into total darkness, except for the brightest green running light he'd ever seen.

Aaron, having achieved the rank of Commander in His Majesty's Royal Navy after a full ten years at sea, was a realist. Yet he could not doubt his own eyes. And, indeed, in tonight's moderate breeze he had just seen, so he told himself, a ketch rigged vessel of about seventy feet with strange pointed sails. It was moving across the water at more speed by half than his very fast ship rigged frigate!

But, he had the weather gage of them, and he would put an end to that Yankee blockade-runner.

Or, he briefly wondered, perhaps it was that confounded woman's ship? Perhaps it was her father seeking her before he continued on to Cadiz?

He passed the word to quietly beat to quarters, and thirty minutes later was but five cables lengths from the ketch which continued sailing on towards Sandy Hook. Yes, the ketch was moving an unbelievable turn of speed, but *Reliant* was closing on it.

'Those Yankees do build damned fast ships,' he thought. 'But, why was that idiot still running with lights on? Didn't he know about the war?'

He considered that perhaps that damned woman was right? That just might be her people, and maybe they did not know of the War. It might be that news had not traveled to New Spain?

Incredulous.

Another ten minutes, and Aaron was another cable closer.

He passed the word to lay one shot across the bows of the Yankee.

That oughta stop 'em, he thought, Yankee or Spaniard.

BOOM! The bow chaser fired, and a huge splash followed, not 100 yards from the silent ketch.

The crash of the cannon instantly awakened Connie.

Oh No, she blanched in terror, hoping that were they were not fighting again. The thought raced through her head that she couldn't stand another bloody battle.

She dashed to the quarterdeck and watched the Captain, following the direction of his telescope.

Her heart felt like it jumped up into her throat! She saw *Anne Marie* in the faint moonlight!

She knew that she was not mistaken; it could be nothing else.

Oh, she agonized, thinking of anything she could do?

Alas, there was nothing.

She had thrown all the foul weather gear overboard days ago. The strobe and EPIRIB had been destroyed anyway. And no, she wouldn't toss away her life jacket; she might need it. *Anne Marie* would probably never notice it in the dark anyway.

But, she rejoiced to herself, tears streaking her cheeks, thank God she wasn't alone!

The tears kept streaming down her pretty face; she knew now that Dad and David were alive! And, they were here too in this god-awful time with her.

She was not alone.

Then as she watched, *Anne Marie's* green running line went out. The ketch tacked and very quickly slid from her view.

Connie quickly dried her eyes and ducked below, down and down to the smelly orlop deck where she was supposed to be.

Corey was wide-eyed after the crash of the shot. She reassured him and sat to wait for quarters to be piped-down. She was smiling, not even noticing the awful odors.

Aaron was shocked! That damned Yankee ketch was already on the other tack! How, he wondered, could any crew tack any ship that fast?

"All hands wear ship and make sail," yelled Aaron.

In five minutes the *Reliant* was headed hard on the wind, two points west of due south, creaming through the seas at over six knots.

But, the ketch had gone? It simply vanished, out of sight.

At the top of a swell, in a glimmer of fading moonlight, John Aaron caught a last glimpse of the damned Yankee ketch, heading a full two points closer to the wind than any ship could possibly sail and throwing a huge bow wave as it crashed through the swells.

It was gone in an instant.

The next morning *Reliant* was riding an inbound current, passing Sandy Hook to port, and sailing upriver to the New York battery. She rounded sharply to windward in the position indicated by the Flagship's signals, and the anchor splashed to the bottom just as she lost headway.

Aaron was pleased to see *Yardley* in port with her gun ports opened to catch the summer breeze. He'd have time to visit his old friend, now Commander of *HMS Yardley*, Ian Sharecross.

Reliant had barely settled to her anchor rode when the huge 74-gun flagship, *Indomitable,* signaled: "*Reliant* to Flag".

Aaron had but a few minutes to dash below and quickly change into his best uniform while Will Thompson got his gig lowered and the oarsmen settled with their best checkered shirts and whitest breeches. Aaron was piped sharply over the side by his Marines, and carefully holding his dress sword in hand, settled into the stern seat of the gig. His sailors smartly dropped oars and pulled sharply to the Flagship.

As they tossed oars at the *Indomitable* chain plates, and as Captain John Aaron's head appeared at the entry port, he heard the Flag Marines call "*Reliant*".

He was piped aboard.

After having spent four years as a Midshipman, and later Acting Lieutenant in *Indomitable,* Aaron was pleased to see so many familiar faces, all of whom he had not seen in the months since assuming command of *Reliant.* The Captain's aide, a Junior Lieutenant with a dandified appearance, as if he'd never swung a cutlass, met him at the sally port.

He offered a bow to Aaron saying, "Sir Wembly will see you now."

Aaron nodded at familiar friendly faces as he strutted aft across the busy main deck of the huge three decker. He entered the spacious Captain's Cabin passing two impeccably dressed Marines at the door. The large Day Cabin was furnished with polished wooden and brass chairs around a long table at the head of which was a large desk. Behind the desk were open windows across the full stern of the flagship. Aaron could see the growing city of New York in a panorama view.

Captain Wembly, a large man with a weather-beaten countenance and a full head of white hair, rose from the head of the table as Aaron entered. He stood behind a display of pure white feathered quills.

"Welcome back to the Fleet, Aaron," he boomed as Aaron entered, "a glass of Madeira?" Wembly was already pouring.

"Please have a seat and tell me how goes the blockade? Or, have ye been to Montauk yet?" he continued his questions. "And, what brings thee to New York? Hadn't expected to see *Reliant* until September."

"Apologies for breaking Orders, your Grace," replied Aaron. "Haven't reported on station yet. Damned Yankees have a new-fangled ketch I'd thought to report. Strange, Sir, the ketch is reported to be a Yankee, but said to hail from New Spain. Damned thing has sails with pointed tops. Never seen the likes of it. She sports no gaffs."

Aaron paused, then continued, "Caught a castaway from her though, strange woman at that. Ere's me Report and trust ye'll want to know of it"

He went on, "Aye, we'll be at sea at first light with the tide tomorrow on your Orders, unless I can water first. And, *Reliant* did destroy a brig loaded with powder at Cape May several days ago; that too is in the dispatches."

Lt. Aaron and the Captain spent the next hour in deep conversation about the condition of the *Reliant*, her crew, her supplies, the need for a careening. The Captain lamented that there'd been virtually no progress in the unending colonial disturbance ashore.

As the briefing was coming to an end Sir Wembly queried, "And what about this Yankee or Spanish vessel, and ye'r castaway?"

"Aye, Sir" replied Aaron, reluctantly, "there is something else, and strange 'tis, yet I'm almost afraid to mention it, Sir, for fear of untoward question."

"Aye, and what be that?"

"Well Sir, two days out of Bermuda, *Reliant* found a castaway at sea, a woman, and as I'm to believe, perhaps a Yankee woman. She says she'd been raised in New Spain. She claims she's washed off a ketch named *Anne Marie,* said to be built in and sailed from a place called Deerford in Connecticut. Methinks tiz the Yankee ketch I've spoken of."

"Harrumph," the Captain replied, "Deerford is but a farming town. No shipyards or even a proper quay there."

"Aye, Sir. This woman had the most strange accouterments when we found her, unfortunately lost 'em at sea. But, she's shown an amazing talent as ships surgeon since our encounter with the brig. Saved a lad's leg she did. She claims she learned healing from Mayan Indians."

"What mean ye of strange accouterments? And how be they disposed?"

"Tiz hard to explain, sir. This lass was found adrift some leagues north and east of Bermuda. Shouldn'ta lived, sir, but we found this orange spot on the sea."

"Orange spot ye say?" interjected the Captain, "strange color."

"Aye, Sir. From the main top 't looked like an orange spot on the ocean just abaft the leeward bow. When I hauled this person into the gig 't seemed 'twas a short and very fat young lad. Now mind ye, sir, some short time after aboard the gig and before we were returned to the ship, this lass reduced the size of the orange coat upon her. For all the world it sounded like a blowing whale. Indeed, t'was then we found she was a woman, sir."

"Further her outer clothing was all of a bright yellow color and there were several strange boxes about this yellow suit that can't begin to describe."

"Anyway, after the sinking of the Brig I couldn't find this clothing aboard. Sorry, sir, should have put 'tall under lock, but in the haste of the engagement, we~," Aaron's speech tailed off.

Wembly broke in, questioning, "ye'r speaking of very strange things. Are thee certain?"

"Sir," replied Aaron somewhat dejectedly, "t'were some wondrous things indeed I saw with this lass. There was a small black box, about the size of your snuff box, sir, but it had no top and no entry. On it was a red light, like there was a candle within, but there was no flame and no heat. I just canna explain, sir. There was more like that. But, the bitch threw it all in our wake before I could stop her."

"Indeed," replied the large Captain, "well we'll worry not about what ye've lost. And, ye'll not be needing a woman on *Reliant* when ye sail for blockade duty on the morning tide. Best send the woman here. I'll keep me eye on her and we've dire need of good surgeons. If indeed she's of importance to the Spanish Crown we'd better care for her well. Perhaps we'll get something from her."

He changed the subject, "Aah yes, and ye'll have ye'r water barge at first light before the ebb".

"Aye aye, sir, but there's one more thing I almost durnst mention, er."

Aaron's speech stumbled, "Last evening approaching Sandy Hook we put a shot towards what may be the same ketch. I am not daft, and I saw it only by moonlight, sir, but that damned ketch beat to windward to a degree and at a turn of heel I could not fathom."

"Aaron," replied the Captain, "should the Yankees have a new blockage-runner with such a turn of speed, and should she be reaching the Connecticut shores, she'll have to pass ye'r position at Block Island. Keep thee a weather eye, and bring her to post. But take care; we'll not be wanting to break our treaty with the Dons."

"And, Aaron," he ordered, "send ye'r damned Spanish woman surgeon here to the Flagship."

CHAPTER FOUR

Stephen Downey stood up on the footboard of the heavily laden wagon and slapped the reins across the backs of his two sweating horses as they strained up a steep hill through the fields away from the Byram River. He was but four or five hours from William's Farm. He knew that he'd arrive in time for dinner.

He remembered his feeling of relief as he'd passed the last British patrol when he'd crossed the river from Manhattan the day before.

Stephen was smuggling several chests of Continental gold, well hidden under bolts of cotton cloth in his wagon. He had spent the previous night in a Tory owned tavern in Port Chester, unable to sleep well for worry about the secret cargo in the wagon parked in the tavern yard.

Yes, he told himself again, he would reach Deerford by tonight.

This was a critical delivery for Stephen. The gold in his wagon bed was destined for Arthur Williams as payment for a shipment of French muskets recently arrived in Philadelphia for Washington's army. However, with the British controlling New York and the Hudson River well past Albany, it was a perilous business to move a cash payment in gold to the French agents in Rhode Island. Stephen knew that it could not be trusted to a sea voyage; the British Navy's blockade prevented that. He knew that this dangerous journey was the only way to sneak the cash through the British lines around New York

But even more critical than the gold, Stephen realized, was the news he'd learned in New York just yesterday.

He had learned from a well placed Tory merchant that Lord Howe was readying to load his formidable army into over 262 ships under command of his brother, Admiral Howe. The British planned to move most of this army by sea, around Washington's Army in Jew Jersey, for a sneak move on the Continental Capitol in Philadelphia.

They planned a frontal assault up the Delaware River to capture the colonial capital by surprise while the Colonial Army was too far away to protect the city.

Stephen knew the plan could succeed. He also knew that General Washington, camped somewhere outside Morristown, had to have this information as soon as possible.

He knew that somehow, impossibly, he had to get this message to the Continental Congress. There was no one else.

Still, smiling briefly, he looked forward to a visit with Arthur Williams, and even more so to a meal cooked by Arthur's lovely daughter, Anne.

It was so easy to think about Anne.

She was tall with long dark hair and amazing green eyes. Still unmarried, she had waited for her whaling fiancé' for years; the lad was now finally thought to have been lost at sea. Oh, but Stephen would love to pursue Anne for himself, but he knew she'd have nothing to do with a runty little poor English immigrant, as was he. Indeed, he smirked at himself; he stood just over five feet and he was all legs and chest.

'I can run all day,' he mused, 'and I can lift heavy loads with any man, but I'm certainly was too pitted and craggy to ever be able to attract a true lady.'

His team of horses plodded down the dusty track pulling his wagon between the stone walls separating the fields that late July morning. The day was warming quickly and a light breeze ruffled the surface of the river to Stephen's right. He pulled off his coat and stuffed it behind his back on the wooden seat, reclining to a more comfortable position as the wagon rolled past the neatly tended fields.

Stephen relaxed into a daydream. He knew he was safe here.

He was well over forty years old and he'd come a long way from the hayloft over the tavern stable in Portsmouth, England, where he'd been born. He was very honored to be a Colonel in the Continental Army; however he did not command troops. Rather, he worked directly for General Washington's staff as one of the many spies employed in gaining intelligence on British movements.

During his recent visit to New York Stephen had dressed as a wealthy tradesman; he was always welcomed in the best drawing rooms. While he'd never look suave and urbane in the city, he was generally welcomed as a successful hemp trader. While he wasn't an imposing figure, standing just barely over 5'6" and being quite slight of build, he was well connected with prosperous planters and merchants throughout the Colonies. Only General Washington, among a very few, knew his real history.

His thoughts drifted back to the first time he'd met General Washington.

Ten years previously, at the start of the French and Indian Wars, Stephen remembered riding into a small army camp somewhere in western Pennsylvania in the middle of a warm afternoon. He'd been dirty and hungry from ten days traveling east from Ohio.

"Who goes thar," he had been challenged by a sentry as he'd approached the campfire.

"Stephen Downey, seeking to enlist to fight Indians," he'd replied.

Stephen had dismounted and the sentry had drawn close, the musket pointed at Stephen's chest. Stephen was then wearing a stained buckskin shirt, worn blue woolen trousers and scuffed boots. The ribs on his horse had been showing, but his long rifle had been openly hanging from the saddle.

"The Colonel's tent is over thar," said the soldier. "Colonel Washington needs troops and thee may do."

As Stephen had approached the tent the front flap opened and a British officer stooped through. He'd then stood up straight, towering over Stephen, perhaps a full foot taller. The officer was slender and impeccably dressed with long blond hair curling on his collar. He had a strong jaw and a hooked nose.

He'd smiled at Stephen.

Stephen had nodded his head towards the imposing red coated officer as he'd looped the reins of the horse around a tree limb.

"Colonel," he'd started, offering his hand, "ye'r the first militia I've seen. I've heard that war is declared and I seek to fight the Indians and their French masters. My name is Downey and I've come from the Ohio Territory."

Washington shook the offered hand as he'd replied, "Downey is it? Well, come on in out of the sun and have a seat. My boys here are mostly Virginia farmers and tradesmen. We may find someone with knowledge of the western territories very useful indeed."

As Stephen had followed the officer into the tent and sat on a camp stool the Colonel had then said, "Thee must be hungry?"

"Aye sir. Ate the last of my jerked beef yesterday."

Washington then had stood and hollered out the tent flap, "Orderly, bring this man a joint of that mutton we had for dinner."

He'd then sat down and addressed Stephen again, "Now tell me about thineself. Does thee truly know the territory west of the mountains? And, what brings thee here seeking to fight the Indians?"

A tin platter covered with a cold shank of mutton and a piece of hard bread had been then dropped on the table.

Stephen took a bite, then answered, chewing, "Well sir, I've lived in the Ohio Territory for most of ten years now, mostly farming in the summers and hunting in the winter. Was married too, and with a child, but they was killed by the Iroquois."

"Yes," Washington had said as Stephen had ripped a piece of bread, "our task is to make the Territories safe for new colonists. Lots of folks are moving across the mountains but the Crown has heard of these attacks by the Indians, we hear incited by the double-damned French. Appears that France want to claim the western territories and they're using the Iroquois to their ends. We aim to establish order."

He continued, "Tell me, Downey, what lead thee to cross the mountains ten years ago?"

"Well sir, when I was landed in New York in '57 I was indentured to a farmer from New Jersey. I was to help him cross to the new territories, and I was also able to teach his children to read."

Washington had interrupted, right eyebrow raised in surprise, "Ye read and write too? Tiz strange to find thee here in the wilderness. How did ye come to read?"

"Well sir," Stephen had replied, "since I was a small lad, back in England, my Da always spoke of the new lands in the colonies. He was a gambler, sir, and after my Mum died he was a drinker too. Got himself jailed in the Portsmouth Debtors Prison when I was but fourteen. Last time I saw him in that prison he told me to get to the port and see if I could work my way to the colonies."

"My Da told me that England was no good fer me there. He said I could only become a thief, or get pressed into the Navy or Army. But he told me that ship's captains might transport me to the new world on something called indenture. Yes, he said I'd have to work the passage off when I got here, but in time I'd be a free man in the clean new world."

"Well, Colonel," Stephen had continued, "I followed my Da's words. I found my way to the port and spent a day walking among the sailors, teamsters, tradesmen and laborers working on the piers. Once, passing outside a saloon, a large red faced Navy boson grabbed my coat, but I ran away knowing I didn't want to be 'pressed into the Navy."

"Several piers away a small two masted ship was loading supplies, and there was a written notice that I couldn't read at a wooden table at the foot of the gangplank. A ship's officer in a dirty ruffled shirt and blue coat was at the table writing something for a thin young man with a girl in a worn dress beside him. I snuck up close to listen to what he was saying."

"He was explaining his indenture contract. He said the ship would transport them and no more than one chest of their belongings to the Port of New York in the New World. There he said the captain would sell the cost of both passages to a new world gentleman or farmer who needed labor. He said it was usually a seven year contract to pay for the passage, but after that they'd be free to seek their fortune."

"I remember the couple looking at each other. They spoke together quietly. For some reason they seemed to have no other prospects in Portsmouth, so the thin girl nodded at her husband. He, then she, both made a mark on a paper the officer offered."

"They then had picked up two bundles of their worldly goods and marched up the quay to the ship."

Stephen remembered, looking up from his empty plate at the Colonel, and then said, "Well, sir, I then just signed my own indenture. It was not easy to convince the officer to take such a scrawny young boy as I was, but I lied about my age and convinced him. I made my mark on the paper, and Mr. Smith, the boson took me to the foc'sl."

"It was a long voyage, stormy and cold too," Stephen had reminisced for Washington, "but in between my duties working the ship Miss Maggie, the young wife, taught me to read from her bible, and to write too."

Stephen's daydreams of his first meeting with the General were interrupted as the wagon bumped through the little village of Greenwich. He followed the two lane track to a ferry crossing at the Mianus River and paid the boatman his four pense. He then paid a full pound to a livery at the ferry landing for a change of horses, and resumed his seat with his coat behind him.

Slipping back into his reverie as the green fields and stone walls slipped by, he thought back to the clear crisp day in March of 1755 when ship had arrived in the Port of New York. As soon as the ship had tied to a small pier the Captain posted a Notice in several local taverns for the sale of indentured servants. Stephen could still remember all twelve of the indentured aboard the little bark, along with the unique fragrance of the cargo of east India tea.

His thoughts went briefly to his special shipboard friends, Jonathan and Maggie. Their indentures had been both purchased before his was sold. They'd gone away with a wagon maker from some other colony. He'd not heard from them since.

Stephen remembered telling the Colonel that first day in the tent, "Captain Abercrombie asked me to remain with his ship, but I wanted none of the sea. So my seven year indenture was bought by a farmer, William McCall, who had decided to move his family to the free land that was advertised, in the Ohio Territory, across the mountains."

"McCall had already sold his little farm in the New Jersey country, and had planned to spend his remaining few pounds purchasing the indenture of a working man. Short and young as I was, I was the best he could afford. At least, that's what he'd told me. He was later pleased to learn that I could teach his children to read."

Stephen remembered that the journey from the pier in New York to McCall's former farm in the little town of Sussex, New Jersey, had taken two days. They'd ridden through New Jersey countryside that looked to Stephen to be almost like what he'd left in England; mile after mile of well tended farmland. Stephen had been amazed at the richness of this land in this new colony. All the farms were all being plowed that early spring day; the rich brown soil seemed easily turned by horse-drawn plows, moving slowly in field after field.

On arriving at the McCall farm Stephen had learned that there were five brothers and their wives all trying to make a living on their small section of the former large family farm. Each parcel, McCall had explained, just was not large enough to feed a growing family. McCall had to have more land, and there wasn't any to be had.

Stephen remembered he and McCall taking five days of heavy work to load two large stout wagons with all the family's possessions for their emigration to the Ohio Territory. The journey west had been said to take eight weeks. McCall's family included the farmer, his stout but friendly and motherly wife, two girls, both younger than Stephen, and two very small boys.

Leaving Sussex on a narrow path to the west, it had taken them three weeks to travel through the forests of eastern Pennsylvania. They had then toiled their two wagons behind teams of oxen on a single rutty path another fortnight through the mountains to the town of Pittsburgh.

There, Stephen remembered, McCall had engaged a flatboat, which was simply a large flat raft. For a week they'd drifted down the widening river. Stephen had had no idea where they were headed, but after ten days on the river McCall put the rafts ashore where a small stream entered from the south. Leading his family up-stream for perhaps a mile, he'd stopped at a vacant and open meadow near the babbling brook and announced that they were home.

Stephen remembered asking himself with dismay, is home? They were in a wilderness of huge trees about a mile from the large Ohio River. There seemed no one else around for miles.

Stephen grimaced even today remembering the endless toil that started with this arrival. He and McCall had labored together, often with the wife, Elizabeth, and even with the little girls helping. They spent the summer clearing fields and cutting down trees that all seemed ten feet around; the trees had grown there for eons. They'd then cut them to manageable lengths and dragged them off to the edges of what were soon to be fields.

They'd still been living in the wagons.

The family had then, as the weather had grown colder, all together built a small cabin, not much more than a hut, in which they'd wintered. That first winter they'd eaten mostly game that William hunted, along with dried peas and cornbread. Occasionally the two chickens had produced an egg or two, but the one sickly and tired cow never had produced but a small bit of milk which Elizabeth always gave to her little boys.

It had taken three years, Stephen remembered, but when he was almost eighteen the farm had grown into its own. It had become actually prosperous. And, he grinned to himself, it had been a good three years.

McCall's migration from New Jersey to Ohio paid had off.

Stephen, finishing his mutton chop, had summarized this all for the tall Colonel in a few sentences.

Then he had said to Washington, "That's when the Indians first struck."

"It was on a Sunday afternoon and I'd taken a pole to the river hoping to catch our dinner. While I was away Indians attacked the farm. I heard the shrieking, but the time I got to the house there was nothing left but a burning pyre. The entire McCall family had been brutally murdered and scalped."

"I buried them all myself," Stephen told the Colonel. "It took me most of two days. After that I walked miles to the nearest neighbors, Aaron and Emily Barnes."

"They hired me on to work their farm. The next spring I married their only daughter, Else. I was planning to spend our lives farming beside the Ohio River."

Stephen snapped himself from his reveries. He didn't want to remember that cold day ten years ago, having come home to find Else and their baby boy also murdered and scalped.

He sat upright on the wagon seat and grabbed the reins. Rounding a bend, his wagon clattered down a cobbled portion of road for several blocks through the town of Stamford, where small trading ships and fishing boats were pulled up fronting a wide bay. Moments later the town fell behind him and the track resumed passing through fields, between more stone walls.

He remembered briefly telling the Colonel about finding his wife and baby killed. That had been just a week before he'd arrived at the Militia Camp.

"After loosing everyone to the bloody Indians, Sir," Stephen had ended his tale, "All I could think of was to ride off and take my vengeance on the Indians myself, but my father in law told me that war had been declared, and suggested I ride east to join the army."

"That was just a week ago," Stephen finished his tale for the tall Colonel

Yes, Stephen smiled to himself. Colonel Washington had made him a scout and a Captain in the Militia. He'd fought through the campaign for two years, always serving Washington.

And, after that war, with Colonial Washington as his patron, he'd become a small success trading hemp, grown as a cash crop from Virginia through southern New England. Rope walks had been growing in the port cities as more ships were being built and re-fit. With an introduction from General Washington to a rope merchant in Baltimore, Stephen had learned to evaluate good hemp in the fields. His first transaction had come from Mt. Vernon.

That had been almost ten years ago, and now Stephen bought and sold hemp in port cities from Baltimore to Boston. It had become a solid and respected business

The previous August, while General Washington was still holding New York and after the Colonies had declared for independence, Stephen had gone to Washington's New York headquarters to volunteer his services. He hoped for a field commission in the Continental Army.

Washington had other ideas.

"Downey," the General had said, "I've more good men trained in field combat and Indian warfare than I can possibly use as field officers, although I could make ye a senior sergeant. I just don't think that would suit ye'r talents."

He went on, "Don't ye have good and loyal trade contacts throughout all the Colonies from Virginia to the North?"

"Aye, General," Stephen remembered his reply, "Although many of the hemp farmers of my acquaintance will never have doings with the King. I've further put some good men of like mind in positions to collect me hemp from other farmers for easier shipment. I certainly know 'em all, I mean, who can be trusted and who not. Of course many of the rope walks are Tory, but their cash is still good," Stephen finished.

"I know of thine growers, Stephen. I've bought hemp from enough of 'em for you at Mt. Vernon to trust your judgment. Because of that I think thee can serve our new Country in a more unorthodox and more valuable position than as an Army field officer".

"Aye, General?" Stephen had queried.

"My belief, Downey, is that this war will turn on our knowledge of enemy plans. And, with the British as thine best customers, and indeed they do need huge amounts of both hemp and rope, ye should remain in a fine position to pass anything you hear of their plans to me. Do ye not also have the trust of the Tory merchants and rope walk factors?"

"You mean," Downey interrupted, "thee'd want me as a spy?"

"Aye, tiz as ye say, and should thee be caught ye'll probably hang," Washington had replied, "Can thee do it for our Independence?"

"I'm ye'r servant, Sir."

"Then ye'll be a Colonel in the Continental Army, with reporting duties directly to me. Keep about ye'r business and act in New York as a perfect Tory gentleman. However, ye can let certain of your collection point gentleman farmers, who are totally loyal to the Cause, know about your true affiliation."

Stephen had replied, "Ye'rself, of course, and Jones at Mt. Vernon, Stanley in Morristown, McWhite in Dover, Andrews in Situate, Williams in Deerford east of New Manchester, and —."

"Stephen," the General had interrupted,"as a Colonel I trust thee to know ye'r contacts, to know who to trust and how far, and to make every sacrifice to get to me with any key enemy information as fast as possible after ye'll learn of it. Ye've no other duties except from time to time an identified agent of the Army might ask thee for assistance or for courier duty."

Stephen had stood, understanding the interview was at an end.

"General, I am at thy Service," and he bowed himself out.

"Stephen," General Washington said as he was leaving, "all ye'll ever need to get my personal attention is your name to my Guard. I trust ye'll not to bother me with details better handled by my staff."

"General, I'm deeply honored by your trust,"

With that Stephen had departed to resume business as usual, or as 'usual' making every effort to learn of all movements of the Kings Army in New

York. That had been ten months ago. All Stephen had been able to offer had been a bit of small courier duty, like the gold under the cloth in the wagon today. He deeply desired to offer General Washington more for his trust.

Then, yesterday, he'd learned about Lord Howe's planned sneak attack on the Congress.

While driving the two tired horses up a rise towards New Manchester his mind was now filled with questions about how he could both deliver the gold to farmer Williams, and also get the urgent news of Howe's planned conquest of the new nation's Capitol to Washington in time. Indeed, he thought, at best, without Army checkpoints, it was a six day ride from William's Farm to Philadelphia. He didn't think he had that much time, and he was worried that with the British Army in the middle it was more like a ten day journey now.

And, Howe was sailing in a week, or less.

Just prior to the early July sunset Stephen turned his wagon off the Post Road at Deerford's small town square and onto a lane that wandered south towards William's Farm. It was late enough that the town was quiet, all the residents being well at home with their dinners. It was still a good mile and a half to Arthur William's fine stone house.

Stephen knew that William's great grandfather was one of the first colonists of Connecticut. He'd claimed over 400 acres of sound front fine bottomland early in the previous century. William's Farm stretched all the way from the east bank of Deerford Creek to the New Manchester town line at the New England River bank, including a fine long point of land protruding into the Sound. Williams had the farm planted in tobacco, hemp and vegetables. He also bred horses and maintained a fine dairy herd.

Stephen, tired, sweaty and dusty, pulled the wagon into the drive in front of Williams" large house and leapt to the front door, banging on the knocker. The door was opened by Anne, Arthur's 29 year old daughter.

"Uncle Stephen!" she yelled with exuberance, notwithstanding that Stephen was close to her own age, "Father, Tad, Mother, it's Uncle Stephen! Oh, sorry Uncle Stephen, come on in, we've just finished supper, but I know there's more mutton and fixings in the kitchen."

"Stephen," boomed a deep voice from a very large man with a long dark beard, white hair, and ruddy cheeks coming into the parlor, "Tiz been since the damned Redcoats tossed our General out of the city that we've seen you, welcome."

"Arthur, you're a sight for me sore eyes," replied Stephen, "and t'was a long and dusty ride. I'd appreciate a cool drink."

After quaffing a pint of cool well water from a pewter mug Stephen quickly took Arthur William's arm and pulled him to a quiet corner.

"Arthur, please have Tad or your best and most trusted person care for me rig; it's got the gold for ye'r French muskets under the calico."

"Aye," muttered Williams, then he boomed, "Tad."

When his tall and well formed 24 year old son appeared he said, "Please, yourself, take Stephen's rig to the barn. Unload it all. Ye'll know what to do with it. Afterwards have Timmy care for the horses."

Tad nodded, and without a word, he disappeared out the front door.

"Come on in and rest ye'r bones," entreated Williams, "and what brings thee here instead of one of ye'r hemp men, any one of whom could have brought the musket payment without ever knowing 'twas there?"

After an hour's conversation over a dinner of cold mutton chops and boiled potatoes Williams understood the urgency of the intelligence Downey had learned about Lord Howe's plans. He quickly agreed they simply had to get the news to Washington, somewhere near Trenton, before Howe landed on the Delaware River. All they could think of was to send Tad with Stephen, riding the farm's best four horses, in an attempt to reach the Army within the week required.

"Stephen," Arthur yawned on their way to bed, "ye're well tired out, and tiz a hard journey that thee and Tad'll be taking. Why not rest the morrow and start fine and early on Tuesday?"

"Aye," Stephen replied, "it'll give Tad and me a day to pack and plan the best route through the lines. I'm thinking we'll still be safe enough to take the farm lanes through White Plains and cross over Hudson at Yonkers; I hear there's a reliable boatman there."

"Thee and Tad can work all that out in the morning. Sleep in, he's always up at dawn, liking to catch a flounder for breakfast he is," said Williams heading down the upstairs hallway,

"He'll have thee called when he's back from the Cove."

Indeed, before dawn the next morning, as was his custom, Tad Williams awoke. He pulled on his breeches, boots, shirt and coat, and slapped his hat squarely on his fair head. He passed through the shed outside the back door for his hickory fishing rod and headed down a path through the woods for the cove.

CHAPTER FIVE

Aboard *Anne Marie,* David awoke very early the morning after they'd anchored in William's Cove, having safely crept up the unmarked channel.

They had sailed from the east end of the Sound all day yesterday without sighting a single boat other than a few fishing dories close inshore. After dark, and as the Sound started to narrow at the west end, they worked to the north shore and were clearly able to see the emerging and familiar outlines Roank's Point on the radar screen.

With a quiet humming of electric winches, the main and mizzen dropped inside their lazy jacks, and the large genoa rolled upon itself. The engine purred to life as the sails were furled. The little ship approached William's Cove.

There were no lights along the Connecticut shoreline, and no navigation markers. Indeed, Jake's assessment seemed correct.

Approaching the cove there were still no channel markers to guide them in. The large estate houses, with their immaculate green lawns and large boathouses had vanished. The shoreline was totally dark and apparently vacant. Roank's Point seemed nothing but empty farmland.

Anne Marie slipped behind the Point, jutting into Long Island Sound, behind which was William's Cove. Jake had to creep the boat along at a mere two knots following a track indicated by their bottom mapping sonar equipment.

"Damn, David," he said, "this channel seems a bit east of what I remembered."

"I'll be dammed again," he said almost to himself as they passed through the narrow entrance to the cove, "I've never seen this place so quiet."

As soon as the anchors were set and the engine shut down, the only sounds were from the crickets, frogs and birds ashore. There was no hint of a light from anywhere outside their own cabin lights. In the bit of moonlight all that they see on the nearby land was dark tall forest.

David and Jake sat back in the cockpit, deep in their own thoughts. They both were aware of the quiet.

"Drink?" David asked, followed by slap as he killed the first mosquito.

"Nah. Damned bugs are terrible; worse in here than I remember," replied Jake, "I think I'm done for today. I'll see you in the morning, but don't make it too early."

David watched him slide below, pulling the hatch closed. A moment later he heard the gurgle of the exhaust as Jake started the generator, and seconds later a second whirr of the air conditioning fan motor.

Three mosquito slaps later David too retired.

Sleep was a long time coming. David couldn't get Connie out of his mind.

He awoke just as the dawn was lighting the eastern sky. He'd slept poorly with all the uncertainty about their strange position and his deep sadness over the loss (to him) of Connie.

He kept worrying if she was really okay.

Certainly, he tried to convince himself, she'd survived the storm and had to have been rescued. He tried to believe that she was perfectly okay, just still over two hundred years in the future.

He'd likely never see her again in his lifetime.

With these continuous tortured thoughts of Connie, no, of course he couldn't sleep.

Finally, he rolled out of his bunk to the cool deck, pulled on a t-shirt and walked to the galley where he started a pot of coffee. He showered, dressed in jeans, deck shoes and a sweatshirt and ascended to the deck with a fresh cup of coffee.

It was a lovely sunrise, and the deserted shore beckoned to him.

'Why not,' he said to himself, 'only take me a few minutes to row ashore and take a walk to sort it all out.'

He pressed the chrome switch that operated the transom door to the equipment hold. With that he gulped down the contents of the mug, then unlashed the canvas covering over the smaller of the two folded rubber Zodiac dinghies that were kept tied in place in the aft hold.

No, he'd realized that he wouldn't need Jake's special semi-rigid inboard; the smaller Zodiac would do fine today.

He attached an air line to the small boat and pumped it up hard.

WOSSSH.

In moments the rubber boat was fully inflated. David slid it over the stern. With a splash it bobbed in the water beside *Anne Marie*. He thought briefly about the outboard motors on the rack in the equipment room, realizing that the effort to drag one out was more than a simple sixty yard row, even in a Zodiac which rowed very poorly at best.

A few moments later he was pulling the Zodiac up the small rocky beach. He tied it to its small danforth anchor in case the tide was rising. He stood and smiled; it felt good to be on solid land after almost three weeks aboard *Anne Marie*.

Looking around he remembered that this was indeed the same place he'd been less than a month ago with Connie. They'd been invited to a party right here, at William's Boathouse, which had stood only a few feet from where the Zodiac was pulled-up on the deserted beach. Then, only seemingly weeks ago, there had been at least five houses visible through the well-manicured grounds surrounding the cove.

Now it was almost impassable forest with empty farm fields beyond.

Looking around in the very quiet morning he heard only the sounds of chirping sparrows, screeching blue jays, whirring crickets and croaking frogs. He saw what appeared to be a narrow path leading into the forest across some rocks to his left. Walking across the shore he started up the path and into the deep woods.

Meanwhile, Tad Williams was almost at the cove, his rod over his shoulder.

He heard a sharp 'crack'; someone had stepped on a branch in the woods ahead of him. Who, he wondered, could be on William's property at this hour?

Tad slipped off the path to the Cove and stepped behind a giant old oak, watching the path.

Moments later the figure of a young man appeared, picking his way slowly through the woods. As he approached Tad's tree, Tad thought that the person approaching was a very strange looking person indeed.

Taking another moment to closely inspect the uninvited visitor, Tad first noted that the man was at best in his early twenties, yet he was clean shaven with an unruly shock of red hair cut unfashionably short, well above his collar. The gray shirt the man was wearing had no buttons on the front; it looked like it must button up the back. Tad wondered how one would put it on, or why one would wear a shirt backwards anyway. The man's breeches were long, clear to his ankles, and he wore no stockings or boots. Instead of proper footwear he wore what looked like tan leather Indian moccasins with pure white leather soles.

Indeed, Tad thought, this was a very strange person walking up the path. Certainly this uninvited man did not belong on William's land!

"Avast there!" Tad called out at the stranger, stepping from behind the tree ten yards ahead of David.

David was startled!

He stopped in his tracks and looked up to see another young man standing in his path, holding a wooden fishing pole in two hands as if he was going to use it as a club.

David gawked at the very strange appearance of the youth.

The young man was dressed in baggy pants which ended at his knees, like the fishermen at Gardner's Island. His stockinged legs disappeared into leather boots. The pants were held up with a wide leather belt, above which was a white cotton shirt buttoned to the neck, but it had no collar. He wore a blue coat that looked like a very strangely cut sports coat, and his long dark hair was pulled behind his head, tied in a small ponytail. The youth's face was framed with a neatly trimmed beard, and on top of his head was one of these silly looking three corner hats.

"Whoa," said David quietly, holding his hands out, palms up, "I mean you no harm. I just stepped ashore for a quick walk."

"What's yer name and where be thee from?" asked Tad.

He continued, "This is William's Farm property."

"I know," said David, dropping his hands. "I think I've been here before. Please tell me, what's the date?"

"Why, July 9th", the youth dropped his defensive stance and lowered the fishing pole at David's simple query.

"Er, sorry, what year?"

"1777," replied Tad, wondering at the queer question.

Tad then started, "Yer name please, and where be thee from?"

David staggered briefly. The simple statement hit him like a blow to the stomach. He really had not wanted to believe Jake's theory, but here was the proof. He stepped back a bit, and then shook his head.

"I'm David Saunders, most recently from Florida," was his weak answer, "and you?"

"Theodore Williams. This is my father's farm," came the strong reply.

After a moment's pause Tad asked, "Does everyone wear those backwards shirts in Florida? Isn't that Spanish? If so, then we're not at war with thee. And, what does thee mean ashore? From what? Where?"

Tad was thoroughly curious now, but he was no longer afraid of this open and friendly acting man of about his own age, regardless of the strange dress and stranger accent to his speech.

David didn't reply for a few moments, gathering his thoughts. He was finally accepting that Jake's instincts were right, and that they had somehow, in that storm, become lost from their world. They had really arrived 240 years into the past!

He leaned back against a tree, his head still spinning with emotions and a with deep sense of loss, plus a little fear.

Finally he spoke, "Theodore, is that how I address you? Or should I call you Mr. Williams?"

"Tad will do," Tad replied, sensing the other's discomfort, but still very curious.

"And, is there a war going on here?" David inquired.

"Aye, quite the case. Damned Redcoats have all of New York," was the reply.

'At least this guy is on the American side', thought David, 'or, was it American? No, they called themselves Colonists'.

"Tad," he began, not knowing really what to say, but seeing questions in the other's eyes, "My fiancé's father and I have sailed here from a very far place and we've had a very strange experience. I don't quite know how we got here, but we've been here before."

Damn, he ceased talking, thinking he was doing it poorly.

'What the hell', he thought, 'Jake might not like it but we may as well start with someone, and at least this fellow looks intelligent and he is on the American side'.

Seeing is believing, so David told himself, let's see how he reacts?

"Tad," he finally began again, "come walk with me down to the beach. I'd like to show you something."

Tad approached him as he turned, "Mr. Saunders," he began.

"Please call me David."

Tad fumbled, embarrassed, but too curious to hold silent, "Thy shirt. How d'ye get it on or off, I mean, it has no buttons, front or back?"

"Look," David pulled at the neck of the sweatshirt, "it has an elastic neck, and I just pull it over my head."

"Elastic?" Tad mouthed the new word.

"In the place where I came from," David answered, "it's a common material for shirts and lots of things. Come along to the beach, I'll show you our ketch."

He turned and headed back down the path assuming Tad was following. Tad did.

Moments later they stepped out of the woods and onto the stony little beach. *Anne Marie* floated before them in the tiny cove. She was looking particularly lovely with the clear morning sunlight gleaming on her deep green hull and sparkling on the shiny stainless steel rod rigging.

Tad's jaw gaped open. He was awed!

He stood there looking, blinking in amazement, for long minutes.

Finally he spoke, the thoughts just falling out of him, "How did thee ever get anything that size into the Cove? Ye must 'av come at night, thee weren't here yesterday. Why does she have silver rigging? And, why the silver wheel? Where are the gaffs on her mainmast and mizzen? Where's ye'r crew?"

"Sit down, Tad," David began, sitting on a large rock at the end of the path. "Let me answer some of those questions."

"First, I'll show you later how we found our way into here. It wasn't difficult. Let me first say though that I am as baffled as to why we're here as are you. And, please hear me out."

"Baffled?"

"Oh, sorry. I meant to say that I don't know why we're here. I mean, and I am perfectly serious, Tad, if I speak with total openness with you, can you keep it to yourself?"

Tad would have promised anything to learn the wonders he'd seen so far.

"Aye, ye've me word," Tad solemnly replied looking directly into David's steady eyes.

He was trying to understand that he should try to believe any strange tale this forthright and strange appearing man might offer.

David thought, and then said, "I still don't believe it is possible, Tad, but I was born in the year 1983, and I am 24 years old. On this voyage we left the port of Fort Lauderdale, in Florida, in June, 2007."

"But –," Tad interrupted.

"Wait!" David continued, glancing into Tad's startled eyes.

"It's true. We suffered a terrible storm in the Atlantic, just last week. We almost sank. And, my fiancée, Connie was lost at sea."

"Oh, I'm sorry," Tad interjected, slipping off his woolen jacket in the warming morning.

David followed suit, pulling the sweatshirt over his head, which revealed the multi-colored t-shirt below.

Tad stared at the shirt for a moment, and then politely dropped his eyes.

"No," David continued, "it's not like it sounds. Er, I mean Connie was most likely rescued, but in 2007. See, we had special radios. Er, you don't know what that is."

He paused.

"Anyway," continuing, "a radio is a way that people could talk to each other from long distances. I can show you one later," he paused, realizing he was making no sense to the young man. Tad was just sitting and listening.

"Anyway", David continued, "after the storm we awoke, and here we are in your time. I don't know why."

"What's that?" asked Tad pointing at the grey Zodiac which was now bobbing to the anchor on the beach as the tide was evidently rising.

Looking up, "come, I'll show you," said David.

He walked down the beach.

Tad followed.

Tad approached the Zodiac studying it closely. It looked like a boat made of four great gray logs somehow fastened together with a bright varnished wooden transom across the stern and two with gray log seats inside. He couldn't imagine why it would float right on top of the water; weren't those huge logs heavy enough to make it settle deeper? It should be nearly awash, not bobbing in the light breeze.

And, why have a boat made of such great grey logs? Why not a simple, and certainly far lighter, wooden lapstrake skiff?

And why the stark white anchor line? Why would someone waste the time to chalk a simple hemp anchor rope?

Then, he was truly shocked!

David simply picked-up a funny looking small shiny anchor.

Tad would have to remember to ask why all the metal was silver instead of iron; these must be very wealthy people.

Then, with the slightest of a tug on the line the little boat danced across the top of the water to the beach! David then simply picked up the bow with one hand and pulled the boat halfway onto the beach with no visible effort.

Tad grew afraid again. He couldn't imagine the strength David must have to simply pick-up those great grey logs so easily for such an apparently slightly built man? He briefly wondered what David could do to Tad if he grew angry?

David sat on the side of the little boat saying, "Come on, have a seat," He patted the gray log side of the boat under him.

Tad cautiously sat.

He jumped right back up.

"It gives under my weight!" he cried.

"Sit, Tad," David repeated.

Tad sat down again, very slowly. He felt the warming rubber give slightly under his bottom. He patted the side of the boat next to him.

He asked, "What be this? Tiz it ever so light."

"As I was saying," David continued, "and it all confuses me because it's supposed to be impossible. Somehow the two of us on that boat," pointing at *Anne Marie*, "got stuck in your time instead of ours. I mean, I studied physical engineering for six years, and I know it's not supposed to be possible to move in time. But we did."

"No, don't look so confused," David continued, "you are sitting on a boat made of canvas treated with rubber and filled with air."

"What is this rub-ber?" interrupted Tad.

"Tad, there are a very many things, in fact most things that I will show you, that we have with us that you will not recognize or understand, at least right away. I'll show you many new things today."

"Rubber, he went on, "is a material which both stretches and is waterproof.

Here," he said, pulling at the sleeve of the sweatshirt now in his lap, "feel how this shirt

cuff pulls out from itself and goes right back into shape. Rubber is in the elastic of my shirt, like I showed you earlier."

Tad pulled at the shirt cuff, stretching it several times. Then he appeared to understand.

"But, why did thee come here?" he quizzed with an open curious expression.

"Damned if I know. It's supposed to be impossible." Jake replied.

He continued, "Oh, you mean why are where at your farm? Well, Jake, who's still aboard, lived very close to here, and he was a good friend of Mr. Williams. The Mr. Williams I knew was likely a descendant of yours."

"Look, Tad, I came ashore to try to sort it all out myself. I mean, everyone and everything I know is lost to me. I'm now here in your time. I know I'm not dreaming. And, I know a great deal more about your time than you can know about mine. But, I've no idea why or how we got here."

Just then Jake appeared on the deck of *Anne Marie*, sixty yards away. He had the ship's ensign under his arm.

He called out, "David?"

"Here, Jake," David yelled a reply, standing and waving.

Jake, apparently not noticing Tad sitting on the Zodiac, just nodded and went to the stern of the boat to raise the American ensign. Further, underneath the ensign, Jake raised his Gadsden flag, the yellow one with the snake and the words DON'T TREAD ON ME. Jake, as a historian, always flew the Gadsden as it was the very original flag flown by Continentals at Bunker Hill. In fact, every boat personally owned by Jake, his father and his grandfather had always flown the Gadsden under the American Ensign. It was a family tradition.

As the large American Flag unfolded in the early morning Tad stared at it.

"That's the new Betsy Ross Flag, isn't it? And Gadsden's? Egod, look at all the stars! Megods, ye tell me we'll win this War?" Tad jumped up excitedly.

"Ah, yes you will. And, George Washington will be the first President."

"Ye refer to General Washington, now encamped at Trenton with our army? And, what's a President? Does thee not mean King?"

By now both young men were standing at the edge of the water on opposite sides of the rubber dingy.

"Tad, come on out to *Anne Marie* and meet Jake. He was to have been my father in law, I mean, I am, er, was, engaged to his daughter. He's one of the finest friends a man could have. He'll probably be better with your questions than me."

"Aye," returned Tad with a quick smile, "let's go see ye'r vessel."

Approaching the *Anne Marie* after rowing across the little cove with Tad in the rear seat, David called-out, "Jake. Ahoy! We have a visitor."

Hearing that, Jake shot up out of the hatch and immediately recognized the colonial garb on the man approaching with David. His suspicions from the day before were instantly confirmed. Yes, he could see that David had a man dressed from 200 years ago in the Zodiac! And, indeed, William's Cove was totally unspoiled by any building.

He'd been amazed to be able to see the grass on the bottom of the cove through crystal clean water when he first woke up that morning. The last time he'd been here there were houses all around the Cove, and the water was just dirty brown murk. While he'd never been an environmentalist, he was amazed to note the clean air and water.

Yet, as a historian, he'd accepted what had happened to them much more easily than had his younger and more scientifically educated companion. He didn't need convincing that they'd moved in time. He simply accepted it, looking forward to a new challenge.

"Come-on aboard," Jake greeted.

He offered Tad, a hand and pulled him up the topsides of *Anne Marie.*

"Jake Shaw," he introduced himself and continued unabashed, "I'll sail out of the river around that Point in something over two hundred years from now. With no reason that I can understand, we have come back home, but in your time, not ours."

"Oh," he slowed down, "David, would you introduce our visitor?"

"Jake, this gentleman is Theodore Williams, although he's allowed me to call him Tad. His father, Arthur, is the current Williams family here."

Tad interrupted, "What do ye mean the current Williams Family?"

"Pleased to make your acquaintance, young man," Jake responded, "I presume it will be one of your great great grandsons who will become one of my closest friends in my time, and who is now probably grieving at my apparent loss at sea. Please, come and let's have a seat. I'm full of questions, but first please take off those hard leather boots. They'll ruin my brightwork."

"What year is it anyway?" Jake continued, "Is Washington in New York?"

Then he directed a glance at David, "perhaps you might get us a cup of coffee? I've just made a fresh pot."

"If ye've some tea, Sir? Only the Redcoat Navy drinks coffee," replied Tad, settling down onto the white vinyl cockpit cushion.

"Is this rubber too?" he asked, feeling the soft smooth surface with his right palm as he tugged off one boot then the other.

"Aye, son", replied Jake.

He understood quickly that this youth would be an ideal first contact for them. Tad Williams had an apparent quick mind, and seemed open to the unusual situation. Then again, Jake recognized that they did arrive on a sailing craft which was not too dissimilar from what the boy had seen.

Further, Jake was comforted by the thought that the youth was both an early American, and the ancestor of his closest friend, as strange as that thought seemed.

"What has David told you about us?" Jake asked quietly while David was below rooting through the galley lockers looking for that old box of tea while a mug of water was 'nuking' in the microwave..

As Tad finished recounting how he and David had met, stumbling through his unsure understanding of the origins of *Anne Marie,* David appeared in the cockpit with a steaming mug of hot water. He plopped two Lipton tea bags into the cup.

Tad looked into the cup with a quizzical expression.

Jake understood.

"The tea is sealed in those little paper bags, and the strings are so you can pull the bags out when the tea is as dark as you like it. Would you like some sugar?"

Tad asked the first question that came to his mind, looking at Jake, "Sir, ye must hail from a very rich place to be able to use so much silver for all the metal on this craft."

"Oh no," chuckled David, sipping his black coffee, "it's not silver."

"Let me see, you know only of iron. Well, sometime in the next hundred years it will be found that iron can be made much stronger by heating it further, and it can be made so it won't rust if some nickel is added. All this metal that looks like silver is what we call stainless steel. It's just a simple improvement on cast and wrought iron. You see, it's the same stuff, just stronger and it doesn't rust."

"But," Jake continued for David, as Tad nodded to the last, apparently understanding, "there are some very big differences in this ketch from anything you've known or thought possible. As an example, we can sail at twelve knots with no wind, or directly into the wind."

"But, Sir that's just not possible!" replied a startled Tad.

David this time offered the answer, "In another hundred years someone will find a way to burn oil in a steel machine which makes the power of a hundred horses with very little weight. Here's an example of this new power."

David continued, "Push that black button," pointing at the 'engage' switch on the electric Lewmar winch at Tad's elbow.

Tad, after hesitating only a moment, pressed on the black switch. He jumped, spilling some of his tea as the winch whirred to life, instantly spinning the chrome drum around.

He let up on the switch and it stopped. He pressed the button again and it whirred again. His mouth was gaped open in amazement!

"Cor, Sir, What makes it do that? Tiz magic!"

Jake shot a fast glance at David, quietly commanding, "Not too fast, now."

"Tad," Jake started again, "There are very many things here which will amaze you, but there is an explanation for all of them. Would you like to see all of *Anne Marie*?"

"Aye, Sir," the youth replied, "I'd like that."

His face reddened a bit as he asked, "Could thee show me to the heads first?"

"Come along," David rose, understanding the fellow needed to relieve himself, thinking that this experience would be fun.

On descending to the salon, Tad glanced at the chart table. It had a multi-colored chart on top of it, and an amazing array of shiny black metal boxes were suspended over the table. Some of the boxes had glass fronts, and there was a confusing panel of switches and round dials. He only had a moment to glance at this strange area because David was just ahead of him, gesturing down around the corner to a varnished wood hallway.

Tad was startled by incredible opulence of the interior of the vessel. It was lined with rich polished wood trimmed with shiny brass fittings. All the sitting places were covered in rich looking fabrics, and there were shelves bulging with bright colored books and other strange shapes. He followed David in a U-turn, David gesturing through a small door.

Tad entered a very little room, as indicated, and with his tri-corner hat under his elbow looked with initial confusion at a little white basin set into a varnished wooden counter with little silver spouts and handles. He puzzled at another white glass pot affixed to the deck. Where, he wondered, was he supposed to - - ?

David ended his confusion, speaking in a clear businesslike fashion, "Look, you relieve yourself there," pointing at the small white head. "And, when you're finished, you just step on this little petal."

David stepped on the flush pedal.

"THUNKTHUNKTHUNKTHUNK"

Tad visibly jumped and went white as the head pump sprang into action, emptying the almost empty bowl and running a clean stream of water through it.

"Tad, calm down! It's supposed to do that. All right?"

David continued as if all was in fact okay, "And, when you're finished you can wash-up like this."

He turned-on one of the spickets at the sink. "The one marked C is cold water and the H is for hot."

"Hot water? Any time? Just by turning that?" Tad asked.

"Yes," stated David emphatically.

"Understand it?" he queried as he stepped out, closing the small door with Tad inside.

The appropriate sound a moment later told him the young man was handling the new situation.

Jake had also descended to the salon.

David sat down at the table across from him and said, "He's playing in the head."

"Wouldn't you if you'd never seen inside plumbing?" quipped Jake. "Did you find out where the hell, er when we are?"

"Yeah. July 1777. How the hell did that happen? You know we're dead to our world. There's no way we can get back. We're gonna have to live our lives here."

"David, son, are you ready to hear the real truth?"

"I know you're right. Yes, we are stuck here," David replied.

Jake continued, "I know that we're stuck because I know the first Shaw in America was named Jake. He started the family shipyard in New Manchester during the Revolution.

"I'm my own damned Ancestor," he exclaimed.

"What do you know of your family history?" he asked David.

"Oh my God," exclaimed David, leaning back shocked, "my ancestors indeed made a fortune in cotton and lumber on the Florida panhandle. We've a family story about Andrew Jackson. Later my great grandfather discovered oil in northern Pennsylvania. Half of the oil and a great deal of the coal in western Pennsylvania were found in supposedly worthless swamp lands and mountains that the family has owned since. Granddad was even reported to have had crazy half uncle that was said to have struck a fortune in California in the 1800's".

"Any family history dating from the American Revolution?" interjected Jake.

"I'm not sure when, but there was some murky history about a colorful old gent who was married to a reclusive witch. It's been family history that he spent a huge fortune that he brought to America on worthless Florida swamp that he developed. It's also been said that he was very active protecting runaway slaves."

"That may be you, and hopefully Connie. We can hope."

"Listen," Jake continued, "and I am deadly serious. We got lucky to have first met this young man who seems both bright and open. I need to keep reminding you, because it's all-important, that we do nothing to impede the flow of history as we know it."

He continued, now deadly serious, "We don't know why or how we got here, perhaps there's a reason, but the fact is we're here and we're apparently stuck. I just wish we could get some word to Margaret and Connie that we didn't die. I'm racking my brain for that."

He was cut-off as the door to the head opened and Tad stepped out with a freshly scrubbed face and combed-back hair.

"I'm sorry; sirs, but I did spend a moment with ye'r hot water machine. I've never imagined the like of it. How do ye do it?"

"Theodore Williams," Jake started speaking in a very serious voice while standing and looking directly into Tad's eyes, "we'll be honored to show you all the wonders of our *Anne Marie*, but I must have your solemn word as a Gentleman and before God that you'll not speak a word of us or this little ship to any living being unless either David or I am with you, or we have a direct and exact understanding of who and why you may so speak to someone."

"Agreed?"

Tad thought for a moment, impressed with these apparent gentlemen, and from all he'd seen. He, so far, thoroughly believed their unlikely story.

He put his hand out, offering, "Ye've both me hand and my solemn word on the matter, sir. I should like, however, to discuss the thought of bringing both my father and our dear friend, and confident of General Washington's, Stephen Downey, who's now at the house, into your acquaintance."

"Aye," replied Jake, "but only them for now. Your descendants speak for you, damned strange way to put it, and we can not live in this time by ourselves."

After that, Jake started his tour of *Anne Marie* with Tad while David cooked them breakfast.

Jake started at the navigation station, explaining very simply all the different navigational aids. He started with the radar, which was easy to explain, and worked through the sonar. He explained why the radios were just so much junk now with no transmitters, except for the VHF with its hand-held sister.

Soon David had finished preparing breakfast. Tad was amazed at the way food was packaged and prepared. The youth had never seen a stove that wasn't over or inside a fireplace.

The morning was complete when Jake popped his favorite CD, Chopin's Interludes, into the stereo.

✯ ✯ ✯

It seemed like moments, but it was actually hours later when a bump was heard along side the hull.

Immediately a male voice was heard calling, "Ahoy there, on the ship."

"Y Gods, what time is it?" asked Tad, just having been looking at the charts of the east coast of America 240 years in the future, "That's Uncle Stephen!"

"You go on deck and greet him," Jake suggested. "We'll give you a moment and be along directly."

"Uncle Stephen," Tad shouted as he ascended the ladder to the deck, "Come aboard. These people are friends."

"Aye, I'm no idiot. I saw her colors," Stephen replied.

"Here, give me a hand. Lord lad, where've ye been? Been expecting thee for hours," Downey grunted as he climbed out of the small skiff he'd rowed out from the beach.

"And, what sort of vessel be this? What Yankee t'would be fool enough to use all this silver when simple iron and hemp would do better? And, how the hell do they sail this thing? There's no main gaff, no ratlines, no belaying pins or cross yards. Hell, they haven't even got a proper capstan. And worse, there's not a gun on her. Some rich dandified fool owns this fancy piece of work, and that's for sure."

As Jake heard this exchange he'd dashed to his cabin and quickly changed out of his nylon warm-up suit and into a plain pair of baggy white duck trousers and a simple blue cotton shirt. He wanted to appear to the newcomer in as normal appearing clothing as possible. He even donned his blue captain's hat with the gold braid and anchor emblem, which he had only formerly worn at Race Committee meetings.

He topped the outfit off with his blue blazer, and then he ascended to the deck expecting the worst. He signaled David to remain below for now.

"Welcome aboard *Anne Marie*, sir, Captain Jake Shaw at your service," Jake intoned formally accosting the visitor.

Jake noted that the man was slight of build and quite short, however he was clearly in the peak of physical condition. He was dressed in clothing similar to that worn by Tad, with britches ending below his knobby knees, white baggy stockings and leather shoes held closed with large brass buckles.

As the day had gotten warmer, the visitor wore a simple cotton collarless shirt tucked into his belt. It was open at the neck.

"Stephen Downey, sir," Stephen replied, removing his hat and making a small bow, which looked a bit silly to Jake.

"I've come looking for me young friend here. We've a hard journey to prepare for, and unfortunately not much time to loose."

"Mr. Downey," Jake said, "might you have a seat here and visit for a few minutes?"

Stephen was too curious to resist, regardless of his pressing need to prepare for the hard ride to the Capitol.

"Aye, sir, I'm most curious about this very strange ketch. She's different from any other I've seen, and without being too forward, why d'ye have her rigged with silver wire? And, why the silver wheel? And, begging ye'r pardon again, what are all those round silver cylinders?" motioning at the winches.

"And, where be ye'r gaff booms? How can ye sail without gaffs?"

Stephen knew he was being a bit impolite with all the questions, but he couldn't stop himself.

"Mr. Downey, I've a strange tale to tell you," Jake started to reply, deciding that this gentleman needed a different tactic than had Tad Williams.

"Sir, if you'll step to the companionway here and look at the Builder's Plate affixed here the day she was commissioned you might understand the reasons for our presence."

Mounted on the face plate over the entrance to the salon was a beautifully engraved brass plate which read:

Anne Marie

Commissioned July 7, 2004

Shaw Shipbuilders

New Manchester, Connecticut

Stephen studied that brass plate for a very long time, his mind first totally confused, then even more confused.

"But sir, there's no shipyard here in New Manchester?" he stated.

"Indeed so, not now," replied Jake, "look at the year she was built."

"Aye, but that's simply not possible." was the emphatic reply.

"Indeed, sir. Not possible in your time nor in mine," started Jake.

He went on, "We sailed from the Port of Fort Lauderdale in what you would call the Spanish Colony of Florida not three weeks ago, in the year of 2007."

"That's right, Two Thousand and Seven, two hundred and forty years from today."

Stephen tried to interject.

Jake held up his hand, "No, sir please let me finish. Thank you."

"Now, we sailed north intending to pass through New York, and return to my home in Deerford on the creek. However we were struck by a violent storm which blew us south of Bermuda. In the course of that storm we were all knocked unconscious. We lost my daughter in a huge waterspout or whirlpool. We don't still know what truly happened, except that when we finally made landfall it was two hundred forty years before we had set sail."

With that Stephen simply descended the rest of the way to the salon and took a seat at the table. Jake sat across from him.

"From ye'r colors it would appear we'll win this damned war?" Stephen asked.

"Aye, unless our presence here does something to change the natural course of history," replied Jake as David entered from his cabin.

Jake stood up nodding at David, "Mr. Downey, this is my almost son-in-law and my companion, David Saunders. David this is Stephen Downey, Tad has spoken well of him," Jake made the introductions.

"We've left Tad on deck."

David and Stephen shook hands.

David then said, "Unfortunately we lost my fiancée in the storm. It's unlikely I'll now become Jake's son in law."

With that he nodded and headed for the ladder to find Tad.

Stephen cleared his voice and said, "Captain Shaw, I do agree that thine origins must be kept in strictest confidence, and we'll have to fit ye both out with appropriate clothing. May I take it that your sympathies can only rest with the Colonies?"

"Indeed."

"Aye, sir, I will share with thee that I am a Colonel in General Washington's service. My duties are unorthodox, but I do have his confidence. Is this oddly rigged ketch as fast as she looks to be?"

"You'll not believe it, Mr. Downey, but this vessel can make twelve knots or more in any condition, with or without wind, and in any direction, as long as our diesel holds out."

"What's diesel?" queried Stephen.

"Sorry. This little ship has an apparatus which operates on a fuel which it burns, not unlike whale oil, and that makes us able to move whether or not we've sails on her. We've about 700 gallons of this fuel in the tanks now, or about enough for over 3,000 miles. Please understand that mankind has made, er, will make advances in the next two hundred years."

"Captain, would thee be willing to employ this remarkable vessel of ye'rs in the services of the Colonies, were ye able to keep her secrets?" Stephen asked, suddenly remembering his current mission and seeing a way to get his urgent message through to Washington.

"Sir," Jake replied after a few moments thought, "I've always been a student of American history, and of particular interest to me, other than finding and salvaging shipwrecks, has been George Washington. He's destined to leave an enormous name for himself in future history books."

"I don't know why we're here, freak of nature perhaps. But if I can be of service without compromising *Anne Marie* or effecting written history in any way, I am pleased to help. My only condition is that I will be the judge of all situations. If I deem this ketch to be in danger of becoming discovered by those who would make a record of her I will instantly scuttle her."

"Aye, sir," replied Stephen, looking deeply into Jake's eyes, "I can commit General Washington to ye'r terms. That's the only way. Would thee be good enough to show me some more of ye'r strange and lovely vessel here? And, perhaps your mate could put Tad ashore? He'll need to find thee proper clothing."

"Ye'r not as stout as Mr. Williams", he went on, "but perhaps Anne could take a stitch in something of his for thee to wear ashore. Tad ought be able to find something for ye'r Mr. Saunders to wear. We should all go ashore later and share this with Arthur, if it's quiet at the house. Ye can trust his confidence."

Four hours later, just as Jake had finished his tour of *Anne Marie* with Stephen, Tad returned with a bag of colonial clothing for Jake and David.

While Stephen had been duly impressed with the main engine and electrical systems, he was most amazed with the special equipment that Jake had hidden in the storage hold.

Stephen had spent a very long time inspecting and coming to understand the potential of the two AK-47 automatic rifles. He was further fascinated by the two long pistols that Jake claimed carried twenty-two bullets, and which he claimed made almost no noise at all. Lastly, he questioned that it could really be possible to stay under the water for an hour using just those little ugly re-breathers?

It all was quite incredible to Stephen.

He marveled at the claimed explosive power that Jake described from those small and innocent looking gray greasy blocks of what Jake called 'plastique'; how could just one brick of it really be more powerful than a barrel of French gunpowder?

And lastly, although he did not doubt Jake's claims, he could not understand how those bright blue pieces of machinery marked EVINRUDE, and which were smaller than his leg, could push their little gray log boats faster than the wind.

No, he thought that Mr. Shaw had to be pulling telling a yarn on that one, but Shaw didn't seem one to stretch the truth. It was likely the same story about the larger boat Jake had said was powered by a silent jet, whatever that was.

"David," Jake suggested, after the tour as they were all sitting in the cockpit under a freshly rigged awning, "what say we treat our guests to a good old fashioned American hot dog and a cold can of beer for lunch? Mr. Downey here wishes us to take him to Philadelphia, or up the Delaware as close as we can safely get. Sound okay to you?"

"You're the skipper," was the reply as David descended below.

Tad followed him to the galley to find out how one would cook a dog for lunch, and what part of the dog they'd be eating.

After lunch, with the two Colonists just a bit tipsy from quaffing four cans of icy Heineken and three hot dogs each, both professing it was the best beer and food they'd ever eaten, they rowed ashore in the wooden skiff. Stephen said that one or the other would return at dusk to lead them to the William's home to meet Arthur and Anne.

They were cautioned to please dress in the clothing that Tad had brought back.

David did look quite the part of the young American colonist after he dressed at sunset. His borrowed blue breeches were properly buttoned at the top of his calves, and the clean white stockings lead down to the heavy leather shoes, which both fit and were quite comfortable. The cotton shirt had lace ruffles that appeared at the sleeves and the neck of the waistcoat. Still, David felt quite foolish, as if heading off to a costume party.

Jake didn't look as good.

Arthur's breeches were far too big in the waist and baggy in the seat. The stockings hung in wrinkles around his legs. Lastly, the waistcoat barely reached his belt. It was evident that Arthur Williams was both a far more stout gentleman than Jake Shaw (as was his great, great, great grandson, Jake's former neighbor), with longer legs and a shorter torso.

No, Jake decided that he would only go ashore in his own white ducks and blue shirt.

"Ahoy *Anne Marie*," Tad's voice came from the beach.

Jake allowed David to row him ashore in the Zodiac after securely locking the *Anne Marie*. As soon as the little rubber boat was again anchored on the beach against the rising tide they set off in single file through the woods.

After stumbling on several rocks, Jake took a small flat flashlight out of his pocket and flipped it on.

"Me God, What's that light?" exclaimed Tad.

"Just a flashlight," Jake replied, slapping at a mosquito.

"It's so bright. Does it have a candle inside? Where's the flame? How did thee light it so easily?" the youth stopped on the path, full of amazed questions.

"It's just something else we have." Jake replied, then asking, "Isn't the house just around the next bend? David, this path seems to go just where the road went last time I was here."

In a moment they rounded the last bend in the path. Jake put his light back in his pocket. Looking up he was surprised to see the same Williams house as he'd last seen not a month ago, except the addition to the left was not there, the garages weren't there, nor was the graciously curved driveway. But, the house was the same. He'd been here before, or more correctly, he would be here again.

He grinned briefly, wondering just how did that work.

And, standing in the soft candlelight just inside the door, Anne Marie Williams welcomed Jake Shaw to her father's home.

As Jake first looked into the dark green eyes in Anne's finely boned face, framed with long dark hair under a silly white bonnet he became breathless for a moment.

"Miss Williams," he stammered.

Her hand was in his and his face was feeling strangely flushed.

"The pleasure is all mine," he managed.

CHAPTER SIX

"*Reliant*," shouted Will Thompson as his gig, with the Captain standing straight in the bow, rounded the stern of the frigate.

Aaron leapt to the chain-plates before his gig was completely stopped and strutted across the deck of his ship, ignoring the piping of his Marines.

He hollered for Willright to prepare to sail on the tide.

"And, get that damned woman to the Flagship," he finished.

Lt. Williamswright banged on Connie's (his) door saying, "gather yr things, Missy and get thee to the quarter-deck. Ye're goin to the Flagship."

Connie had little to gather except her somewhat cleaned bloody clothing. She was dressed in Willright's shirt and knee length (mid-calf on her) trousers. She wore the deflated life jacket under her shirt, out of sight.

As she exited the little cabin she smiled at him, "Thank you for the cabin, and may I please borrow these things? I'll try to find someone to leave them with for you, if I can, or give them to you if you find me when you return."

"Nary mind, Missy," Willright replied, "keep 'em till ye find urself proper ladies clothing."

On ascending to the deck she found Captain Aaron impatiently standing at the rail. He gestured her into the waiting boat.

But, she paused a moment, worried about leaving the injured young seaman, Corey, in the clutches of the grizzled sail-maker. Surely he'd not see to sterile bandages, and the leg would certainly get infected.

"Captain," she quickly asked, "must the injured seaman Corey remain here? I am afraid for his recovery on the voyage you plan. May he not be transferred?"

Aaron thought a moment and realized her request made sense. Damn, but he should have thought of it himself.

"Willright," he yelled, "quickly now. Get Corey to the deck. He's in the Orlop. And, send a hand to bring his chest aft."

Moments later Connie was handed down to the rear seat in the little boat next to the sailor, Will Thompson, who was holding the tiller. Shortly Corey was roughly handed down to the other side of the seat. His leg was beginning to bleed through his trousers.

'My God,' thought Connie looking around,' "this is New York?'

As the little boat rowed her towards the biggest sailing ship she'd ever seen, she stared around her at the unbelievable sights of New York Harbor that clear and warm July day.

On Connie's last trip to New York, some three months past to her, the island of Manhattan was covered with skyscrapers, and this East River was spanned by a score of bridges. Now, looking ashore at the bottom tip of the island where the Staten Island ferry piers were supposed to be, where the Trade Center used to be, surrounded by Battery Park and the huge buildings of Wall Street, Connie only saw a low two story stone fort with red coated sentries marching along the top. Round mouths of, she presumed, cannons were sticking through holes in the stone walls.

To the right and left of the fort there were wooden piers as far as she could see. Most of the piers were crammed with square-rigged sailing ships of every description, loading and unloading boxes and bales of cargo. The piers were crammed with jostling wagons, neighing horses and shouting workmen. The din was apparent across the quiet water.

Behind the piers and the fort she could see the red bricked buildings of New York, with nothing appearing higher than three stories at the most.

To her right across the river, where the Brooklyn Bridge used to end, there was a small village surrounded by green fields with but three little piers jutting into the river.

Anchored just off of these piers was a large and apparently very old sailing ship at anchor without masts or rigging. It had three faded and stained yellow bands around it, all with open square holes, she presumed former gun ports. However iron bars, not cannon mouths, crossed the lower two rows of square ports.

To her left were two muddy little islands topped with grass. Of course, the Statue of Liberty was not in evidence. And the shores of New Jersey on the far side of the Hudson were apparently no more than tilled fields and some green forest.

Indeed, Captain Aaron had said it was the year 1777. The sight of New York brought it all home to her. It was 1777 indeed.

The harbor was busy. There were all sorts of small sail and rowing craft bustling between what looked like over 200 anchored ships. Some were clearly war ships and others were apparently cargo ships. There were several two masted smaller ships sailing up river, and one three-masted ship was drifting clear of a pier, just shaking out her jibs and top sails.

"Ahoy *Indomitable*," the man beside her hollered as the boat rounded under the stern of a huge ship. This one had three bright and fresh red bands painted around her. From under the stern there were not less than two layers of gold guided windows with walkways above her head.

"Toss Oars," the steersman yelled, and the boat crew stood their oars on end in perfect lines.

The boat slid to a stop at a little landing that had stairs up the side of the ship. Connie didn't ask; she simply rose and, as daintily as possible, stepped up to the deck of the huge sailing ship.

The officer who greeted her looked over the side and said to the boat below, "take ye'r wounded man there to the *Jersey*," gesturing at the old ship she'd noted with no masts, anchored off the Brooklyn side of the river.

"Aye, missy," the officer continued, looking over Connie standing there with her dirty little bundle of belongings and dressed in the baggy white pants and white shirt given her by Lt. Williamswright. "Captain wants a word with thee."

He gestured at a young boy, also dressed in the heavy woolen uniform of an officer, "Midshipman, escort the lady to the Captain and attend her 'till the Captain's seen her".

The boy, who couldn't have been over thirteen, saluted the Officer and solemnly waved at Connie to follow him. He turned towards the rear of the ship and picked his way across the bright white decks between huge black iron cannons. Connie followed as he threaded his way around scuttleways and dodged working throngs of sailors, entering a varnished door under the poop deck.

Inside the varnished door was a gloomy dark room with lighting only from a small skylight above. The pervasive odor here was almost unbreatheable; a far stronger mix than on the frigate she'd left. It was a nauseating mix of old tennis shoes mixed with wet wool, vomit, spoiled meat, sewage, and a whiff of tar. Pheww! This 'room' was furnished with a long table with ten chairs bolted down on each side. Another young officer was silently working on papers at the end of the table.

"Lady from *Reliant* to see Sir Wembly as Ordered, Sir," barked the young guide.

The other officer stood, saluted back said, "Aye, the castaway, The Captain'll see thee presently, Wait there."

"Midshipman, ye're excused."

He gestured at one of the chairs before rapping sharply on the double wood stained and highly polished doors at the other end of the gloomy cabin. Then he went through the door, leaving Connie at the huge table alone.

Moments later he re-appeared stating, "This way, miss,"

Connie followed him through the doorway.

The after cabin was huge. It was airy and bright, furnished with beautiful wooden tables and brass-bound leather chairs. The entire stern end was filled with open windows above deep blue cushions, with the city in plain view. A large man, formally dressed and wearing an officer's blue wool coat with golden lower sleeves, rose from the ornate desk in front of the open windows and gestured Connie to a straight-backed chair in front of the desk. The dcsk was clear of all papers. Connie couldn't help noticing the carved wooden stand with four large white feathers. She puzzled about the feathers for a brief moment then realized that they were quills for writing.

Connie then observed with almost a giggle that while the Captain was hatless, his florid face was ringed with a pure white wig. She struggled to hold back a grin at the silly appearance of the fat man with the silly powdered cotton strings that looked like a dust mop on his head.

As she sat down the Captain fixed her with an uncomfortable stare, taking in the dirty white clothing, the shirt buttoned to the neck (to hide lifejacket underneath) and the calf-length white trousers with the now dirty white sneakers still on her sockless feet. Her small bundle of her own blood stained outer clothing was dropped at her feet.

"Madam," he began in a superior tone, "may I please have your full name."

"Constance Anne Shaw," she replied meekly.

"And, from where d'ye hail?"

Connie knew to be careful with her answers. She'd lived with her father, and knew of her father's interest in history. This man, she knew, could blow holes in the claims she had made to the frigate captain about Spain. And, as a daughter of Jake Shaw, she knew that she could leave no unanswerable recordings in the future history books.

"I was at sea on my father's small ship," she replied, "washed overboard in a storm and *Reliant* rescued me."

"Aye," the Captain said sharply, "I got that from Commander Aaron. Please tell me ye'r port of departure and the destination of ye'r father's vessel, and her name."

This should be safe, thought Connie, replying, "We departed the east coast of Florida two weeks ago, bound for New York."

"Aye," queried the man, "the whole of South Florida is in the control of the Queen of Spain and, while not at War with England, 'tiz little legal cargo there for New York. Hmmmm, methinks there's but a small settlement in that Colony. What be its name?"

"And again, please Miss, what were thee carrying, and what was the name of ur vessel?" he demanded again, sharply.

"Sir," replied Connie thoughtfully, "*Anne Marie*, is the name of my father's ship. It's not large, and I don't know what cargo he had aboard."

"Unlikely," came the reply, "and what be thine home? Aye ur speech is different, be thee a Colonist from New Spain? Be thee loyal to King Phillip?"

There it was, just as Connie had known it would come. She could hardly claim loyalty to England and their King. Further, just a trip ashore would reveal that she knew nothing of the dress or the culture of the times, other than what history books and movies had shown. Indeed, it also occurred to her that her Country, the United States, would not even come into being for another ten years or more. She simply had already figured to claim herself as a Connecticut resident, marooned with the Spanish for years, and hope for the best.

"My original home is in Connecticut," she simply stated.

"Then ye be a colonist. Do ye'r people support the King, or be they damned traitors and rebels," thundered the Captain.

He was loosing patience with this unusual castaway. Wembly knew from Aaron that she had a most unusual way of healing; indeed Aaron had offered that it seemed almost sorcery. Her speech was very strange clipped English. Yes, he could clearly understand her English, but in a time when all Englishmen virtually gave away their station and nearly their home city by their diction, this woman's speech was unlike anything he'd ever heard.

He pursed his hands under his double chin and took a moment to look her over carefully.

Yes, she was in castaway sailor clothing. She had woefully short hair that was somewhat dirty and stringy, but it did appear carefully clipped. Her completion was fine and clear, a good indication of high station, and her hands were neither calloused nor red. Again she was no ordinary serving wench or rough sailor's daughter. Hmmm, and yes, he considered, she must be of high birth somewhere, but where? And from where came the gift of healing?

Connie took a chance, interrupting his thoughts, "sir, my mother and I took passage to Havana in the Cuba Islands several years ago. Our little ship was attached by pirates. My mother was killed, and I was taken as a hostage. The Pirate ship fell into a storm and was wrecked on the coast of the Floridas where, by the grace of God, I was spared my life. I was taken in by a tribe of natives. They called themselves Seminoles. It was they who taught me to heal."

She continued, inventing her tale as she spoke, "Over the past year I managed to pass several messages to missionaries, hoping to get word to my father, a merchant from New England. Just last month he did finally find me. With great joy he purchased me back from the Seminoles."

She went on, "but I was cast off his little ship in a great storm just weeks ago, and here I am. Our ship and crew is small, too small to be of interest to your Navy. And, it's been, I think, five years since I've been home. I've only heard of this rebellion since I was saved, but I can not say anything of the feelings of my family in Connecticut until I can see them. Can you offer me passage?" she implored, "It's not far."

The bewigged Captain said nothing. He was deep in thought. Indeed, perhaps the lass was telling the truth, but, her tale seemed very far fetched indeed. Yet she clearly had a true healing gift. Clearly, no matter what she said, she was not from these Colonies. He'd heard every sort of use of the King's language from all these so called Colonists, and none spoke anything like this lass.

"Nay, Lass, I'll do no such thing now," he finally said. "We're loading the Army for a sortie South under Admiral Howe's orders, and I've good men dying in the *Jersey* yonder," he waved at the old ship with no masts seen through the corner of the rear windows.

"I hear ye'r a medical person, and we've need of thine talents. If ye'll give me ur parole I'll find thee lodgings ashore. If not, ye can nurse me boys on the hulk until the Fleet's return. Then we'll ask the Senior Admiral to decide what to do with thee."

"He may find it be best to turn ye'r case to the Admiralty in Portsmouth. Indeed, that's the best thought. Aye, there's a brig clearing for Portsmouth with dispatches. Methinks I will send a message to Lord Howe and ask him what to do with thee."

He paused and looked back at her saying, "still, we'll not see ye harmed. Will thee offer ye'r parole?"

Connie was not about to give her parole, which she understood as a promise not to escape. No, she'd promise nothing until she better understood where she was.

"No, Sir, I can't give you my parole for my father could sail in at any moment," of course Connie knew that to be very unlikely.

"However," she continued, "I will work on your hospital ship and bunk there for now. I shouldn't want to be taken to Portsmouth or anywhere farther away from my father."

"Indeed, sir," she implored, holding back tears, "why not let me simply work as a nurse to your injured and earn the funds for my travels in search of my family? "

"Nay, Miss. I shan't do that. Methinks ye need the protection of the Crown right now. And, if ye'r father is a proper English sailor he'll be sailin into this fine harbor any time to seek thee out. If he fails to appear then we'll know ye haven't been completely truthful, and with ye'r clear high upbringing, methinks Lord Howe will need send thee to higher authority in Portsmouth. I'll not bear their wrath for letting thee slip through our hands and getting ye'rself hurt."

He finished stating, "It'll be the Lord's decision, when he's time for the likes of thee."

"Aye," he went on. "ye'll be safe enough. There 'r a score or more women nurses living on the hulk, and hundreds of disloyal Colonists, men and women, in the prison holds below. Now, off with thee, and I'll discuss ur status with Admiral Howe next we speak."

As she rose to leave he volunteered, "Still, I'll leave word that if a small green ship bearing ye'r father appears in port and asks ye'r whereabouts, we'll turn thee back to him. But don't get ur hopes up. It'll be not likely ye'll be returning to Connecticut until we quash this little rebellion. Ye may get to London first."

"Midshipman," he bellowed, "escort this woman to Captain Spence on *Jersey*. Pass me regards 'n tell 'm that this woman appears not a Rebel, but canna be returned to her home in enemy territory. 'E's to make use o'er nursing skills 'till the Fleet returns. We'll address her case then. He's also to accord her every courtesy of a fine lady; she's not a trollop, ye hear."

Connie was crushed.

She bit back her tears as she followed the boy out through the maze of men and activity on deck. She was left to wait at the quarterdeck at the top of the ladder. Down the side a boat was being brought-up.

Connie had truly hoped she could find passage the short forty something miles to Deerford. She just knew she'd find *Anne Marie* and David waiting there.

While she was waiting at the sally port for the boat she looked again at the huge ship, amazed at its size and at the activity. All around her on the main deck rough and grizzled looking men were rushing back and forth engaged in various tasks which she little understood. Looking up at the three masts festooned with their yardarms, the maze of black rigging seemed to reach the sky. And, all the way up on all three masts she saw men working, some with pots of black stuff coating the ropes, some making splices, and some were just clearly loafing.

Then she noticed at the top of each lower mast there was a little platform and, yes, she saw a small brass cannon on each platform. She knew she was on a British three-decked ship of the line, the modern equivalent of a Battleship. Her Dad had given her a 'Hornblower' book some years ago, and although she'd had little interest in it at the time, she never could have imagined the sheer size of this monstrous sailing ship, It was jam-packed full of hoards of sailors, petty officers, officers in blue coats, and even a group of red coated soldiers on the bow doing a close order drill under the barking orders of their leader. There was activity everywhere.

She wondered where they all slept.

A far bigger rowing boat than the one she had arrived in, the Midshipman had mentioned a cutter, came along side with its twelve oarsmen. Connie was hastened down the stairway and into the rear seat of the cutter. It cast off, and with twelve sailors pulling on oars, it rounded under the gold-painted 'poop' of the *Indomitable*, and headed for the old hulk with no masts, the *Jersey*.

While the cutter was crossing the harbor the coxswain, sitting near Connie, volunteered what he knew of the *Jersey*.

"That old three decker has been here for years," he said. "She's been used by the Navy both as a prison and as a hospital. The lower decks behind those bars is where the Yankee prisoners are kept."

"Why are they prisoners?" Connie asked.

""I guess, Miss, that they are mostly sailors taken by the blockade. 'Course there's likely some soldiers left from the battles in Brooklyn last fall. I hear the upper gun deck as well as the main deck is the surgery fer our injured soldiers and sailors."

As the cutter drew close Connie could hear a muted rumble of wails and curses from every corner of the ill-kept hulk. As she looked up the tall stairway to the entry port, past barred gun ports and peeling paint, Connie hugged herself. She was dismayed that this was where she must stay.

She carried her small bundle slowly up to the top deck. The coxswain followed her up and handed a packet of papers to a one armed sailor who met them.

"New nurse for thee," the coxswain said, handing over the packet.

The sailor grabbed the packet and gestured for Connie to follow him saying, "I canna read this, but tiz certain ye'r t'go to Mrs. McAdams. She 'as charge of all the nursin'."

Connie noted that the main deck of this ship was covered over with canvas awnings which kept out the hot sun, and allowed the breeze. There were cots lined up in neat lines under the awnings, each with a convalescent assigned. Many were sitting and talking in small groups or playing cards. Some of the cots held sleeping men. Amidships a large area was sectioned off into what appeared a large galley with a seating area for those who could walk.

She followed the sailor aft to a stairway down to the upper gun deck. He lead her through a doorway and into what she recognized as a gunroom, or officers mess, however the once large open cabin was partitioned into small 'rooms' with canvas hung from the low beams overhead. The only ventilation was an open skylight above. It was both very hot and the smell was even worse than on the flagship that she'd just left.

Connie, thoroughly exhausted and perspiring heavily under her layers of clothing (the life jacket under her shirt was especially uncomfortable), wanted most a bath and a chance to sleep in a clean bed,

The sailor pointed her to an empty canvas cubicle with a hammock hung inside offering, "Ye can wait in 'ere for Mrs. MacAdams, She's the head nurse.

Connie collapsed into the small hammock. She was asleep in moments, regardless of the heat, odors and discomfort.

"Aye, there ye be Missy," Connie awoke to a woman's voice, "I'll be Mrs. Mac Adams, and I've heard ye'r especially gifted with the wounded. We can use ye'r gift here, and God knows it," she prattled.

Connie looked up towards the canvas door-flap at the woman to find a pert small middle-aged person with her graying hair in a tight bun, clothed in a floor length cotton print dress buttoned to a high collar. At least she was smiling.

"Might I have a bath?" asked Connie, "and, perhaps I might borrow some clean clothes?"

"A bath?" was her incredulous reply. "There'll be no bath on the *Jersey*. Heavens child, you'd take a chill in the cold water. Goodness, ye should know that more than one bath a month is unhealthy. Still, we can find thee something to wash-up with."

She looked at Connie's rough and dirty sailor's clothing with distain and said, "Miss Betsy is about ye'r size. Let me find thee something more suitable to wear until we can get thee ashore for proper things."

She left the canvas stall, giving Connie time to quickly slip out of the dirty shirt and hide the life jacket under the folded blanket on the hammock. Mrs. MacAdams was just re-entering with a wooden pail of water and a bar of yellow soap in one hand and a handful of clothes including a print dress in the other just as Connie was re-buttoning the smelly shirt.

"Ye'r name is Constance Shaw, so I'm told, and ye're not to go ashore unless so ordered." she chirped, laying the clothing across the bed.

"I'll leave thee be to dress ye'rself, proper now, and don't ye forget the corset. This ship is filled with men, and we must remember ourselves. Aye and ye'll receive six shillings a week as a nurse, plus of course the use of this cabin. Please get ye'rself dressed and I'll be back to show ye the rounds".

The little lady bustled out leaving Connie with but a bucket of cold water, a slab of yellow soap, and a piece of rag to clean herself. The clean clothing was thrown across the hammock.

Connie felt like simply tossing herself across the smelly blanket and giving in to the sobs she was barely holding back. How did she get to this dark little smelly dungeon of a place? Where was her Dad? And David? She did see the *Anne Marie* the other evening, didn't she?

Stripping off the almost crusty shirt and pants she was aghast to notice the hair growing in her armpits. Oh, and even her legs were sprouting spiky blonde hairs. And worse, she could even smell her own rancid body odor. She'd give anything for a hot shower, her razor, her little blue package of Secret deodorant and, oh heavens, a toothbrush!

On top of it all she really needed to go to the bathroom, and had no idea of where to go, or what crude form it would take.

The dreary mood passed, and Connie did as she was told. Really, she told herself, there was no choice. She made the best of the bucket of water with the harsh soap, and finished by squeezing the soapy water through her hair. Feeling a bit better she looked at the dress and underclothing left for her. The underpants were not a problem, and despite that they drooped below her knees, at least they were clean soft cotton. The corset however looked like an appliance from hell.

She wrapped it around her back, the ribs in it already uncomfortable, and pulled it across her stomach feeding the laces into the appropriate holes.

She then and rested her small breasts into the rigid and bony cups provided. Every time she moved it seemed to pinch and bite. AAGH! But, she had been told she must wear it.

Damn!

Finally, with the rigid corset laced as loosely as she could wear it, Connie pulled the blue print dress over her head and buttoned the front up to her collar. Y'gads, it was hot.

Last were the white socks and the shoes which, thankfully, were just a bit too big, although it took some time to lace them up past her ankles.

Connie left the hot canvas-walled little cabin looking, more urgently now, for a bathroom. Just as she reached the door to the deck Mrs. MacAdams entered.

"Ah, my dear," she exclaimed, "Don't we look the proper lady now."

"Thank you, Mrs. MacAdams, would you tell me where the head is?"

"Head? Aaah, there wasn't a chamber pot in your cabin? Should be. Herman, our orderly, keeps them emptied. Let's look. It's supposed to be there."

Returning to the cabin with Connie in tow the older woman simply pointed to a blue ceramic bowl under the foot of the hammock,

"There, miss, are thee blind?"

She exited and allowed the now blushing Connie to use the pot. Damn again, but it felt so unclean without a roll of toilet paper.

Her following tour of the crowded upper deck was not unpleasant. Mrs. MacAdams pointed out that these British officer and petty officer patients were kept on deck under the awnings as they were all on the mend, and would shortly be returning to their duties. The more unfortunate who had lost a leg or arm were waiting for transport home to England.

Well forward, resting on a pallet of straw, she found Corey, the seaman from *Reliant*, resting comfortably. He sat up and greeted her enthusiastically.

Looking at Mrs. MacAdams he said, "Cor, tis saved me fr sure she did, me wiz a splinter in me leg an all. Thought I were a gonner I did,"

"I'll be up and around in a few days," he continued, "and no more of *Reliant* fr me. No. I'm to be posted to yonder transport," waving his arm at the large anchorage of ships.

"Rumor has it Howe's to move the Army on Philadelphia forthwith and when she returns from that I'll be off to England in 'er."

Connie squeezed his hand saying, "Well Corey, it is good to see you, and you have healed so very well."

Walking away and towards a scuttle leading below decks Mrs. MacAdams quipped, "T'was a fine piece of work on that young man, and ye'r not even a surgeon. Let's use ur talents below decks".

Stepping into the gloom of the upper gun deck was entering into a totally different world. Here there was only a hint of a cross breeze from the open ports, with more dim and flickering light provided by smoking lamps hung from the low beams overhead. The smell of putrefying flesh from unwashed wounds, and the cries of men in pain with no drugs to ease it made Connie reel with dizziness. There were several other ladies in the long low chamber, mostly doing little for the injured men except to bathe their foreheads with damp cloths. There were no supplies of fresh sterile bandages in evidence, and only one man, described as a doctor, was working on a patient. He was dressed in a dark suit of clothes with blood clearly caked on this sleeves and shirtfront.

'My God,' Connie wanted to scream, 'Clean this place out! Get those men some fresh clean bandages! Get more light in here, and fresh air! There must be something for their pain?'

But, she said nothing. She merely gritted her teeth and followed MacAdams on her tour through this particular hell.

Connie promised herself that she would simply have to find a way to escape.

Eight bells rang through the hulk. MacAdams explained that it was time that the volunteer ladies tending the sick and injured would be transported ashore and further that Connie's duty would begin at eight the following day.

Connie professed extreme fatigue and begged off dinner with the on-board group of two doctors and twelve nurses. She asked if she might simply take her meal in her canvas cabin and retire early.

She did get her bowl of boiled pork and carrots, and then she did put out her lamp, falling quickly asleep.

But, she pressed into her memory her determination to wake herself at midnight. She had thought of a plan. She'd considered her options carefully and, yes, it should work, with luck.

It would be dangerous, but it was really her only option anyway.

Sure enough, she awoke as eight bells struck midnight. There was no light from the skylight above. Connie had no watch, but she was certain her brain had indeed awakened her as she planned. While eight bells could also be four in the morning, Connie was certain that she had it right.

Yes, reconsidering, she knew that Jake and David would try for Deerford, and that it was just over but forty-some miles from New York Harbor to

Roank's Point. And yes, she further had noted that the ebb tide had begun just at six, when she had last been on deck. The flood would be turning about now.

Connie knew the current flooded up the East River towards Long Island Sound at well over four knots; she'd been up the East River enough times to know that for sure.

And, in fact, she knew very well that her father would never sail *Anne Marie* into this crowded harbor where all could see the modern ketch for what she really was, especially as no one on *Anne Marie* would know she was even there anyway. They probably thought her either dead or left back at home in the 21st Century.

Connie crept silently out of her little hammock and pulled the clothing she'd been given over her sweatshirt, but without, of course, that damnable corset. She slid the life jacket from under the hammock and, in her stocking feet, tiptoed up the scuttle to the main deck.

"Who goes there," the Officer of the Deck challenged softly.

"Nurse Constance Shaw, unable to sleep and wanted a breath of air, Sir," Connie replied.

"Keep thee to the poop deck," he cautioned softly. "I'll be close if ye need me."

With that he resumed his 'rounds of the upper deck.

As soon as the sentry was out of sight Connie steeled her resolve. She jumped lightly to the wide cap rail, and she dived cleanly over the side!

It was at least a 30 foot drop to the black water, but Connie dove smoothly, head first, into the harbor without a noticeable splash. She curved neatly under the water, swimming as far from the ship as she could before she surfaced. The limp inflatable lifejacket was still in her hand. Surfacing well out of the glow from the oil lamp on the poop deck she took care to look up and back to check that her dive had not been noticed.

The water was cold, but bearable. Connie slipped the jacket over her head and quietly blew into the inflation tubes. The jacket inflated. It held her head well above the water.

She felt the current start to tug her slowly up-river. She swam with it, moving silently through the darkened fleet. From time to time she had to paddle a bit harder to clear a looming hull, but the exercise simply kept her warm.

Within a half hour the current had increased to full power, bowling her along at five knots. For four hours Connie held herself in the middle of the river. The moon had risen and she could see the dark forest on both sides slide by as she drifted with the flooding current, swiftly upriver.

Once, it must have been after three hours in the water, with her teeth chattering in the growing cold, she banged her knees into a barnacle-covered rock.

"Ouch!" she cried aloud.

There weren't any rocks in the middle of the East River the last time she'd sailed through! In moments the rock had passed.

Less than an hour later she was startled to see in the faint moonlight a string of boats roped together in her path. Yes, it must be Hells Gate, at the top of the river where the sides were closest together and the current was at its strongest. Yes, the Triborough Bridge would one day be high over her head.

She swam backwards, slowing her rush through the flooding current to take a good look at the obstacle.

Aah. There were soldiers in the boats, and she could see the glint of the steel gun barrels. Yet they were talking and laughing. They were clearly not expecting trouble.

She had to get past them, but how? But, she had no time to think about it; the current was dragging her down on the boats far faster than she could hold herself back.

Connie quickly pulled the little rubber plugs from the inflation tubes of her lifejacket. The cold water was forgotten. She allowed the jacket to deflate, and aimed herself to drift between two boats, not breathing as she approached.

She ducked her face into the river and passed, unnoticed, between two longboats. She hoped that this was the end of the British Lines. She hoped that perhaps there were Americans on the other side?

She was very tired, but she managed to slowly re-inflate her life jacket. Her limbs were now really stiffening from the cold water; she couldn't even feel her hands and feet in the cold. It was ever so tempting to just to lay her head onto the life jacket, close her eyes, and drift off to sleep.

She slapped herself sharply on both cheeks, her hands feeling like two dead fish. Then she started to swim, vigorously kicking and moving her arms. The exercise warmed her.

Resting again, she noticed the sky brightening over Long Island; dawn wouldn't be far off. She knew also that the current was weakening. Looking to her right, she could see a dark point of land quite close by. She searched her memory about her several recent trips through the eastern end of Long Island

Sound and the approaches to New York Harbor with her Dad concluding that the dark point of land could only be the southern end of City Island.

Connie also realized that she had to get ashore very soon or she'd be washed back down the river with the ebb tide.

Stroking through the frigid water as strongly as she could, Connie swam towards that bit of land on the north shore. The activity warmed her again and as soon as the current fell slack her stockinged feet touched the rocky bottom.

Wading into shallower water she looked at the shoreline trying to find a remembered landmark. While simple logic told her that this was City Island, the last time she'd seen this point, in 2006, it had been covered with houses, boat yards and docks. Buildings had festooned every inch of the dirty shoreline, with the brown water of the polluted sound lapping under docks. Yet, this very early July morning the water was clean and crystal clear. There were no buildings in sight, and a line of tall bulrushes blocked the view of the land from her location, waist deep, staggering with cold towards the green wall of greenery.

Slipping through the bulrushes, Connie peered over a low stone wall and saw a small farmhouse and barn several hundred yards away. Working herself slowly around the shoreline to her left, she soon saw a village across a little inlet. Wondering if it was friendly, she decided that she couldn't take a chance.

Finding a little hidden patch of dry sea grass between some large rocks, Connie huddled down, thoroughly chilled and miserable, waiting for the July sunshine to bring its warmth. With her life jacket as a pillow she curled-up on the soft grass and was sound asleep even before the first rays of morning sun struck her drying reddish hair. The sun was up. Her clothing dried on her as she slept soundly through the day.

When she awoke it was late afternoon. Connie was hungry and very thirsty; she was also very bedraggled-looking. No, she knew she couldn't simply walk up to the farm house, introduce herself, and ask for food and water. She thought she might still be in British territory, and might find herself dragged back to the hulk!

She considered her options.

Yes, she was free of the British, at least for now. But, she was still was still a long way west of Deerford. She also didn't know and had no way to find out if the people living here were friends or not. Still, she had to find water. Her dry, parched, throat was growing more painful as the day warmed-up.

Deciding that she had to stay hidden, she considered her options. If she could find clean clothing, was it possible to simply walk to the Post Road, turn right, and follow it home?

Dismayed, she rejected that. If this was City Island, the bridge probably was not yet here, and any boatman taking her to the New York shoreline would certainly question an unknown single woman.

Then again, she realized, if this was indeed City Island, well of course there'd be boats. She'd simply have to try find and steal a boat.

With a plan in mind, she returned to her grassy hiding place and waited for dark, suffering through the now hot and muggy afternoon, well bitten by mosquitoes and thirstier than she could ever remember. Finally she slept again.

Well after dark, she guessed it to be before midnight because all the lights in the village were finally out, Connie woke up abruptly. She instantly felt the searing pain in her dry mouth and throat from the salt water she'd inadvertently swallowed in her escape. First, she simply had to find fresh water.

She looked across the cornfield to the dark farmhouse. Knowing they'd have a well, she crouched through the field to the back of a wooden fence. There, not twenty feet away, was a well with a bucket hung over a pulley.

Connie slid silently around the fence and crawled across the dirt farmyard to the well. Reaching up, she untied the rope holding the bucket. It ran quietly through the pulley as the bucket descended. When it stopped, she pulled it up ever so quietly. As it cleared the stone top of the well, Connie stood a bit higher and pulled the bucket to the well cap. She tilted it and let a long cool drink slide down her throat. She then tilted it towards her, rinsing the stinging salt from her face and neck.

She released the bucket, but it fell away from her, clattering back down the well! A dog started to bark inside the house!

Connie dashed back into the cornfield and kneeled in the dirt. The farmhouse door banged open.

A man in a white nightshirt stood in the doorway peering at the farmyard. He looked for long moments, and then shut the door.

"Get ye on back to sleep, dog, ain't nothing there," Connie heard the man growl.

Feeling greatly refreshed and much more alert, Connie stood up in the field. She could see a small village several fields away. She quietly crossed the fields and climbed over three stone walls that separated them, until she drew closer to the sleeping little town.

Skirting the small group of houses, she saw that there were four small boats pulled up beyond the high tide mark in front of the village. She crept up the rocky beach for a look. The smallest of the boats had oars and a rolled-up sail in the bottom.

Connie felt a surge of joy! With this little boat she knew she could get home in just a few hours, and the tide would again shortly be flooding to help her along.

She carefully tugged and pulled at the small boat with the oars, which appeared to be about sixteen feet long. Yet, no matter how hard she tugged and pushed she could barely budge it towards the water. It was simply too heavy.

Not yet quitting, she stood back to catch her breath. Looking around in the dim moonlight she spied a smooth round log further up the beach. If, she reasoned, she could get that log under the keel at the back of the boat she might simply roll it into the water.

It would be noisy, but there was no other way.

After fifteen minutes of straining her small body to haul the smooth log to the back of the boat, and barely able to lift it's stern onto the log, she was ready. She crept again to the bow of the boat, noticing that the closest small houses were no more than twenty yards away. She took a couple deep breaths and told herself it would have to happen now, and fast, or never.

She heaved upward and pushed back on the bow of the wooden skiff with all her strength. The boat inched back and stopped. She stood back, stretched her aching muscles and put her shoulder to the bow, heaving up and back again with all her might.

This time the boat surged backwards, thundering across the rocky beach. It sounded like drums beating as the log bounced across round stones with the boat on top! It splashed its stern into the shallows, and Connie heaved on the bow to float it free.

Suddenly she heard, "Stop, Thief!"

A huge booming voice in the dark rang out again, "Charles, James, grab ur muskets! Someone's stealing the smack."

Connie flopped over the rail into the boat, dropping the lifejacket into the water and forgetting it in her haste. She quickly polled the boat into deeper water and fit the oars into the thole pins. She flopped on the wooden seat and rowed for her life, seeing three men halted at the water's edge.

"Stop Thief or we'll fire!" bellowed one.

Connie saw the glint of a gun, and saw a flash; CRASH, the gun fired.

In less than a minute, CRASH, another fired. Connie felt a huge slam in her right calf, and a hole appeared through the boat at her hip. Still, she never stopped rowing. Before they could re-load she was lost in the dark.

She heard a commotion of cursing and yelling from the village behind her as she rowed past the point and into the Sound. Apparently the villagers did not get another of the boats into the water in time to find her.

Once clear of the little inlet and into the open Sound Connie looked down at her leg. In the gloom she could feel warm blood coursing over her foot, and although it wasn't yet terribly painful she knew it would be, and soon. She moved it and found, thankfully, that nothing seemed broken. Quickly she ripped a large swatch from the hem of the bedraggled skirt, soaked it in salt water over the side, and wrapped her leg as tightly as she could. The bleeding seemed to stop.

After a half hour of painful work, Connie had the small lug sail set and was ghosting east in the moonlight, looking for landmarks that would guide her to Deerford. Hopefully *Anne Marie* would have found Deerford too.

The boat was weakened from the shot, but it didn't leak too badly if Connie kept it healing just a bit to the right. She had to bail with a small wooden scoop, but she could stay ahead of the trickle of incoming water.

Some time later, she didn't know if it was minutes or hours, she woke up with a start. She was angry with herself for falling to asleep, and her leg now burned like fire. She was again dizzy with thirst, and she knew she had a fever from the exposure.

Looking carefully around her little boat, she hoped that she could she recognize where she was. And, yes, in the pre-dawn's light she could barely make out the familiar rocks just west of the Deerford inlet. Somehow the little boat had sailed a straight course while she had dozed. But she was both too close to the rocky shore, and the boat was almost swamped.

She knew she'd have to get across the inlet or she'd not make it to the William's farm before full daylight, although it was amazing to her that she had sailed and drifted so close after nodding off.

She took her seat again at the oars, nearly waist deep in the sinking boat, and somehow summoning the energy, rowed the heavy swamped boat across the inlet, almost passing out with each pull on the heavy oars. In her weakened state it was all she could do just to get the last few hundred yards into the black muddy shore.

She did it. At first light of day the swamped little boat slid through the ooze of black mud and into the tall bull rushes. Connie more fell out than climbed, and pulled herself ashore with her arms, hopping on one leg. Her hands grasped a stick of driftwood. Hobbling further up through the deep mud and tall sea grass, using the stick for balance, she finally collapsed beside a small dirt track.

Sitting with her injured leg stretched in the dirt, she looked around in the brightening dawn. The last time she'd been here, only last month, there'd been a road around this point of land and a public beach to her right. The empty fields across the road had been dotted with pretty little houses, while now there was only a single dirt track wandering off through open fields to her right and to her left.

And, she could barely stand-up. She tried to choose which way she would find help.

Relying on memory, Connie figured she had landed about half-way down the mile long point of land. She remembered that the William's house was nearly at the bridge which crossed the inlet. She could see no bridge this morning, still guessing that it was to her left she used both hands to hold the stick as a crutch as she stood again and hobbled up the path.

Anne, Arthur William's daughter, was gathering eggs.

She saw a blur of dirty white and blue gingham briefly at the end of the field, and then she glimpsed it again. Curious, she set down her basket of eggs and walked up the pathway.

Shortly she saw, to her surprise, a young woman in a filthy dress with a bloody bandage about her leg struggling to rise to her feet. Running to the young woman's aid, Anne bent down and helped her up.

"Aye, Missy, t'will be all right. Let me get thee to the house. What happened to thine leg?" she said as she helped Connie to her feet.

"Is this the Williams Farm?" Connie asked weakly.

"Aye 'tis," replied Anne. "I'll be Anne Williams, and my father'll be at the house. What happened to ye'r leg? And, who be thee anyway?"

"Tell me," Connie gasped with the last of her strength, "do you know of a ketch named *Anne Marie*, and of Jake Shaw?"

"Aye," replied Anne, looking more closely at Connie, "thee must be the daughter that he refused to believe lost. Ye'r father and thine friend David were here, but they've sailed just last night for Philadelphia."

CHAPTER SEVEN

Just the previous evening, *Anne Marie* had made a fast passage of it. It had seemed the winds were always in their favor as Jake, David and Stephen cleared the Point and rounded to the east. The same southwesterly breeze that had carried Connie to safety had pushed them up the Sound. In less than nine hours *Anne Marie* was over a hundred miles away, again at the Race, the narrow exit from Long Island Sound between Fisher's Island and Orient Point.

As they approached Fisher's Island in the morning twilight David shouted to Jake, "radar shows a ship in the Race"

Jake looked to the east and through his red filtered binoculars could barely make out the outlines of a square-rigged ship.

"Betcha it's a British blockade vessel," he quipped. "We'll fix that."

He spun the large chrome wheel to starboard.

As soon as Stephen recognized where they were heading he yelled to Jake, "aye, sir, 'tiz a large risk ye'r chancin' to sail the Gut. Why t'wasn't a few years ago, before the big storm in '67, when farmers were drivin cows across at low water. 'Tiz narrow and dangerous."

"I trust the captain of that ship thinks so too," replied Jake, gesturing at the approaching frigate while bending over to press a silver switch on a little panel beside him. The diesel engine purred to life, startling Stephen who had not yet seen it work.

Jake then slid the screen of the bottom mapping sonar into place, which clearly showed him a deep path through the channel ahead. There were no channel markers, of course, but none were required with the eyes of the sonar working for them.

"Aye," said Stephen, comprehending, "tiz a marvelous piece of work here."

Anne Marie shot quickly through the very narrow Plum Gut, luffing straight into the wind against the strong flood tide for about a mile. Jake then steered the boat back towards the Gardener's Island, filling the sails as they reached towards the open Atlantic Ocean. He kept the big diesel running. *Anne Marie* exceeded fourteen knots, racing to the south until only the topsails of the frigate could be seen over the ridge of Plum Island.

"Nope", Jake laughed, "that frigate will have to go the long way around, through the Race. She'll never see us again."

As soon as *Anne Marie* cleared Montauk Point the wind veered further to the west offering them a brisk close reach along the Long Island south shore, kept just out of sight. Still, David kept a close watch on the radar repeater, watching for possible approaching vessels.

The ocean was empty that first day but late that night, as they passed off shore from Sandy Hook, the entrance to New York, David called Jake and Stephen on deck.

"Look." he pointed at the radar screen.

There were dozens of tiny blips ghosting across the radar screen, stopped just inside Sandy Hook

"Aye," Stephen said,"that'll be part of Howe's Fleet, anchored and waiting for the rest of 'em. They're certain to all weigh tomorrow. It'll be very close to see if we can get word to the Congress in Philadelphia before they attack."

The next day *Anne Marie* 'rounded Cape May into Delaware Bay under a lovely sunset. Since leaving the farm, Stephen couldn't keep from continuously remarking on the incredible, to him, sailing speed of the little ship. He'd been on the helm almost every waking hour. A good sailor himself, he simply loved the feel of *Anne Marie*'s large chrome wheel as she scudded along in perfect trim averaging over twelve knots. Every time the wind would shift or veer a bit he could delicately and ever so easily adjust the sails back again to perfect trim with a mere touch of an electric winch.

Stephen was also amazed at the food. It seemed to him that unbelievably tasty concoctions were being created in mere minutes, as if by magic, each time mealtime approached. Stephen still did not quite understand how a frozen solid package, covered with frost, could first even appear on a warm and sunny July day, and then how that frozen block could be reduced to steaming plates full of delectable dishes in mere minutes. It seemed pure magic to him, noting that his former seagoing fare was limited to salt pork, sea biscuits and cabbage.

He also delighted in the loose and comfortable clothing that David had offered. At first he felt it terribly immodest to walk about in nothing but short pants and a light cotton blouse that David had called a t-shirt. And, yes, the first day his legs had gotten painfully sunburned, but Jake had spread some magic crème on them. They healed overnight. Now he had some other crème called 'Sun block' that he remembered to put on his exposed white skin. It worked.

But, the thought of that huge armada, just a day or so behind them, had him constantly worried.

"Jake," started Stephen, looking at the Jersey shore as the deep forest glided past about a mile on their right hand side, "I'll be needing to go ashore at Cape May Courthouse, which lies about twelve miles on ye'r starboard shore. Y'know of my urgent message. Seems Lord Howe and his damnable brother, the Admiral, are already sailed from New York with a veritable Armada to sack Philadelphia. I durns't know quite how, but I've got to let our Army know of' it. T'would be better if we could sail closer to the city, but ye can be sure the double-damned English 'll have a blockade force in this river; probably a sloop or small frigate. We'll not be lucky to get as far as Chester."

He continued, "I hope to find a fast horse and get to Camden sometime in the early morning. Think my only choice now is to get warning to the Congress, if they'll listen to me. So, ye'd best let me get in me proper clothing, and run me ashore here. And, thank'ee for ye'r fast passage. Thee alone may have saved our Congress."

"Don't you worry now," replied Jake as he slid his laptop computer across the deeply varnished table in front of the chromed wheel, "look at this."

With that, Jake stroked a few keys and a nautical chart of the lower reaches of Delaware Bay appeared on the screen. It could be aligned with the screen on the radar repeater, displaying the exact position of *Anne Marie* as she rounded to the northwest, heading upriver.

"My god!" Stephen exclaimed, "That looks like a chart, but like nothing I've ever seen, and tiz in colors."

He pointed at the screen, asking, "what be those red and green dots?"

"They're navigation markers that probably won't be there for maybe another hundred years," replied Jake.

"See," he pointed at the screen again. "Here's the Delaware Memorial Bridge which won't be built until sometime in the 1940's. But, no matter, with our radar, this chart and our sonar we can still safely navigate upriver without the buoys."

"Ye'll sail up the Delaware at night?" queried Stephen. "Tiz not been done before. Tiz nearly a hundred miles to the city. How'll thee see the shoals? And ye might run smack into a British picket. I truly can not allow thee to place yer fine ketch and ye'r good selves in further danger. Ye should simply run me ashore in one of ye'r fine fast little boats and sail ye'rselves back to New England."

"Have no fear, friend", came Jake's reply. "See here, we can look at the bottom of the bay ahead of us or in any direction we want on this screen. We'll also see any picket ship on the radar, here, long before they'll see us."

They sailed smoothly nearly five hours northwest up the Delaware Bay in a warm offshore breeze. The wind died as the Bay narrowed to the entrance of the Delaware Rive; they were still nearly fifty miles south of Philadelphia. The sails were lowered and furled. *Anne Marie* continued her push up the Delaware River towards the Colonial Capital with the quiet diesel thumping her along.

At a few minutes past four in the morning, with the Capital only eleven miles away, David, who was at the helm, suddenly cut the engine off.

Jake arrived on deck moments later asking, "What's wrong?"

"Looks like a picket ship anchored there," David pointed at the radar repeater to a spot about a half mile up-river. "It's anchored in mid-stream, just downriver from Little Tinnecum Island. She's in the middle of the narrow part of the channel; we'll not slip past without notice."

By then Stephen was also on deck dressed in his own clothes.

He quipped," just put me ashore here. Surely from here I can easily make to the Capital by morning. I'll rent a rig, get to the General and can get meself back to William's Farm sometime next week. Y'all 'v done enough."

Jake thoughtfully replied, "Nope, Stephen. There just isn't time. We know that Howe's already sailed. He'll be only a few days away."

"And, Stephen, I know for certain that Howe's fleet will anchor in two days time behind Cape May. I also know that they will not attack Philadelphia."

"But," Jake concluded, "the only thing between the British Armada and our Congress is ourselves."

"How do you know that?" asked Stephen. "I expect our General will have a company or two along the river, and the militia in Philadelphia always keeps a number of gunboats manned at the port."

"History proves you wrong, Son. The Army is about four miles north of Trenton tonight on the east bank of this river."

Stephen wondered how Jake would know that.

"David," Jake redirected, "the tide's high. Bear us off to your port at 350 degrees."

"See," he pointed to a little indent on the radar screen, "that's the entrance to Darby Creek, and if these charts are still right, it should have deep enough water for us to slip in close under the trees, right here."

Anne Marie slowed to a bare crawl and veered to the northwest side of the river, creeping along as close to the Pennsylvania shore as her sonar would allow. Her keel was mere inches off the muddy bottom.

In the starlight, the three masted outline of the British sloop of war could just be seen at anchor a mere 300 yards to their north. It was just below the end of a little low island which was in the center of the channel.

The sonar found the deep cut into the creek. *Anne Marie* followed the cut through reedy marshes and almost to the edge of a growth of trees that rose darkly up almost to mast height. They quietly slipped anchors to the bottom, fore and aft.

"David," Jake whispered, "I've a thought. What say you take Stephen upriver in the jet boat while I divert the attention of our friend there? If you can get moving quickly, you can slip past Philadelphia before first light and get to Trenton in time to catch the General in the morning."

He smiled, continuing, "I think that I can arrange a surprise for that Sloop. She's gonna find her anchor is dragging before morning, may even go aground downstream. Then, I'll be waiting for you right here in the Creek tomorrow night."

Stephen had thought he'd seen it all, but he was open-mouthed in amazement when David walked to the rear of the Ketch and uncovered a boat that was hanging in the davits there. It was another small boat made of the same rubber 'logs', but this was bigger than the first one. David pushed another silver button, wire hummed through pulleys and the boat dropped gently into the water. He then jumped down into it, looked quickly at the control panel, and then pulled himself back up the stern of *Anne Marie*.

"Jake," he whispered loudly, "what kind of boat is this? I've not seen it. Is it new? Do I need to know anything special on how it works?"

Jake replied, "Oh, it's my new Seal Delivery Boat. I just demo'ed it to the Navy. It's pretty cool. Jet powered. Just hold the red starter button down about five seconds and the motor will wind up. It's almost totally silent, and with no propellers it can be grounded. Be careful, though, it's really fast."

David nodded, jumped back in and gestured for Stephen to get into the boat. Stephen shrugged. He sat down on the stern of *Anne Marie* and dropped into the small gray boat.

A few minutes later Jake reappeared at the rail of *Anne Marie,* but he was dressed in a suit of the same dark rubbery material that the boat was made of. He lowered himself into the boat, and then lifted in a round silvery tank with lots of valves at the top and a heavy canvas bag. Stephen did not know what was in that bag.

"Okay, let's go, but quietly," Jake said softly.

Stephen was looking for the oars and oarlocks when he heard a high pitched squeal followed by a muted rumble. After a quiet thud, the water at the back of the boat gurgled and bubbled. The small boat silently pulled away from *Anne Marie,* without oars. David guided it through the night towards the river.

Stephen sat frozen in place, wondering what made this boat move.

Once outside the Darby Creek channel, the boat turned up-river, hugging the north shore. It presently passed the picket vessel. As they reached the lower end of Tinnecum Island Stephen sat open-mouthed as Jake attached the heavy tank to his back, tied a heavy belt festooned with many strange objects around him, and lastly pulled a black mask with a glass face over his head. Jake then simply dropped backwards over the side of the boat with his tank, and sank below the river surface.

"What's he doing? Is he safe?" queried Stephen quietly.

"Shhhh. Don't worry," whispered David. "Jake knows exactly what he's doing. He'll be drinking scotch back aboard *Anne Marie* in a half an hour."

David turned the small boat up-river, creeping slowly.

In what seemed only a few minutes a loud hail was heard from the sloop of war and all her deck lanterns were quickly lighted.

"All Hands, Anchor Adrift. " the cry came across the quiet river.

Jake had simply swum down the chain and unshackled the anchor. The sloop spun south on the ebbing current, out of control.

At that moment David whispered, "Hang On!".

Stephen was thrown to the floorboards of the little boat as, with an increasing but still silent whine, little boat was thrown wildly forward. Stephen felt a huge wind blowing across his back and, terrified again, he raised his eyes to see if David was all right. His first thought was that they'd suffered the near-miss from a cannonball fired by the Sloop of War.

And there sat David, resting calmly on the rear thwart behind a small black steering wheel with his hair blowing straight back.

Stephen then understood that this little boat was literally flying across the top of the water at enormous speed. He swallowed twice, understanding that this was just another amazing machine. His fear subsided.

Crouching on his hands and knees in the bottom of the flying boat, Stephen, of course, had never had a thought that anything could move as fast as this little rubber boat was skimming them over the water! The gray box in the center of the boat was vibrating with a mild humming sound. Still, after a few moments of literal terror, he sat up and realized that he was perfectly fine. It was apparently all quite normal to his host. In a minute or two he relaxed to find that the ride was actually enjoyable.

He looked at David who simply smiled and waved, hollering, "Hang on!"

Long before dawn the boat passed the junction from the Schuylkill River and without slowing, zoomed silently to the east and south of the two muddy little islands just down river from the colonial city of Philadelphia. They were almost a mile away on the New Jersey side. There were no lights from the little dock at the sleepy town of Camden as they silently skimmed past.

They continued north, up the twisting river. The port across the river was jammed with sailing ships tied to wharfs while David's attention was glued to a glowing screen on the black box in front of him. Stephen guessed that David was watching a map of the river.

Clearly David knew how to keep the boat skimming quietly in the river's center near the darkened towns they continued to pass.

Stephen wondered what the local folks would think if they should see the machine? He knew it was best they didn't.

They arrived south of Trenton before Stephen could believe they had traveled so far. As a few pre-dawn lights in the town came into sight ahead. David aimed the little boat to the left side of the river, away from the town. The silent jet boat again snuck past the quiet waterfront ferry dock; the machine making almost no noise.

Moments later David steered the boat into the muddy river bank to their right.

"Grab the painter and pull us in," he whispered to Stephen. "If Jake is right, we're very close to Washington's camp."

Stephen and David pulled the light jet boat up a muddy bank and covered it with a tarpaulin, then some branches and dead leaves.

Stephen turned to David saying, "keep thee with ye'r machine, David. Stay well hidden. I'll walk into the camp, hoping its close, and get my message through to the General. After I pass the news to Washington I'll get meself a horse and see ye both back at William's in a week or so."

David responded, "How long will it take you to find him?"

"The Army was last at Monmouth Court House, perhaps a day's ride, unless Jake was right and the Camp's been moved close by."

"OK," said David. "I'm guessing that Jake knows exactly where the Army is. He was quite a student of this War. Trusting they're close, I'll wait here to tomorrow night. If you can get back here you should travel back with us."

"Canna promise," replied Stephen, "but I'll accept ye'r offer. Remember do not stay past tomorrow night. If ye do not get *Anne Marie* clear of the river soon ye may get bottled in by the invasion. Ye'll certainly be sighted then."

And with that, he slipped away, fading into the forest.

David was too tired to argue. He simply slipped under the boat cover, onto the rubber deck, nestled himself on life preservers, and was soon asleep.

It seemed he had no sooner wakened briefly to pull his jacket tighter when a hand slapped on the boat from the top.

"David? " he heard a loud whisper

He pulled himself out from under the canvas cover, instantly getting soaked by a driving rain. He stood up in the driving rain with wet leaves stuck to the side of his unshaven face. Blinking twice he saw Stephen, wrapped in a heavy cloak. He was standing next to a very tall figure, likewise in a dark cloak, but with long white hair slicked down on his neck under a large gold tri-cornered hat.

David scrambled over the side of the rubber boat, stumbling only a little. Twinkling blue eyes looked David over from the tousled mop of red hair to the leaf-spotted face and the soggy sweatshirt and jeans.

"General Washington, may I present David Saunders, from the Twentieth Century, of whom we recently spoke." Stephen formally and with a slight bow introduced David to the tall General.

"Tiz an unlikely tale that Stephen's brought to me," the General started in a deep voice, holding out his hand, "but tiz clear from ye'r clothing and ye'r strange boat there that there's truth to what Stephen has said. Tell me, will that thing yonder really fly silently across the top of the water faster than a full gale o'wind? And, can ye truly swim like a fish under the water and breathe too?"

"G-General George Washington?" stammered David, picking a leaf from under his collar.

He continued, "my God, Jake will never believe it. Aah, he's my father in law, or soon to be, aah, ummm, I mean as soon as we find —,"

David stopped stammering, straightened, and wiped the wet leaves off his chin. He looked into the kindly gaze of those incredible piercing eyes.

The General spoke again softly, "It's all right, son. Stephen's well told thine plight. T'would seem that Providence has brought a tremendous boon to assist our cause, yet we'll do well to concur that thine very existence in this era must be kept a great and urgent secret. T'was very fortunate that Mr. Downey found me at Middlebrook Camp here in Trenton."

He continued, "It can only be the Grace of God that has brought ye unbidden to these troubled times. I've greatly, and in the secret of my soul, despaired of our meager chances of prevailing in this great struggle. But, from what Mr. Downey tells me, yerself and thine unbelievable vessel hail from near this same place, but from a time in our future? More, ye and ye'r Captain, nor anyone alive, can fathom how ye came to be here.

"Y-Yes sir," again stammered David, "apparently so. I mean we were just sailing home a few weeks ago and we were caught by a hurricane near Bermuda. We woke up here, I mean, in this time, not ours. And neither Jake, my father in law, er, I guess he'll be my father in law if Connie is here, ahh—"

"Aye," the General replied in a soft voice, "Y've lost all ye'r family and all that was dear to thee. I understand it must be very difficult. But, ye'r very appearance here, and the very story that Stephen tells me, that ye hail from a great and strong Country called, what, the States of America?"

"It's the United States of America, General," David interjected.

"Aye, and that its birth was this very struggle upon which we are embarked?"

"Yes, General, but Jake tells me that we can not ever be even seen here in this time. We must let history as it was written take its course. I mean, if we were to do something out of place, or worse, get caught, then the world as we knew it might change."

"Aye again, son. Ye'r mentor, this Jake, is a very wise man. Methinks ye may be here for a grander reason than ye think. Why just the plot that we've hatched with Mr. Downey here will foil Mad Dick's plans to capture our Capitol, for certainly without yer'selves we've no way to keep him from sailing up the Delaware tomorrow and destroying our Congress."

"More than that, ye'r very appearance and ye'r truth of the future will buoy my own endeavors through this terrible time. I know now, in my heart, that we will prevail. Ye've brought me a wonderful gift."

"Please return with Mr. Downey to your amazing vessel. He and I have hatched a plan that, with ye'r help, may well confound the approaching enemy without compromise to ye'r selves. We hope ye'll agree to assist our Cause as he'll outline. I must be back to my troops anon, but my regards to thine Captain and convey my sincere respects. I trust I will personally make his acquaintance."

"Now", General Washington smiled, "would thee show me this little amazing boat before ye depart?"

He rubbed his hand along the smooth rubber curve of the jet boat.

The two young men dragged the boat easily back to into the river. Stephen held the bow while David hit the red button producing the usual soft whine of the starter followed by a puff off blue smoke as the jet motor purred to life. He then backed the boat into the swift current as Stephen jumped aboard. They planed off in a small circle, throwing spray high into the air, and returned to the muddy shoreline.

Washington bent over the rubber boat again, pushing gently on the side.

"What be this made of?" he queried.

"It's a canvas boat coated with epoxy, er rubber, and filled with air."

"Canvas, aye", replied the General, stroking the little plastic running light on the bow, "but I know nothing this rubb burr and e coxie of what you speak. How to you ever light the wick in this very small lamp?"

David leaned to control panel and flipped the small running lights switch. The bow light instantly lit.

Washington stepped back, startled.

"My God, Sir!" he exclaimed, "That is indeed a miracle!"

"Nothing but a battery powered lamp, Sir," shrugged David.

Washington blinked and straightened.

Turning to Stephen he said, "Mr. Downey, dost thee truly believe ye can confound the Lords Howe into believing that my Army is encircling the Capital, instead of encamped here, a week march away?"

"Aye, Sir. With the help of our new friends methinks our plan will succeed."

"Godspeed then. Perhaps some day I can visit ye'r amazing ship," and with that the General waved briefly, and was instantly swallowed in the rain and woods.

David and Stephen pushed off into the current.

"Stephen, was that really George Washington?"

"Aye, in the flesh."

"And we're to — "

"David, can thee get us back down river to Jake, quickly and without being discovered? Methinks we need discuss the General's plans together."

Just under two hours later the two young men, thoroughly wet and cold after pushing at cruising speed through the continually driving rain, were south of Philadelphia, idling along the eastern bank. The dismal rain had hidden them well from any curious eyes along the river.

David un-snapped a pocket in the boat and took out a small hand-held radio.

Snapping it on and tuning to Channel 16 he voiced, "*Anne Marie, Anne Marie.*"

The black box, much to Stephen's surprise, squawked back, "Ah, David. Good to hear your voice. Where are you?"

"We're mid-river just passing north of Tinnecum. I don't se the picket ship"

"OKAY, you're clear to enter the creek," the radio continued to speak, "the sloop's not in sight. I'm tied to the west bank just where you left us. Look closely, it may be hard to see me. I've run some branches up the masts."

Coming around the end of the little island and into Darby Creek the young men in the boat saw nothing of *Anne Marie* until they were less than 100 yards from the shore. Then they could just make out her green hull against the mud of the riverbank. Indeed, Jake had run some branches up the masts. The little ship was virtually invisible.

Shortly they were aboard, dressed in warm dry clothing and sipping large mugs of hot chocolate.

After sharing with Jake his excitement about meeting General Washington, David suggested that Stephen now divulge what the General had requested of them.

"Aye," started Stephen, "the General had a runner from the Amboys late yesterday confirming that a great fleet of over two hundred sail had weighed from New York and cleared south. It can only be the Lord Howe; they call him 'Black Dick', for Philadelphia with his damnable brother's army."

"By now, be the weather fair, they'll be rounding under Cape May tonight sometime. The fleet will anchor in the lower river by morning. General Washington believes that Howe will send a scouting party up-river to land above the Schuylkill. From there tis but a few miles on a good secure road into the Capital. If they find no opposition landing on the north bank, they'll drop back to the fleet. As soon thereafter as there will be a fair southerly to push them upriver, we can expect a sacking of the City within days by both bombardment from capital ships and an Army assault."

"And General Washington thinks that we can stop this?" asked Jake.

"Aye, if ye'r willing."

"I bespoke to him of ye'r guns that shoot hundreds of times without loading and of ye'r ability to see through the night. I also proclaimed thee loyal Colonists, and even told him ye call ye'r selves Americans. The General felt that only thee, through the Grace of God, might able to slow Black Dick from his mission, as else we'll loose the Capital without warning. Methinks his sight of ye'r little boat gave him comfort in the plan."

"Simply, there's naught he can do from his encampment at Middlebrook before the Redcoats have the city sacked. If we so loose our Congress and our Treasury, our citizens will loose heart and our struggle will be lost."

"Will thee help?" he implored.

Jake leaned back, eyes closed, deep in thought.

After a moment he looked at David asking, "son, I know you've never been to war. You've never fired a weapon in anger, or at another human. Could you do it?"

David thought for a few minutes, then replied slowly, "yes, if it's the only way to protect that which is in the right, I could. But, I'd need to be convinced."

"Hmmmm, this is interesting," started Jake.

"In our histories of this Revolution, Lord Howe did depart New York with a great fleet of 262 vessels to sack the Colonial Capital in July 1777, which is I guess now. But, he didn't succeed, and there's no record of his landing at the Delaware River at all. He's reported only to have anchored his fleet at Cape May Courthouse, then to have proceeded back to sea."

"The English didn't then approach Philadelphia until some five weeks later. They came then overland from the Chesapeake Bay and won a major battle crossing Brandywine Creek, some twenty miles west from the Delaware."

"Revolutionary scholars," he continued, "have often puzzled at why Howe didn't press his advantage and attack the Capital immediately, today or tomorrow, by simply sailing up this unprotected river on the first favorable tide and wind."

Stephen interrupted with a quiet whisper, "Ye'd be the reason, sir, would thee not think? We must stop 'em".

Jake held up his hand and thought for a long time.

"Aye boys, we'll do 'er. Let's make our plans. But, at all costs, we can not be discovered. I'll scuttle *Anne Marie* if she comes into danger."

"Truly," he continued, "we can't be even seen by anyone, and we can't be documented as having been here. We can't even have any questions left behind that there might be anything other than what is understood as perfectly normal going on."

"And, while doing that, we three have got to stop the largest armed force on this Continent from its path towards an assault up this River. Stephen, now what the devil does General Washington suggest the three of us are going to do to accomplish all of that?"

✫ ✫ ✫

Lord General William Howe, resplendent in his red uniform, heavily decorated with gold, campaign ribbons, and medals, leaned back in a large chair in his brother's, Admiral Howe's, great cabin on the three-decker HMS *Victorious*. The ponderous ship was anchored near the town of Cape May Courthouse, in the lee of Cape May, accompanied with an invasion squadron of over 260 navy vessels, transports and supply ships of all descriptions. The lower Delaware was virtually covered with ships, sailors and 15,000 miserably wet and seasick soldiers this cold rainy evening.

"Damned bloody wilderness!" the General stated to his brother, dressed in the blue and gold lace uniform of a Kings Admiral, "we ought to just give the muddy damned place to the bloody Colonists."

"Aye," grunted the Admiral, "t'would likely do so 'cept they've tweaked the ire of our Lords. Harrumph, they canna just walk away from the King. It's our duty, my dear brother."

The marine sentry at the door rapped sharply and presented a visitor, "Lieutenant Bristol, your Lordships."

"Aah, bade him enter," replied the Admiral.

Then to his brother he stated, "This be the son of Sir Bristol, Earl of Wickersham. 'EE's a bright lad and methinks the right sort to lead our foray upriver to sniff out any Colonial defenses about their muddy little pigsty of a Capital."

"Our loyal spies in the city report it was undefended just a fortnight ago, and Washington's said to be still encamped near Trenton, at least four days march north," replied the Lord.

"Canna be too sure," was the reply.

"Enter," he then said to the sharply dressed young lieutenant who'd appeared at the doorway.

The young man stiffly approached the oak table and formally saluted the two portly gentlemen lounging in their seats, "Lieutenant Bristol, Sir".

"Know thee what we're about, Lieutenant?" queried the Admiral to the young man.

"Aye, Sir. Tiz common scuttlebutt that we're to sack the damned Yankee's capitol city in Philadelphia. Me boys think 'twill be a lark as the 'tween decks rumor has the Yankee Army encamped elsewhere."

"At ease, Lieutenant." spoke Lord Howe.

"Indeed we've good report that General Washington's Militia is some forty miles north of the City, and on the wrong side of the river. But, we be seeking a fresh scouting before we land our troops and commit our ships. Mind ye now, we're not afeared of a handful of rabble colonists, but a large force could make a bit of trouble."

The Admiral interjected, "We need thee, sir, to take the cutter *Fencer* up this river, anchoring just South of this island", pointing at Tinnecum on the chart.

"Ye'll take two boats of Marines onward up-river and scout out any Rebel defenses above the junction of the Schuylkill River, here. We'll need a complete report on any Yankee defenses south of their muddy little city, as well as on the most likely places to land our armies."

"Aye aye, sir," the Lieutenant saluted and turned to depart the Cabin.

"And. Lieutenant," the General barked as he was leaving, "don't get ye'r Marines spotted by that rabble. T'wouldn't do to have them fore warned."

At dusk, still in the sheeting rain, the small cutter, perhaps only fifty feet on deck and propelled with strong sweeps as well as sails, hauled anchor and ghosted away from the anchored fleet, enroute up-river. She was towing two longboats. Two platoons of Kings Marines were laboring in the rain with the crew of the sloop, heaving at the heavy sweeps to increase their speed.

Each of the sweeps, large oars, was just under eighteen feet long and there were five thrust through the deck scuppers on each side of the little vessel. The inboard ends were roped together, and four men worked each. They alternately raised the inboard ends to lower the paddles altogether, then pushed, running forward together. At the end of each stroke they would push the handles to the deck and trot smartly to the rear. Forty men were so employed running and pulling back and forth on the slippery wet deck, rowing the thirty ton ketch upriver at about three knots. It was exhausting work. Still, they had another three knots of a flooding tide to push them along.

Within a few hours the rain stopped and a land wind picked-up from the south west, giving a welcome break to the oarsmen and speeding their trip.

Bristol timed his arrival for dawn at the head of the Bay and the narrows to the river, still thirty miles south of the City. And, just as the eastern sky was brightening, the breeze shifted to the south west and the channel veered to a narrow cut to the left of a swampy little island. Before noon the rooftops of the village of Chester appeared on their left side. And, just ahead, the picket sloop appeared. The smaller cutter sailed closer.

Lt, Bristol softly hailed, "Picket sloop, ahoy."

A voice replied, "Acting Lieutenant McKenna, sir."

The ships moved closer together.

Bristol spoke again, "McKenna, ye'r station is five miles up-river in the Tinnecum Channel. Why be thee so far south?"

"Our anchor chain parted in the wee hours, sir, and we've not had the breeze to move back on station until just now. And, sir, we've but a small crew. We can not sweep her against the current."

""Quite so, McKenna," retorted Bristol from the cutter. "Carry on. Ye may as well drop down river to the Fleet. There'll be an action soon and ye may be needed."

"Aye aye, sir."

The cutter then moved to the west side of the channel and continued up-river, entering the narrow channel to the west of Tinnecum's Island. Their anchor finally splashed to the river.

Lt. Bristol turned to the Acting Lieutenant Sharft, the young Captain of the ketch saying, "Soon as it's dusk me and me boys are going ashore to scout. We'll return by first light. If ye don't have us aboard then ye'll want to drop down the river out of sight below the island and come back for us after dark tomorrow."

"Aye aye, sir," replied Sharft.

And with that Lt. Bristol ordered his Marines to get what sleep they could.

At dusk, and after their evening meal, the troop of Marines climbed down into the small boats.

"Heave away."

Scharf set an anchor watch on the bomb ketch and retired his crew below.

An hour before dawn he was awakened in his tiny cabin by the sound of a muffled boom somewhere in his bilges. He briefly thought that a log floating down river had bumped the hull. He went back to sleep knowing that the Watch on deck would call out if anything hove into sight.

Yet, moments later, while thinking of Mary, a buxom and willing serving girl in his favorite New York pub, he was awakened by his boson beating at his cabin door,

"Captain, we're sinking! Water's already to the 'tween decks. The crew's on deck; we must take to the boats."

The Lieutenant swung his feet out of the gimbaled bed to the deck of his tiny cabin, and into almost knee-deep water.

"Abandon ship," he cried as his head appeared out of the scuttle, just as the deep river was rising over the main deck.

His twenty-five man crew could not all fit inside the small launch that was cut free of it's lashings before the ship sank. However, as the river was only twenty feet deep, and as the ship went down upright, her crew simply climbed into the rigging perching on the yardarms like seagulls. They clung to the rigging all through the damp night until the sun rose and burned through the clouds above the Jersey shoreline.

As the sun came up Lieutenant Sharft found himself sitting at the maintop, his back to the slanted mast, wearing only his drawers and shift. He was mortified.

The boson was at his side.

"Evans", Sharft asked after he got himself under control.

"Aye, sir"

"Who was on watch, Evans?"

"Cor, sir, t'were a fine evening what with the rain slacked off, sir. Jus like now, sir, we could see the river side to side and there were nothing near a'tall. Sir, I canna guess, sir, how her bottom could be stove in, and so fast, sir."

"Aye," the young Lieutenant was almost wailing, "*Fencer* was almost new, just taken from the French. She was sound and tight, hardly pumped an hour each day on the crossing.

"Could it have been a cannon from the shore?" he asked.

"Nay, sir," the boson replied slowly. "We'd a seen a flash of powder, sir. We saw nothing. Felt like sommat banged her keel from under the river, and hard enough to break 'er back and stove in most o'the planking too. I heard of a whale doing that at sea."

Lt Sharft held on to the mast, knowing that his career in His Majesty's Navy was likely over, and he really didn't know why or how. Still, he knew that he'd not pass the certain Admiralty Inquiry on this sinking.

Meanwhile, Lt. Bristol's two boatloads of Marines, having left before the cutter sank, did reach a small quay on the Schuylkill River just north from it's junction with Delaware. It was clearly a ferry landing where the main road to the south crossed the river. Yet it was deserted and quiet. Even the ferryman's house seemed empty. The house had not been abandoned; there were several scrawny chickens in the yard, and the Marines found a pair of fine sucklings in a shed.

Bristol left a token force of four armed sailors with the boats, and marched the Marines with the rest of the sailors north on a fine road alongside of the river, north towards the Capital. It was said to be only three to four miles away through fenced fields. He threatened the four left as guard with a flogging if they were to start a fire to eat a chicken, and ordered them not to slaughter the pigs until his return.

Lt. Bristol's Marines had covered half of the four miles to the city when the road dipped down through a marshy grove. His plan was to approach to just under a mile from Philadelphia, then scout to the edge of the growing town. He was expecting to find no armed forces in the area.

BLAM! BLAM! BLAM! BLAM! BLAM ! Without warning the forest erupted with rippling of musket fire. It seemed like over 500 muskets all fired within the space of a minute or so!

Bristol's instantly terrified force was decimated by the first volley. The head of a man beside him exploded into flying bone and a spray of blood. The trained Marines dropped to the ground and returned fire with all twenty-four of their muskets, but it was merely 24 single shots against a volley of over 500 single shots; indeed a poor showing against such a massive opposing force.

Muskets spent. His men cowered in the darkness in mortal terror, trying to reload while crabbing in the mud.

From their left another volley of hundreds of shots flew harmlessly over their heads. They continued to lie, belly-down, knowing they were vastly out numbered. Indeed, Bristol himself was wounded in the arm.

Megods, Bristol thought, they were cross-fired by two large groups, all probably re-loading their muskets now for the kill. There was no choice. He was crestfallen.

"Quarter!" he shouted, "QUARTER!"

"Cease ye'r fire," he heard.

Then louder, a command was yelled to him, "Throw down ye'r weapons, Redcoat dog."

A slight figure dressed in a Yankee Army officer's uniform presently appeared through the gloom of the darkened grove.

"Redcoat there," the Officer called, "throw down ye'r weapon and offer ye'r surrender, else we'll cut thee all to ribbons."

"Quarter sir," shouted Bristol again, weakly.

The Yankee officer approached.

Bristol, rising to his feet, couldn't help but say, "Sir, I was to believe that ye'r Army be encamped leagues north. How can thee be here?"

"Ye foolish British," the Yankee snarled, "O'course we knew when Black Dick sailed that ye'd try for Philadelphia. D'ye think our General Washington be stupid? Our General marched my boys almost to the death, but we've beat ye'r army here, have we not. Aye, and we'll take the lot o thee to the gaels," he paused.

Bristol said nothing. The clearing grew silent except for the soft moans from several of the wounded.

The Colonist continued, after apparent thought, "Nay, if ye'll give thine solemn pardon to quit this war and return to where from thee came I'll release ye to crawl back to ye'r Lord Black Dick. Ye tell 'em to bring on his twice damned army and fleet. We're ready."

Lt. Bristol knew he didn't have much of a choice. He and his men could be hauled off to a colonialist prison with little food and no medical help, or he could promise as Gentlemen to withdraw himself and all the survivors from this War. He knew his Colonel would honor the Parole, and he'd likely be sent on to France with no black marks on his career.

"Aye," Bristol replied, "ye've my Parole, and that of me men."

With that, and no further words, the Yankee officer and silently disappeared into the trees, as Yankees were so wont to do. The entire Yankee force then vanished with hardly the cracking of a twig.

Bristol ripped off a piece of his sleeve and tied it around his wound. The tongue-tied boy, still carrying the red flag, stood by his side as Lt. Bristol motioned for his men to arise from their prone positions in the mud and re-form.

"Stack ye'r muskets and re-form," he commanded. "Be sharp. Those Yankees are certainly watching thee."

Three of his Command were never going to rise again, and another two had wounds; one of which likely wouldn't last the night. They slowly and painfully helped each other back down the muddy trail two miles through the wet fields and back to the landing. They arrived just as dawn was breaking.

The four sailors were there with the two boats. There was still no evidence of the ferryman or his family, and the sailors were ready to grab the livestock.

On Bristol's arrival the boson ran up to him.

"Sir," he yelled, "aye, you'll 'ave skirmished with the Yankees. Let's get thee into the boats and back aboard *Fencer*. Aye, sir, but that was a strange thing a bit ago, made me boys worry a bit."

"Aye, boson?"

"Probably nothin, sir, but t'was sure we heard a growlin' from the river but a half hour past. Strange, like a, well I dunno—", trailing off.

"God knows, boson, what creatures lie in these miserable forests here. Forget it and let's back to *Fencer*. And, tell those goddamned sailors to leave the ferryman's livestock be."

"Aye", continued Bristol, "we were set upon by at least a brigade of crack Colonial troops. Nary saw but one of the bastards; kilt three of me best. They're likely still watching us. Hear now, place the wounded and dead in one boat. Leave the other for us, and let us together get this urgent news to Lord Howe."

"Damn," he continued, "but my Parole does include all except ye healthy sailors. Nomatter, let's thee quickly row us all down river to *Fencer*. We need get word to Lord Howe that this Colony won't be an easy sack up this river."

And, an hour later, as the two boats dropped past Tinnecum Island, they saw to their collective dismay the two masts of the sunken cutter poking up from the water's surface. It was festooned with her exhausted crew, almost two score of them hanging on to whatever piece of rigging would hold them out of the swirling current.

"Lt. Sharft," called Bristol, spotting the former captain of *Fencer* perched at the main top, "how came thee to be sunk?"

"I durnst know," replied the exhausted young lieutenant, "and Howe'll have me stripes. She was a well found new cutter, yet she sank at anchor. I'd suspect Yankee skullduggery t'were there any Yankees in the river, but we've seen none."

Then noticing the bloody and moaning wounded men in the towed second boat, "Sir, seems you've crossed swords yer'self."

"Aye," replied Bristol, "indeed there's Yankees on the river. Methinks tiz a brigade, not less. Ambushed us last night not two miles up river from the Schuylkill ferry. Best get ur crew on these boats and we'll manage down river to the flotilla."

"Lord Howe won't be pleased. He's got a hornet's nest ashore here."

The two longboats were loaded past capacity, with their gunwales just inches above the river surface, as they were loaded with the entire crew of

Fencer and the troop of Marines. Still, the surface was calm and the sailors managed to slowly work the boats back to the fleet.

Two days later, just as the sun set over the green fields to the west, the huge British fleet simply sailed into the Atlantic, away from Cape May. Lord Howe and Admiral Howe were secure with the knowledge that they had saved themselves a disastrous surprise defeat at the hands of that too clever General Washington. Still, they thought it best not to report this ignominious little defeat in their formal dispatches to the King and Admiralty.

No, they'd report that they had hatched a better plan, that to approach the colonial Capital overland from the head of the Chesapeake Bay.

While, at the same time on *Anne Marie*, still invisibly tied to the riverbank under the bluff in Darby Creek with the branches in her masts, the only sound was quiet snoring. The little inflatable Zodiac boat and the larger jet boat were both tied to the stern. There was a still just dried wet suit and scuba tank, used by Jake to affix a pound of plastique explosive to the sloop, on the floor of the cockpit. And, resting on top of Stephen's dirty Colonial Officer's uniform on the cabin sole there were two AK-47 machine guns waiting to be cleaned.

Yes, the British Fleet would attack again, and soon too. But, Howe's next assault on Philadelphia would come after a secure landing from the Chesapeake with a proper overland march. Of course the Colonial Government would not be surprised, and when the British did prevail a month later at Brandywine there'd be nothing remaining of the Colonial Government or Treasury in Philadelphia.

Even the cows and pigs were taken to the new temporary Capitol at York, Pennsylvania, leaving nothing behind but an empty city.

CHAPTER EIGHT

Lt. Aaron stepped to the rail of *Reliant* this beautiful late July morning with his glass under his arm just in case a Yankee could be found again trying to 'round Fisher's Island, several cables to windward. Indeed, having been on blockade station less than fortnight, Aaron was frustrated and ready for some action. Those damned Yankees had eluded capture so far.

T'was just like he'd told Admiral Wembly. T'would take two King's Ships to seal-off this piece of important coast line, for the blockade-runners were slipping out always at the opposite end of which ever inlet he was patrolling. Oh, for another ship to put a cork in the bottle.

And, he could swear it was that same damned green ketch that had again totally baffled him with her strange and impossible tactics just after he'd arrived on station early last week. He was not able to bring himself to enter her tactics in his Log, as certainly nobody at the Admiralty would believe him. They'd think him daft.

Reliant had spotted the little green ship reaching fine down the Sound a week ago in a stiff Southwesterly, breasting the flood tide. *Reliant* had beat to quarters. It was simple to merely wear back and forth on the Connecticut side of The Race, certain in the knowledge that the approaching ketch could only either sail directly out through The Race, under *Reliant*'s guns, or wear ship and haul West back up the Sound, with the bigger *Reliant* hot in her wake.

No, Aaron had thought, this time this un's as good as captured.

But, to his absolute shock and dismay, as soon as the strangely rigged little ship was abeam of Plum Gut, the only other exit from the Sound. The Gut was known to be not navigable, blocked as it was with barely submerged rocks. Still, incredibly, through the rocks and against a flood tide of five knots with a strong southwesterly, the ketch simply hauled wind and sailed straight through the Gut!

That damned green bitch ketch with the pointed sails seemingly sailed straight and impossibly up-wind with her sails luffing for almost a mile. It was simply impossible!

Aye, the Admiralty and his peers would think him daft if he logged it.

Reliant, downwind, down current, and on the wrong side of Plum Island never had a chance. The ketch was hull-down, a mere speck on the eastern horizon and long gone before *Reliant* could give chase.

Aaron was still fuming. No, he knew that it simply could not have been possible for that crazy Yankee bastard to have pulled that trick, but he did.

Yet, this time Aaron did get a good look at the little green ship through his long glass. He'd noted the distinctive mainsail with the pointed top, apparently without a gaff boom on that spar. It also had an unusually large jib with a stubby little bowsprit. Even the smaller mizzen sail had one of those strange pointed tops.

No, he'd not let that one get away again. But, he was intrigued by the strange rig the Yankees had put on her that seemingly allowed such unusual performance.

Breaking his thoughts, Aaron heard, "Sail ho," as the lookout hollered, "to seaward, one point larboard of the Race."

Aaron nimbly dashed up the main ratlines to the t'gallant yard and trained his glass to seaward. Aye, there he saw a fully-rigged ship in the offing. He saw that it appeared to be a British sloop, probably with dispatches.

Two hours later Aaron welcomed the young lieutenant commanding the newly arrived Sloop, *Samantha*. They retired to Aaron's tiny cabin.

"Aye, John," continued Lt. Richard James from *Samantha*, "tiz a strange one at that, but the Captain thought you'd be the best to chase it down".

Between them on the deck of the small cabin was an orange deflated life preserver embossed *Anne Marie*.

Richard had recounted how Aaron's heretofore female prisoner had apparently escaped from the prison hulk. Presumably with Yankee help, she had slipped somehow past the boat boom at Hells Gate and had come ashore near the village of Whitestone. Of course, she must have had help. Still, her escape party, while stealing a boat, had apparently been discovered by loyal Tories. This very life jacket was found ashore after the scuffle.

"So," finished Richard, "Captain Wembly asked I relieve thee at this station while ye make haste to re-capture this prisoner. He's told Black Dick of her and wants her back when the Admiral returns. He feels she may be in the town of Deerford, which is on the Connecticut shore well inside the Yankee lines. It's not thought to be well defended with only a couple of farms in the area. Wembly said that once ye may find the prisoner ye'r to return her to the Captain, but ye'r cautioned to sail the east end of Long Island as most vessels trying the East River find themselves on the rocks."

"Aye, and, how is the Captain's humor?" queried Aaron.

"'T'iz foul, John. He'd planned to sail with the fleet to sack the Yankee Capital in Philadelphia, but Howe transferred him to the hulk, taking *Indomitable* with the Fleet. Wembly fears he's left in a backwater. And, he's down with the gout, worse'n usual."

"Aye Richard," started Aaron after a pause, "tis some action he'll be wanting. Best I get that lass recovered quickly."

Aaron's heart picked-up a beat thinking about the lovely young red head that he'd soon see again. Little doubt that Wembly would want to present her to Howe himself, and perhaps t'send her on to the Admiralty to support his claims about that strange Yankee green ketch with the pointed sails. Aaron thought that perhaps, with a bit of luck, he could arrange to take her to Portsmouth in *Reliant*?

Continuing to address Richard, Aaron continued, "and be certain to keep a sharp lookout for a strange Yankee green ketch."

"And what strange ketch be that?" inquired Richard.

"Aye, ye'll know if ye spot her. She is a strange one that. Hull's bright bottle green and she rides low in the water. She's fore 'n aft ketch rig, and has no gaff on the mainsail or the mizzen. Damned sails haul to the mast tops with no gaff booms at all. Flys an oversized jib. Methinks she's the place where this oddity came from," kicking the flat rubber deflated jacket with his buckled shoe.

"Aye, tis all strange enough," he mused on.

"Richard," Aaron started quickly after a moment, "where are thee bound from here?"

"*Samantha's* under orders to sail under ye'r command to tighten the blockade on Buzzards Bay and the Sound, sir," replied Richard.

"Aye, with two vessels we'll bottle 'em tight," said Aaron. "*Samantha* and *Reliant* together ought to grab all those dammed blockade runners, even the green ketch on her return. We'll find some fat Yankee prizes, soon as my short mission to recover the little lady and deliver that baggage to Sir Wembly is finished."

Continuing, John asked, "As I'm to raid a Yankee settlement might I borrow ye'r Marines? Indeed, our complement gives us few enough, ye'r extra men may be very helpful."

"Wish I were off on this adventure with you," came the reply. "Indeed, canna see where I'll need 'em the next few days here on this station; ye'll have all twenty. And, good luck to thee. How soon 'r ye off?"

"It's but a day's sail up the Sound," replied Aaron, "might as well take advantage of the current flood tide. If all goes well we'll return by here in two days time with our prisoner, and to turn back ye'r Marines. Another three days should see her safely on the old hulk with Sir Wembly, awaiting transit to their Lordships."

"And, soon as that chore is done we'll catch us some Yankee prizes."

An hour later *Reliant* was hard on the starboard tack, holding nearly due west up Long Island Sound, leaving *Samantha* with her former lonely blockade station between Fisher's Island and Block Island.

✲ ✲ ✲

Connie awoke as a shaft of yellow sunshine flashed across her eyes. A light breeze blew the blue chintz curtain aside from the open window. She stretched, inhaling the mixed fragrances of the daffodils beside her bed mixed with the cedar tree outside her window.

She stretched herself in the feather bed. Yes, her leg felt almost normal after three days of blissful rest under the care of both Martha and Anne Williams.

Or, maybe, she considered, her recovery had been so fast now knowing that she was not lost and alone in an alien time? Yes, both her Dad and David had been here in this very house, only departing the evening before she got here. And, they would return soon; something about a quick and urgent message that had to get to the Capital in Philadelphia. Oh, it was strange to realize the Capital would not be in Washington DC for another twenty years.

She giggled at the silly thought. Anyway, her David and her Dad would be back any time now, and that's all that mattered to her.

Sliding out from under the sheets, reluctantly deciding to leave the comfort of the feather bed, albeit mostly because nature was calling, she wrapped one of Anne's print cotton robes around herself and stood. Her leg was still sore, but she could trust it to hold her. She knew she had to exercise it back to complete health.

She pulled a blue china chamber pot out from under the washstand, used it, poured fresh cold water into the washbasin and splashed her face, feeling now completely awake and refreshed. Oh, but a hot shower would feel great, followed by a mug of steaming hot coffee. She lamented that she'd just have to make do with a cold splash-bath and the strong English tea offered by the William's.

Connie was looking forward to the day ahead. Today she was going to ride into Deerford with Anne. It had been agreed the day before, although Martha did insist that Connie must wear the hated corset and proper ladies attire to appear in public. She'd been gently told that the now tattered but clean and serviceable sports bra just would not do.

Still, the appeal of visiting her home town of Deerford, even two hundred years in it's past, and having lunch with Anne at the same Post Tavern, sounded too good to miss. She wondered how much of the little village she would recognize.

Anne and Martha had decided to introduce Connie to the locals as the fiancée' of a privateer's officer who was staying at the farm while the ship was pillaging British cargoes. This would be a popular introduction in Yankee Deerford, certain to have Connie invited to Sunday Tea at Pastor Allen's fine home, along with the leading families of the area after Church the coming Sunday.

Dressed in a lace trimmed yellow gingham frock and descending the stairs which wrapped around the huge center fireplace of the farmhouse, Connie first greeted Arthur who was at his large desk, apparently working in a big ledger book.

"Mornin' to thee, missy," thundered Arthur, his big red face smiling at her, "seems ye're not favorin' that leg so much today."

"Yes, sir, and good morning," replied Connie, who was still a bit shy around the big buff farmer.

She smiled at him and walked behind his chair into the great room seeking Anne or Martha. Finding Anne seated at the table industriously pouring fragrant melted wax into candle molds, Connie felt enough at home to pour herself a cup of tea and cut a slice of the fresh bread on the table. She coated it with blueberry jam from a newly opened jar. Anne was, as was Connie, dressed in a print dress, well corseted and buttoned to the neck. Her thick long dark hair was tied in a severe bun.

"Mother's havin' the boys hitch the wagon for us," she simply stated, wiping her hands on a rag after the last mold was filled.

"Really, Anne?" asked Connie. "I thought when you said we'd ride into town that you meant we'd actually ride the horses, not that I'd really mind a buggy. I do like riding on horseback."

"Well, we could ride if ye'd wish, I'd like that myself," Anne replied thoughtfully, "but have you ever ridden side-saddle? Riding astride, as you mentioned last night, just won't do for ladies."

"Okay, let's leave the riding for another day. I'd really like to look at the town. Really, Anne, this house isn't too different from what it will be in two hundred years, but you'd be amazed to see this area when I left, er a long time from now. This whole point will be built-up with houses everywhere you look," Connie prattled on as the girls walked to the barn to find a small wagon hooked-up behind two horses, one brown and the other gray.

Anne climbed up to the seat, and after waiting for Connie to join her Anne wheeled the horses smartly around. They trotted off down the lane. Reaching the end of the lane to the house, they turned right on the sandy trail, not far from where Connie had landed nearly a week ago. They turned then along a dusty rutted dirt road that ran beside the tidal inlet through cultivated fields. Each field was lined with stone walls, and curved over the gently rolling rises and dips in the land.

"Wow," started Connie, "you maybe won't believe this Anne, but I was right here not much more than a month ago, to me that is. Things are so very different."

"How so?" queried Anne.

"It's different in ways I wouldn't have expected," Connie paused for a moment, "for instance, this whole area," waving her hand across the stone wall to their right indicating four large cultivated fields, "will be covered in deep forests except where the houses will be. And, there were a lot of houses with pretty green lawns."

"That whole field will be broken into lots of maybe a half acre each. Yes, and there were, er will be, a lot of little paved roads through the woods."

"And, over there," Connie pointed with her hand to the left, "was a stone bridge across the inlet, with a dam under it to keep the water on the upstream side," she waved to the right.

It made a very pretty pond with a lot of willow trees around it. We used to ice skate there in the winter," she continued.

"And there, just across the creek, is where the yacht club was. Oh, and our house was up on that little hill over there," she pointed across the creek to a low hill crowned with a grove of apple and birch trees.

"Gee, I never would have expected there to be almost no trees here, I'd kind of thought those deep woods had always been here," she remarked, again waving her arm, this time indicating the acres and acres of cleared fields neatly outlined with straight stone walls through which they were driving.

In fact, other than the copse of trees around the farmhouse far behind them in the dust, the grove on the little hill across the creek, and a few appearing to grow in the town about a mile ahead at the end of the tidal inlet they were following, there seemed no trees at all. Everything was neatly cultivated fields from rolling hills to the North back to the edge of the Sound.

The Williams farm was one of the largest in the County, over 200 acres, and it was planted in tobacco and hemp, along with ample vegetable gardens for the table, fodder for the animals, and a small apple orchard.

Anne puzzled, "paved roads you said? Whyever for? They certainly must have cost a lot in horseshoes."

"Oh no, Anne," giggled Connie, "nobody will ride or 'drive' horses here in 200 years, or perhaps only for sport. No, we drove everywhere in cars, hmmm, no I mean motorcars. They are something like having a small wagon, like we're in, only much lower to the ground and instead of horses to pull it there's a mechanical motor inside that has many times the power of a horse."

"Whatever is wrong with a simple horse and wagon?" Anne was looking at Connie sharply.

"Aah forget it Anne," said Connie a bit sourly. "There's no use discussing things I can no longer have. Really, I need to learn your world, this world."

"Oh look" she brightened. "There's the First Congregational Church. It hasn't changed a bit, except for the community center which just isn't there yet."

Just then they were clattering across a wooden bridge at the head of the creek they'd followed for nearly two miles. They drove the wagon into the small village of Deerford.

The town in 1777 only ran from the Church at the west end to the mill to the east along what would eventually be Main Street. It was now just a wide dirt lane between the two landmarks with houses and a few stores irregularly spaced. Anne explained that Main Street was the primary road through the Colony, running the between New York to the West and Boston to the East.

Connie giggled, "Anne, this will be called the Boston Post Road for all time."

"Oh and look," she exclaimed waving at the General Store, a new white clapboard building with a wide shaded porch.

"Who is the owner of the store? Why when I was here a month ago it was a liquor store and old Mr. Coggin bragged that it had been open for over 200 years."

Anne was startled, "Connie," she said softly, "John Coggin just opened that store a year ago. The old store was burned 'cause the owner was a Tory."

Connie was in such a good mood. She had to drag Anne to every corner of the town looking at each house, remarking which would still be in place in her time, and what changes she could remember. Anne followed Connie about the town, reminding her to speak softly so the townspeople wouldn't remark on Connie's strange speech. At every shop they visited Anne introduced Connie to the merchants, town residents and other visitors from area farms.

At lunch time they entered the Post Tavern, Anne explaining that no Lady would enter the bar room, rather Ladies used the large front dining room. They each ordered a hot mug of strong tea and a bowl of stew from the steaming cauldron in the fireplace. Connie was just bubbling over with her discovery that this room had changed so little.

As the sun fell low in the west late that day the two young women clattered back into the farmyard in the wagon, several purchases from town in packages in the back.

Martha greeted them from the door saying, "wash off the road dust at the well and come ye in for some hot tea; it'll refresh thee"

Connie was effusive that evening, eating little at supper, as she regaled the Williams family on the changes and similarities she had found in the area since she had left it a month ago. And, while they did show interest, Arthur Williams finally had to caution Connie that she'd need to be very careful to never let her thoughts on the matter go past their small family group.

"Aye," she agreed as she said good night to the family.

The next morning Anne knocked on her door. It was early.

"Connie, time to dress for church."

She got up, washed in the pitcher of fresh water and dressed herself again in the formal colonial clothing, this time in a brown cotton dress that Anne had asked her to wear. Oh, but she hated the corset, yet Anne had told her it really was necessary for church, and she'd advised that it really needed to be laced completely up.

After she dressed, she descended the stairs to find Anne, Martha, Arthur and Todd all likewise formally dressed and at the table with tea, boiled eggs and warm bread. Martha fixed her a plate.

Tad and Arthur were in black knee britches with fine white stockings covering their calves. They both wore polished high shoes with brass buckles. Each had a lace shirt on, with a black vest and a formal coat that looked more like a fancy tuxedo jacket than a current day sport coat or suit jacket. It was a warm morning and both men already had red faces. Martha and Anne were in similar dresses to hers, likewise buttoned to a closed and tight collar.

After breakfast Tad got to his feet saying, "will look to the coach."

Soon, hearing a horse neigh outside, Arthur rose, as did Martha and Anne. Connie followed them out the door. She had not been in the coach house next to the barn, so she was surprised to see a shiny black formal coach with gold leaf and bright brass trimmings hitched to four matching chestnut horses. Raymond, Arthur's overseer, was in the box of the coach with Jane, his wife, beside him. Connie guessed that the three children on top of the coach, all likewise solemnly dressed were their children. Tad held the door open and Martha climbed in, followed by Anne then Connie. The two men got in last and Raymond slapped the reins.

They followed the same road as yesterday into town. Today, when they turned onto the Post Road towards the town center, they joined a long line of other wagons of all types heading the same way. All were loaded with families and local workers dressed in their Sunday best. Martha and Anne were waving to and greeting many of the people they passed.

They drew to the rear of the church yard which was now filled with horses and wagons of all types. There were only two other coaches similar to the Williams, but none quite so new and grand.

Alighting from the formal coach, the Williams family, with Connie, mounted stairs to the church and stood in the lobby. Connie was introduced to dozens of local men and women; she couldn't begin to remember the names. Just before nine they all filed into the sanctuary. The Williams Family sat themselves in the second pew from the front on the right, apparently their regular place.

The Anglican service seemed to Connie to go on forever.

She was used to Sunday services in this same church, which usually lasted about an hour, perhaps sometimes a little more. But, it was noon before this service ended. Meanwhile, today, the church grew hotter and hotter in the lovely July morning. By the time they all filed out Connie was dripping with perspiration, and the scratchy corset was rubbing her sides raw under her arms.

The entire congregation then stood around on the church lawn, seemingly for hours, just socializing. The men were talking about the war, their crops, and a lot about their horses and about local fishing conditions. The women's topics were their children, their cross stitch projects and the shortages of good cloth due to the blockades. Connie, of course, heard no topics of interest to her so, hot and miserable, she had to just stand beside Anne, smiling sweetly when introduced, and trying not to appear as totally bored as she was.

At long last Arthur called for their coach. They were almost the last to leave the church yard.

Arriving back at the farm they all remained in their Sunday clothing while Martha served a large hot meal. Finally, in the late afternoon, Anne and Connie were able to find some cool breeze and a pair of comfortable wooden chairs under a shady tree.

"Anne," Connie started, "is this the same every Sunday?"

"Why, of course, what do you mean?"

"I mean, does everyone go to Church? Is the service always so long?"

Anne looked at Connie appraisingly. "Why of course. Really, Sunday is the only time we get to see most of our neighbors. And, nobody would ever miss going to Church, unless you're sick. It just isn't done."

"You didn't have Church on Sundays?" Anne asked.

"Well, we usually went, when we were home, but it was usually not longer than an hour. And, of course it was air conditioned. We wore much cooler clothes too."

"When did you get to talk to your friends and neighbors?"

"Oh," Connie was a bit abashed, "we had telephones. Heck I could call anyone anytime from my cell phone."

"Cell Phone?" Anne tried the new words.

Connie blushed, "Oh, Anne, I'm so sorry. I'm behaving like a spoiled child. Yes, we did have something called a telephone. It allowed us to simply put some numbers into a little box and we could talk to anyone, anywhere, who had a similar little machine. Most people had them. Oh, it was really so marvelous, I do miss it all so."

Anne looked at Connie, asking, "does thy father miss it all too?"

"Funny," Connie replied thoughtfully, "I really don't think so. He really adjusts to things ever so quickly. But, really Anne, I haven't seen him since the storm, and I do miss him. David too."

"Oh, and mostly, David. When do you think they'll be back?"

"Well, Stephen said no more than a week, and it's been over that now."

With that thought the young ladies went back into the house. Connie went up to bed early and drifted off to sleep.

✻ ✻ ✻

"Back Topsails," ordered Williamswright as HMS *Reliant* 'rounded to the wind just south of Roank's Point at four bells of the morning watch. The sliver of the quarter moon showed the Point to be a cable-length to the north as the anchor splashed from the cathead.

"Captain Aaron requests ye in the cabin, sir," a sailor said to him softly as soon as the anchor had set.

Williamswright descended the scuttle, knocked twice and entered the cabin to see Aaron poring over an Admiralty chart.

"Willright," the Captain started, "methinks the girl we seek can only be here," taping on a black mark about a mile up the west side of Roank's Point.

"This mark is the known whereabouts of William's Farm, an advised hotbed of rebels. And, the girl mentioned William's name. I need thee to take the longboat and our Marines along with those we borrowed. Scout the area. If ye can grab the girl without raising an alarm, do so. But, if ye find a large force at the farm just scout it out and return by first light."

"Aye aye, sir."

An hour later the longboat, loaded with red coated Royal Marines armed with muskets, cutlasses and pistols, and with their bayonets glinting in the moonlight, was ghosting up Deerford Creek. The oars were well muffed with rage in their thole pins so they would make no noise.

At a break in the bull rushes along the eastern shore of the creek Willright softly commanded, "Coxswain, pull to larboard. Aye, ground 'er in yonder dark shadow."

The sailors were designated to stay with the boat to keep it from stranding with the falling tide while Willright and the contingent of Marines stealthily crept up a pathway towards the peacefully sleeping farmhouse.

A horse neighed. Sam, the old sheep dog, started to bark. That got the rooster going, and that racket all woke Anne Williams.

She lay awake for a few moments, hearing the clock downstairs ring five bongs. Rising out of bed she saw that it was not yet daylight, and there was but a silver of the moon casting a very faint light outside. She wondered what could have startled those darned animals.

Then, there beside the barn, she saw the figures of several men darting across the yard to the hog pen! She briefly wondered if it could be thieves, then thought that unlikely.

Looking closer she could just made out distinctive white belts crossing the dark shirts of the intruders.

British raiders, she finally realized, galvanizing her into action!

With her heart pounding, Anne dashed across the hallway to Connie's room. Awakening her silently, Anne whispered, "looks like trouble. Here, let's into this hideout. 'Twas built against Indian raids. Looks like British sneaking into the yard. Let's take no chances."

Anne dashed to the wooden wall at the top of the stairway and pulled on a little piece of railing. A section of wall hinged inwards.

"In here, Connie. They mustn't find you." she whispered, shoving Connie into the hideaway.

She then pushed closed the hidden little panel in the stairway with Connie inside. She ran towards her parent's room, but at that moment the front door downstairs burst open and a hoard of red coated Marines smashed into the house.

She dashed back to the hideaway, re-opened the secret panel and stepped inside with Connie. There was barely enough room for both girls, squashed between the rough stones of the fireplace and the paneling of the stairway.

"Williams, Get ye down here 'fore we burn thee out!" came a rough shout from below.

Martha and Arthur quickly arose and, clothed in heavy robes, descended the stairs to find their sitting room full of armed British Marines in red uniforms, brandishing muskets with bayonets. They were lead by a blue coated naval officer. The blue coated officer quickly lunged for and grabbed Martha, spun her around and placed a huge cocked pistol at her head.

"We'll 'ave no games with the likes of ye Rebels now," growled the officer. "We be 'ere but to find a prisoner escaped from the King at New York. She'll be a bit of a lass, and said to be at ye'r farm. Now ye'll find that lass and bring her here, else ye'r lady'll pay fer ye'r foolishness."

The officer cocked hammer of the heavy pistol with a loud click

Williams replied stoutly, hoping the two girls had hidden themselves as he had so often drilled his children in their youth, "there be nobody here but the two of us."

"Then ye'll not mind we search," sneered the officer, motioning at the largest of his men. "Sergeant, 'ave a look around."

He held the cocked pistol at Martha's temple.

After clomping around on the second floor the Marine sergeant reappeared stating, "this man be lyin'. There's nobody in sight up there but there's two beds 'been just slept in, still warm they are."

The Officer quickly re-aimed his huge double barreled pistol and calmly shot Arthur in the leg.

CRASH, and Arthur fell to the floor, his shin bone shattered.

The Navy lieutenant jabbed the pistol barrels again at Martha's right temple and growled, "t' other barrel 'll splatter her rebel brains on the wall. Now whar is she."

Just then a squeak was heard from the top of the stairway, and Connie stood on the landing still dressed in her nightgown and robe.

"Here I am."

"Grab her, men," ordered the office.

"Tie up these two. We'll be off before the hired help can rally."

Connie felt herself roughly handled. Her hands were quickly lashed behind her, and she was dumped into a large smelly cloth of some sort. Moments later the small detachment of Royal Marines retreated out the door, joined-up with the lookout in the farmyard, and bounded down the lane. Connie, trussed like a deer, was carried like a sack of potatoes across the shoulders of a very large and smelly Marine.

Just as the sailors cleared the yard with their cloak-wrapped prize over the shoulder of the huge marine sergeant, Anne ran down the stairs, also in her robe. She rushed to her mother and father who were both on the floor. Martha was already wrapping a clean rag torn from her shift around the bullet wound in Arthur's leg.

She'd never heard her father curse so!

"Damned bloody arrogant thieving swine," he was cursing, "Damn them all to bloody hell! Ah that's just why we need to throw those bloody bastards back off our shores," he raved on.

Knowing both her parents didn't need her at that moment, Anne thought immediately of Connie. She had to know were they taking her.

She dashed out the door, mindless of any danger to herself, ran to the stable, and leapt on the back of the first horse she saw. Fortunately it was Prince, her father's old and gentle gelding. Without a saddle, she urged Prince to a gallop, chasing down the lane the way the British had come.

As she reached the end of the point Anne saw their boat pulling towards the Sound. She followed it with her eyes from the shoreline until it cleared the point. There in the misty dawn she saw a large frigate a mere cable length away.

The little boat pulled alongside the large ship, was hoisted aboard, and the ship spread her sails. It swiftly picked up speed in the morning's westerly and vanished.

Connie had been re-captured.

✲ ✲ ✲

The rattling of a heavy chain awakened her. At first, Connie didn't know where she was; then, she drew in a breath and the stench told her. Rolling over, she found that every part of her body felt bruised.

She had been almost suffocated while wrapped tightly in that smelly boat cloak, and she'd been jounced on her stomach over that giant's shoulder running back to their little boat. She remembered being tossed in the bilges with a boat rib smashed against her back while a foot held her firmly down, but she'd been too busy trying to simply breathe to pay much attention. She knew she'd been again hoisted back to that hard shoulder, and twisted around several times presumably after reaching their ship.

Lastly, she'd been unceremoniously dumped into this dark smelly room with no light whatever. As she had been dropped she must have hit her head and blacked out. How long had it been she wondered?

The chain rattled again against the door as she sat up.

Her heart beat faster as she wondered what would come next.

In a few minutes her breathing slowed down, and she realized that at least she had the cloak to keep her warm. But, she questioned why and how had they found her and why they couldn't just leave her alone ?

All day Lt. Aaron conned *Reliant* east towards the Race and the open ocean. No, he was not afraid of anything the Yankees might have afloat in the Sound; he was guiding the ship himself because there were unmarked shoals and he was anxious to make the fastest passage possible back to New York, returning his prize to Captain Wembly.

He was increasingly conscious of a knawing desire to see that alluring witch again. He couldn't put her from his mind.

After the first dog watch he retired to his cabin for his supper. And, after quaffing a full bottle of Madeira he told himself that it couldn't hurt anything if he just checked on her.

He placed his hat on his head and called for the Master at Arms.

"I'll 'ave the keys to the chain locker," he demanded.

Connie heard the chain rattle again.

The door had opened awhile ago and a plate full of greasy pork and peas had been shoved inside with a mug of green buggy water. She'd only been able to choke down a mouth full of peas. A single swallow of the water had made her gag it all up.

Her thoughts raced as she considered who might be at the locked door now? Perhaps, she hoped, all they wanted was their grubby plate.

John Aaron had a picture in his mind of the girl, Connie, the last time he'd seen her several weeks ago in New York. She'd been standing then against the rail of the prison hulk in a thin dress with the wind pressing the fabric against her body. The shape of that young female form had kept Aaron awake nights. And, here she was again his prisoner!

He thought that perhaps were he to offer her pardon and the lieutenant's cabin she'd warm up to him?

Pushing the door open and entering the small locker with his lantern held up Aaron saw the object of his dreams sitting against the swell of the hull. Green vomit dripping from the boat cloak wrapped around the small figure huddled in the rough wool. Then he noticed a rat rooting at the uneaten food thrown as far from the girl as was possible in that very confined room. Her eyes were glassy. She was vacantly staring at him.

Aaron came quickly to his senses, the effects of the mederia he'd drank vanishing quickly. He knew he'd need to get this girl cleaned up and made presentable before the ship anchored in New York.

"Ye'll be all right", he said, picking the girl up in the cloak and tossing a corner of it across her head to protect her from derisive stares from the crew.

He carried her aft and once again into his cabin. Aah, but he'd like to undress her, but he daren't. He simply unrolled her from the boat cloak and laid her on his gimbaled bed, covering her with a clean blanket and closing the doorway behind him. He left his little sleeping cabin.

Connie wasn't unconscious. She had simply faked sleep while being carried aft.

As soon as Aaron left, Connie arose and flung open the window to the rear of the cabin, bringing in a cool fresh breeze. She went into the small head area, took the pitcher of water from behind the door to the cabin, and then cleaned herself as she was able. She then spotted an opened and re-corked half bottle of red wine.

Two swallows of the stuff warmed her stomach. Yes, she recognized that this was the same damned ship she had been on. And, yes, it was the same double-damned captain. Why, she wondered again, had she been kidnapped? What was their fascination with her?

She wrapped the clean blanket tightly around herself, tossed the smelly boat cloak in a corner and huddled on the cushions under the open rear windows. The ship was moving easily, and Connie was asleep in moments.

She awoke to a shaft of sunlight peeking over a wave top and striking her face. It was a bright sunny morning. The ship was healed over and a glance out the window showed no land in sight; they were apparently making very good speed. Connie stood up, finding herself ravenous and thirsty; her tongue a bit fuzzy from the wine. She managed a couple of swallows of the vile water by holding her nose, feeling quickly better. She snickered, wondering if there was food value in the green stuff suspended in the water.

Awhile later Aaron knocked, thereafter entering. Connie was seated in front of the windows still wrapped in the blanket. She simply stared at him, making no sound.

He offered her a pair of large white duck seaman's trousers and a striped shirt, both too large, but familiar enough. They were at least clean and serviceable.

Taking the clothes she addressed the scar-faced officer in the formal uniform with the silly looking gold braid shoulder cap on the right shoulder. "Captain, why have you kidnapped me and why am I so important to you?"

"Miss Shaw, thine origins, ye'r speech and ye'r equipment when we found thee have started the interest of Post Captain Wembly whose strong desire is to present thee to Lord Howe and perhaps then take thee to London when he is relieved of Command in August. I've also ventured to him there's likely some connection between thee and a certain green Yankee ketch what's been seen to sail in strange patterns."

"Methinks the Admiral will find favor in Court for presenting thee."

"Captain, I've nothing to tell you. My speech is from Florida. I know of no ketch that can do strange things. On what grounds do you attack my family in the night, shoot my Uncle and drag me off to a different country? Your actions prove the Revolution's cause is just. Who do you British think you are? In fact I think the Colonies are gonna win this little war."

Aaron reddened with anger at her outburst, but contained himself.

With that Connie stopped her tirade, realizing that it would do no good.

"Captain," she began in a quieter tone, "might you find me some scissors, a needle and some thread so I can alter this clothing to fit?"

The captain gave a little bow and departed.

Ten minutes later Ian, his wizened little steward, appeared with the sewing materials that allowed Connie to make, from the remains of Anne's nightgown, a crude but serviceable set of underwear and to cut the seaman's clothing down to a better, if baggy, fit. She did feel better.

And, Connie reflected, given the way that Captain was leering at her, the baggy fit was probably a good idea.

"Sail ho," Connie heard the lookout holler, "hull down fine on the larboard quarter."

She then heard drums rattle and the pounding feet of running sailors. From her past experience on this same ship she knew the walls to her little cabin would come crashing down in minutes, and that she would again be needed back in that verminous smelling orlop deck, presumably again to assist the drunken surgeon.

Horrors.

The cabin door banged open. Aaron entered and said, "We've sighted a sail running up the Sound behind us. Damned if I know how he got passed us. When she saw us, the damned Yankee turned tail and is running. But that little cockleshell will not escape this King's frigate on this fine sailing day. We'll be about and have her on in an hour or two. Would ye care to join me on the quarterdeck for the chase?"

Connie nodded and followed him out the cabin door, through the gunroom and up the short ladder to the quarterdeck. The crew was running madly about placing cannon shot and powder near all the guns on the main deck. Another crew was knocking down the cabins aft and uncovering the great guns in the cabins. Sails were flapping overhead as the ship was turning to chase the sail back they way they'd come.

The activity was furious for about ten minutes, and then all fell into silence. Gunners were assembled in groups of eight around each of the guns and sand covered the decks. Red coated marines could be seen with muskets and small cannons at the mast tops. The *Reliant* was ready to fight, and the day was beautiful. A strong warm breeze, at least twenty knots, pushed the Sound into white capped waves bowling the frigate along under a full press of sail. She was healed to starboard, and the wake creamed by.

"Twelve and a half knots," yelled the sailing master, reeling in his log.

Aaron and Willright were both standing in the mizzen ratlines above Connie, their eyes plastered to their spyglasses.

Connie looked forward in the direction they were looking and yes, she saw a tiny white flash of sails in the distance. Her heart leapt to her throat! Yes! She knew at a glance that she was looking at *Anne Marie*.

But, she controlled herself; she must not let anyone know.

"Appears we're overtaking 'em," muttered Aaron, "but not as fast as we should. Damn but that ketch is fast."

"What the Devil is that?" exclaimed Willright.

"Damnedist thing I ever saw," retorted Aaron, again looking through his glass. "What the bloody hell is that yellow sail? And, that damned sail is round."

He then hollered to the sailing master at the helm, "Smith, get the studding sails on her, fore and main, both courses and t'gallants!"

Smith replied, "She'll not take it, sir. The rig's overstrained now, and the helm is powerful to weather."

"Damn your eyes, man, I gave an order. Tie hawsers to the main top to stiffen the rig and get the damned studding sails on her. Do it now, damn ye'r eyes; they'll ease the helm."

In a moment a swarm of sailors ran up the ratlines at the foremast and main. Slender booms were rigged outboard of the two lower square sails on each mast, and a sail was rigged to each. Another crew of men tied long brown ropes to the base of the main top mast and dropped the ends to the deck, where more men carried the ropes aft, ran the ends through deadeyes and pulled tight.

"Haul home," yelled Smith.

Reliant lurched to leeward as the four additional sails filled with a crack. The newly run braces drew drum-tight and almost seemed to vibrate while four men on the big wheel struggled to keep the large ship from broaching under the huge press of sail. The ship recovered, and with the leeward rail now awash, seemed to leap forward.

"Fourteen knots and a half," the boson cried.

Connie ran back to the windward rail, looking forward and hoping that *Anne Marie* was no closer. Indeed, as she spotted the ketch, still far off in the distance, another yellow sail appeared at the mizzenmast; Jake had rigged the reaching staysail.

With that Anne knew that the handy little ship would easily top sixteen knots in this breeze. She relaxed and turned away.

Aaron would be screaming with anger and frustration, but there was no way that he could catch *Anne Marie* today. She actually found herself enjoying the exhilaration of riding the fully rigged ship under the massive cloud of straining sails while slyly watching *Anne Marie s*urf east until the tiny spec of sails in the distance vanished over the horizon.

After awhile Aaron stepped back on the deck next to Connie, snapped his spyglass closed, and said, "Aye thar, 'pears 'twas the same strange-rigged ketch that I've been chasin' these past weeks. This time it's got not one but two round yellow sails with the Yankee snake on 'em."

"Is that ye'r vessel?" he asked Connie sharply.

Not waiting for an answer he continued, "it's damned impossible for a little cockleshell of a ketch to run away from a Kings frigate in these conditions, even it we do have a mite of weed on the bottom . It just canna happen."

Turning back on Connie, Aaron demanded loudly, "Now missy, ye'll be telling me what ye know about this mystery green ketch with the pointed sails?"

"I know nothing of her, sir", she replied, casting her eyes down.

He was in such a rage she was afraid he would strike her.

"Harrumph." he finally grunted, "get thee back to the cabin. We'll let the Sir Wembly in New York sort thee out."

Indeed, minutes later the 'All Hands Stand Down' command was heard, the strange ketch having vanished over the horizon.

Later that day Aaron entered Connie's cabin, his former sleeping quarters, and without asking simply sat on the bed and looked at her.

After a bit he started, "Miss Shaw, *Reliant* again gave chase to that same green hulled ketch with strange rig as we've seen twice. This time it was passing hull down on a reach, and sported a large round sail at the bow and another at the mizzen. Ye were on deck, did thee not see it? Would ye believe a round sail? And a yellow one at that? Lieutenant Williamswright said he saw through his glass that it even had the same snake on it as was on ye'r Yankee flag at Boston. Now, how could that be?"

Connie's heart was jumping in her chest. No, she recognized that he'd not know that the mystery ship could only be David and her Dad. Nobody else would have a yellow spinnaker with the Gadsden image. Heck, in this time nobody even knew what a spinnaker was.

Of course these oafish Brits would not know of *Anne Marie*. There was no way she could begin to tell them what the ship was, let alone why they were all here instead of arriving for a Deerford wedding, as they should. No, she resolved, nobody would ever get the secret of the *Anne Marie* from her. And, yes, she had seen it leaping across the waves it. Yes, it was right here.

Damn though, she realized that if *Anne Marie* hsd just come home one day sooner this second ordeal of hers wouldn't have happened. Still, she knew that her Dad and David would learn of her plight soon, and they'd be certain to find her.

She was sure of it.

She replied coolly, "Captain, I know nothing of round sails with snakes on them. Are you sure you are seeing right? This makes no sense to me."

"Aye methinks ye know well enough. Harrumph, perhaps time will tell."

With that he stomped out.

Two days later Connie again was treated to sailing up into New York Harbor where *Reliant* anchored close to the same old hospital/prison hulk from which she'd so recently escaped. It was truly depressing to see those brown slab wooden ship-sides again.

But, this time the harbor was almost empty. Connie wondered what had happened to the hundreds of ships that had been here only two weeks ago.

An hour later she was again pushed up the side of the old hulk, Aaron closely behind her. They were escorted aft along through the invalids to the main cabin.

"Sir Wembly, allow me to once again present Miss Constance Shaw to thee. Ye've met this lady before," introduced Aaron to the grossly fat Post Captain in the Cabin of the prison/hospital hulk *Jersey*.

"Indeed Miss Shaw," began the fat and still be-wigged senior officer with a scowl, "Mrs. McAdams was upset to loose ye'r talents a week ago when ye fled up-river. We'll see that ye've not the chance to do so again. Still ye must have 'ad help. How else could a little lady get so many miles at night, and through our pickets too? Now, who spirited thee away? Tell me and we'll make thee comfortable here, perhaps even let thee ashore to some of the shops."

He continued, "I am further interested most deeply in ye'r practice of healing, which could save many good English lives. Aye, and I have other questions. "

"Sir, you are nothing but a gang of criminal kidnappers," Connie blustered, "I was dragged from my bed and my Uncle was shot!"

"THAT WILL DO," the fat Captain thundered.

Just then Mrs. McAdams knocked at the door and entered, dressed in her usual tight corset and floor length cotton print dress.

"Mrs. McAdams," the Captain addressed her, "can thee keep this person below decks so she canna escape until either Lord Howe returns or I can arrange transport for her to London?"

"Aye, sir," McAdams replied, "I'll put 'er to work on healing the fine English lads wounded at Monmouth, and she'll sleep in the orlop under guard."

"Now missy, what will it be? Will ye tell how ye escaped and who helped thee, or shall we have to confine ye to the lower decks and chain ye in the orlop at night?"

Connie was angry.

She started again, "look sir", she blurted back, "I am a free woman, simply visiting friends at their farm when your bully boys kidnapped me and shot my host. By what rights do you pillage a peaceful countryside and kidnap women? Is this how your great King treats innocent women? I demand you put me on a boat or whatever you have and return me to my friends."

"No ma'am," interrupted the Captain, his fatty jowls wobbling under his wig, "ye clearly have secrets our King and Parliament need to know. Ye have things that came with thee that we canna explain," throwing her battered life jacket on the deck at her feet.

"Ye can wait here for the next picket to Portsmouth and travel like a lady, else Mrs. McAdams will have thee work daytimes and we'll chain thee at night. What'll it be?"

"You can have me work on ye'r English boys, and I will, but I require equal time on decks three and four where the wounded American boys are confined. But, you'll not have my promise not to try to get away."

"Captain?" queried Ms. McAdams

"Aye and make it so" replied the Captain, "Allow the witch to tend both English and rebels, but make her quarters guarded in the orlop below decks so ye'll not loose her again. Mind, she must be chained and we'll set a marine guard too. She'll nae be on deck daytimes 'thout an armed guard either."

With that, Connie was dragged off to begin a temporary life of service to the wounded of both sides. Her billet was a hammock in the orlop well below the waterline of the smelly old hulk. It was an airless little hole, with nearly unbreathable air. She was locked in every night with two marine sentries outside her door.

It stank of sewage and vomit.

CHAPTER NINE

Anne Marie had cleared Cape May without onward incident and was broad reaching northeast on the port tack with a comfortable twelve knot breeze. There had been no ships of any kind sighted since they'd departed Darby Creek. The Kings fleet had sailed away.

"Well, guys, that's about the end of the fresh food," quipped David as he set a large plate full of baked chicken and vegetables on the table on the saloon.

"We're down to staples now," he continued, "It'll be lots of tinned meats, canned vegetables, frozen stuff and rice. We've got plenty of basic dry staples, but the refrigerated stuff's gone."

"And, didn't we finish the last of the beer yesterday celebrating our success?" followed Jake. "I've still got a case or two of good scotch though."

"Speaking of supplies", Jake continued, "After we cleared Cape May this morning I took an inventory. We're OK on water, and we can get more. The diesel though is down by a third, about 500 gallons is left in the tanks. We've used up one of our three propane tanks, and your boat ride the other day leaves us just four ten gallon cans of JP-5 in the after lazarette."

Stephen looked blankly at the two having the conversation, interjected, "I suppose it's the fuels that make these amazing things work that you're discussing? "

"Yes, Stephen," replied Jake, "*Anne Marie* uses diesel oil for the main engine, and about six gallons more each day to run the generator to make electricity, uh, the power for the, well, the electrical stuff. The stove uses propane, a different fuel, and the motor on the little boat takes JP-5, yet another type of fuel. And our small outboard takes gasoline, but we've used none of that. I am very aware that we can't get any of these in this time, so when the fuels are gone all these motors and things they run will just stop."

"I'm most worried about the diesel fuel because most of our systems depend on it. We can do without the gas and the propane if we need to, heck we've probably got enough propane to last a year anyway."

David thoughtfully interjected, "what about whale oil?"

"Whale oil?" popped Jake

"Yes, whale oil."

"Whale oil will run a diesel engine," queried Jake?

"Yes, Jake", replied David, "it should. The properties are very similar."

He continued, "whale oil has very similar burn temperatures to kerosene, which is but a refinement of the #2 Diesel you use. I can think of no reason it wouldn't work, of course it would need to be carefully filtered. In fact, with a good blacksmith and the right materials I may even be able to refine some into a workable gas replacement, but I'd need to know more of what is really available in this century."

"Damn, son", replied Jake, "I guess you do know your chemical engineering."

Continuing, he mused out loud, "whale oil should be in good production at Nantucket and New Bedford. As I remember my history, neither town was too much disturbed by the Revolution; the British wanted the oil as much as the wealthy Colonists".

"Aye, tiz dear though," interjected Stephen, "a mere pint of the stuff will cost a gold half guinea, which is the wage a workingman makes in a week. Most common working people and farmers use simple tallow candles for their light."

"And," David blurted, "Whales are thinking and sensitive mammals. We know that now. Whaling is outlawed in our Century. I'd not want to reward the killers of Whales."

"David," Jake butted in, "in these times whales are viewed as just big dumb fish. We're absolutely not going to make any statement in these times about the practice of whaling, but we will need fuel for *Anne Marie* and I doubt there's an alternative. Heck, David, it was your idea."

"Further, I'd like to fill our tanks with it while we're still half full of good diesel. I think a blend of the two will do better than whale oil alone, at least until we know it works without fouling the filters and injectors."

"Jake, ye'r whale oil 'll come dear," repeated Stephen.

"If a mere quart of the stuff costs a half-guinea then a hundred gallon barrel will be over a hundred quid. And ye'll be needing four barrels. Thank the stars that General Washington gave me a purse for thee."

He tossed a leather bag on the table that clanked heavily on landing.

"Methinks we need make for Nantucket 'fore we revisit Deerford. The folk there are close mouthed as any, and we'll need be in and out in a single night."

It was a dark night several days later under overcast skies when *Anne Marie* crept silently through the sand bars south of Cape Cod towards Vineyard Sound, between Nantucket and Martha's Vineyard. It was a quiet night too with the seas almost calm, allowing Jake to pilot the yacht through the treacherous sand bars. When the radar showed Nantucket to their right, Jake veered around and slipped into Nantucket's Salt Pond, showing no lights. The Zodiac inflatable dinghy, unstowed and inflated in advance, was pulled along side as soon as they were anchored.

"Docks should bear 083 degrees," said Jake as Stephen and David dropped into the little boat, "it's only 220 yards away."

Stephen and David rowed silently along the compass bearing towards the town on the course plotted with the radar. It was pitch black.

They smelled it before they saw anything; a strong odor of rancid oil was combined with the unmistakable odor of unwashed men. Then, in the dim light of lanterns, they saw the outlines of a deeply laden ship-rigged whaler tied to a pier.

"Aye, David," whispered Stephen, "pull to the quay just under her bows."

As the rubber boat silently bounced against a piling Stephen hopped up with the painter.

"Wait here," he whispered, pulling himself to the dock.

David sat back on the center seat of the Zodiac, under the dock, with the boat painter looped around a mussel-coated piling. It seemed like hours of total silence before Stephen again dropped silently into the little rubber boat.

"Sorry. The captain was ashore and the mate had to fetch him. Just arrived from a three year voyage today and the crew's all at home. The captain had just learned of our struggle today. Yes, they're Patriots; captain needed the crew's vote to offer to help us. They won't even take a shilling for the oil."

"We're to show a light at four bells. A longboat'll come alongside with ye'r four barrels. Let's be back to make ready."

At 2AM David, not wanting to use a bright electric light, flipped on a small battery powered white light that was normally used to illuminate the cockpit at night.

"Ahoy thar," came a hoarse whisper from the starboard side.

In a few moments David heard the command, "toss oars."

David just had time to dangle a fender over the side to protect *Anne Marie* from a scraping from the approaching heavy wooden longboat. And, indeed, there were four heavy wooden casks lined down the center of the boat.

"Mr. Peabody," instructed Stephen, "if ye'r men will be good enough to rest easy there we'll pass a line and sling for the first barrel."

With that, using the main boom as a crane arm and with an electric winch silently helping, well out of sight, the first barrel was hoist aboard and lashed to the rail. Three more barrels soon followed. By the time the sun rose in the east *Anne Marie* was long gone from the Nantucket's Salt Pond.

As soon as they were safely away Jake took a quart of the oil to the engine room. He drained the Racor fuel filter for the generator and filled it with the whale oil. He then pressed the starter for the little machine and was amazed that it lit off just as always, with not even a miss.

"Damnation," he exclaimed to himself, "this stuff actually works."

The whale oil was then simply siphoned through a cheesecloth strainer from the casks on deck into the fuel tanks. To Jake's continued delight, the big diesel fired-up with no noticeable difference, without even a hint of the black smoke at the exhaust that dirty fuel produces.

He spent another twenty minutes in the engine room watching the glass bowl of the Racor fuel filter to make sure the fuel was clean, and found nothing amiss. Last, he popped-in a fresh Racor fuel filter, noting that they still had a case and a half of this essential item left aboard.

Meanwhile, on the foredeck of the whaler two grizzled seamen were leaning back on the capstan.

"Cor, Johnny," the elder seaman ventured, "never seen the likes o'her. 'Er topsides waz smooth like glass, and where was 'er crew? Did ye se they pulled a hunnert gallon bar'l topside with nary a whisper. Waddya make o'it "

"Aye, she be a strange 'un. Thar's no tellin' wat with the war on 'n all. Mebbe she's a frenchie? But z the mate said to keep our lids on't so I'm tellin nothin. Still, they musta 'ad twenty men below decks to 'eave up those barrels. Wonder they dinna allow 'em on deck. Prisoners perhaps."

Meanwhile, *Anne Marie* was motoring slowly, with no sails up to avoid notice from the shorelines. They had crossed the narrowest point of the Sound between Vineyard Haven and Woods Hole, seeing no signs of life. But, they knew to expect something of a British blockade between themselves and home.

✲ ✲ ✲

Anne Marie was knifing up to the Race, the entry to the sound, broad reaching on the port tack and making her usual cruising twelve knots when Stephen sighted the square tops of a full rigged ship reaching towards them.

"Jake, David," he yelled, "looks like a ship is closing up on us. Might be a blockade frigate."

Jake dashed up and looked around. Seeing the ship in the distance he ran to the masts and hit the winch brakes, instantly dropping the sails. With bare poles, *Anne Marie* wallowed in the small waves while the frigate charged past, apparently not noticing the green ketch in the distance against the green shoreline.

After the large ship sailed past, and well out into Block Island Sound, Jake had all the sails re-hoisted, and the little ketch sped due west, slacking sheets.

Looking back again, Jake saw the frigate wear about, apparently intending to give chase. Still, it was a long way in the distance.

"Keep an eye on that one'" he said to Stephen, handing over his powerful binoculars, "I don't think they can catch us, but let's be sure."

"Damn," Stephen called out after twenty minutes, "I can't believe it. They've spread studding sails. They just might catch-up now."

"Nah," retorted Jake.

Turning to David he said, "David, we'll want the chute and the mizzen staysail."

David rigged a long aluminum pole from the foremast to the bowsprit and tied a bagged bundle on the deck under the straining jib. He quickly connected several ropes to different places then called to Jake, "hoist away."

A huge yellow sail snaked out of the bag on the deck, and as soon as it was at the mast top Jake sheeted it home using a second electric winch. The sail popped open and *Anne Marie*'s bow lifted as the sail yanked her faster, creaming through the waves.

Within another few minutes David had hooked a second yellow sail to a ring in the deck at the base of the mainmast, and hoisted yet a second round sail to the tip of the mizzen mast. It too popped open, and the little ketch literally flung herself from wave top to wave top.

"Seventeen and a half," shouted Jake, with a huge grin, "and broke twenty on the last slide down the last wave."

Two hours later the frigate was a mere speck on the horizon astern.

David quickly dropped all sails, and Jake ran close into the north shore using the motor.

The Frigate bowled past in sheets of spray, never seeing them.

Anne Marie then resumed her original course, re-hoisting the cruising rig an hour later. They enjoyed a beautiful summer sail up the Sound making the run up to Williams Cove in record time. As the sun was rising on the second morning from Nantucket, *Anne Marie*'s anchor dropped to the muddy bottom of the cove.

While all three aboard were anxious to get ashore to learn any news, they decided that Jake ought to go on ahead while the younger men tidied the vessel, to follow soon after.

"Oh Jake, it's you!" the door crashed open and Anne came flying across the cleared yard as soon as Jake stepped out of the woods. She simply ran into his surprised arms and hugged deeply. As he put his arms around her he felt her sobbing against his chest, and also felt her firm unfettered breasts against him and realized with a start how desirable she was!

He stroked her long shining brown hair, calming her. "Now what's all this?" he asked quietly.

"The British came night 'fore last," she managed between sobs, "they took Connie and shot Father."

"What? Who's Connie?"

"Th-Th- Thy Connie," stuttered Anne, looking up at him.

"Yes, she had escaped from the British in New York and somehow got herself here just after you sailed. She was almost done in. And, somehow they found her. Raided here early yesterday morning. Shot Father and took her back to their ship. It happened only yesterday. "

By then, unconsciously hand in hand, they had reached the farmhouse. Anne stepped inside, Jake following, to find Arthur in his usual big chair, his leg wrapped in a bloody bandage and propped on a stool.

"Shaw, me friend, tis good t'see thee", he thundered, "bloody damned rascal Brits raided here totter night an' gave me this," waving at his leg.

"Took ur daughter too, the' bloody bastards."

Anne chipped in, "Jake, I really don't like the look of this wound. We've set the bone but it seems not healing well."

She unwrapped the bandage to reveal foul smelling pus leaking from the black and blue hole where the ball had entered the leg. The exit wound appeared healthier.

"The doctor'll be by later today, but he's worried too. Said if he can not bleed off the bad humors he may have to take the leg."

"Anne, run quickly on down to the cove and have David bring the First Aid Kit ashore. He's had some medical training and can maybe help. I wish Connie were here; she's best at this."

Anne dashed out, running all the way to the cove. She arrived quite out of breath.

"Stephen," she yelled towards *Anne Marie* at the top of her voice.

Two heads appeared through a hatch.

"Come quick! Father's hurt. Jake said something about an aid kit," she yelled across the water.

When they got back to the house Anne was amazed as David took charge. First, he had her boil a kettle of water. As she tossed logs into the fireplace under the black pot he opened a white case and took our several white paper wrapped packages. He approached Arthur and told him to relax while he looked closely at the wound. Noticing that the bullet had passed through, David was relieved that at least he wouldn't have to try to probe for it.

"Sir, I'm going to inject you with some morpheme. It will make the pain go away, and you won't feel me cleaning up that wound."

Arthur nodded while the shots were given.

David then cleaned the wound with rubbing alcohol and trimmed the ragged and yellow edges with a small surgical scissors. Lastly he coated it with some slimy stuff from a tube. He lastly sewed it closed. Then he gave Arthur a shot of penicillin

Anne and Martha stood by watching it all.

"Tiz a godsend," mouthed Martha, amazed at David's deft actions with the small scissors and his fast neat stitching with the silver needle he's pulled from a paper wrapper. She couldn't imagine why he'd stuck a sharp needle into the leg, but she ignored it.

An hour later with Arthur resting quietly, well doped-up with some penicillin and codeine pills, David sat with Anne, Jake and Stephen in the kitchen.

"Anne, it's an incredible relief to know that Connie is okay," David started, "did she tell you what happened to her?"

"She didn't say too much, except that she was picked up by a British frigate and returned to New York where they worked her on the *Jersey*, a horrible old hulk they use as a hospital. It's said to really be a death ship. Anyway, somehow she got free and actually swam the river to a place she stole a boat. Somehow she got shot in the leg, and arrived here one morning in the holed little boat, more dead than alive."

"My goodness," commented Jake, "I can't imagine swimming up the East River! And, she stole a boat; what spunk she has."

"I don't know why," Anne continued, "but those raiders yesterday seemed to know exactly where to look for her, and she's all they took."

Looking at David she continued, "And, David, she was so very worried about you. You were almost all she talked about."

Jake ventured, "Waddya bet that that ship we saw in the Sound yesterday was the one that took her, but why would they go east? Why not simply sail back west and into New York?"

Stephen replied, "Ye canna sail down the East River. Tis too dangerous with all that high current and the rocks everywhere. Aye, a small boat or longboat with oars p'rhaps, but no sailin' ship can go there."

"You're right, of course", said Jake. "The rocks and shoals to the west of Welfare Island weren't cleared until the early nineteenth century. Indeed, they've got to sail clear to Montauk and back. No wonder this area will see so little action this War; it's a literal backwater."

"Still", he continued, "we'd have no trouble with *Anne Marie*; I wonder ——."

Just then there came a knock at the door. Anne opened it and a formally dressed old gent in a powdered wig entered. He walked over to Arthur and looked at the bandaged leg.

"Well Arthur," he started in a wheezy voice, "lets us first get ye bled to draw off the evil humors, and then we'll see the wound."

"Dr. Gladstone, thank you for coming," Anne interrupted, "but I think we've got Father well treated. Please greet our friends, recently arrived from the South, and Mr. David there has had some medical training that seems to have worked on Father."

"Aye," said the Doctor, greeting the three guests, 'Bleed him well did thee?"

"He's resting comfortably now," replied David, avoiding the question.

The Doctor walked to Jake and began to pick at the ace bandage clipped over the dressing.

"What be this?" he queried sharply, pinching the material up between two fingers.

Martha rescued the moment, drawing the Doctor's arm towards her, "Tiz but a new fangled bandage that Dr. David learned from the Spanish Indians. Has Arthur quite comfortable; is that not so dear?" nodding at Arthur.

"Quite so," he responded, quite groggy from the drugs.

"Come, Doctor," Martha continued, "come and have a glass of my fresh raspberry juice. Anne just picked the berries yesterday."

"Aye then," Gladstone replied, "Sorry Arthur, canna visit overlong as Mrs. Fitch also needs me services. I'll be by to check on thee tomorrow."

And with that he quaffed his juice. Anne escorted him to his rig. The three men and Anne were silent for awhile after the doctor's little wagon clattered out of the yard.

David broke into the quiet thoughts of the group, "Jake, do you really think that there's any way we could get her back, I mean, under the noses of the entire occupation Army?"

"The whole Army is out at sea with Howe, lad. T'will be but a token force at the port now."

"Aye, and if ye canna get me ashore in the city a day in advance I can mebbe find the lady," offered Stephen. "I know Wembly well."

"When do you think that ship will get her there? We only passed them yesterday, and they were still sailing east?" queried David.

"Well, with this westerly, if they cleared the Race on last night's tide, they'll need to beat back to Sandy Hook. Could take them perhaps two more days, unless the wind shifts."

☆ ☆ ☆

They agreed that it was worth the use of half their remaining precious gasoline and the JP-5. Did David not say he thought that he might be able to make more, eventually?

After several days of planning, *Anne Marie* sailed west at sunset on a deserted Sound. They anchored just before midnight behind Whitestone Point, showing no lights, of course.

Stephen, fully dressed in his finest, with a small bag beside him, climbed down into the jet boat and seated himself on the forward thwart with David at the helm. They started the motor and quietly sped to a point about a mile up-river of Hells Gate, shutting down the motor close to the Long Island shore. Their first obstacle would be the British boat boom and they could not allow themselves to be seen.

Allowing the little boat to drift with the current, and paddling quietly, they slipped up to the Long Island end of the blockade, about half a mile from where the boom was tied.

"Are you sure there'll be no sentries where the boom is tied?" David whispered to Stephen.

"Tis unlikely here," came the quiet reply. "At this side it's swamp and wilderness for miles. The boats are here to protect the city from approach by water. There'll be nobody in those wilds of Long Island."

"Okay then," David said.

As agreed, David then waded through the muck to the shoreline leaving the very properly dressed Stephen in the jet boat anchored in the shallows. David moved silently through the underbrush towards the lamp glow on the boats.

There it was! The cable holding the longboats full of sentries was a full two inch hemp rope stretched drum tight in the full ebb tide. It snaked ashore to where it was tied to a huge oak tree.

David, lying in the shadow of the tree, went to work with his razor sharp knife, fraying the rope at the back of the tree. He was trying to avoid a clean cut; hopefully it would look like an animal had gnawed it through.

It parted with a loud snap.

"Cor, bloody damned cable's broken again," was heard from the closest longboat as the five knot current swept the string of soldier-laden boats down-stream to bump ashore on the rocks at the mainland side of Hell's Gate.

Now, unseen by the British soldiers, David hurried back to Stephen in the jet boat. They pushed off, and they silently guided the little craft through Hell's Gate with their paddles, hugging the south shore as closely as possible. Once out of ear-shot of the cursing soldiers in the stranded longboats David started the motor, and they quickly sped south as close to the shores of Manhattan Island as David dared. He didn't need to pile-up on a rock tonight, however the charts did indicate that the Manhattan side of the river should be more rock-free than the Long Island or Welfare Island side.

A lantern's light appeared ashore on their right bow.

"Aye, David," Stephen tapped him on the shoulder, "it be thar."

David pointed the small boat slowly towards the shore several hundred yards north of the light, which was just inland of a little wooden dock. He shut off the motor and paddled the last few yards until the boat bumped the rocky beach.

"You sure you know how to work that radio?" queried David, "remember, leave it off until just before you call us."

"Aye, tiz not difficult, but still seems the work of the devil that I can talk to ye from miles away," Stephen quipped, "But, I'll follow ye'r plan."

David pushed off, paddled back into moving river, and was lost to sight in moments. He slipped quietly back up upstream through Hell's Gate, the same way he had come down river at slack tide. The British boat boom was still tangled on the north shore. He was back aboard *Anne Marie* well before the new flood tide began.

"Are you sure you want to risk *Anne Marie* in that river tonight?" David asked Jake, "who knows, we might be seen this close to the town? "

"That's the plan, son. If we don't pass through the boat boom before it's fixed tomorrow we'll be seen anyway; at least now no one knows we are here. We'll just have to chance that the area behind Welfare Island is the swamp I think it is. And, if we don't move right away we'll need to push against the full flood. They'll hear our engine for sure."

Anne Marie, under diesel power in the total darkness after the moon set, slipped slowly down the river. She glided, once again, past the broken boat boom just as the flood tide was starting.

Their radar guided the way.

As the sun began to lighten the sky to the east *Anne Marie* anchored fore and aft, close in to a swampy forest behind a field of tall bull rushes on a swampy little island. One day in the future this island would be paved over with high rise apartments, and it'd be named Welfare Island. But, today, it was just a bleak swamp.

The day dawned dreary and rainy.

After breakfast Jake picked up his binoculars saying, "gonna go up the mast and see if I can look at the main channel on the other side of the island."

He then climbed the main mast to the lower spreader. He squinted through the glasses to get a look at the channel down the river on the other side of Welfare Island. Indeed, it did look scary. With the flood tide now at full force rushing up-river, Jake could see water gushing over the many boulders barely hidden below the river's surface. There was no way that *Anne Marie* could ride that maelstrom down river there and maintain enough control to avoid the rocks. He wondered how Connie had ever managed to swim through that without getting herself killed.

Still, as he had guessed, looking way over to the Manhattan side of the river, there seemed to be a narrow navigable channel. The only way Jake could imagine getting get *Anne Marie* through the rocks would be to push against the flooding current under full diesel power. He hoped the shoreline was as deserted as it appeared for if anyone heard them, with the engine on full power, they'd be sitting ducks.

Dropping back to the main deck he shook his head at David in the light rain.

"Gonna be real tight in that channel. One mistake and we could be dashed onto the rocks, and of course we'll be making a lot of noise," he said.

"Can we get through?" David asked, "It's the only way to get Connie."

"If Stephen gets back to us tomorrow we'll try just after midnight, when the tide turns upriver. That way the tide won't be full strength against us. I think we'll be okay," retorted Jake,

Stephen had banged the door to the tavern open at two hours before midnight and pushed himself to the bar through a throng of rowdy red-coated soldiers.

"Megods," the blonde barmaid exclaimed, "If'n 't ain't Stephen Downey, the hemp man. Whar ye been keepin ye'r self, lovey?"

"Aye, Mollie, I'll be 'avin a pint o 'ur best, and a bed upstairs. 'Tis been a long ride from upstate, and the pickin's was slim. Damned Colonists must mark me fer a Kings Man," Stephen nodded in apparent disgust.

"Aye lovey, but u're late tonight,"

"Fell in with a platoon of Hessians at the ferry and rode in with them. It's not safe to ride the upper end of this accursed island at night alone, y'know".

"And ye dinna bring ye'r troop of beer swilling Hessians to me bar for a pint of me finest?" she asked sharply.

"I offered 'em a pint each, Mollie, but they was pressed to get to their barrack at Fulton Street. Nay, they parted with me just up the lane."

"Take ye room six then, ye'r regular. Ye're lucky 'tiz empty tonight," the girl replied, fetching a brass skeleton key on a chain.

With that Stephen quaffed his pint and retired up the narrow stairs, his bag in hand.

The next morning Stephen dressed again in his usual colonial best; lace shirt, cravat, blue woolen pants and silk stockings. He surprised himself to find how uncomfortable these clothes were in the already sticky late July morning, when compared to the loose-fitting cotton clothing he had worn on *Anne Marie.*

Nevertheless, cramming his tri-corner hat on his head at a jaunty angle, he descended to the taproom for a breakfast of strong tea, warmed bread and several thick slabs of bacon. He didn't see any of the other traders he often met here at the Crown Tavern, nor did he know any of the red-coated British officers in the tap room. .

After making arrangements with the innkeeper to keep his lodgings for a few days, Stephen stepped out to the muddy street and followed west to Broadway, then south to the Battery. Perhaps, he thought, he could get some information from the duty orderly?

Yes, he learned at the head of a Navy pier that that Sir Wembly was now the ranking officer in the Port , and that he was aboard the *Jersey.* Apparently he was using the hulk as his day offices, and he retired to a commandeered large residence each evening .

"Aye, Lieutenant," Stephen finished the exchange, handing him a printed calling card, "tis at the Crown I am lodging and if ye'll be good enough to pass my regards to the Post Captain, p'raps he'll wish an audience?"

With that, Stephen departed.

Having little to do until a message could be sent to the flagship, and a reply hopefully returned to the Crown Tavern, Stephen strolled down Front Street, remarking to himself how empty the port appeared. Yes, there were several trading vessels at various wharves loading or unloading cargoes, but there was hardly any sight of the huge occupation army. The harbor was devoid of the usual bustle of British Navy ships. There were only two frigates at anchor and one small sloop.

Stephen wondered briefly which ship had carried Connie, hoping that their guess was correct, and that she was here.

Following a lunch of fried fish at a waterfront tavern, Stephen walked back up Front Street to the landing to see if his request to meet with Post Captain had been accepted. He'd thought that he might intercept any reply here and save himself the walk to the Crown and back?

A Midshipman, indeed, had a brief note for Stephen.

It said, "Mr. Downey, Sir, The Captain's compliments. He'll receive thee aboard *Jersey* at ye'r pleasure. He has also asked the pleasure of ur company to take supper with him tonight at his residence."

"Aye, Sir," Stephen addressed the young Midshipman, " 'Ave you a boat for I'm able to attend the Captain at the moment,"

A short while later the duty longboat pulled into the lea of *Jersey.* Stephen couldn't miss the rank stench coming from the hulk. It was some fine flagship indeed, he thought. \

Stephen climbed to the sally port, was piped aboard and he was escorted aft to the main cabin where Wembly bade him enter without delay.

"Downey, me lad how be thee?" growled the grossly fat Post Captain, sitting behind an ornate desk with one foot wrapped and propped on a stool, "forgive me for not standing to welcome thee but this gout has me down," waving at his foot.

"I am well, sir, Av been upcountry beyond Westchester seeking likely crops for the fall harvest. Looks to be a good year for the hemp crop, but the damned Yankees will be careful where they'll sell. Fools are more dazed with their damned new flag than with solid gold. Still, they'll take me gold. No doubt the ropewalks and merchants here will be pleased."

"Aye, and have thee news of any Rebel movements?"

"Nay, tiz been quiet. Heard some whispers though of Gentleman Johnny marching south across the lakes to meet our Army and to cutoff the head of the Rebel snake."

"Aah, tar be something to that, me boy, but the Hessians under Burgoyne are wanting horses, an' they'll not be fighting' much thout we pay the rascals. And in gold too. Damned supply ship is late. Should be a two decker carrying the gold for that damned German army. Latest dispatch from Montreal was claiming a delay until the ships with the Hessian's horses arrive. Damned hirelings are too good to walk with the Army, y'know".

"What of the fleet here?" queried Stephen, "port looks damned empty."

"Aye, and ye didn't know that Lord Howe sailed last week to sack the rebel's little capitol in Philadelphia. I've had no news. P'rhaps this sorry little war is already over."

There was a knock at the door. Wembly hollered, "'Enter".

His orderly, the same mere boy of a midshipman, stepped in and announced in a shill voice, "Commander Aaron, *Reliant*, Sir,"

"Send him in"

"Aye aye, sir."

And a tall sharp looking dark haired Commander with a nasty disfiguring scar on his face appeared in the cabin. He snapped stiffly to attention.

"Lieutenant Aaron, Sir!" he barked his name with a salute.

"At ease, Captain, and may I present Mr. Stephen Downey."

" Mr. Downey is a hemp trader by trade, bringing much wealth to His Majesty's merchants, and also from time to time some valuable information gleaned from his travels throughout this foul backwoods colony,."

Stephen stood and bowed from the waist.

The Captain continued, addressing Stephen, "Aaron commands *Reliant*, waving his hand at a pretty frigate in view through the open stern ports. "He's one of our invaluable blockade picket ships, just returning from a bit of special duty."

"On ye'r way are ye, Aaron?" Wembly continued, addressing the l.

"Aye, sir," Aaron replied, "we're fortunate to have found fresh water, the lighter will cast off in time for us to slip afore the evenin' flood."

And, re-addressing Stephen, the Commander said, "Tiz back to Montauk for us."

"Ere's ye'r orders then Aaron," stated Wembly handing over a packet of papers. "I'll be placing *Samantha* under ye'r command. P'raps with two of thee at Montauk ye'll better cork up the Yankees."

Wembly then asked, "What of that strangeness I gave thee on ye'r last short mission? I'll be wanting to pass it to the Admiralty and let them ponder over it."

"Aye, sir., 'ere tiz," Aaron reached down and passed a small canvas bag to the Captain,

"And ere's that thing," pulling out the orange life jacket .

Stephen stared at it. Wembly noted his gaze.

"Aaron ye fool," he thundered, "Ye should left 't covered!"

He continued in a quieter tone, "Aye, Stephen, this is a curious business. Aaron found a little lady adrift, dressed in strange clothing and wearing this. We had 'er here, treating 'er well, but she escaped. Worst is, she got away with the entire bloody fleet in the harbor, and nobody knows how."

"There was something very unusual about this lady," he continued, "so I sent Aaron to recapture her, and ee's done well at that. Methinks she's a Yankee, but there's enough question 'bout this lady so I'm sending her on to London as soon as I've a ship returning; perhaps that doubledamned two decker with the Hessian pay, if she ever gets here."

"And where be this creature now?" queried Stephen, hoping his off-hand remark would get a reply.

"She'll be safe enough this time, damn her eyes. The lass has unusual healing skills so she'll be four decks below ur feet tending the sick and wounded, but she'll not escape again. We keep 'er locked in the orlop after hours as she's inclined to run. Fact is, I've asked for her to look at this gout.".

Aaron interrupted, "by ur Leave, Sir"

"Aah yes, ye're excused Aaron, and good hunting,"

Aaron snapped back to attention and saluted. With a sharp about face he departed the cabin. Boson's pipes shortly trilled at the sally port as he left for his ship.

"Have a seat, Downey," the Captain offered waving at an ornate chair. "I sent for that Yankee baggage just before ye arrived. She'll be up presently. Now that Aaron slipped out about 'er ye may just as well rest here 'till she's tended me. P'raps with ye'r knowledge of these colonies ye can place her?"

The two of them discussed current New York gossip, the departure of the Lords Howe for Philadelphia and other news of the war until there was another knock at the door and the same Midshipman entered with a slight young lady nudged ahead of him.

"Indeed, Downey, this be the lass," offered Wembly.

Stephen saw the person was indeed a small trim girl dressed in baggy white duck pantaloons and a striped baggy sailor's shirt. Stephen could easily see a strong resemblance to Jake.

"Captain," she started in a clear voice, "I've told you there's nothing I can do about your damn gout. And, the bleeding your local butcher doctors are doing on you is less than worthless. The only way to rid yourself of discomfort is to eat far less fatty foods and get some exercise. Please allow me to return below decks where there are men with real injuries that I can help. "

"Damned ye, impertinent woman," Wembly replied, "curb ye'r tongue else I'll clap thee in irons."

And to Stephen he quipped with a raised eyebrow, "Sassy lass is she not?"

"All right, midshipman get 'er below again, and be certain she's locked in the orlop at dusk. And, get me a real physic who'll properly bleed off the pain from this gout."

Turning to Stephen he said, "sorry, sir. I'd thought she'd be civil, but apparently she's of unusually independent mind for a woman. Can thee place her speech though? Tis a strange sounding English she uses. Have ye 'eard it's like?"

While Stephen knew exactly what the Post Captain meant, he simply shook his head venturing, "Av 'eard it said that there's a colony of settlers in the Floridas that's under protection of the Spanish Crown, but 'av never met one. P'raps that's her people?"

He continued, "And, Sir Wembly, I must be off. I've business in town yet today, but will be honored to be at ur residence at eight."

"Thank'ee Stephen. It'll be a small dinner , but ye'r always welcome."

As the longboat rowed Stephen ashore he could see two large ships beating up the harbor. Indeed, on closer look the leading ship was a two decked ship of the line, her commission pennant streaming back from her main mast. He raised an eyebrow, knowing that the ship would certainly be carrying the paymaster's gold.

Later at dinner he learned how the British were going to secretly move two thirds of the gold south to the Lords Howe, and the balance north up the Hudson River to General Burgoyne.

No, it had not been a light dinner. The guests included the captains and several lieutenants from the newly arrived ships. The discussion ranged from the crossing weather to current gossip from Portsmouth. Still, Stephen was politely excused when the five Navy officers retired to a private discussion.

The dinner had started with a clam bisque, proceeded to steamed fish, followed by a rack of lamb with broiled potatoes, and was finished with a plum pudding, all accompanied by never ending refills from the Captain's cellars. Stephen wondered what Wembly would call a heavy dinner?

He needed the four mile walk up-river to the Crown, where he settled his bill and retrieved his bag.

"Nay, Mollie," he said after grabbing his things, while leaving the tavern, "just finished dinner with the Sir Wembly and couldn't think of a pint, even of ye'r best. Am off for a sail up-river to Albany so I'll need rush off. Ship's weighing at dawn."

He then walked three miles north to the little deserted pier on the East River landing.

Not really believing it would work, Stephen pulled a little black box from his pocket and, following Jake's exact instructions, he carefully turned the tiny knob on the upper left to the left. It gently clicked and a red little window lighted up displaying number "16". Then he turned the knob on the upper right also to the left.

Yes, as it had on *Anne Marie,* the little box squawked at him. He turned the right knob to the left until the box was quiet. He raised it to his lips, pushed the larger knurled button at the bottom and said, "*Anne Marie,* David are you there?"

Then he took his thumb off the button, as instructed, and waited.

The box replied, as he was told it would, "Hi Stephen, what can you tell us? Do you know where she is?"

Stephen was amazed! It sounded like David was standing beside him.

Remembering to push in the little button at the bottom before talking, Stephen replied, "Aye, David, I've seen 'er and spoken to 'er, She be fine and we can get 'er as we planned, But, thar's a fortune in gold sailin' upriver. We need to see if we canna find a way to help the King give that gold tae General Washington. Mind ye, there'll be the prize master's share in 't for thee."

In a few minutes Stephen heard the nearly silent whine sound of jet boat motor as David appeared at the water's edge to pick him up. Stephen stepped into the little boat. David made the boat swim backwards, turn around, then return upriver through the rapids at the usual breath-taking rate of speed .

Stephen again held on for his very life, again trying not to be afraid of the nearly flying machine under David's steady hand.

"So, Jake, that's about it," finished David an hour and a half later.

"Yes," he summed up, "there's no reason we shouldn't be able to slip onto *Jersey* and snatch Connie without being seen or heard."

"But after that," Jake replied, "what do you think about all that gold? Might we be able to take it too? Can you think of a way to get both Connie back safely, then steal a king's ransom from under the nose of the British Navy?"

David and Stephen took another half hour to unravel the rest of their plan.

"Yes," Jake replied afterwards, "but aren't we taking a terrible chance that the ship might not sail on the morning tide? And if it doesn't, your gold will be lost forever in the muck of the East River."

David thought a moment, then said, "Yeah, if we miss the sailing, the ship'll go down in the river and we'll never make a recovery at night before the tides scatter the spoils. What do you think, Stephen?"

"Aye, methinks the Hessians with Howe, and those with Gentleman Johnny 'll be clamoring for their gold, mercenaries and all. I was just with the Post Captain and the Captains of those ships. While I was dismissed before their plans was set, my bet is that the two-decker'll re-water and re-provision before she goes anywhere. Therefore, they'll quickly transfer the gold to *Emily*, a fast sloop of war, and she'll be down river for Howe to the South with most of the gold on the ebb tomorrow. We need to strike her while we can; our Cause needs the money."

"Aye," he continued, "some of it will go up-river by armed cutter to Burgoyne, perhaps even tonight. Seems we won't have much of a chance of that portion, but,"

David cut him off with, "Let's see what we can plan. Still, Stephen, do you mean we'll turn it all over to the Colonial Government?"

"Aye, me boy, but not all of it. Washington 'll let ye keep the usual privateer's share."

"How much is that?"

"Last I heard, the usual is one third."

The only disagreement to Stephen and David's plan came from Jake.

"David, you've made one error. It's you, not me, who needs to stay with *Anne Marie*."

"No way," David retorted. "It's my job to get Connie back"

"Sorry, son," Jake answered kindly, "Remember you're the career pacifist. I'm the one who has done work like this before. I won't flinch if it gets tough. You might."

After an hour of preparation the little jet boat drifted with the current directly down river towards the huge triple-decked hospital and prison hulk. Stephen was at the motor, having had a quick course in its operation. Jake was dressed in his black rubber suit with the strange breathing apparatus at the top.

As the little boat crept to a line directly up-current from the bow of the prison hulk Jake gave a signal and Stephen killed the motor.

They both crouched down, hiding in the bottom of the small boat while the boat drifted up against the anchor chain. Jake grabbed the rusty chain and quickly tied their bow line to it.

They were safe directly under the massive bow of the prison ship where they could not be seen from the deck.

"Are ye sure ye can do this?" queried Stephen.

Jake nodded. Silently he dropped over the side and into the black water. He flipped his mask over his face and placed the re-breather mouthpiece between his teeth, breathing in quietly as he sank below the surface.

He allowed himself to drift back with the tide, along the side of the barnacle and grass infested hulk, until he thought he was almost past the stern. He flipped his feet and pulled himself neatly around, next to the great weedy wooden rudder. With only his head above water, he took a portable cutting torch from his pocket and pointed the tiny blue flame at the wooden planking in front of him.

He stopped. And reconsidered the plan quickly realizing it was not smart to cut through the hull. It could sink her too fast, or it might start a fire. He looked for a better way. With the doused torch in hand he swam around the left side of the hulk. Not more than twenty feet forward of the stern he found an open gun port just within his reach over his head.

Levering himself up to the opening by pulling on the cast iron bars bolted over the port, Jake was able to see that the square hole in the hull had only had iron bars heavily bolted to the interior, presuming to keep the prisoners in. There was nothing to un-bolt, at least not without creating a nasty racquet.

He looked closely again realizing that any sparks from his small cutting torch might start a fire, or be seen, but his fiber hacksaw ought to make short work of the old soft iron bars.

He started sawing, leaning on the two handles of the fiber saw, pulling first on one side then the other. In a few minutes the first iron bar sank quickly to the bottom of the harbor, followed quickly by the one next to it.

Jake slithered in.

From the diagrams studied with Stephen, he knew he was on the lower gun deck, the one used for prisoners. From his position, crouching just inside the gun port, he could see by the faint glow of a lantern on a bulkhead out of sight row upon row of hammocks filled with sleeping bodies. When he pulled the facemask off the stench of those sleeping unwashed bodies, of sewage, and of rot almost made him retch.

Connie was said to be locked in the orlop, supposedly two decks below and as far aft as possible. Jake briefly questioned how could she stand this foul place?

Hooking his swim fins to his weight belt, and with his K-Bar knife in-hand, Jake crept with his elbows on his stomach silently through the filth under the hammocks, seeking the ladder downwards. Using brief flashes from his pencil-sized flashlight he found the ladder and silently scooted down past several locked store room doors. He found yet another ladder, and crept still further downward.

The stench got worse.

He heard a murmur of voices and saw the glow of a lantern coming up the lower ladder. Looking carefully over the edge of the combing, Jake saw two British Marines, their coats unbuttoned, and their muskets lying on the deck next to them. They were seated at a table playing cards under a smoky flickering candle lit lantern.

Jake was surprised to find sentries on duty. He'd thought British would trust their stout doors and iron padlocks to protect the store rooms from the prisoners. Still, there they were.

He and David had thought there might be someone he'd need to silence quietly, so he had a packet of six shark darts. These were small darts filled with a strong and instantaneous sedative, fired from a pistol by compressed air.

As Jake pulled the dart pistol from his belt and aimed down the hatch at the back of the Marine closest to him he briefly hoped that the dart would merely knock these men out, not kill them.

Phfffft.

The feathered shark dart, filled with a drug that would immobilize an attacking shark in a split second, hit the Marine between his shoulders.

He fell as if pole-axe'd. A few seconds later his card partner followed. Jake dashed the rest of the way down the ladder and checked the pulse of the fallen Marines. He was pleased that they remained alive.

Moving past the fallen sentries into the gloomy passage beyond, he passed a number of unbolted doorways on either side. At the very end of the catwalk Jake found a double bolted hatch secured with a huge padlock. Jake's hacksaw made short work of the lock. Slowly and quietly throwing the bolts, he quietly opened the right side door, aiming his little light around the chamber inside.

He saw a number of empty cots with tie-down straps and a large wooden table, also with straps at each corner. And, yes, there appeared to be one sleeping body on a sole hammock strung-up at the end. It could only be his daughter.

In this hot, airless and incredibly smelly hole at the bottom of this rotten old ship, there she was! How could he miss the short curly mop of red hair?

"Connie," he gently rubbed her neck and shoulders as he had done when she was a baby, "wake up, it's me."

Connie stirred, and woke.

"Daddy?", she started, "but how?"

She threw her arms around him to make sure it really was Jake.

"Ssssh," he cautioned, whispering, "Talk later. Let's get you out of here."

He handed her a pair of white ducks and a shirt that he grabbed from the end of the hammock, whispering, "Come on."

She pulled the clothing on and grabbed his arm.

He lead her silently down the passage and into the area where the sentries had fallen. Jake remembered to stoop down and pluck the spent darts from their red coats as he and Connie crept by.

They silently climbed up the two ladders. At the lower gun deck Jake motioned Connie to crawl under the hammocks to the starboard side. Pushing and sliding through the evil muck on the deck she gagged at the smell.

They reached the side of the ship, but the closest port was fully barred.

Jake stopped, looking about him for the one he'd cur through.

He heard a noise, but it was only Connie, retching into the slime on the deck.

Knowing he had to get her out, and fast, Jake guessed that the open port had to be still farther to his right, more towards the rear of the ship. Indeed, he made the right choice. As he elbowed onward through the slime he found the next gun port where he could feel that the bars were gone.

Connie was right behind him. He motioned for her to drop through the open port and into the dark water. He followed, quickly slipping his feet into his swim fins and silently pulling Connie against the current to the rubber boat at the bow.

Moments later Stephen reached down and pulled Connie first, then Jake, over the side and into the jet boat.

Connie threw her arms around her Dad and sobbed into his neck, "Oh Dad, I was so terribly afraid I'd lost you and David forever. How did you find me? Oh, and how did we get to this terrible place?"

"Sssssh, baby," Jake whispered as he stroked her wet head, "it'll all be okay now. David is waiting for us on *Anne Marie,* not far from here. Shhhh, we need to slip away before anyone hears us."

Jake untied the painter from the anchor chain of the *Jersey,* and the boat drifted down-river with the current until they were out of immediate hearing. When Jake felt they were safe he smiled again at Connie.

"Here," and he gave her a wet t-shirt so she could wipe the gun deck filth from her face.

He spoke in a whisper, "Connie, this is Stephen Downey, an American, who's helped us to find you."

"Pleased to meet thee, Maam," whispered Stephen, realizing this was the nurse he had met with Sir Wembly.

He then directed himself to Jake, "Any trouble?"

"No, Stephen, 'cept a couple of Marines will have a headache in the morning. They'll know we've gotten Connie, but not how," he opened his hand, showing Stephen the spent darts.

"Didn't I see you today?" Connie sharply asked Stephen.

"Aye miss, that's how we found thee."

Jake started the motor and the jet boat silently motored up-river. Somewhat later, in the moonlight, Connie saw *Anne Marie.*

It's hard to tell if David was happier to again see Connie, whom he simply hugged for a very long time, or if Connie was happier just to be back with her Dad and David. Still, after reassuring them that she was all right, albeit thinner than usual, she could only think of a hot shower, her razor, her deodorant, her blow dryer and her own real and clean clothes.

She basked for twenty minutes in the hot shower while the men discussed their next plan. She spent another full five minutes brushing her teeth. Oh, but it was so wonderful for her to be back with her little electric shaver, her hair dryer, her deodorant, a touch of lipstick, and clean, fresh soft clothing!

Soon enough, dressed in a clean pair of running shorts and a T-shirt, legs shaved for the first time in months, her hair blown dry, and just a bit of makeup, she emerged into the sultry evening air back on deck in the cockpit.

David slid to her side, "You look great," he exclaimed, kissing her cheek lightly.

"You too," she murmured, snuggling closer to him.

Continuing, she looked up saying, "God, I'd thought I'd never see you or *Anne Marie* again. How did we get here? Dad, how soon can you get us back home?"

"I just don't know what happened, Kitten," Jake replied softly, using her pet baby nickname, "and, I'm not sure there is a way back."

"But it's so dark and dirty here," she instinctively barked back, somewhat shrilly. "I want to see Mom, and what about my Lab? You mean it's all gone?"

"I'm afraid we'll have to make a life here, Connie. Thank goodness that you're safe, and that you and David have each other,"

Meanwhile Stephen was in shock! His eyes were wide open, and he had to force his jaw from gaping open. When he first saw this girl she had been dressed decently in sailor's clothing, albeit she appeared plain looking. The next time he saw her was when she was dragged over the side of the rubber boat, wet, dirty, stinking and bedraggled. Certainly though, she had been still decently dressed from neck to toe.

But now, when she'd re-appeared a few moments ago, she was nearly naked! He was dazed that her father and fiancé' would let her out in public in this indecent nakedness? Her long white legs were openly showing from a point nearly at their top, starting from only the briefest of shimmering blue bloomers, all the way past her ankles to white moccasins on her feet. Why, any decent Lady, heck even savage Indian squaws, wore bloomers that fall below the knee under her dress, and only the worst tart would ever even show an ankle.

Even more shocking, above these shimmering blue 'bloomers', this Connie wore only a light cotton T-shirt, very like the one he had worn. But, but she had no corset or apparently any undergarment whatever under it! Aye, as she turned to hug David he could clearly see the full outline of her small breast and the hard nipple at the end framed by this light shirt!

He'd had to look away in embarrassment.

Her hair in the dim light looked like spun red gold, and her big blue eyes, moist with tears when Jake told her they'd not return, looked huge, and outlined against her face. Her lips were a soft shiny pink with snow white pearly even teeth.

Stephen, again, had to gaze away into the darkness to collect his thoughts.

Swallowing his shock, nearly outrage, he could only assume that this was clearly how women will dress in Jake's time to come, for neither Jake nor David had made any comment at all on the way she was dressed in Stephen's presence. Still, he knew that this Connie had best learn to cover herself up here, or she'd be startin' riots with both men and women! After considering further for just a moment he thought it best not say anything, except to Jake, and perhaps not tonight.

Just as he was remembering to talk it over with Jake, David spoke up.

"Connie," he said, "we didn't get to properly introduce our friend Stephen Downey."

Stephen extended his hand, trying to keep his eyes directed to her face, away from her far too evident chest.

"Again, pleased to meet thee once more, Miss Connie."

"Yes," retorted Connie with a smile, "you were with that fat grumpy old fart today, Captain Wembly, with the gout."

Jake took up the introduction, "Stephen is a part of the colonial government, Connie. And, we've been helping their effort with a few things, but we need to be really careful not to be caught or too well seen, if you understand."

"But, I did see you with the fat old Captain?" she queried Stephen sharply .

"Aye, Miss Connie," Stephen started, "But —"

David interrupted, "He was there to find you. And he did."

"Okay," she replied, "I guess thanks are in order. I am ever so happy to be away from that horrible place."

Then she said to her Dad, "I guess I do understand that we are in another time, and I guess it wouldn't be cool for them to catch us and go through *Anne Marie*. We'd be like a flying saucer, or something from outer space in our time."

"Exactly," Jake nodded.

"But, Connie," interjected David, "I did get to meet General Washington, you know, the first President? Stephen knows him well. And we helped him out near Philadelphia."

Connie looked at Stephen asking, "Where do you fit in this picture, Mr. Downey? Now, I did see you in that overstuffed gouty Captain's cabin. How can you help us and still be so friendly to those English monsters?"

"Aye, Miss, its fittin' fer thee to be askin. I'm an irregular Officer of the Continental Army, and also known to be friendly disposed by certain Tory and British folks both here in this city and elsewhere. I undertake special missions for the General."

"You mean you're a spy," Connie interrupted.

"Aye, if ye'll put it that way. Rather, I take it as a Patriot doin' all I can to wrest our Colonies from King George. Of course, if I should be turned by the Redcoats I'll likely hang."

"In fact, miss," he continued, "if'n ye'll allow me to change the subject?"

"Jake," Stephen said, "if'n we durnst get movin soon we'll be here in the light 'o day and will miss our chances at that British payroll what won't be long sittin' in that two-decker."

An hour later *Anne Marie* was passing between the British anchorage to the west and the dark shore of Brooklyn, riding silently on the now ebbing tide. They were using the muttering diesel to keep maximum distance from the anchored ships on her radar screen as the silent ketch passed through the anchorage unseen in the darkness.

Just before they cleared the harbor mouth they anchored *Anne Marie* at the Staten Island side of the Verrazano Narrows.

Jake and Stephen dropped back into the jet boat.

"David, tell her what we're doing and keep a watch for us," Jake said as the little boat disappeared in the near darkness.

"What are they doing? Is it dangerous?" Connie queried.

"Well, it is bold, but it shouldn't be too dangerous, especially for Jake. Here's what they plan to do," and he continued.

Captain Eddleston had returned aboard his ship, the 74 gun first rater, at midnight. He was sobered with the Post Captain's plan and harsh admonishments. Immediately he commanded his second lieutenant and his Captain of Marines to his cabin.

Eddleston gave them concise orders, and within a half hour the ship's cutter had pulled away in the dark, guarded by a company of Royal Marines.

The new sloop, *Emily,* was then warped along side Eddleston's ship. No lights were showing, and the crews of both ships had been banished to their hammocks below; the scuttles were secured and guarded by marines.

The officers of both ships, themselves, worked ropes run through through pulleys rigged from the 74's mizzen yardarm. Twenty-one heavy wooden boxes were swiftly pulled from the bowels of the two decker and stowed in a tiny locker under the sole of the captain's cabin in *Emily*. She was then warped back to her bower anchor, awaiting the ebb tide just before dawn.

Next, a second 28 foot sailing cutter was likewise brought to the starboard main chains of the 74 gun ship, and 9 heavy boxes were gently lowered and lashed amidships under the thwarts. She was placed under the command of the ship's First Lieutenant, Mr. Ward.

The job was done. The lower deck gun ports were allowed again open, and the crew was allowed back on the top deck in the warm evening.

"Mr. Ward," the Captain instructed the cutter's commander in his cabin, "it's just six bells of the morning watch. Ye should still have two hours of flood tide, followed by six hours of ebb, but ye've a nice southwesterly to push thee upriver. Ye're to proceed directly under sail and oars, at utmost speed, to the town of Nyack, on the west bank, just here", pointing at a chart of the Hudson River.

"A dispatch rider has gone ahead, and ye'll turn over ye'r cargo to Colonel Burgess for his onward transport."

He continued, "Lieutenant Ward, ye'r mission is essential to the winning of this war. Thee must not fail. I've given thee a company of crack Marines under Captain Milton in a second cutter. Choose ye'r boat crew carefully; they'll need pull hard through the night and ye'll be fighting the ebb tide ."

"Aye, aye, sir," Ward saluted sharply and departed.

The Lieutenant flashed a lantern at the cutter filled with marines. Descending to the stern of his own cutter, the one with the nine heavy boxes, the two boats rowed swiftly around the Battery and set their lugsails, speeding north up the Hudson River with twelve oars pulling hard on each.

Also, as ordered, just after dawn as the ebb tide started to flow, *HMS Emily* ghosted down river under topsails. The small ship reached Sandy Hook just as the sun rose, bloody red, out of the eastern sea.

Following his strict Orders, Lt. James put his helm down and sailed along the coast of New Jersey just within sight of land. He felt safe in the knowledge that there was not a proper harbor that could conceal a superior Colonial force until he crossed the Delaware. Once past that, he was again safe to the Chesapeake, where he would rendezvous with Howe's Fleet and rid himself of those damned twenty-one chests of gold secured in the little hold under his tiny cabin.

Emily was entrusted with this very special and secret duty because she was the fastest ship in the fleet, newly arrived from Portsmouth with a clean bottom. Her orders were to outrun any sail she saw, safely delivering the special cargo. James knew that his little ship alone could only flee an enemy. Her eight little guns couldn't do much damage to even a small Yankee privateer, but *Emily* was very very fast. She really could outrun almost anything afloat.

Meanwhile, just west of *Emily* on the Hudson River, the moon set just before dawn. The crew at the oars of the two British cutters had found their pace, and on both the Marines were sitting ramrod straight between the oarsmen. Their muskets were loaded and primed with the bayonet blades pointed to the sky. The lookouts in the bows of both boats could see nothing in the inky darkness, save the faint glow from a single lantern in the stern of the lead boat. Lt. Ward was watching his small candle-lit compass, and was whispering helm orders to the coxswain.

Of course they could not see *Anne Marie's* dark gray jet boat floating silently, dead in the water ahead of them. Jake and Stephen had sped the jet boat past the New York Battery, well ahead of the cutters in the darkness. They drifted and waited in the center of the quiet river, between the Palisades to the west and the wooded heights of northern Manhattan Island to the East.

Stephen was the first to hear the creaking of oars through the darkness, coming towards them..

He whispered to Jake, "Center of the River. Close. Look closely, you'll see a small light"

Squinting through the inky darkness, Jake could just barely make out the shape of a boat in a flickering small glow at the rear of the first boat. Two of them were coming, rowing fast and silently up the river.

As they'd discussed, he quietly idled the motor, guiding the inflatable silently to a position just ahead and to the left of the oncoming and unsuspecting cutters.

The first cutter's outline came clear, not fifty yards away. Jake let it pass. He then knelt on the rubbery side of the semi-inflatable boat and without warning, he opened fire with an extended burst from his AK-47 on the trailing cutter full of Marines. He emptied the magazine. As the jet boat closed on the drifting cutter he emptied a second magazine into the boat, now filled with dead and dying British sailors and Marines. They never knew what had hit them.

Stephen then quickly twisted the throttle of the motor and shot up alongside of the lead cutter. Lt. Ward got one pistol shot off before Jake's AK-47 cut him in half. The surviving sailors all immediately leapt into the river, holding on to their oars.

As the rubber boat gently bumped the side of the slowly sinking cutter, Stephen climbed in. He pushed away the gristly body of the officer, and almost fell over nine boxes of gold coins.

One by one he grunted them to the gunwale, and slid them to Jake.

As a final gesture, just before jumping back into the rubber boat, Stephen blasted a hole in the cutter's bottom. It swamped, like its sister, and drifted down river.

Jake hoped some of the sailors would make to shore, regretting that they'd had to kill so many.

The jet boat, now heavily loaded, idled back down the western side of the river to her rendezvous with *Anne Marie*. Stephen sloshed the blood off the chests as the heavily laden little boat waddled south.

David and Connie were waiting on *Anne Marie,* anchored behind the little island that would someday hold the Statue of Liberty. Nine heavy wooden chests were manhandled up the side of the ketch, and were stowed away. David stowed the little boat.

Just after dawn, refreshed with hot coffee, they watched *Emily,* close hauled to the wind, slip down river towards Sandy Hook under topsails and jibs. She was a lovely sight.

Aboard *Emily,* Lt. James cleared Sandy Hook, tacked south, and could just hold her parallel with the shore. As soon as she was settled on course he set the watch, left his second officer on the quarterdeck, and repaired to his cabin for his breakfast. After finishing he reclined on his cot, exhausted from the previous all night's efforts.

He dozed off.

"BLAM", the deck jumped under his hammock!

"What the bloody hell!" he shouted, hitting the deck with both feet, running.

He reached the Quarterdeck, dressed only in his smallclothes in the early morning sunlight, looking quickly all around. There was nothing in sight except the green shore of New Jersey miles away. Shaking his head, he knew they could not have hit a reef, and there was no ship in sight. Regardless, E*mily* shook with a sickening lurch to leeward.

Lieutenant Richard James knew his career was gone at that moment.

Still, with a fading glimmer of hope he called out, "Boson, See if she is taking water?"

The grizzled boson nodded and dove down an open scuttle. He appeared in a few moments, wet to the waist.

"Aye sir, 'tiz already six feet in the forward well, and rising. Don't know what we coulda hit but 't has killed her I fear,"

"Run quickly," James ordered, "find all the lines you can and tie 'em together afore she founders. Nail the end to an empty water barrel. My God, if she founders at least we'll be able to find her. Tiz somewhat shallow here."

He then commanded, "Wear Ship, Helm up. Sail due west."

Emily was sinking as she moved more and more sluggishly towards the sandy beaches of New Jersey. Before she covered a miles her bows were nearly at the water's edge and still dropping.

James yelled more orders from the quarter-deck, " Make for shore until she goes under. Launch the boats. Prepare to abandon."

Amazingly, *Emily* stayed afloat for another half hour. She put three miles behind her before she simply sailed under the waves and sank. James and the crew took to the boats, keeping in sight of the sinking ship until he was assured that the barrel with the nailed line was afloat. *Emily* could be in no more than a hundred feet of water for he could look down and see her main top ghosting at the limit of visibility below him.

The top of the main mast was eighty feet above the keel. Grasping at any shred of hope in his despair, James knew that the only way the Gold (and his career) could be salvaged would be if there were native pearl divers in the fleet? Could the Royal Navy not dive that deep?

He simply didn't know for sure.

He carefully took and recorded bearings to the shore, then directed the crew to set the lug sails of both boats. Assisted by hard rowing, they made all possible speed back towards Sandy Hook and the Port of New York..

James' mind was reeling. He wasn't sure that it was possible that a diver could dive to *Emily,* but he hoped it could be done. Then again, he thought that the Army engineers might be able to raise the wreck enough to move her to shallower water? He clung to the hope that someone in New York would know how to recover those strongboxes from their shallow watery grave.

Soon the long boat and the gig slid from view, rowing up river towards the city.

Anne Marie's small gray jet boat cleared the entrance of a small inlet two miles to the South of the wreck. As it approached the estimated location of the sinking, David raised the radio to his lips.

"Damn, Jake, they even marked it for us."

"And how," Stephen asked of David, "again, did you sink the Sloop from so far away?"

"It was simple enough really. Last night Jake simply pasted a line of plastique Semtex along beside the keel, and we detonated it this morning with a radio device."

Stephen shook his head. David's answer was totally incomprehensible to him. Still, whatever they had used, it was a simple miracle that all the King's Gold was right there, less than one hundred feet under the bobbing cask. Certainly Jake's magic breathing equipment would make recovery simple.

Three hours later the salvage was completed. It was really quite easy, as the *Emily* had settled almost upright on the bottom. Jake and David merely descended the eighty feet with re-breathers. They entered the cabin through the open skylight, and pried the lock from the little store room in the decking. In short order the twenty boxes full of newly minted gold coins rested on the salon floor of *Anne Marie*, next to the nine boxes taken from the cutter.

"How much is there?" a breathless Connie asked of Stephen after he had finished counting the plunder.

"I make it just over two hundred thousand Crowns," he replied, "and a full third will be granted to *Anne Marie* by Congress as ye'r share."

"Worse the bother," he continued, "my Commission makes me unable to share it with thee."

"Aye," he went on, addressing Jake, "Can thee get me upriver to Bayonne? I've a trusted colonist farmer there who can take Congress' share to General Washington. Ye may as well just keep ye'r ten boxes here."

"Stephen, Stephen, slow down," cautioned Jake.

"The whole damned British Fleet's gonna be sailin' south at any moment. Just as soon as the crew of that ship tells them what happened, they'll be charging out in force, and the wind is fair for them. No, I can't take *Anne Marie* anywhere except straight to sea, and right now."

David chimed-in, "Jake, there's just under an hour's worth of gas left in the jet boat, and we'll not get any more JP5 for quite awhile, if ever. Let's let Stephen take it, and the gold, while we turn and sail east? The other Zodiac with an outboard is still here anyway."

"That 'll work," quipped Jake.

"OKAY with you, Stephen?" he asked, "but you'll have to cut the boat to ribbons ashore and bury it deeply before you leave."

"Aye, and thankee. I'll be sure to sink 'er where t'will never be found, and the General will owe ye yet another debt of thanks."

In a quarter hour the jet boat, weighted down beyond her design with twenty boxes of gold aboard, was a spec on the horizon, pushing like a barge away to the northwest. *Anne Marie* was on a broad reach at twelve knots headed due south.

Jake felt he could clear New York several leagues to the South, then bear to the East, and on to Montauk Point, His instinct told him there would be a far tighter British 'gauntlet' to run while returning to Deerford this time.

"Dad, just how much money is that gold we got?, Connie asked.

"Well", he replied pensively, "that's a bit of a tough question. Money in this century is very differently valued than in ours. But, in rough estimation, a golden Crown, which is an English Pound, is worth something like a $100 dollar bill."

"So", she said, after some thought, "We have, with our estimated seven thousand five hundred guineas, the approximate of seven and a half million dollars. I mean in 2006 money?"

"Aye, my little girl, but it will go a lot farther in this century. If we can manage to keep it, and to use it right, it is enough to set us up well and comfortably in this time."

"Oh God Dad", she wailed. "I want only to go home!"

She continued, "I don't want to live here with all these smelly people, and the blood, and the dirt, and the horrible clothes. I want my pretty room, my clean office and my lab. I want to hear good music, and watch the news on TV. My little Miata is gone, and mostly I miss Mom and my friends."

She started to weep.

David had silently come on deck and heard her . He was looking into Jake's eyes as the girl turned and sobbed in his arms. Jake nodded at him as David hugged her to him.

"Connie, my love," David began gently, "we are simply stuck here, in this time, but not in this place. I promise you we can find a clean and gentle place to live. Somewhere warm, and without the dirt and the rules of where you have been. I know you liked the William's farm."

"It was okay," she said in a small voice, "but the people in the town were insufferable. Their rules and the clothes are horrible."

"Can you trust me to find a clean and new place for us? Somewhere without the rules? Somewhere warm and friendly? I know Jake will help us look in the right place, and we're rich enough to buy our own ship to get there and back."

Jake was nodding, "He's right, Connie. I can think of a dozen places where the living was gentle and relaxed during the nineteenth century. We can't help that we're stuck here, but with this", kicking the gold boxes, "we can make the best of it."

Connie nodded, wiped her wet eyes and David lead her below to their cabin.

Jake held his ketch on course due east all afternoon and into the evening. The wind died after the sun set; the changed motion of the boat waking David and Connie. Allowing her to go back to sleep, David headed up the stairway, knowing Jake would need a break.

"Connie feeling better?" Jake asked.

"Yeah. She's had a rough time of it, and she's really unhappy here. She really liked the Williams family, but I guess she really misses her life as it was. Do you really think we can find somewhere she'll be happy?"

Jake started the engine, moving the boat forward under the stars on the flat ocean .

He replied to David, "I'd think that somewhere in the South would suit her better. Certainly you two can afford a gracious life style where ever you go, but it would seem that a less populated area, somewhere where the climate is gentle may be the best. Let me think about it."

He continued, "Meanwhile, are you okay to keep us on course for a few hours ? I'm bushed."

"Sure, Jake."

Jake awoke hours later when the sound of the throbbing diesel engine stopped. As he awoke he felt the ketch heel over and pick up speed under sail.

He dressed himself and poked his head up the hatch. It had gotten quickly colder. He pulled a sweatshirt over his head, slipped on a windbreaker, and stepped up the deck as the new day was brightening the eastern sky. He found *Anne Marie* sailing close to a freshening northeasterly wind, and he could see two points of land ahead, one on each side of the bow.

"Mornin, David," he said, stepping to the big chrome wheel.

David stood and stretched, saying, "That's Block Island on the right and Montauk to the left. I was guessing that you wanted to again run under Gardner's Island and back through the Gut."

"I'm not too sure about that," Jake replied. "Stephen heard the Brits saying they'd beefed-up the blockade here at the east end of Long Island. We may find it a bit tougher to get past them. Let's sail closer in to Block Island and drop the sails there so we can move closer. For sure, the sun on our sails will give us away if we sail in."

Anne Marie emerged from under the lea of Block Island in the damp 25 knot Nor-Easter several hours later. Jake noted two faint 'blips' on the 'scope, one just inside Plum Gut blocking the southerly entrance to the Sound, and the other just to the east of Fisher's Island, about four miles south of Watch Hill. Both were clearly Royal Navy Blockade Vessels, and they could be presumed to have sharp lookouts.

Worse, the Nor'easter would favor them sailing a broad reach in chase, should they spot *Anne Marie*.

Jake thought his best approach would be to run under power, 'hull down' from the patrols, almost to the Connecticut shoreline. They'd slip as close to the rocky shore as the depth mapping sonar would allow. If they could sneak past the cruiser in Block Island Sound, and run full speed up Fisher's Island Sound with all sails flyin', Jake thought that they ought to be able to break into Long Island Sound, and with a sufficient lead to run past the frigates.

It would have worked, except for Commander John Aaron.

Aaron had specifically called his crew to Quarters two days ago and addressed them sternly, "Ye 'av all seen the Yankee witch ketch we've lost hereabouts. And, ye can be sure she'll be back. We'll be doubling all watches at the mastheads, and me own glass will be with the lookout at the maintop. Ye'll be looking for sail, but likewise be looking for a green hull moving without a sail, for that'll be how she moves. And believe it."

"Aye, and the man what spots 'er 'll have a gold crown for 'is pleasure!"

His actions had paid off. Just the day before they'd spotted a fast brig breaking for New London. *Reliant* pounced and chased it neatly to the waiting *Foxhound*. The cargo of rum and cotton would fetch a nice price in New York.

At mid day it was in fact Ian Sharecross at the main topmast with the Captain's glass who spotted a large unusual burst of spume against the rocky shoreline. Looking hard towards shore he saw a dark green hull dive over one wave top, and into the next. Above the hull were two white masts, ketch rigged, and showing no sail.

"Sail Ho, er Green Ketch in Sight, Cap'n!" he bellowed at the top of his voice just as the ketch broke out from behind the island.

"She's on the larboard bow, close in to the shore."

Aaron ordered *Reliant* to beat to quarters.

In minutes the usual blockade reefs were shaken out of the courses and t'gallents. Under full plain sail they streaked up the Sound on a broad reach, the wake creaming off behind, as the frigate bowled along on her best point of sail.

"Willright, have the log thrown," bellowed Aaron from the windward side of the Quarterdeck.

"Aye aye, sir."

And in several minutes, "Captain," Willright yelled, "Log reads almost 14 knots."

"KABOOM","KABOOM", *Reliant* fired two 32 pounders as signals to *Foxhound*, her Sloop of War consort riding just outside Fisher's Island. That signal told *Foxhound* to clear west under full sail, hopefully to catch the blockade runner as *Reliant'* pushed her out bchind Fisher's Island.

Connie popped up the hatch. She looked around and gasped at the sight of two square rigged warships chasing them, not a mile away!

"Please, Dad, don't let them catch us," she shouted.

"Don't worry, kitten," Jake flashed a grin back.

He was just a bit faster than Aaron had thought possible. As soon as Jake saw the frigate on his weather beam loosening her reefs, he and David immediately raised the main and set a large reaching Genoa. He also had David run a reaching staysail on the mizzen. That kited *Anne Marie* through the water at almost thirteen knots in the increasing nor'easter.

At 13 knots they were fast enough to shoot out from behind Fisher's Island a good mile ahead of the second ship, now also hot on their tail. Further, while the second three masted ship was smaller than the first they had seen, it was also slower. It was visibly drawing behind, while the larger ship seemed to be drawing closer.

Anne Marie was still picking up speed as the mizzen staysail bellied with a crack. Her knot-meter ran up to sixteen as she slid down the back sides of the steep swells, ducking her rail to the cabin house. She slowed to fourteen knots as each swell rolled under the keel.

The frigate seemed to fall slowly behind when Jake saw studding sails appear again on her fore and main t'gallent yards. The large ship healed over sharply, then seemed to leap forward again.

He made a quick decision.

"David" he cried, "Rig the small chute."

"No way she'll carry it," shouted David back.

"She'll have to," Jake hollered as a puff of dirty smoke erupted from the weather bow of the chasing frigate, a water spout appearing but a few yards in their wake.

David, with Connie helping, had never rigged a spinnaker that fast in his life.

Within minutes David was calling to her, "Take up the guy; sail is flying behind the reacher."

The yellow spinnaker popped open, yanking *Anne Marie*'s masts now sharply to leeward, almost pulling the ketch into a full broach.

Connie slacked the spinnaker sheet just in time to get Jake's rudder back under control, then with the sheet winch in low gear, the Spinnaker was more slowly filled with wind. *Anne Marie* leapt forward, the knot-meter literally 'pegging' itself at the 20 KT mark. She was surfing over and through the waves, outrunning the swells.

Jake had never pushed *Anne Marie* this hard, and was thrilled at her performance.

The frigate, studding sails notwithstanding, was no longer gaining. Jake saw her try to add more studding sails to the leeward yardarms, but each time they tried, the sails were simply blanketed.

It was a wild ride, but it was less than 100 miles up the Sound to the Roank's and while *Anne Marie* was outrunning the Frigate, the large ship kept doggedly on their tail.

An hour after the chase began, and with the frigate now about two miles behind, the mizzen staysail blew apart with a huge bang. David and Jake wrestled the shreds to the deck.

Aaron saw the sail on his prey disintegrate. He knew this was the break he needed!

Within fifteen minutes Jake realized they were no longer running from the frigate. Both ships were apparently making the same relative speed giving *Anne Marie* no chance to slip away. He had to do something, but what?

"David," he finally spoke after they had passed Roank's Point in the early evening, "stand by. Here's the only way we may be able to get past them."

Aboard *Reliant*, Aaron was gleeful.

He knew that the damned ketch with the funny round sail simply couldn't get away. Yes, she was fast as the devil, and no. he couldn't quite close with her. But, there was less than thirty miles of Sound, less than two hours at this speed, before the ketch would run into the boom at Hells Gate. He'd have her before sundown!

Suddenly, in a cloud of spray. The green ketch stopped dead in her tracks. Her sails disappeared like magic, and in mere minutes she came back headed right at *Reliant*'s bows. The damned ketch was smashing through the waves, directly up-wind with no sails, and it was moving incredibly fast !

Within a very few minutes Aaron could see her skipper, dressed in yellow, sitting at the helm as the damned ketch headed directly towards *Reliant*'s bow, as if to ram. Both ships were closing on each other at almost 30 knots. Worse, the ketch was aimed to pass under his lea rail, mere yards away. With *Reliant* heeled over in the strong wind, all her guns on that side pointed only at the water rushing by, mere inches from their muzzles.

Aaron, thinking quickly, had but time, himself, to run to the leeward rail, aim the forewardmost six pounder swivel, and pull the firing lanyard as the green ketch ploughed by a stone's throw away.

Instantly he grinned. His chance shot had gone home. He saw that the green ketch was holed!

"Helm Up! All Hands, Wear Ship!" he screamed, knowing it would take him miles to get the studding sails in and work the heavy frigate back to the damaged Yankee witch ship that had almost out-foxed him again. He hoped the ketch would still be floating so he'd have a very unusual prize!

"WHAM."

Aboard *Anne Marie* the round iron six pound ball from the frigate's quarterdeck slammed through the doghouse window, continued through the dinette seats and on through the steel hull, leaving a huge hole. Each time *Anne Marie* nosed down off a wave a fire hose jet of green water spouted upwards. In minutes the water was rising above the floorboards.

David acted by instinct, without asking Jake. He simply tore open the engine hatch

above the screaming diesel and reached under the rising water. His Leatherman knife found the seawater intake line and he sliced sharply through it. Then he ducked further under the rising water and yanked the seacock valve to 'off'. The huge diesel now sucked its coolant water from the bilge instead of the Sound.

He then ran up the ladder to the cockpit and quickly reported the damage and actions to Jake.

"Aye", Jake said following David's quick report. "Let's get her main and jibs up. We'll lay her on the port tack and stack those ten boxes of gold to starboard. That ought to keep the hole above waterline enough for the intake to keep her going. We can duck behind Great Captain's Island and heel her over long enough to do a wet-patch."

"If we can hide until dark," he continued, "we can then slip back to our cove. With any luck we'll be rid of that bastard, for now anyway."

He was staring at the frigate who, having struck her studding sails, was wearing to the same tack. But, clearly the large ship was at least five miles down wind. Jake doubted it could possibly get close enough do any more damage.

Anne Marie was safely hidden in her secret little cove by midnight. The damage was ugly, but not critical..

Best of all though, not only had they recovered Connie, they had successfully stolen the payroll of the British forces in the Colonies. The share earned by Jake would insure financial security for them all in this crazy century.

Aaron watched the Ketch slip behind some small islands as darkness fell. He knew he could not sail that close in shore in the darkness. The ketch was gone.

Reliant returned to her Blockade post.

A week later more dispatches arrived from New York. John Aaron opened a sealed package marked for his personal attention. He read:

My Dear Captain Aaron,

I am loathe to convey that your female prisoner escaped a second time. We know not how she managed to slip from the locked orlop deck past two armed Marines, but she has vanished.

I pray you, Sir, to break your blockade duty and repair to New York forthwith. It is most important that we re-capture this colonial viper and dispatch her to the Admiralty along with the strange materials we still hold.

Sir Wembly Bellows, Post Captain

CHAPTER TEN

"Nope", Jake said aloud, frowning, "that'll need a better fix."

He'd checked David's quick patch over the hole in *Anne Marie*, and found it was leaking slowly at the lower seam. Still, tapping on it, he was sure it would hold a few more days

They had returned to the little cove after their successful return from New York, and after eluding the British frigate. As soon as they were safely anchored the four of them, quite exhausted, slept through the day.

Connie awoke first in the late afternoon

She snuggled closer to David, then remembered her friend Anne.

"David," she whispered in his ear, "we need to let the Williams know that we're okay."

"Hmmmmm," he rolled over and held her tightly, whispering back in her ear and stroking her back, "in a little while, okay?"

She let her fingers play along his chest, "Hmmmmm"

Awhile later, as the sun was setting, they got up and found Jake quietly replacing the shattered window in the salon. He had already removed all the broken pieces the shot had shattered from the seat, exposing David's hasty patch.

"Can you fix it, Dad ?" Connie asked.

"The window and that hole will be easy", he replied, "I'll just careen her tomorrow and weld in a patch. The seat and the cushions, though, are likely more than I can repair with what we have."

He continued, "Oh, young Tad came down to the beach an hour ago and we're invited to dinner. Guess I'll clean up and finish this tomorrow; we should be on our way soon."

Then he glanced at his daughter in her shorts and halter top, "Err, Connie, you might wear something else. These folks are more formal than we're used to."

"Oh Dad !" she spluttered, "you're right though, but I hate their clothes. Let me see what I can find."

Presently the three of them stepped out of the path through the woods and into the yard in front of the house. Connie had found a mid-calf length yellow cotton 'granny skirt' and a long sleeved white eyelet blouse. With a half-slip underneath she looked as 'proper' as she could manage.

The Williams' door was flung open. Anne ran across the yard to hug Connie.

"Oh, ye'r saved! I was so worried. They did not hurt thee? Oh, t'was a terrible thing. Father's even now hired some lads from Bridgeport to guard us."

She stepped back, glanced at David then caught Jakes eyes. She and Jake both held each other's gaze. For long moments neither said anything.

Anne blushed and recovered.

"Please do come in. Father's recovering nicely, and I am sure he wants to hear of thine adventure. How did thee find Connie and get her back?" she chattered as they entered.

They stayed late at the house with the Williams, recounting the events of the past days. Arthur and Tad really could not understand the parts about breathing under water, but they accepted the story. They loved the account of the fracas with the longboats on the Hudson, and were thrilled with Jake's account of 'head-charging' the frigate on the Sound.

All evening Jake sat close to Anne. They stole glances at each other like teenagers.

Anne asked Connie if she would prefer to stay in the house, but Connie demurred. She wanted her hot shower and electricity.

When Jake, David and Connie were finally leaving to go back to the boat Arthur said, from his chair with his bandaged leg up on a stool, "Tiz a fine purse you've won, Jake. Have ye any thoughts of what ye'll do with it?"

Jake shook his head as the three of them walked away.

All the next day, while patching the side of *Anne Marie,* that thought was on Jake's mind. What would they do now?

To make his patch in the hull permanent, Jake warped *Anne Marie* close to the shore and anchored her bow and stern. He then ran a line from the main halyard to the base of a tree and heeled her over. From there he was able to neatly weld a steel patch over the hole, grind it smooth and reapply black bottom paint.

As he then re-anchored the boat and made his way back to Williams' house for dinner he thought he had a plan, which would, of course, take

Arthur's agreement. And, under his arm were the sodden remains of the cabin cushions. Anne had volunteered to do what she could to sew them back together, although Jake didn't think that quite possible.

A week later Jake was standing in the orchard on the hill in the center of the two acres of land he had just purchased from Arthur. It was, of course, the same plot of land he'd left that June. He'd also hired twenty lads from Bridgeport, and another ten locally. These were his laborers, digging a foundation for the house he'd drafted, while also serving as sentries and guards against further British attacks.

Yes, he smiled to himself, he would have the same house he'd left; it was perfectly re-planned. It would be exactly the same.

His next task would be to cross to the little bay behind William's Cove and purchase the same plot of land on which his shipyard had stood. Now it was simply a rocky small farm with a small house and barn that had been owned by a Tory family who had fled to New York. Arthur had advised him that it could be had for a good price.

Jake was anxious to begin building ships again.

Yes, he'd told himself that he could design and build ships that would be just barely ahead of the current times. In fact, he'd decided that he would primarily design large ships for others to build and use his yard for smaller fast coastal and fishing vessels. After all, he remembered, that was the family history, was it not?

Aaah, but it was a hot afternoon. He was sweating inside his heavy cotton shirt and woolen pants with knee high silk stockings, as was proper summer dress for a colonial gentleman (or so he had been told by Anne and Arthur Williams). He supposed they were right. His life was in this Century now and he felt obliged to blend into the culture. But, oh he longed for his air conditioned Dodge Ram V12 Crew Cab pickup and a light cotton T-shirt today!

He saw dust rise off the road. Then a wagon appeared plodding down the lane. It was just a little two wheeled affair, shabby and well worn, drawn by an old and bony horse with ribs like a washboard under a swayed back. A grizzled stout old man with a white beard was the sole occupant. A pile of boxes was stacked about him on the wagon bed.

"Hallooo, be thee Mister Shaw?" the gent hollered as the wagon entered the cleared land from the dirt roadway.

Jake walked his horse towards the now stopped wagon.

He answered, "Yes, I'm Jake Shaw."

"Heard in t'village that ye may seek shipwrights here?" the old guy ventured.

"Yes," replied Jake, holding his hand out and shaking the other's, "it is right I am planning to start a shipyard. In fact my friend Mr. Williams is offering on the land for me as we speak. I want to build small coastal merchant vessels. I've good designs of ships, but will need a foreman who's experienced in the building. My name's Jake Shaw."

"Aye, Thaddeus Jones at ye'r service, sir," spoke the older gent with a twinkle in his sharp blue eyes.

"Heard tell that ye had a mite of good fortune with a prize at sea, and wantin' to settle ye'rself here to build ships. Least that's what I heard at the Crown Pub in Deerford."

"Can you follow plans?" Jake asked, "I've no shipyard yet, that will take some time, but I need to get my house built."

He rolled his house drawings out across the back of the little wagon asking, "Can you follow these?

"Aye, sir. Tiz a fine set of drawings ye've here. Aye, can see ye need masons for these stone walls and good carpenters too."

"Mr. Jones, if you can start for me here as my foreman on this house we can move you to my shipyard when I get the land purchased. Would that work for you to start?"

"Aye sir, 'tiz work I'm needing. If ye'll give me a chance I think ye'll be pleased with me work," Jones replied gazing directly into Jake's eyes.

Jake returned the direct eye contact replying, "Thaddeus Jones what brings you to the Roank?"

" Mister Shaw, I were owner of a small yard at Fulton Street in New York, left to me by me departed wife's father. The double damned British took over the yard, but not afore their soldiers was quartered in me house an' raped me little girl, Turned 'er inter a little trollop they did, and it kilt me wife. I couldna stand 't so when the wife passed I done burnt the yard in the night 'n left the city. Been fixin' blockade damage to Yankee traders at Norwalk since, but wantin to git to building 'em again."

"Aye, Mr. Jones," Jake then told the story he had hatched with Arthur.

"My father sent me to the Continent in '55 to study ship building with the French, but when I came home in '62 the family needed captains and traders, not ship builders, so I've been to sea since. Got lucky with a rich British prize last year. Family yard was burned out in Tidewater so I've come here. Need a good foreman to build to my plans, first this house and then I'll build a shipyard, the location I've in mind is but two miles east of where we stand."

Continuing, he said, "Mr. Jones, you seem to know of shipbuilding, and if you don't I'll soon know. Ye'll find my plans may be a bit different from what you've built in the past. If I hire you as my foreman, what pay do you need?"

"Well," Jones replied, "if I'm to do thee a proper job I'll need live at ye'r yard when it's built, and if ye'll provide a house I'll be ye'r man. But it'll not be cheap to get me best. An' it'll not be Continental dollars neither, golden guineas only. Seems a guinea per month plus ten percent of each vessel sold will —"

"Woah there!", stopped Jake, "ten percent?"

"Aye, it dinda hurt to ask thee now," Jones replied, looking abashed.

"Five percent, and only after the ship's sold and paid, unless I keep her myself in which case I'll still pay you your share of the fair value."

"Agreed," said Jones, "And me hand on't."

He firmly shook Jake's hand again.

Together they then walked over to where the young men were digging the foundation, stripped to their waists in the heat. Jake introduced Mr. Jones to the work crew, after which they sat under an apple tree while Jake outlined the plans for the shipyard. Mr. Jones had only compliments for the layout, and was anxious to get started just as soon as Jake could secure the land.

"Okay, we'll give it a try," finalized Jake.

He then called to the young men digging behind the ropes pegged to the ground in the foundation, "lads, this is Mr. Jones. He'll be the foreman for me."

"Mr. Jones", he continued, directing his voice to the older man, "it is time we ended work for today. If you'll come back at eight tomorrow morning and get these boys started I'll be up later. I may have more news about my purchase of land for the yard. Is that satisfactory?"

A simple "aye." was the reply.

Jake headed back down the lane towards the farm..

Jake and Arthur had worked long into the night a week ago, the second evening after Jake, Connie and David had returned from recovering the gold from the sloop they sank. They enjoyed each other's company and Jake learned a great deal about the culture of his new environment from his new friend. Arthur had offered a room in his house to Jake, who was happy to accept. He wanted to leave the privacy of *Anne Marie* to Connie and David.

Arthur had tried to have Connie move to the house too, explaining that it was really improper in those times for an unmarried couple to live alone. Still, Connie could not be budged. She insisted on staying where she had the comforts of home and the privacy to wear her own clothing. And, no, Jake really did not want to intrude on the young couple.

He'd simply have to find a way to get them properly married, and soon.. David and Connie only wanted to spend some time alone together.

She had been unhappy and irritable after they'd all truly faced the simple fact that the crew of *Anne Marie* was likely never going to be able to return to the twentieth century. Connie had been doubly anxious to clean-up the mess below decks in *Anne Marie*. Yes, she had understood that the three of them would need to learn to adjust to eighteenth century, like it or not , but she decidedly did not like it.

After their first night ashore, Connie simply had taken David's hand and walked him to the boat, hardly saying goodnight.

Anne had whispered to Jake, "She'll need some time, sir. She misses her home so. Ye'll be welcome here while we find thee a place of your own."

That second evening, satisfied with his repairs to the ketch, and after a sumptuous dinner, Jake had seated himself in a straight backed chair with Anne across from him, and Arthur to his right. He was uncomfortably aware that he could hardly keep his eyes away from Anne, really wanting to speak just to her alone, but also very aware that he was technically still married to his wife, Martha, left behind in the twentieth century.

Still, Anne had let her long dark hair down, falling over her shoulders. It highlighted her strong jaw line and her startling green eyes. She wore no make-up, and clearly needed none. Regardless that her proper dress covered her from her neck line to her ankles, the slender and firm body under the dress was alluring to Jake. It wasn't easy to focus all his conversation primarily towards business with Arthur, allowing Anne to interject her thoughts from time to time. He really wanted to spend time alone with Anne.

He'd banished the thought, at least for now.

It was Arthur who first offered Jake a home site, accepting Jake's request for the orchard. He further knew of the parcel on the river for the shipyard, and he who suggested that Jake represent himself as a former Virginian who had moved to Nassau and owned a pair of privateers, from whence came the source of Jake's newly found fortune. That also would explain Jake's differently accented English language. It allowed him some degree of eccentricity and deviations from the local Anglican Church strict behaviors.

Still, Arthur and Anne were both emphatic that none of that relieved Jake of the half-day every Sunday attendance at the local Deerford Church, nor of the need that he purchase and learn to wear a complete colonial wardrobe of mostly hot and tightly buttoned clothing.

He did refuse the wig. And, he hated the clothes, as did Connie.

At the end of that first evening Arthur also offered him a guest room.

As Anne escorted him up the stairs she'd quipped, "And, thank you for naming your beautiful little ship after me, although it's probably just happenstance."

"Pardon?", queried Jake, turning on his way through the guest room door.

"Aye, my full name is Anne Marie."

She turned away with a swirl of her gingham skirt towards her own room, just next to his.

As Jake undressed and climbed onto the high feather bed he could hear Anne next door, also getting undressed for bed. Jake's mind filled with thoughts of how she'd look, outlined in a sheer nightgown with the moonlight glowing through the window.

"No!"

He told himself that she was Arthur's daughter, and he was married to Martha.

Or was he, he mused as he drifted to sleep? Was he not really now a widower? Could he think of a future with Anne? In any event, he knew he should not stay here for long; he'd perhaps move up to the inn for awhile.

He fell asleep smiling.

The next morning when Jake went to the boat for his clothes and the personal things he would need at the inn Connie was even more adamant. She wouldn't wear the colonial clothes. And, while she liked both Anne and Arthur Williams, she was haunted by that British Captain. She was simply terrified that, with David by her side or not, and regardless of the now thirty man private security force, the British would keep hunting her down.

Jake agreed that Connie and David could, at least for now, enjoy the comforts and privacy of *Anne Marie*, safely moored in the hidden little cove. The two enjoyed an idyllic break from the times, notwithstanding that Jake was sure Anne would always disapprove of an unmarried couple living together.

He'd seen them again yesterday, on a Sunday morning, when Jake had strictly told the couple that they must appear in church in Deerford with the Williams Family. Connie protested, but Jake had his reasons.

"Darling," he had reasoned, "in this century you two can not continue to live together. It's just not acceptable. You need to get married, and just as soon as we can arrange it.".

David had chimed in, "we're overdue anyway, Connie."

"So, why do I need get dressed in that horrible hot clothing and sit all day in a stuffy church before we marry?" she'd asked.

Jake replied, "I'm sure you've noticed that things are a lot more formal here, girl. To be properly married means you both need the advance blessing of the parson, and we need to post banns so anyone with an objection can voice them in advance."

"And how long are these bans?" asked Connie archly.

"Usually at least a month," Jake had replied, "but, Anne tells me that since we're newcomers to the area, and we're sponsored by Arthur, we can do it in a week or two. But, you need to be in church every Sunday in the mean time."

"Really, Dad, what's with you and Anne anyway? Sounds like she's running our lives."

David interjected, "Hey Connie, leave your Dad alone. He just wants the best for us, and so does Anne."

Then he said, "Its okay, Jake. We'll be ready in a few minutes."

They'd all gone to church in the William's coach, and the Parson had posted their bans, formally introducing them to the congregation. They were to be married, in the same church as originally planned, a week from the coming Saturday. It was just a couple hundred years earlier than they had thought.

Yesterday afternoon, after they'd arrived back at the farm, Jake discussed his wedding present with David.

"Son", he'd said, "we both know how unhappy Connie is here. She barely leaves *Anne Marie*, and dresses in local clothing only once a week. Heck, you both won't even come to the Farm for dinner with the Williams and me unless I come and drag you over. Even then, Anne is a bit scandalized by Connie's freedom of dress. And, it'll get worse when the weather gets colder."

He continued, "Now, I do understand that women particularly, in this century, are a great deal more restricted in most things than Connie likes. I can't blame her."

David nodded, "Yes, she really isn't happy. It's hard to keep her from actually crying every night."

"Well, I've an idea," forwarded Jake. "What would you think of a sailing voyage, perhaps south, to a safe area?"

"You mean, you'd let us take *Anne Marie?*"

Jake replied, "That may not be the best idea, David. Anywhere you go, she's simply too different in rig and appearance. It'd only bring you trouble.

No, I was thinking of a small, fast coastal trader. Of course, we could make if comfortable for Connie. *Anne Marie* needs to stay hidden here in the cove covered with tarpaulins just in case a casual traveler might pass."

Jake continued, "Arthur told me of a sweet little six-gun brig of about eighty feet with a crew of fourteen and a fine young mariner named Phillip Strong as Master. She's just finished building in New Bedford of cedar built on a proper oak frame"

"David, she's finely sparred and said to be quite fast" Jake concluded. And, she's for sale?" David asked.

Jake replied, "Arthur knows her master and owner, a fine young Patriot named Phillip Strong, who commissioned her building to go privateering. He apparently lost his money in another privateering venture. He's got to sell to clear his debts."

"Where is she," David queried?

"She lies now at Essex on the Connecticut River, a comfortable two day ride. It's only about sixty miles. Are you interested in her? If so Arthur will draft us a letter of introduction to Captain Strong."

"Okay, Jake", replied David. "If I like her I presume we could simply sail her back here to the Cove."

That was just yesterday. Yes, a lot had happened since their foray to New York.

Jake walked back down the hill and towards the William's farm, leaving Mr. Jones to dismiss the lads from their digging. He was feeling better knowing the house work would go onward while he and David could go look at the brig Arthur had found.

The next morning, in a light shea drawn by two horses, Jake and David stopped at the site of the new house while on their way to the Post Road and Essex. They found Mr. Jones just rising from a bed he'd made in his wagon.

"Morning, Mr. Jones," greeted Jake, "I thought you'd be staying at the Crown?"

"Nay, Sir. Must be careful with me funds these troubled times."

"Aaah, cannot have my foreman sleeping in the open, can I? Here, sir, is a Guinea, your first month paid in advance. And, until we get a shipyard started, I can pay you a two Guineas each month. Will that keep you comfortable at the Crown for awhile?"

"Aye, sir," Thaddeus bowed his head, "ye'r most generous. I'll be making sure ye'r house proceeds."

"We'll be away for a day or so. If you need anything you can ask at the Williams farm."

"Aye, sir," came the strong reply.

Jake wheeled the two horses around and guided the little surrey back down the lane.

Late that the next evening Jake and David arrived in the exceedingly pretty little town of Essex, which Jake noticed had been largely unchanged into the twentieth century. As instructed by William, he inquired at the Inn for Captain Strong. The word "Crown" on the inn's sign had been painted over. Crude hand lettering replacing it with the word "Patriot". Still, everyone still called it the "Crown Inn" as it had been for over 100 years.

Phillip Strong kept a room at the Inn, and shortly met them in the Pub Room.

Jake liked him immediately. He was a short stout young man, built like a barrel, with long thick arms and short legs. He was apparently enormously strong and well suited to his name. After the bar maid left a pewter pint of warm beer for the three of them Jake and Phillip began to negotiate for the brig.

After several hours and a shared leg of lamb the three reached an understanding. They retired to their rooms, agreeing to meet the next morning to inspect the vessel before a deal could be struck..

Phillip explained on the way to the pier in the morning that he, as second mate of a privateer, had shared in two successful voyages clearing just less than three hundred pounds. He'd used a part to start construction on his little ship, planning to command her himself on another raiding voyage. And, with the larger share of his winnings, he'd invested in the fitting out of his former ship for her next voyage.

She had been captured by the British, and with it went his ability to pay the note on the completion of the new ship.

"Have you named her yet?" Jake asked.

"Nay, Sir. She's just finished fitting out. I was knowing I may have to sell her. Should be the right of the first owner to name a vessel, although I was hoping to find someone to put up the funds so I could command her against British cargos. I could return thee a fat profit."

He looked at Jake beseechingly, and waved at a two masted vessel of about eighty feet length.

Jake smiled, said nothing, and walked the pier looking critically at the ship. She bobbed slightly to the small waves in the river, apparently quite light and agile. He appreciated the rake of the masts and the simple but clean single flush deck.

He walked aboard, followed by David. Strong waved off the single armed guard.

Below decks Jake took hours crawling through every accessible opening.. He then climbed to each masthead. David, especially, noted the large and airy Master's Cabin in the stern with its large opening ports in the transom.

Finally Jake looked at David asking, "Will Connie like it?"

David just nodded.

Jake addressed Captain Strong saying, "Aye, Captain she'll do nicely. I'll want a bit of reworking on the rig, but should not be much of a bother. Let's go back to the Pub and discuss terms."

Four hours later Jake owned a new brig, which he promptly named *"Martha Shaw"*. He also engaged Captain Phillip, as he now referred to him, and the captain's suggested mate with fourteen known youths as crew. Jake had clearly stated that the ship would not be used as a Privateer, but mostly for a voyage of exploration. Still, he promised that the Master and crew would be well paid.

David had started to object to an outside Captain, but Jake silenced him quickly.

"Just what do you know about how to handle a two masted brig with square sails and a crew of fourteen?" he asked with a twinkle in his eye.

The next morning Jake went to work with drafting paper, sketching the changes he wanted made to the rig of *Martha*. He took the finished plan to Captain Phillip. At first Captain Phil objected, as it was a departure from current standards, but Jake showed him the benefits of additional fore and aft sails and fewer squares.

"What do ye call this rig?" Phillip asked.

"It is a brigantine," replied Jake.

"She'll be just as fast off the wind as any brig, but she'll claw to weather like a witch. It's my own design, and, when you get her rig altered you can bring her to the inlet behind Roank point."

"Aye, Sir, be that near Deerford? I hear all that land is the Williams Farm and tiz no place to go ashore."

"You'll be welcome. We'll be staying at the inn in town. You can find me there."

"Aye then, we should be there within in ten days time, that is if the damned redcoats don't have a blockade vessel in the Sound."

"Good then", and turning to David Jake said, "We've still several hours' daylight, perhaps we can get to that nice inn in Branford?"

For David and Connie's honeymoon Jake had thought to send them south in *Martha* to search for live oak trees on the Florida Gulf Coast. He knew he'd need a source of that precious wood for the knees and ribs of the ships he would build, as well as for the floor beams and roof joists of his house. He was also aware that there was little British activity in the Gulf of Mexico, so they should be safe. In fact, it was reported that the French controlled the area, and they were friendly to the Revolution.

On the ten hour ride back from Essex, and during their dinner at the inn at Branford, Jake discussed his thoughts deeply with David, educating him on exactly what he sought. He suggested that David and Connie take a hold full of hardware and tools as trading cargo.

"And, he suggested, "a dozen barrels of rum may be useful too."

David thought it all was a grand idea, quipping, "It's interesting that my family history is claimed to have roots in Pensacola anyway."

As soon as they arrived back at William's, David jumped down from the shea and headed for the path to the cove.

"I'll tell Connie about our plans," he said over his shoulder as he walked across the yard, "I think she'll like it."

Jake was certain that David, with Captain Phil's knowledgeable assistance, could elude the British blockades in the fast and handy brigantine. And, Connie would have time with David to reconcile herself to their fate. If they left the last week of August they should be back in about six weeks, before it would start to get cold.

Jake turned the little wagon around and headed back up the lane to town, uncomfortable to seek more of Williams' hospitality. Yes, he was more and more attracted to Anne, not wanting to admit to himself that he really didn't miss Martha terribly. His solace was to throw himself into the building of the house, and he was looking forward to getting involved in the shipyard as soon as he could.

For now, he told himself, he should see Arthur and Anne only on Sundays during those interminable church services, and perhaps for Sunday dinners.

Just as the sun was setting through the trees ahead of him Jake pulled his shea off the lane to allow a large farm wagon to pass in the rutted Post Road. It was Tad Williams.

"Mr. Shaw, greetings sir," accosted the handsome youth, "what brings thee to town on a Wednesday evenin? Had thought ye'd be at the Cove all week? "

"Hello, Tad. Indeed, I've finished the repairs, and have started work on my house, but I've had the good fortune to have engaged a skilled foreman to work my crews. I've trespassed on your family's fine hospitality too long already, so I'll be comfortable at the inn for awhile. It's off to the Inn for me, at least for now."

"Nae, Sir! If Anne should learn that I let thee pass on to the Inn she'll 'av me hide, older sister and all. An' me father e'll 'av the rest. No sir, ye must return to the Farm with me, tiz almost closer than the Inn from 'ere. Anne keeps saying she's seen almost none of thee."

Jake knew he'd have to accept, so he hitched his horses to the wagon and climbed up next to Tad.

It wasn't that he was avoiding the Williams, he just was uncomfortably aware of his growing feelings for Anne which he was not sure were reciprocated. Yet, as they crossed the yard pulling to up the grassy lane to Arthur's house Jake was thrilled to see Anne bustle out the door, recognize him in the Wagon, set down the pail in her hand and flash him a warm, seeming very personal, smile.

He smiled back warmly, jumped down from the wagon and walked towards her. Without even thinking he put his arm around her and smiled into her deep green eyes. Jake had an irresistible urge to bend down and kiss her smiling lips when they both heard the pounding of another galloping horse clatter into the clearing.

It was Stephen! It had been over three weeks since they'd seen him. Still, he was unexpected.

Stephen leapt off the horse and grasped an astonished Jake's hand, clapped him on the back, and exclaimed, "Jake, sir, 'tiz pleased I am to have found thee so quickly. I've news for ye, and, throwing a meaningful glance into Anne's eyes, we hope ye'll again help our cause? Let us find Arthur and I'll explain"

CHAPTER ELEVEN

Stephen looked terrible.

As soon as they got inside the house he sagged down in an armchair next to Arthur. Jake noted that he apparently hadn't shaved for days, and he had deep fatigue lines etched under his eyes. His clothes were crumpled and dirty, and he'd not bathed in awhile. No, Stephen had not arrived in Deerford for a social visit; he must be on another serious mission.

Stephen quaffed a tall class of water that Anne had brought in and attacked the plate of bread and cheese. With his mouth still full of bread and cheese he addressed Jake.

"First, I did get thine gold to Washington. He is still camped near Trenton, but is preparing to march south to meet Howe's army. The Red Coats have come ashore in Maryland, on the Chesapeake, and will soon march on Philadelphia."

He continued, "The General sends his deep thanks for ye'r package, which was sent on to the Congress. The whole Government is in readiness to move to York in Pennsylvania if Howe gets close. He asked me to again let thee know he's deeply thankful for ye'r successes in New York. Without the win o'that pot o' gold, both Continental Armies would be mostly deserted by now. Seems like a lot of money, but truly t'was just enough to pay the creditors and a little to the troops, without which many would have deserted."

"From there I was sent to Albany in New York with urgent messages for General Gates and General Arnold."

"These are terrible times."

"Howe is advancing on Philadelphia and Bergoin has an army of regulars and Hessian cavalry marching south through New York. When I reached Arnold he had just learned that Fort Ticonderoga fell to Bergoin and he's on the move again. If Bergoin's army can get past Gates and Arnold, there's nothing to stop them from cutting our Colonies in half."

"We'll not survive that."

Stephen rose to his feet.

"Jake, might we take a bit of a walk? The rest I've to tell thee is really most urgent and secret."

He bowed at Arthur then nodded towards Anne, "I trust ye'll excuse us for a few moments?"

Jake followed Stephen through the yard and around the paddock to the lane that ran to the end of the point. As soon as they were well away from the house Stephen started again.

"Aye, terrible times. We can do nothing to help Washington's plans to thwart Howe's march on Philadelphia. Those army's will come to the test somewhere south of the city. But, Jake, we may be able to help Benedict Arnold in New York."

By now they'd reached the end of the point. The sun was setting into the Sound in a red blaze of glory. They sat on a large flat rock. Seagulls were wheeling overhead and horseshoe crabs were creeping through the mossy rocks at the water's edge.

"Aye", Stephen resumed, "Washington has moved from Trenton where he hopes to bottle-up Howe before he gets to the Capitol. But the more dangerous fight will be in New York somewhere north of Albany. Should Arnold and Clinton be defeated the Red Coats can take the Hudson. They will have split our colonies asunder."

"With all of New York from Canada to the sea in their hands, and Howe in our Capital, we'll be finished. Our Colonies, split north from south, can not stand."

Jake stood up and paced a few steps back and forth along the muddy beach, deep in thought. The moon appeared to the east, almost full.

He stopped, looking out at the Sound, and said, "Hmmmm, Stephen. I can tell you, and in strictest of secrecy only, that my studies of this period tell that Benedict Arnold will prevail at a town named Saratoga. I also remember something about his Hessian cavalry being short of horses. Hmmmm, something about horses lost at sea."

Jake sat back down on the flat rock next to Stephen.

"Have you heard any reports about any shortage of horses in Burgoyne's Army?" he queried.

Stephen looked puzzled, "Horses? How could thee know?"

"Yes," Jake interrupted, "I remember studying this Battle. Unless my history studies were wrong, Burgoyne's Hessian cavalry does not have the large horses they need, and they're marching on foot."

"Tell me Stephen, is there not a valley or town in New Hampshire that is well renowned for raising fine large horses? I seem to remember a battle won by a colonist leader named John Stark and 2000 of his Vermont army in, hmmmm. Yes, it was Bennington."

Stephen looked almost stunned.

He asked quietly, "how could thee know of our urgent mission? I've traveled 120 miles in just two days to see if thee can help Mr. Starke in Bennington. Arnold just learned two days ago from his Indian scouts that a body of eight hundred Hessians is marching on Bennington afoot. They plan to raid the horse farming there. If they are mounted our boys can't stand against them."

He went on, "but, Jake, methinks ye'r recollection is wrong. John Stark does not have an army of 2000 Vermont lads. Nae, those lads are with Clinton and Arnold already. I saw him just two days ago; he left Albany with me."

"Yes, John Starke has ridden ahead to Whitehall Junction and Bennington, but he's no militia of thousands. Nae sir, he fears the only resistance he can find will be old men and young boys, and not many of them either."

Jake stopped pacing.

"I can't doubt you, Stephen but my history lessons were very clear. There will be a battle in Bennington in just over three days time, and Starke will win it."

"Tiz not possible." Stephen interjected, shaking his head.

"A few farm boys and old men simply can not stand to eight hundred hardened Hessians, even if they are afoot."

Jake digested this then sat back on the large stone, deep in thought.

"Stephen," he said thoughtfully after awhile, "it's against everything in my nature to do anything here that will make a change, but it seems we just have to make certain that the damned Hessians do not get those horses. I mean, Starke must prevail in Bennington. That's the way it happened. But, if he has not the men, then perhaps we do need to be there to help."

He paused and thought for awhile, then said slowly, "guess it couldn't hurt to be there to make sure things turn out as history will be written."

"Well, then," Jake stood to return to the farm, " I know our mission."

"If those Hessians overrun Bennington, and get their damned horses, then the path of history will change. Indeed, Stephen, we need to get there to help Mr. Starke if he truly needs it. It's truly critical."

"But", he continued quickly, "the Battle in Bennington was fought on August 16th. Today is the twelfth, which leaves us only two days to get north. How can we travel a hundred and twenty odd miles in just two days?"

Stephen replied, "If Arthur will give us his coach and four we can ride straight through. We can buy fresh horses on the way. If we start right away we have a chance."

"No, " answered Jake, "we've a lot to do before we can leave here. It may take us all night to get ready, and I'll need your help. Here's what we need to do."

Jake outlined his plan.

When they arrived back at the farm house it was quiet. Jake thought all the William's had retired. They all had, except Anne, who was sewing by candle light as they entered.

"Stephen," she said as she stood and stretched, "ye'll not mind sleeping in with Todd?"

She then lit a candle and handed it to him,. "And, Jake, good night to thee."

Jake interrupted, "Anne, we can't stay. Stephen has brought a most immediate situation to me. We must prepare now and leave tonight. Is Arthur still awake? I don't know if he can help, but the loan of your coach for a few days would be most appreciated."

Anne stopped and turned to Jake, "ye'll not be in any danger, will thee?"

Stephen smiled to himself as Jake stroked Anne's shoulder lightly. My, he thought, but they made a fine looking couple.

An hour later found Jake and Stephen on the trail back to the cove and *Anne Marie*. Jake had explained that he was very short on bullets for the machine pistols. Apparently he had recovered all the casings from all the rounds fired so far, but they needed to be re-filled.

When Jake had purchased the weapons, years ago in Miami, he had picked-up a cartridge press and a small box of caps. The store had been overstocked and gave them away almost free. He wouldn't carry gunpowder on *Anne Marie*, that was too dangerous, but he knew that the box of projectile moulds and caps was somewhere in his equipment locker.

They arrived at *Anne Marie* with a small keg of black powder and a very heavy sack of lead ingots. Connie and David were curled on the couch in the salon watching a movie on DVD.

"Sorry to break in on you two," Jake started, "but Stephen and I have some urgent business for a few days and we need to do some work here to get ready."

"Where are you going, Dad?" Connie yawned.

"Just a little side trip for a few days. We'll be long back for your wedding."

Then Connie saw Stephen.

She and David both stood, David saying, "Hey Stephen, didn't expect to see you so soon. Will you be here long enough to be in our wedding?"

"Nay, wouldn't miss it."

David continued, "Time we were off to bed anyway. Connie, I'm sure your Dad and Stephen have things to do. We'll just be in their way."

After the youths went forward to their cabin, Jake told Stephen that he too should get some rest; Jake said that he could do what he needed alone. Stephen didn't argue. He just stretched out on the cushions and was snoring lightly in moments.

Jake dug through the equipment room and appeared back at the table in the salon with a sealed metal box. He cleared the salon table and covered it with a blanket.

Simply, after the past two excursions the cartridge clips for the AK 47's were almost all empty. Still, each gun had a cartridge-catching bag to recover the spent casings, Fortunately Jake had what he needed to refill those empty clips.

He and Stephen had come aboard with a small keg of gunpowder, No, it was not modern smokeless powder, it was old fashioned black powder, but it would do.

Jake went to work.

He put a small bar of lead into his black iron pan and set it over a high flame on the propane stove. He then set a heavy black steel cube on the blanket. It was a projectile mould designed to cast bullets to fit the diameter of the AK 47 casings. The lead went into the top and, in a few minutes, after it cooled, the bottom could be slid off and a quick dunking in ice water made the new lead bullets slide out.

Jake refilled the mould over and over for several hours, making a large salad bowl full of perfect lead castings.

He then opened the cartridge press. He inserted twenty casings in their little slots, then dropped a percussion cap in each. He carefully filled each casing with black powder to the top of the ridge, the lead bullets going in the top half of the press. Pressing the halves together Jake had twenty new cartridges. It took him about five minutes to make them.

After three hours his eyes were bleary and his hands were aching, but he'd made 2,000 fresh new loads. He then re-loaded the gun magazines. Exhausted from the night's work he set his watch to wake him in just two hours, at first light.

"Hallow on *Anne Marie*."

It was Todd, calling from the rocky beach just before dawn.

"Hello Todd", called back Jake, "please bring the coach and four to the head of the path, we've quite a bit to load."

The youth nodded, waved, and ran back towards the house.

Within the hour Jake and Stephen were inside William's large coach with two of the local militia boys driving the four horses at a gallop. They headed east on the Post Road in a dash to try to get to Bennington and to find John Starke.

Jake fell asleep for most of the morning, awakening when the coach stopped to cross the river on a ferry at Bridgeport. Then he woke again at a small inn on the other side of the river.

"Change of horses," Stephen quipped, "'Eees be done in for now."

The four horses from Williams' Farm had barely been able to haul the heavy coach up the stony river bank from the ferry. While the four tired beasts were lead away and four fresh horses bridled Stephen passed some coins to the inn keeper who returned to the coach with a slab of cold meat, a slice of cheese and some bread.

"Don't mind we eat as we move?"

"Not at all," said Jake, "I'm worried we'll not get there in time, or that the Hessians will be in front of us."

"Think we'll be all right," Stephen offered with a mouth full of food, "Hessians'll be marching from the west. I've us following the coast and we'll cut north through Sturbridge and Worcester. If the weather holds, and providing we can keep finding fresh horses, we should get to Bennington late tomorrow night."

"Fresh horses could be difficult then?"

"Nae, sir. I've paid back there to board Jake's matched foursome to our return; he'd not like to loose the set. But 'tiz usual that 'orses are traded along a busy highway as we'll be following. May just have to wake an innkeeper or two as we pass through the night, and tiz good ye've ye'r purse."

Busy highway, thought Jake? It seemed a mere dirt roadway wandering alongside brooks and between green fields in the mid-summer afternoon. They passed farm after farm with all the fields lined out by rock walls. The only trees were those left alongside the dirt road and a few for shade in the yards of the farmhouses. The coach bounced and swayed as it was skillfully driven behind the four horses, who seemed able to go on and on at an easy canter. They, slowed down to a trot only going up the hills.

Jake was amazed at the differences in the countryside from his last drive to New England from his home. Yes, he had come pretty much the same way, driving up Route 95 to Stratford, cutting over to the Merritt Parkway and following that to Hartford where he would pick up I-84 to the Massachusetts Turnpike and on into Boston. His last trip had taken three hours in his Ram pick-up. But, the last time he was here the ride was through deep green forests almost all the way, except through the more industrial areas near New Haven and Hartford. There had been no cleared fields, barns, or herds of dairy cows.

He sat in the upholstered back seat of the plush coach all afternoon gazing out the open window as colonial Connecticut rushed past at breakneck speed; at all of nine to ten miles per hour.

It was after dark when they crossed the Thames River on another ferry just south of Hartford. Jake bought a pot of stew and bread from another inn and traded the spent horses and four guineas for their fourth fresh set of mounts. They rattled again off in the darkness. Jake and Stephen dozed on the soft seats while the lads from Bridgeport took turns driving.

Late the next day, the fifteenth, they crossed the Connecticut River by ferry at White River Junction, and posted on toward to the horse farming communities of Andover and Franklin.

At the inn in Franklin they asked the whereabouts of John Starke.

"Aye," the innkeeper had replied, "Ees but arrived this afternoon and in fact 'ees booked a room 'ere. If ye'll have a seat and a flagon 'eel likely be back soon."

Just then they heard horses gallop up outside. The door banged open and a wiry short man wearing buckskin trousers and an open white cotton shirt entered the inn, followed by several older farmers.

"John, ye've made it. Pleased t'see thee," smiled Stephen.

"Aye, and be this the stranger of whom ye've spoken?" the wiry man asked looking at Jake.

Stephen made the introductions, after which they sat in a booth at the back of the taproom.

"I canna be telling thee how he knows, John, but Mr. Shaw here has a convincing belief that ye'r Hessians can be stopped in Bennington. What have thee for a force to turn them back?"

"I don't know where ye get ye'r information, Mr. Shaw," Sharpe scratched his beard, "but if'n we can get all the able bodied souls who 'ave any gun at all, t'will be not more than eighty souls. And, Bennington still is a fair piece from 'ere. What makes thee think we few old men and a small number of boys can turn back a ten-fold force of hardened Hessians? And, why Bennington instead of here? Lord knows I tried to get that damned Arnold to give me a brigade of 'ees troops, but he'd not let 'em go."

"John, Mr. Shaw insists it can be done in Bennington. And," glancing with an eyebrow lifted at Jake, "if ye'll give Mr. Shaw a bit of ye'r time he can take thee for a bit of a private walk and show ye how we can help stop the blasted redcoats."

"I've little time for foolishness but, aye, shall we take a walk, Mr. Shaw?"

Jake nodded and led the wiry bearded man out to the coach. He opened the boot in the back and withdrew a canvas bag.

"Please walk with me over that small hill where there are no people about."

Stephen waited five minutes, heard a volley of shots, and then followed. As he strode up to the two men at the crest of the hill and behind a stone wall Jake had the canvas bag closed again.

"What think ye, John?" Stephen queried.

"Coor, sir, 'av never seen the likes ov it! And 'ee say ye've two of these horrible French secret guns? Mr. Shaw tells me there's but two of those wicked Godless things ever made and 'ee's got 'em both right 'ere."

Jake just nodded as Sharpe continued

"'Ee also says that ye'r arrival here is the work of the Lord meant to prevail 'eer, and that if we can keep the damned Germans from our 'orses, it'll end in winning our freedom. Hard to believe, that."

Both Jake and Stephen continued to smile quietly at Sharpe as he continued, "and, that we must resist at Bennington? Indeed, I know the perfect field there where the road comes out of a forest. But, Mr. Jake Shaw here demands I'm sworn to secrecy about both of ye, and can never speak of those terrible weapons."

Stephen then replied, placing his hand on Sharpe's shoulder.

"John, indeed ye're right. Our cause is clearly blessed by the good Lord as there canna be any other way for these miracles to have come to us. Still, ye can never speak of it, for surely if ye do anyone who hears thy words will think thee daft anyway. Come, let's make a plan."

Early the next morning outside a white stone church in Bennington, Sharpe had assembled his total force of only eighty-two armed men. Most of them were older farmers, many with sons in the Militia fighting under Washington or Clinton. And, the rest were mere boys of twelve or so carrying small rabbit guns. Some of them only had bows.

He introduced Stephen.

"Patriots," Stephen began, "I am with General Washington's Army, and I've learned that the Red Coats have just marched from Montreal for Albany They've taken Ticonderoga. They intend to split our Colonies, and conquer us after we are broken in two."

"Can we allow that to happen?"

"Nay," came a roared reply.

"And," Stephen continued, "With the Red Coats are 800 Hessian Lancers whose horses were lost at sea. They are afoot, but if mounted they'll present a terrible force of cavalry that General Gates may not be able to stop. We must keep these Hessians from capturing your horses."

"Yes, where will they try to get these horses? Why right here, away from you. Will thee help me to stop them from stealing your horses and pillaging this lovely valley?"

A tall grizzled colonial in a stained buckskin shirt stepped forward, spit on the ground and asked, "'Ow, sir, are 82 of us, mostly without a proper musket 'n all, goin' to stop 800 fast marchin' Hessian troops? Best we could do is slow 'em down by shootin' some of 'em from ambush. But, we'll not stop 'em all; no sir, not without more than just us. All we could do is slow them long enough to allow our womenfolk and children to git hiding up in thar' in the hills."

"Patriots," Stephen continued, looking at the old colonial, "would you believe me if I said we can stop them? We do have a plan. We can not share all the details of it with thee, but we need thee to do exactly as this gentleman says," gesturing back at John Sharpe.

"Ye need harass the Hessians as they approach, as this Patriot says," Sharp thundered.

"We are going to ambush them before the road forks in Burlington. We'll have a real surprise for them at this end of the meadow. And all ye need to do is move them quickly from the woods at the west end towards the place where the road passes between the trees at the east end."

He thundered on, "My friend here and I will have plan that will truly stop 'em and send the bloody bastards running. I don't think they'll go further."

"Are ye with us?"

"Sir", came a voice from the back of the crowd, "Taiz all fine and good for ye to talk of a surprise and all, but, sir, I'm afeared that I'll need get me herd and kin to the hills. I canna see how just two gents as yer'selves can stop such an army."

Stephen whispered to Jake, "Ye were right to plan ye'r little demonstration."

Jake had taped a stick of C-6 Semtex to the base of a large pine tree at the end of the meadow. In his hand was the electric detonator.

"Okay, I'm ready," he whispered.

Stephen replied to the crowd at the top of his voice, "my friend here is just landed from France, and he's come with some terrible French new weapons which was given to Dr. Franklin. Turn about and look at that line of trees."

They all turned towards the forest.

"BLAM," and largest pine tree with a base of at least four feet simply leapt into the air. It hung above its stump for a brief moment, then crashed to the ground. There was not even a puff of gun smoke.

The crowd was dumbstruck.

"Do ye believe me now?" cried Stephen.

"Aye," came a joint roar from the crowd.

"Cor and Glory," the Colonel exclaimed, spitting a wad of tobacco juice, "come on me boys, let's have a look at that tree. How was it done?"

"Hold it!" commanded Stephen at the top of his voice.

They stopped and looked at him.

"We can not allow anyone to see Dr. Franklin's secrets. They are but few in all the Colonies, and they come at very great expense. In fact I need a promise from all of thee that ye'll never speak of it again. Is it not enough that we've the good fortune to be here with Dr. Franklin's weapons today to save your homes and herds?"

"Aye", the grizzled Colonel said, then louder, "can ye'all keep this secret, me lads?"

A chorus of Yeas followed.

"Then let us post a watch on the road with our fastest runners. Let us have a full hour advance warning so we can get into place. Where is John and Henry? They are the fastest."

Two slender youths, one with a musket and the other with a mean looking double barreled pistol emerged.

The taller simply stated, "We are the fastest in the Colony, I'm John McRay and this is my brother Henry."

Four hours later, on the afternoon of the 16th, Henry McRay crashed into the farmhouse where Stephen and Jake were awaiting the Hessian advance.

"They're comin," Henry panted, "There's thousands of em."

"Keep ye calm, son," Starke said calmly, "now it's off to the church with ye and ring the bell. Just keep ringing it, for about ten minutes. Then it's off with ye and ye'r boys to ye'r ambush positions. Y'all should be in position when the Hessians come up the road."

He continued, "And, remember to tell the boys to take one shot while the Hessians head towards us in the trees, and re-load. We'll turn them back and ye'll get yer second shot at them as they run back up the road."

The youth ran off to the church. The bell began to peal.

Stephen and Jake, each carrying a black case and a canvas bag of loaded magazines, trotted their horses a mile east of town just to where the woods narrowed in close to the road. They climbed pre-selected trees into pre-selected positions and sat back waiting.

Oberlueutenant Hans VonStollen was hot and miserable. His woolen uniform scratched against his skin spreading the prickly heat rash. His feet were big balls of pain, with huge blisters after marching for days on end in his riding boots. Marching, Haah ! He was a Hessian Lancer, and Lancers did not walk; they rode! Damnation to all English sailors for allowing their fleet to get lost in a storm, and the transports with his horses lost or sunk.

Aah, well, he was certain that in just a day or two his men would be astride again. His map told him the first of the colonial horse farming villages was just ahead. Only a mile or two more, and he'd be on horseback again. And, soon after, they'd find mounts for the entire battalion. Then let these damned upstart colonists beware.

"BLAM"

Private Luten dropped in place, the top of his head vanished and a huge glob of red and gray matter sprayed the troops to his rear.

"BLAM" BLAM" BLAM" BLAM""BLAM"

Five more Privates and one Sergeant likewise dropped with mortal wounds. Puffs of black powder smoke appeared from the woods behind stone walls on both sides of the trail.

"BLAM","BLAM","BLAM","BLAM","BLAM"

More Hessians dropped to the sharpshooters in the woods. And, there was nobody visible to shoot back at.

"DOUBLETIME, MARCH," yelled the Oberlieutenant, running forward into the open meadow, towards perceived safety where there could be no enemy hiding.

"Keep running to safety. We'll wheel and drop e'm all from the other end of the meadow," he commanded to his troops.

He'd make short work of these ragged colonists!

They made it just to where the woods pulled back closer to the road on both sides. Just as the Oberlieutenant was preparing to issue his next command, the dusty road erupted upwards as four deeply buried casks of gunpowder exploded, set off with a detonator Jake had made. It sent men and pieces of men cart wheeling into the sky. Others fell screaming to the earth.

"BLAM","BLAM","BLAM","BLAM","BLAM","BLAM","BLAM"," BLAM","BLAM","BLAM","BLAM","BLAM","BLAM","BLAM","BLA M","BLAM","BLAM"

The guns were firing without stop faster than anything the Oberlieutenant had ever heard, even in the midst of a fully pitched battle! Huge clouds of black gunpowder smoke were now coming from the trees in front of him.

His last thought, before a bullet tore his head apart just over his right ear, was to wonder how the whole Colonial Army had managed to get ahead of his column?

The remaining Hessians dropped their muskets and ran back up the road. They charged blindly through the woods with the Yankee militia men dropping any stragglers in their tracks. By evening, when the militia reassembled back towards town, they were shocked to see, out on the field, the women kneeling beside the wounded to try to help them. No one thought to ask about the two out-of-towners who had precipitated the battle until later that night, long after, of course, Stephen and Jake had silently slipped away.

Jake was very pensive for the entire three day ride to Deerford from Bennington. They stopped at inns in Concord, Sturbridge, and Saybrook. Stephen kept trying to draw Jake into a conversation, but Jake was too deeply in thought. Even after dinner at each inn Jake would withdraw to himself, often taking long walks through the fields and farms.

Finally, with Deerford just an hour ahead, Jake said softly, "Stephen, I have made a very difficult decision. I will need your cooperation, and I trust you can convey my thoughts to General Washington."

Stephen leaned back in his seat and looked at Jake.

"You see," Jake said, "I know now how this war will run. I know that the Colonies will win it, and I know of a lot of the history to come. Yes, there will be more battles, and yes, many good men will suffer and die, but the outcome is foregone. Or, perhaps, the outcome is foregone only with the interference of me and my *Anne Marie?*"

Jake paused, deep in thought.

"You see, I don't know why we're here, or how we got here. But still, here we are. Having accepted that, I can finally piece together what we're doing. Let's stop for awhile; I need to clear my thoughts."

They stopped the mud splattered coach in a clearing and Jake asked the Bridgeport boys to tether the horses. He withdrew with Stephen out of their hearing to sit under a lovely chestnut tree. It was cooler under the tree, and a gentle breeze was blowing.

Jake then continued slowly, "You see, Stephen, I've been terribly concerned that we do not change history. Yet, that's just what we've done now. Twice."

"The first change was when we convinced Howe to sail away from the Delaware. Indeed, he did land at the head of the Chesapeake and he will win Philadelphia. But, we delayed him long enough to get the Government safely out to York. Now, had we not been there, it seems likely he would have pressed his attack"

Jake continued quietly, "Yes, the British will occupy Philadelphia, and Washington will have a terrible winter at Valley Forge, but in the end he and these Colonies will prevail."

"Still," Jake ended, " there is yet one more job for me and *Anne Marie*."

"What be that, Jake?" asked Stephen quietly.

"Franklin needs to know the outcome at Saratoga."

"Well, tiz not yet been fought."

"Still, Franklin needs to know it's won, and he needs to know before November 15th."

"You mean Dr. Ben Franklin? In Paris, France?" queried Stephen.

"Exactly so."

"But by the time Burgoyne gets around to attacking, and if we win, it will be still be weeks, perhaps months, away. News of it won't reach us until at least a week after the Battle. The soonest we could know anything would be the end of October, and it's just not possible to get a message to Paris, France, from here, in less than about eight weeks, in the winter."

"Yes," Jake replied, "these are strange times, and I suppose I should not bet on my foreknowledge of events. Still, Stephen, if memory serves me right, Arnold will prevail in Saratoga on October 3d. And, even in winter, *Anne* Marie and I could get word to Paris in no more than four weeks."

"No", he mused aloud, further, "I just can not bet on my historical knowledge. If I move *Anne Marie* too early and make claims in France before the event could happen, I may be seen as a quack. We'll just have to be ready for an immediate fast voyage the minute the battle is won."

"Stephen", he spoke up more sharply, having made a decision, "you will just need to make sure I receive news of the outcome at Saratoga immediately after the battle, which I still believe will be October third."

"Can you arrange that?"

CHAPTER TWELVE

"Reliant," cried out the quartermaster of the watch on *Jersey* as Lt. Aaron's longboat pulled around the stern of the hulk.

It had only been a fortnight since Aaron was last here. He wondered at the urgent summons from his blockade duty, so soon after regaining his vigil at the east end of Long Island?

As soon as he was piped aboard the old hulk, Wembly's pompous young aide was at his side. "Post Captain will see thee right away. Mind ye, 'ees gout is worse than ever and 'ees always in a foul humor."

Aaron nodded and followed the younger man, removing his hat as he entered the great cabin. And, indeed, Captain Wembly did not look well, He was propped up on the seat cushions across the rear of the cabin, his enlarged leg wrapped in white bandages. His wig was skewed and he held a half glass of Madeira drooping in his left hand.

"Aah, its Aaron," he turned his head, "Me gout has me down me lad. Pull a chair over. What be the news of the blockade?"

"Sir, ye've not given me time to barely begin."

"Suppose that be true. Have ye 'eard of the losses we suffered here in New York a fortnight ago?"

"Nay, Sir," replied Aaron, "I've heard just some scuttlebutt of a sloop lost and 'er captain sent off in chains, but 'tiz only focsul talk."

"Nay, tiz worse than that, and thee must keep what I'm to tell ye in strictest confidence. We've suffered a terrible loss that I fear will be placed at my doorway. Methinks that only you may be able to make sense o'it and perhaps salve me good name. I fear, without proof of reason for the loss, I shall be recalled and dishonored."

"Sir," retorted Aaron, "What in God's name could possibly do that to thee? Ye've had a distinguished career in the Service."

""Methinks ye'r Yankee witch had 'er hand in it. Please drag over that large box and open it," the Post Captain waved.

Aaron lifted the lid on the box and withdrew four iron bars.

"Look at the ends closely," Wembly directed.

John Aaron had never seen iron cut so cleanly. And, in peering sharply at the sawn ends of the bars, he could see circular cut marks.

"Very strange iron cutting," he spoke.

"Indeed so. Seems your doxie again escaped, but this time from the orlop deck under the noses of a pair of Royal Marines. Now those two Marines are clapped in irons for they said they fell asleep on duty and saw nothing. But the only strangeness, after a deep search of the lower deck, was these cut bars. Anyway, the vixen has again vanished. But, that's not the worst o'it."

He took another gulp from the wine goblet and continued, "Day after the doxie disappeared I had sent two armed cutters upriver to Gates with a payroll. The cutters were attacked and sunk almost within sight of the city. The only two survivors babble about a shipload of Yankees firing a huge fusillade."

His chin quivered, "Worse even, we'd sent the *Emily,* a fine new sloop, south to Lord Howe with the larger portion of the King's payments. She sank almost in sight of Sandy Hook on a clear morning."

"Me gods, Man," Aaron retorted, "*Emily* was nearly new, and the fastest ship in the Colonies!"

"Aye, and that's more o'it," the gouty Captain continued, "Er crew was spared. Came up in the boats they did with their tale of *Emily* having, they thought, sailed over a swamped hulk as 'twere no colonials about. Anyway 'er Captain, the lad Sharecross, fastened a cask to her before she sailed under. Damned if the sloop rested straight upright in but about fifteen fathoms."

"Course the frigate what brought the booty cleared back to Portsmouth a'fore this tale was told, and I've kept the crew of *Emily* jailed. But *Jersey* here had a Lascar steward aboard who claimed to dive for pearls. We took him to the sinking and he swam down with a stone. He was so long under that we feared he drowned, but not so. He popped back up, bleeding from ears and nose."

He told a tale that he had swum through the open hatch of the sloop and into the cabin, and even found the strong room. The damned Lascar claimed the lock was broken, the hatch was floating free, and not a farthing was left."

"Now, Sir" Wembly raged, "I ask thee, how could that be?"

Aaron was stunned. The ship sank on a clear morning. Its location had been watched almost continuously, save the few hours immediately after the sinking, and yet the secret cargo was not there.

"Sir," he ventured a reply, "as thee saw the cargo go into the ship ye'rself, and as the vessel proceeded almost straight to sea, and as the cargo was gone the next day, well then the only answer can be skullduggery. Yet, I've known young Sharecross since he was a Midshipman in *Indomitable*; I canna believe he's a streak of larceny. That can not be the only answer."

Wembly replied, "Aye can be only that, or the bloody Lascar was lying, hoping to go back for the treasure another time. But, I fear that was not the case as we flayed the poor sod to where a witch would have unfolded the truth, and his story was unwavered. Unfortunately he did not survive the questioning."

He went on, "Fortunately we only consigned half the Crown's gold, keeping half here. I had hoped to pay off our burgeoning debts in the city, but I've had to reship what I could to Lord Howe and to Gates. That leaves our coffers here quite bare."

"I've also not told anyone here of the thefts. Instead, I dispatched Sharecross in irons directly to Portsmouth on a slow small brig with a letter suggesting that he may be involved in some skullduggery and noticing a partial loss of the treasury."

He finished, "I'm convinced the Admiralty will want me own 'ead in this affair, and that I'll be summarily recalled in disgrace as soon as the word can get to Portsmouth and back. Yet, with luck at this season, that could take five or more months. My only thought is to produce proof of that vixen, and perhaps of that green ketch of which we've spoken. If I can return on the packet when it's back here in several months or so, before a demand arrives from their Lordships, then I perhaps can take this proof with me."

"Aye," replied Aaron slowly, "seems unlikely that such a slight lass could cut these bars like this. Are ye certain she'd not cast herself again into the harbor? And what could mere small lass have to do with the loss of *Emily?*"

"I know not what, my friend Aaron, but I feel we need make an attempt to find the lass, if she lives, and perhaps her green ketch too. Lord knows if we can bring a startling new discovery to their Lordships I'll fare far better. And, Captain Aaron, were thee the ship to deliver such with us, t'would not hurt your career either. I imagine you could be presented at Court?"

Aaron thought quickly. Yes, he would love to get that Connie lady back aboard *Reliant*. Perhaps he could break her down, especially were he to transport her to England. And, it would do his prospects no harm to return with such a strange little package, especially if he could find some more of those unexplainable trinkets that she'd first appeared with.

"Hmmmmm," he mumbled, it just might get him presented, which would assure his post captaincy..

He replied, "Captain Wembly, we know the nest of rebel dogs that took her in last time. We do not know if she drowned on this escape, or of she's even returned to their blasted Connecticut farm. And, I fear we'll not again have success with another direct grab. But what do ye think of "

~~~~ (he went on for some time).

☆ ☆ ☆

Having grown up in Brighton, a small seaside town, John Aaron was a poor horseman. Yes, he could sail anything, and he'd been in the Kings Service since he was eleven years old, but he'd never learned to ride a horse well. Yet here he was, bumping along the Boston Post Road on a bony old nag trying to look like a down-on-his-luck fisherman. His old clothes, taken from a prisoner in the hulk, stank in the hot sun and his growing beard itched.

He wondered if he was finally getting close.

He passed a hay wagon going the other way and hailed the driver, "how far to Deerford?"

"Bout a mile. Over the rise. Good day to ye sir," and the wagon rolled past in a cloud of dust.

A short while later he rode up to the general store in Deerford and dismounted. He tied the horse to a rail and clomped inside in the ill-fitting old boots.

"Can I help thee, Sir?" asked a rosy-cheeked plump woman in a gingham dress.

"Might I get a drink of water f'r meself and me 'orse?" slurred Aaron, deliberately hiding his formal language.

"Help thyself, the well is in the side yard."

After drinking deeply from the tin cup beside the well, and after watering the poor old horse, Aaron re-entered the store.

"Would ye be knowin if'n thar's any work to be 'ad hereabouts?" he queried the woman.

"I'd not know," she replied, "but if ye'll ask Mr. Sims at the pub, p'raps he'll know of something. Tiz just up the road on ye'r left. Sign's down for re-painting don't ye know, what with it used to being the Kings Pub and all. Heavens knows that name would never do for a fine patriot like Mr. Simms, now."

"Ay, er, thankee maam."

Clearly Aaron knew he was in a hotbed of the rebellion. He walked the horse up the street and found the pub. It was empty except for a short round man who was hanging pewter mugs on hooks on the back wall. The man turned as Aaron entered.

"Can I help thee, sir? We've some fresh baked bread, some slices of mutton and cheese if ye'r lookin' fer a bite?"

Aaron sat at a table, stretching his sore legs.

"Aye, a bit to eat and perhaps a pint of ye'r ale?"

After bustling behind the bar the innkeeper brought a plate of bread, meat and cheese in one hand and a pewter mug of cool ale in the other. Aaron was hungry. He tore at the bread and took a mouthful of the ale.

"Four pense," stated the innkeeper.

"''Aye," mumbled Aaron through a mouthful of bread and cheese, tossing the coins on the table.

After eating he engaged the innkeeper, Mr. Simms, in conversation. Aaron told him that he'd lost his small fishing smack to the British when they crossed from Long Island the previous fall, and that he had worked as crew on a brig out of New York, just having been paid off that week,

"T'was a good fishing man I was, before the war," he finished up, "but just weren't suited to sea voyaging. It's looking for a situation I am. Know ye of anything about here?"

Simms sat at the table, bringing them both fresh pints.

"''Heard tell," he mused, "that a gent named Jones was hiring hands to work a new shipyard being built in the bay east of here about four miles. Dunnow if 'ees still building, but sometimes his people come in here f'r a pint. Still, rumor is that Jones don't own the yard. Tiz said to be built by that new fellow, friend of Arthur Williams. And o'course any friend of Mr. Williams is welcome in Deerford indeed."

"Who be this Williams gentleman?" queried Aaron..

"Only about the biggest farmer in these parts. Aye and this new friend of Williams, a Mr. Shaw, 'as been in town fer awhile. Said to've been be a successful privateer captain. Some say his prizes from the Red Coats is what paying fr 'ees new house and shipyard."

The innkeeper rambled on with Aaron smiling at him, encouragingly.

"Aye, t'was even a fine wedding here in the church Saturday last," the innkeeper finished his tale. "Seems this fellow Shaw 'as a daughter was married 'ere. Lovely little lady that, but speaks like a foreigner."

Aaron's interest was keen, but he yawned, appearing bored.

"And, who did this fancy little lady marry? Was it a local gent?"

"Nay, never seen him afore. Perhaps 'ees an orficer on Shaw's vessel."

"So, where be this privateer now?"

"Dunnow much o'that neither. Just repeating local talk, y'know. I suppose it'll be moored in Norwalk as there be poor moorings on our little river."

Aaron wouldn't get much more from the innkeeper, so he asked for directions to the new shipyard.

As he left Simms said, "I often 'ave folks 'ere an hour before nightfall or so. If ye've no luck with Mr. Jones p'raps someone'll know of sommat later on.. The missus is cooking a fine stew fr supper."

It was easy to find the just started little shipyard, about three miles east of the town on a field between the dusty road and the Sound. There was a lane leading off the road towards an old barn that was being rebuilt and enlarged.

As he drew closer, Aaron could see workers drawing stone boats full or rocks down to the shore where they were being tossed into a form to make a large pier. He noted that it was a fine place for such a venture with apparent deep water close to the rocky shore. There were several tree covered small islands at the mouth of the shallow bay, protecting it from the open water in the Sound.

He stopped by the barn and hailed a carpenter asking, "Whar be Mr. Jones?"

The man pointed at a white haired old man.

"Mr. Jones," Aaron accosted him, "me name is Aaron Smith and I be seeking work. Ave ye anything? I turn a fair 'and with an adze?"

Jones looked the applicant over. Yes, he was dressed like a working man, and he really did need a bath, but something just didn't ring true. Aah, it was the man's hands. They were softer than they should be for someone who worked every day, and there were not the calluses he'd expect. And, he smelled beer on the man's breath.

Hmmm, he thought this one would not do for Mr. Shaw.

"Sorry, Mr. Smith, but I am very busy just now. As ye can see, we've a full crew 'ere and just don't have anything needed just now. P'raps if ye'll ask around at the pub in Deerford later today ye may find a farmer what needs a 'and."

Aaron cursed the old man's bloody Yankee heart as he simply nodded and re-mounted the bony nag. It was still too early to return to the inn, and the ale had made him sleepy. About halfway back there was a fine oak tree in a seemingly vacant field. He stopped, hobbled the horse, and leaned back in the shade, dozing off.

He awoke to the sound of a clattering wagon and of a man cursing aloud, "Bloody damned Yankee sons of sods."

A very skinny man was talking aloud from his seat in an approaching wagon.

Aaron stood up and waved, calling out," Hail, friend."

"There be no friends of mine in these parts. They're all traitorous colonials wat won't even part with a farthing for a fine load of fresh potatoes from an honest farmer wat's only crime is loyalty to the King."

"Whoa, friend. I meself be loyal to the King."

"Ye be true to the King?"

"Aye, sir, and more too. Might we talk a bit?"

Aaron followed the farm wagon back east on the Post Road, then north a mile on a small lane between stone walls. After awhile the wagon turned between two gate posts and stopped in front of a small one level house, indeed just more than a hut, standing near a rickety barn that had clearly seen better days.

He followed the scrawny farmer across a creaking porch and into the dim single room structure.

"Can't offer thee more than a roasted potato and a cup of tea. Blasted colonialists wouldn't buy me 'arvest."

"Perhaps", Aaron ventured, "if ye be truly loyal to the King we can come to an arrangement?"

He dropped a heavy leather purse on the planked table.

"What be ye'r name?"

"Jonathan Stone, sir."

"Aye, ne thee the same Jonathan Stone that's been sending messages to New York?"

"Aye," Stone admitted cautiously, eyeing the purse, "there've been certain promises made t'me".

Aaron nodded. He'd found the right man as described by Wembly. Indeed, Stone had been promised the William's property when the King won this little rebellion, and for that he had been said to have been very loyal.

"Well then, Stone, here's what I'll need. And, I'll leave this purse with thee.

Four days 1 as an advance on ye'r services. O'course, it" be doubled when ye'v had success. Now, here's what we seek."

Aaron spent a half hour outlining his plan.

Ten days later Aaron was back with Captain Wembly in *Jersey's* great cabin advising of his pending success.

CHAPTER THIRTEEN

Connie loved her wedding present from Jake, *Martha Shaw,* the new little ship. She had first come aboard just after the long wedding party in the churchyard, still dressed in the formal colonial garb that she hated. From the head of the gangplank Connie couldn't help but notice the clean flow of the single deck, without the usual raised poop, or quarterdeck.

The small brig had been still refitting next to the rickety wooden pier in Jake's new yard. The foremast was being replaced, and workmen, directed by bellows from Thaddeus Jones, were bustling overhead, hanging new blocks and running new sheets and braces under Jake's studied direction.

Walking aft on David's arm, they almost reached to the large wheel at the very stern, then David led her down through an open hatchway to the main cabin. This 'owner's cabin' had both a direct hatch to the wheel as well as a doorway to a second area which served as wardroom, with a cabin on each side of that. One cabin was larger, perhaps for a senior officer to starboard, and there was a smaller cabin for the mate along with a charthouse to port. Forward of that was the hold.

Connie could tell that the owner's cabin had been refit by David and Jake just for her. It had a large double bed under opening windows through the transom. There were beautiful built-in drawers and a closet along the port side. There was a polished wood table to starboard with a reading nook at the head of the bed. A small door at the foot of the bunk opened to the head which emptied simply under the ship's counter. Everything was upholstered in blue chintz cloth, and the woodwork was polished cedar. It all smelled fresh and new.

"Oh," she said to David with a hug, "she's lovely."

David smiled, "She's even named for your Mom. Now, come on up and meet the crew."

At the foot of the mainmast David stopped beside a stout young man who was directing a couple of young boys at the mast top.

"Tie 'er off there", he hollered, "and don't forget a double coat of tar."

He turned to the couple and put his hand out.

"Ye must be the new Mrs. Saunders. Phillip Strong at ye'r service," he took Connie's hand and made a slight bow.

"Oh, Mr. Strong," Connie started.

She was interrupted, "Nay missy, tiz just Phillip to thee."

"Phillip then. I understand you built this ship. She's really beautiful."

"Aye, miss. She'll be fast too, but a tad wet to weather. Ye'r father made some changes to the rig that we're just finishing now. Hope ye'll be ready to sail on the morning ebb"

Connie looked to David who nodded, "of course, Phillip, as planned."

Philip started again, "that man there," pointing at a middle aged seaman leading a crew of youths who were hauling barrels into the hold, "will be me mate, Ees me uncle Howard and has been at sea since a mere whelp. We'd thought to have ye'r husband work as mate but ur father thought it best he use this voyage to study the ways of sailing ships with squares."

"I really wanted to work my part," David began, "but ~~."

Connie cut him off, "Jake is right, David. You need to work beside Captain Phil and learn everything he knows. Anyway, that way you can spend more time with me. It's our honeymoon, isn't it?"

Just then Phillip made a gesture at Howard who let out a sharp whistle. Within moments the rest of the thirteen crew dropped what they had been doing and assembled behind Howard on the deck.

Phillip turned and addressed them. "Lads, this fine young couple 'ere be our owners and will be sailing with us. Mr. David Saunders will be working the ship with us, and 'ees pretty bride will be on board. They're to 'ave ye'r every courtesy."

He looked at Connie saying, "now then Mrs. Saunders, this grizzled old sea dog is our cook", nodding at a tiny older man, almost toothless, but with a smile and twinkle in his bright blue eyes.

Connie spoke up, "I hope you've plenty of fresh food and vegetables aboard. I won't hear of a diet of salt pork and pease like the British live on."

Cookie nodded, "aye Missy. We'll 'ave the sows, the cow and the fowl aboard tonight. Captain Phil himself sampled the salt beef, and he found two casks of fresh limes in the market at Bridgeport."

One by one David and Connie were briefly introduced to each man. Still, there were twelve of them and Connie knew she would take a few days to remember the name of each. After awhile Connie and David took the farm wagon around to the next point of land and to the cove where *Anne Marie* was moored.

As they were packing to move back to the *Martha Shaw* David asked Connie what she had to wear on their trip.

"Well," she replied, "I guess I can't wear my shorts and halters with all those young guys. I really don't have a lot. I've just one sun dress, these two pair of slacks, this one shirt and these t-shirts. Doesn't Jake have a sewing kit aboard?"

"I think so", David said, as he disappeared into Jake's vacant cabin. "Here it is," he said.

He also plopped a handful of Jake's jeans and shirts on top of her bag.

"I'll bet you can make these fit well enough?"

"One other problem," she smiled shyly, "I have only three bras, and there's no elastic material. It'll be tough to make more, but I'm not wearing a damned corset."

David disappeared again and came back with a spool of ¼" shock cord. He cupped her breasts with his palms and whispered in her ear, "I'll have some fun helping you make what you need."

Dawn the next morning found *Martha Shaw* on a reach, scudding east in the Sound. They slipped quietly through the Race before dawn, and were clear of Montauk Point without ever seeing a blockade ship. The twelve day voyage south was perfect. Captain Phil sailed southeast nearly to Bermuda to avoid the Gulf Stream. They then veered south and skirted the outer banks of the Bahamas, bearing then west to the Keys.

"Damn, but it's hot!" thought Connie, standing in the breeze by the taffrail of the swift little brig.

The ship was reaching along at over nine knots with the palm fronds of Key West just visible to starboard. Connie had wished she could wear just her T-shirt and shorts, but David was probably correct to insist that she wear long duck trousers and a full shirt when on she was deck. Yes, she had even made some ill-fitting jeans and two serviceable bras. The crew seemed to take no notice her more informal clothing at sea anyway.

Unlike her last sea voyage on that smelly British ship, on this trip she always felt clean. David had fixed-up a shower in their little head next to the large main cabin. It was only a large wooden bucket with some holes in it, but it worked. He would have Cookie warm up several buckets of water so her showers could be warm, then he'd pour water into the shower bucket as often as she wished. Sometimes these shower times ended in fun, she blushed to herself.

Indeed, thinking back, Connie had enjoyed this trip. It was said to be but several more days northwest across the Gulf of Mexico to Escambia Bay. Old Thaddeus had advised that there was a plentiful supply of live oak in West Florida, and had recommended the small Spanish town of Pensacola as a possible safe port. It was last known to be away from the British and the War.

David had lived in Pensacola as a small boy, and he was anxious to see the town now. He didn't remember much of the history of the area except that it had been traded back and forth between the French, the English, the Spanish and even the Confederacy a number of times. Still, he remembered a gentle climate, neither as hot as the tropics in the summer with never a hard freeze in the winter.

The most serious concern was the possibility of a hurricane in these southern waters. David and Phillip watched the barometer hourly. They had told her that at any suggestion of dropping pressure they'd sail back to the North. She knew that it was a bit more dangerous in the Gulf, but Captain Phil seemed confident that he could read an oncoming storm and keep them out of its direct path.

Four mornings later they made landfall on the gulf coast about twenty miles east of the pass into Escambia Bay. *Martha* sailed in a gentle southeasterly breeze along the whitest sandy beaches Connie had ever seen.

She climbed to the main top with David. They could see across the brilliant white sand barrier island to a lovely blue protected lagoon beyond. On the other side of the lagoon was another narrow spit of land, again with no growth other than green scrubby bush. Beyond that there was yet another sparkling emerald bay in the far distance. It was stunningly beautiful but there was no sign of any civilization at all, not even a fisherman's hut. Still there were at least a dozen porpoises dancing under the bows of *Martha Shaw*.

Somewhat later they could see a pass through the barrier island in the distance. It was guarded on both sides by large earthwork forts. The bay beyond the protective barrier sand island widened to the east, and the small settlement of Pensacola, further up the large bay, could be seen from the mast top.

"David," Connie cried from the main top, "Bring up your binoculars. That looks like an English flag over that fort."

Sure enough, several minutes later David clearly saw the red English flag waving over the fort at the pass.

"Haul down our flag," he hollered down to Phil at the helm. "Hoist the English one and assemble the crew."

David and Connie climbed back to the main deck. He then looked at the faces of the fourteen young men assembled around the main mast.

"We made an error," he started.

"We thought this place was under French control, but very clearly the British have it now. Still, there's nowhere else we can sail to get the bent oak we need, so we just have to act like we're not an enemy. I doubt these folks ashore know a lot about the war back home. We all need to keep our home port to ourselves."

"Where do we say we hail from?" asked Nathan, a tall young man.

"Hmmm", thought David aloud, "I don't want to say anywhere in England since we know so little about it at this time. We'd trip ourselves up."

"How about Halifax?" suggested James, another of the crew.

"That's a great thought!" David smiled.

" Remember everyone," he spoke loudly at the assembled faces, "don't talk of New England when we get ashore. We must maintain that we're from Halifax in Nova Scotia. Is that fine with all of you? Captain Phil ?"

"Aye, sir", came a joint reply.

As the brig approached the two forts, breasting the strong ebb current and flying the red British ensign, a boat approached. It was rowing fast down-current with a young officer in a familiar red medal-covered uniform in the stern sheets. It came close quickly.

"Heave to," the youth hollered, brandishing a large pistol.

Martha luffed her sails and Captain Phil ordered the foretopsail backed, stopping the handy little vessel which now drifted back into the Gulf of Mexico in the ebb current. Moments later the boat pulled along side and the officer was pulled through the railing. David and Phillip were there to greet him.

"Brigantine *Martha Shaw* from Halifax in Nova Scotia," Phillip stated formally, "David Saunders, owner and Phillip Strong, master," he introduced, holding out his hand and nodding at David.

The officer ignored the outstretched hand, removed his hat and bowed towards David.

Standing straight again, he addressed both men saying, "Welcome to the Crown Colony of West Florida. I am Sub-lieutenant Charles Potter."

He continued, "What brings thee here? And, have ye news of the progress of the war in the North? Have we whipped those rebellious rascals yet?"

"Sir," David replied, "we know little of the occurrences in North America. We were warned to sail well clear, so we stopped briefly only in Bermuda enroute here. We've been told we may find a cargo of bent live oak for our family shipyard."

"Aye, perhaps, and ye'll have a cargo to sell? Tiz a poor place here, just our small garrison and several planters, and o'course the Indians. Ave thee any rum? Our Garrison is damned near dry."

"We have mostly hand tools, saws and axes, and some fine Nova Scotia cotton cloth," replied David slowly.

"And yes," he continued with a smile, "We've twelve barrels of Barbados rum."

The red uniformed officer broke a huge grin, displaying his very crooked teeth. He bowed again.

"I can state with certainty that our Colonel Scott will pay a fair price in gold for thy rum. Doubtful ye'r trade goods will find a market here, but John Porter's got a small trading post and runs a schooner to Mobile every week or so. That's a French area, and likely unsafe for a British visit. Porter may be able to trade off ye'r cargo."

"I see the tide has changed," he continued, "please be welcome to our little settlement and thee may warp urselves into our pier."

"What did he say, David?" asked Connie after the officer had returned to his boat and pulled clear of the brig.

"We are invited to moor at the main wharf," he replied.

Then he addressed Captain Phil, "can you get her up the bay?"

Phillip nodded, then he shouted at the top of his voice, "Trim sails. Helmsman, make for the pass. Foretop there, call out for shoal water."

The tide had indeed changed, making it an easy and fast reach up-current to the entrance of the pass and then into the bay between log forts on both sides. It was also easy to see the deep water as the channel was clearly deep blue colored. The yellow water over the sandbars was to be avoided. Once through the pass, *Martha* had to make four quick tacks back east, with the new flood behind her, before they cleared a long point of land. Then they could bear north into the Bay.

Thirty minutes later the town appeared on their port side. The long narrow town wharf was evidently the only place to moor. There were two squat ships with English flags at anchor, and a number of small fishing craft dotting the emerald bay.

David was impressed with the handy way Phil jibed the brig into the dock, stopping exactly where he had planned so his sailors needed only to jump from the railing of the ship to the dock and tie the lines to the pilings.

Before the lines were doubled the arrival of the little ship had caused a stir in the small town, which appeared nothing more than a collection of small wooden houses outside the open gates of a wooden fort. One building, larger than the rest, appeared to be a market of sorts.

It was mid-morning, and already the sun was warm, Connie was on deck, now dressed in a long cotton dress buttoned to the neck. The cool breeze blowing across the barrier island from the south cooled her off and made the weather feel quite pleasant. She and David stood beside the gangplank and watched a as two men in white trousers and red coats walked down the lane towards the pier.

"That must be the Colonel and his aide," David whispered to Connie She nodded.

The two British officers walked up the pier. One was a tall and very thin man with gold insignia on his jacket. Accompanying him was the same youth who had met them at the pass and who had rowed in ahead of them. They both approached the gangplank to *Martha* and bowed deeply.

The young officer straightened and said, "Greetings again from the Governor of the British Colony of West Florida, Colonel Henry Scott. Welcome again to our Colony."

David responded, directing his comments to the Colonel. "We are here with a cargo of tools and cotton cloth. We seek to trade for a return cargo of oak. We've also twelve barrels of rum that Lieutenant Potter claims you may need."

"We bid thee welcome," the Colonel replied. "Indeed we'll buy ye'r rum if the price be fair, but there'll be small market for ye'r trade goods here. We're but a small and poor colony, just a few farmers and our garrison, plus of course the Indians and the blacks. Perhaps John Porter who runs the store here may be able to help with ye'r cargo."

"I understand ye hail from Nova Scotia" he continued, "so I'd not suggest ye sail to Mobile to trade. It be French, and they're not inclined to trade with British vessels. In fact, they'd likely impound thee were ye to sail there. However, if ye've the funds ye can hire some men from the small village at the head of the bay to help thee fell and trim a cargo of oak. Beware however, they'll be a rough lot up there. Most of the trees near the sea have already been removed, so the settlement at Scratchankle is ye'r nearest location."

David replied, "thank you for that. We'll look over the trees tomorrow. For now I'd like to meet Mr. Porter, and certainly my wife would like to step on dry land for a bit. Shall we?"

And he stepped towards the gang plank, taking Connie's hand. The two British officers followed. David started negotiating the price of his rum while walking up the pier.

Porter's store was a single story log building about forty feet square with a low porch roof over the entrance and a large fenced yard in the back, filled with various used equipment. The yard included used anchors, ship's capstans, wagon parts and a great deal of jumbled equipment of all sorts, a lot of which David couldn't identify with a quick glance. As they approached the building a huge man with a shaggy black beard rose from a chair made of a half barrel. He held out his hand to David with a smile on his craggy face.

"John Porter, sir," he greeted David, then nodded at Connie with large green eyes that didn't quite focus together.

"Ye'r pretty little brig 'pears well loaded indeed. What av thee to trade? Unfortunately since these soldiers ran the French off to Mobile there's not much we have to offer here, but come on inside out of the sun."

The inside of the building was more jumbled than the back yard. There were piles of wooden crates and pyramids of barrels and casks of all sizes. Tables were heaped with clothing, and the back wall was hung with an assortment of muskets, pistols, several swords, and a collection of knives. Sides of bacon hung from the rafters along with coils of different sizes of rope. It was a mess.

"Mollie," John Porter called out.

A short round woman with a large round face and a tangled mop of mousy brown hair stood up from behind a stack of wooden crates.

"Oh John, I see we have visitors. Oh and even a lovely young woman. My goodness, what brings such a lovely lady to this desolated outpost?"

She smiled warmly and ambled over to them, her gingham skirt swirling up tendrils of dust from the floor.

"I'm Connie Shaw, er Saunders. This is my husband David. We're not married that long. Anyway, we're just in from Dee, er Halifax," Connie stopped talking, having stumbled almost into a serious error.

David picked up, "Pleased to meet you Mrs. Porter. Yes, we have a cargo of cotton bolts and tools; mostly large saws, mauls and axes. This is our first voyage here, but seemed reasonable that if there was lumbering there would be a need for tools and clothing.

"Aye" replied the big man, "there be lumbering up the Blackwater all right but 'tiz done by folks transported here. Rough lot they be."

"Transported?" Connie queried.

"Aye, Missy. The Crown in their wisdom sends convicts to cut the trees and drag 'em to the mill where they're cut for shipping. Most o'it goes straight back to Portsmouth fer the King. And ye're right, they seldom send proper tools fer the convicts t'work with. Likely thee could trade ye'r lot of tools for a cargo of bent oak, but since tiz the King's oak ye'll likely not get more fer it than a load of wood."

He thought a moment more, then said, "Ye'r cloth is a bit more bother. No one hereabouts will buy much o'it and tiz so few folks here since the Army ran the French off to Mobile that I can't pay ye fer it and carry the stock. More the bother, it's likely not safe fer thee to sail it to Mobile yerselves. Those Frogs may impound a British vessel. Anyway, might we have a look at ye'r cargo?"

With that Molly, Porter's wife spoke up, "Perhaps Mrs. Saunders would rather rest here with me on the cool porch while ye men walk down that hot pier? I've some cool iced tea."

"Why thank you," Connie replied. "That would be very nice, and please do call me Connie."

Late that afternoon the two men stomped back onto the porch. The Colonel had purchased the dozen barrels of rum for a nice profit to David, and John had agreed to trade the cotton cloth for enough supplies to get *Martha* back home. Lastly, the Colonel had offered to send a squad of soldiers with the young Lieutenant aboard *Martha* for a short trip to the lumber camp at the mouth of the Blackwater River.

David and Connie stayed with the Porters for dinner.

"I'm afraid I've made thee a poor bargain on the cotton," John said as they finished the lime pie, "but as ye've seen, the few folks in town and the small farmers hereabouts simply are always strapped for cash. Tiz a poor place."

Connie replied, "Yes, seems so. Still I am surprised that most of the people here are black. Really the only white people here seem yourselves and the Army. Yes, all the people I've met seem very nice, but I guess I'm surprised to see so few white faces."

John answered, "Aye, that's an easy one. First, yes, the British ran all the French settlers back to Mobile several years ago."

David interjected, "the same thing happened in Nova Scotia a hundred years ago. The British deported all the French to New Orleans, or perhaps some came to this area."

John continued, nodding. "True. And the nigras mostly all walked here from plantations to the North in Alabama. See, we British won't abide slavery, so if the nigras can get here they have a safe haven. Yes, from time to time a band of slave hunters will come seeking them for a bounty, but the Colonel runs them off. Aye, the nigras here are a pretty decent bunch. They ain't got much. They farm a bit and some are pretty good at building stuff. Kinda stick to their own little villages, but we see them in here when they can afford to buy anything. And, of course, that's where I get my beef and bacon for the ships."

Then he addressed David. "Those sojers'll be aboard ye'r ship at eight in the morning. The tide will be flooding so ye'll want an early start."

"Well then, thank you both for a fine welcome and a good diner," David stood up, reaching for Connie's elbow to head to the door.

"David," Ms. Porter said, "ye may not want ye'r pretty wife to sail to Scratchancle with ye. Tiz a very rough place. They're all really the scum of London. A few women perhaps, and fewer underfed children, but most are very rough men."

She looked at Connie and continued, "My dear, would thee not rather spend a day or two here with us while ye'r husband seeks ye'r return cargo? The place they're going is very hot and damp, and also infested with mosquitoes as big as bats."

Connie glanced at David who gave a small shrug.

She replied, "Well, you make it sound much nicer here and perhaps safer too. If it isn't any bother to you?"

Early the next morning Connie dressed in loose slacks and a cotton shirt. She packed small duffel and as a squad of soldiers marched up the pier she kissed David and skipped down the gangplank to the dock. She skirted the puffing troops and waved at Molly who was waving back from the porch of the store. By the time she reached the shady porch and looked back, Phillip and his crew had already filled the topsails and jibs of the brig. The ship was gathering speed, headed north up the bay.

With the southwest breeze on their beam it was easy to sail the small ship up the wide bay. It looked wide, but it was really quite shallow except for a narrow winding channel, easily seen by the color of the water. To their left were tall white sandy cliffs with deep green forest on top. To the right the bay gradually shallowed and blended into miles and miles of swamps.

After passing the cliffs they sailed for two hours up the narrowing bay towards apparently more endless swamps. At one point the Lieutenant pointed at a branch of dark water forking to their right. The sails were trimmed to the diminishing sea breeze, and the little ship continued slowly up the winding channel.

A mile further and the bay narrowed to a river. Mosquitoes found them. Clouds of large ferocious bugs settled on everyone. The soldiers, marines and sailors buttoned their shirts and coats to their necks, pulled their hats down, and simply swatted at the insects landing on sweating cheeks. It was hot.

Just as the zephyrs of wind ended, the little ship slid next to a rickety pier that materialized from the swamp. The further they had come up the bay the more mosquitoes had attacked.

Phillip carefully had the brig turned to face down river before he ordered the sailors to secure the ship to the pier. As the ship was swinging about David gazed at the shore. The pier ended in a path through the bull rushes that rose up a shallow embankment. Just out of sight, behind the dense green vegetation, he could see smoke rising. He guessed that there must be a village up there.

There was. Within a few minutes, just as the last lines were made fast to the dock, a group of four skinny little children dressed in rags scampered up the pier waving at the ship.

"Off with thee," hollered a grizzled sergeant.

He looked at David and said, "Little bastards will steal anything wot's not nailed down."

David slapped at another mosquito and asked the Lieutenant, "How soon can we see whoever is in charge here so we can make our trade and get out of this place?"

"Come then," the Lieutenant replied, "Lets go ashore and find Mr. Smoat. I've met him before. Seems he's in charge of the work parties hereabouts and if anyone can trade ye'r tools for a cargo of bent oak it'll be Smoat."

"Is it dangerous in there?"

"Aye, the townsfolk are ruffians; former prisoners ye know."

"Then I'll be just a moment," David replied.

David descended to his large cabin and rummaged in a special leather case he'd hidden in the false bottom of his locked sea chest.

As the two of them strode up the embankment and through the ramshackle huts that comprised the village, the Lieutenant appeared to pay no attention to the listless collection of too thin children and ill dressed women staring at them from the drooping porches of the mean little houses they passed. David tried to ignore them too, but he couldn't ignore the stench of rotten meat and open sewage.

After walking through the village, stepping around piles of garbage and assorted offal in the dirt lane, they reached a tall wooden fence with a stout gate guarded by two well fed men in good cotton clothes.

"We seek Mr. Smoat," queried the Lieutenant.

""E'll be at the 'ouse," mumbled the taller of the two as he spat a wad of tobacco juice on the ground. He gestured over his shoulder with his thumb.

It was a different world inside the gates. The wide lawn was trimmed, and a well shaded pathway wound through a stand of tall old oak trees to a lovely one story white house with a wide shaded veranda. There was a pretty white barn off to the right, and a sparkling pond to their left. They stepped up onto the verandah and knocked on the oak door.

A moment later the door swung silently open. They were greeted by a strikingly beautiful dark haired girl of perhaps sixteen dressed in a formal green gown.

"Ye'r here t'see Mister Smoat?" she asked, making a small bow which caused her young and large breasts to almost pop out of her very low cut dress.

"Foller me then."

They followed her through a cool interior hallway and out a side door to a shaded porch. A large rugged looking man dressed in white cotton trousers and a loose fitting yellow shirt rose from a cushioned chair.

"Lieutenant, good t'see thee again," his crooked teeth flashed through the full beard, "and who's ye'r companion?"

"Mr. Smoat may I present Mr. David Saunders, owner of the brig *Martha* just arrived at ye'r pier."

"Pleased to meet thee, Mr. Saunders. And to what do we have the honor of your presence in this godforsaken hole? Aye, but please sit thee down. Suzanne, please fetch these men a drink."

The girl turned back into the house, reappearing with two clay jugs and set them on a small table.

"Rum and cool water is the best I can offer," Smoat stated, mixing three tall mugs.

David started, "Mr. Smoat, I'm given to understand that you run a logging operation for live oak trees?"

"Aye, but tiz for the Royal Navy. They send a transport from time to time, every month or so. They bring me vermin from the London gaols for workers, and barely enough to feed'em. Hard t'keep the lazy bastards workin' as they're always sneaking off to hunt or fish. And, since we've hardly any saws or axes left that'll cut a tree I'm afeared the navy will be disappointed their next arrival unless they bring the tools I've been askin for a year. Still and all, from time to time I'll find a pretty doxie like Suzanne; born on a transport she were."

David interjected, "Mr. Smoat, I've heard that you may need tools and by chance I've a cargo of lumbering tools. Would you trade for a cargo of live oak?"

"Sit thee down," Smoat directed, "and let's see what ye can offer. May as well stay for supper. We've a fresh side of beef. Appreciate company anyway; Suzanne is fine to look at and play with," he winked lewdly, "but she ain't much fer talking."

Smoat revealed that he had hidden a load of cut oak from the last transport, and had sent them back half empty, insisting the Admiralty send proper tools along with the jailbird convicts on the next voyage. He was happy to trade the tools for a deck cargo, but he managed to squeeze David for a cash payment of twenty crowns. It was exorbitant, but it was in fact less than half David's profit on the rum.

Smoat and the Lieutenant kept quaffing the rum through the early evening and through a simple dinner of roasted beef and cabbage. As it was getting dark David stood to leave.

Smoat offered, "Ye can spend the night if ye wish. Ye've paid me fairly and I'll even send Suzanne or her sister in to play with thee. I've done had all I want of 'em both earlier today anyway."

David shook his head and started for the door.

"Coming?" he queried to the half drunk young lieutenant.

"If'n ye don't mind I'll stay here for some o' Mr. Smoat's entertainment."

Smoat then spoke up, "Be thee armed? Can be dangerous walking through the village, especially if the men folk are back. I can have me boys walk with thee to the docks."

"Thank you, Sir. Yes I've a pistol," David tapped the shoulder holster he was wearing under his shirt with the loaded .38 Special.

"Ye've a pistol under ye'r shirt all day? Can't be large enough to do any damage. And how do ye keep ye'r powder dry in this heat? What 'av ye got thar?"

"Thank you for your concern, sir, but I'll just be on my way. It's easy enough to find the pathway back, and it's not dark yet." He waved and departed.

But he'd miscalculated. It was quite dark by the time he reached the tiny ramshackle village. As he was striding through, slipping on the garbage and sewage in the dirt, he became surrounded by a pack of boys.

They started to whine and yell at him, "Aye, tiz a fine gentleman ere. Look at 'ees fine clothes. 'Ee must be a rich man. Ay sir, ye'll ave a few coppers fer us? Take us to ye'r ship for a few crumbs?"

They badgered about him. David ignored them and just kept striding.

But, as he passed a large tree, a meaty paw slapped him in the middle of his chest, abruptly stopping him in his tracks. He took two fast steps backwards peering through the gloom to try and see who had stopped him.

"Ees alone," a shrill voice cackled.

With that, four or five men in rags for shirts wearing worn leather hats, all brandishing mean looking machetes, encircled him.

The leader spoke again, "Now sir, ye're a fine gentleman all done up proper like, and we're certain ye've a purse about ye. If'n ye can spare ye'r purse we'll let thee pass."

David did have a small leather bag tied inside his belt, and it did have the balance of his profits from the rum sale inside. He thumbed it.

"Aye, ees got a purse alright," the leader shrilled.

"Pass it on over and we'll let ye pass on."

David reached into his shirt and yanked out the revolver.

"Back off," he commanded.

"Don't be afeared o'that peashooter," cried the ruffian, "tiz but a tiny French woman's gun. Even it hits ye it'll be but a prick."

"All together," the leader shouted, "at him!"

The four men lunged towards David swinging their wicked looking knives.

David didn't hesitate. He simply aimed the revolver at the shoulder of the leader and pulled the trigger. Spinning, he made four fast additional shots, hitting two others. He then simply pushed past the dazed and shocked leader who was grasping at his bloody shoulder, and ran quickly down the path to the pier.

"What was that?" Phillip shouted as David leapt onto the ship, winded.

The Sergeant popped up from below, "I've 'eard shots! Are we being attacked?"

"No, Sergeant. They tried to rob me passing through the village but I got away."

"Whar did they get guns? Them prisoners ain't allowed firearms. If we find one with a gun 'eel hang fer 't. I'll call me troops and we'll turn that pesthole upside down until we find the vermin with a gun. Cor, there was four or more shots; that'd be too many guns fer comfort"

David thought fast, then replied, "No sergeant. I carried two pistols with me. Damned fine French models with two barrels each. Bloody sorry to have lost 'em in the river on the way down the pier, but they ran off my attackers."

He continued, "Just post a close watch tonight. We should have a cargo loading in the morning and perhaps we can get down river on the afternoon tide."

With that he went below to his cabin. He took of the shoulder holster and the pistol. After carefully cleaning the gun he slipped it back into its hiding place. He went to bed, covered himself from head to toe with one of Connie's fine sheets to keep off the mosquitoes, and fell asleep.

Three mornings later Connie and David were comfortably seated in the crook of a large bent oak log, part of the deck cargo on *Martha,* as the brig cleared the Pensacola Pass and rose to the first of the Gulf swells. It was a beautiful cool morning with porpoises again playing around the bow of the ship and seagull wheeling overhead.

"David, it just sounds like a perfectly horrid place up in that camp. I mean, it sounds so different from the lovely time I had with Molly while you were gone."

"You must have really liked Pensacola to have promised another cargo of cloth and gave away my last twenty crowns for a burned out stone house." he chided.

"Darling, I really enjoyed my stay here. This is the only place I've found people I like in this awful time, except the Williams' of course. It's not just Molly and John. No, it's all of them in that little town. And, it's the climate, Molly says it's really perfect all year. Even William, the old guy who took us to the bluffs in his wagon, was wonderful. Even his family was terrific when we went there for dinner. Really, David, didn't you like that ten acres on the bluff? It's really the only place where the trees were never cut."

"Connie", he looked deeply into her eyes, "my family history starts in Pensacola. It was just five years ago that my Dad sold Grandma's old plantation house on Scenic Highway. Connie, the land you just bought was the same place. No, not the house, but the land. I guess Jake's right. We are our own ancestors."

Regardless, Connie was finally content. She knew now that she and David would return to Escambia Bay and make it their home. She really just wanted her privacy to be able to live as she wanted, and in her own clothing. She knew she could live her way in this place.

A week later Key West was in sight again, this time on their port beam.

"Morning," David stepped to the rail next to her, handing her a steaming mug of coffee, "Key West to weather there, huh."

Turning his back to her he yelled out, "Watch to the braces. Step lively now. Slack braces, Haul sheets," and to the sailor at the helm he spoke out, "east nor' east, quarter north."

"Aye, sir", the youth at the wheel replied, guiding the brig two points off the wind as the eight men on deck scampered about trimming the yards on both masts to the new course.

Looking back at Connie, David commented, "We'll pick-up the Gulf Stream in a couple of hours, and if the weather holds we'll be 'rounding Montauk in ten or twelve days."

"Yeah", she replied, "I can't wait to see Dad and Arthur and Anne, but I really hate the clothes I'm forced to wear there. I'll be so happy when we can move for good back to our new little house on the bluff."

"Sail ho," came a cry from the masthead lookout, "Three points abaft the port bow."

David leapt to the ratlines, followed closely by Captain Phil and Uncle Howard, who both emerged from below decks carrying their telescopes as soon as they heard the lookout.

At the main top David could see the other ship, a large topsail schooner, bowling down wind under a full press of canvas with studding sails set to windward. It was perhaps ten miles distant. Phillip had his glass on her.

"What do you make of her?" David queried to Phillip.

"I don't like 'er looks," came the muttered reply. "She's too narrow and tall built to be a merchant, and her rig is raked for speed. Further, there's no reason for her to be on that course unless she means to take up with us."

Moments later he added, "Damn, she appears to show five guns per side. We need wear ship and see what she does."

Then addressing the lookout he hollered, "Henry, keep a close watch and tell us the minute she changes course."

With that Phil simply grabbed a backstay and slid smoothly down to the deck, eighty feet below. David followed.

They wore ship, changing course ninety degrees.

Within ten minutes the black pursuer likewise changed course.

"Tis no doubt, David, she'll likely be a pirate, or at best a British privateer under Letter of Marque. In any event, it'll not do for them to board us," observed Phillip.

"All hands," he cried out, "lay aloft the studding sails and booms."

With the additional press of sail *Martha* surged faster. But, they just couldn't pull away from the black pirate clinging to their wake, now just four or five miles behind.

Over the next hours the black ship crept closer.

As soon as the black ship tried a shot with their bow chaser, which fell about 300 yards short, David ordered the deck cargo of logs tossed overboard. That did help their speed, and caused the big pirate to drop behind again as she had to dodge the barely awash logs which would hole her had she hit one.

Then, just before sunset the wind died. Totally. It left *Martha* slopping back and forth on the swells .

Worse, within minutes the black ship had two boats in the water, each filled with a dozen or more men rowing as fast as they could towards the hapless and becalmed *Martha.*

When Phil saw the approaching boats, filled with men heavily armed with cutlasses, pikes and pistols, he dashed below and re-appeared with his loaded one-shot pistol in hand.

Turning to David he proffered the gun sadly saying, "Aye, David, they'll be upon us in a quarter hour. I fear we've no defense left. Tiz too bad ye lost ye'r fine double barrel pistols. Ye'll not want ye'r lovely little lady taken by the likes of them. Ye'll want this for her. Can thee do it?"

David looked sharply at Phil, then spoke grimly, "No, Phillip".

He spoke quickly, "I need you and your crew to take Connie below. You may hear things that you'll question, but your crew can not know how I am going to keep those pirates from boarding us. I will keep them away from *Martha,* and from Connie too."

"But, how?"

David cut his protest off, "Not now, Phillip. Get you and your crew below decks. Fast."

With that, and with the sails slatting empty of wind, the crew marched, protesting, to their foc'sl below. David dashed to the main cabin and took a black case from another hiding place under the built-in bunk.

When he got back on the main deck the boats were closer, and the deck of *Martha* was empty.

David slipped a magazine into the slot under the AK-47 machine pistol and simply leaned against the railing as the closest boat approached the starboard side. His cleaned and reloaded .38 Special was at his shoulder.

"Strike ur Colors and Save ur Lives," came a cry from a tall sailor in the stern of the boat. He was wearing a red rag around his head and a blue and white striped shirt.

"Return to your ship and save yours," cried David in reply.

"Damn their Yankee eyes, Board!" yelled the same the leader to the crews of the two longboats..

When the first boat approached to about 50 feet David quietly raised the machine pistol and in less than three seconds shot a line of holes into its waterline. Several rowers howled in pain as their legs were shattered.

"Come no closer, I warn you," David called out.

Meanwhile, the other boat slipped around the bow of *Martha*, out of his sight.

"Board thee and be damned!", screamed the leader, "Pull hearty, Mates, they'll not have any loaded balls left to fire."

With that David had no choice. He simply fired the rest of his magazine at the men in the boat as almost point blank range. It sank. The pirates, mostly wounded, clung to the sides.

Just then David heard a howling screech behind him. He had no time to smack a new magazine in the AK-47 as he spun around to see the other boat crew pour over the bow railing, running at him with pistols and cutlasses raised.

David yanked out his revolver and squeezed-off eight shots. Six men fell to the deck. The rest of the oncoming pirates slowed their charge just long enough for David to slide a new magazine into the machine pistol. In less than five seconds the attackers were all dead.

David ran to the railing and shot holes in the second longboat. It swamped quickly. Then he quietly slipped down to the cabin and returned the machine pistol and the revolver to their hiding places under Connie's wide eyes. He hugged her for a long time. He then called to Phil to allow the crew on deck. Presently he heard faint splashes as the dead attackers were tossed overboard.

"David", hollered Phillip from the quarterdeck, "come on up, we need thee."

The moon had risen showing the black-hulled raider, still just out of cannon range, slopping back and forth on the calm sea. Phillip was watching them through his telescope.

As David approached Phillip said softly, "They don't know what's happened. And, there can't be more than ten or twelve of them left on board. Quickly, let's make them believe we're lost. Can thee find the shirt and red scarf of the leader?"

David instantly understood. He ran forward. Over the bow, floating face down in the water, the dead body of the leader sloshed against the hull.

He turned to one of the crew saying, "Samuel, can you grapple him up?"

Meanwhile, Phillip lowered the colonial flag from the gaff. Minutes later he leapt to the taffrail dressed in the sopping wet blue striped shirt with the red bandanna around his head. He waved a cutlass over his head as a slight breeze filled the sails.

A cheer was heard from the black schooner.

Phil jumped back to the deck and called to his small crew saying, "Men, load our three guns on the leeward side. Load 'em with grapeshot and small musket balls. Aim for the decks."

"You mean to load with grape shot?" interjected David, "I'll help them."

At that moment Connie appeared up the scuttle to the Quarterdeck, looking ashen and shaken.

"David, what the hell are you doing," she started shrilly. "You just murdered twenty men, and now you are planning to shoot more. David, let's us please just get under sail and leave them alone. We don't need more killing."

She stopped, quietly sobbing.

David put his arm around her and said, "Honey, it's just not that easy. See, there's only fifteen of us with three small guns per side on our little *Martha*. There could be twice as many or more of them, and something over twice our guns. Also, they're a whole lot faster. Either Phil and I trick them now, or we'll be in much bigger danger later. Please go on below. They don't need to know we've a woman aboard."

"Here, David, put this on." Phillip was offering another damp tattered pirates shirt.

David slipped the smelly shirt over his shoulders and jumped to the mizzen ratlines as Connie slipped back below decks. He kept the AK-47 down beside his leg where the crew couldn't see it..

Martha then hauled wind, backed her foretop, and drifted to leeward. All her other sails were left to flap in the slight breeze. The black schooner approached. Still, the schooner's gun ports were closed, apparently believing that *Martha* had been won. Meanwhile David climbed to the mizzen top with his last two magazines. He simply sat and watched the pirate bear down on them.

The bearded leader of the pirate ship, still unknowing that he had lost the majority of his force and his two boats, could see what looked like Zeke, his first lieutenant, clearly at the helm of the captured ship. He rubbed his hands together in anticipation of adding this neat little brig to his flotilla, and her cargo to his coffers. He smirked wondering if there might even be a woman aboard?

As the schooner rounded under the stern of the drifting *Martha,* the crew remaining on the pirate's ship was ranged along the ship's rail, several with grappling hooks in hand.

Just as the grapples flew David shouted, "Now."

"KABOOOM"

The three short fat deck guns on the starboard side of *Martha,* each filled with little lead balls, smashed into the pirate's crew at the rail of the schooner. At the same moment David opened up with the AK-47 from the main top, clearing the quarterdeck of the schooner, and insuring that the heavily bearded fat fellow in the gold trimmed coat, her obvious captain, was down. It was over in moments. There were only seven survivors from the pirate schooner

As soon as the very brief battle quieted, Connie appeared from the cabin and ran to the wounded pirates, now under guard from the *Martha* crew. She bandaged three with bullet wounds, none very serious. Then, over her protests, Phillip placed all seven of them in one of the swamped longboats. He gave them two oars and waved in the direction of Key West, just over the horizon.

"Ye can't leave us abandoned on the ocean in a sunken boat," one of the pirates wailed.

"Ye'd have done a lot worse to us," David hollered back.

Phillip then said to them, "Follow the pole star and ye'll reach land by morning if ye keep rowing."

"Do I understand that we can keep this ship as our prize?" David asked Phillip as the swamped longboat waddled away in the dark.

"Aye, she's yours now. Fine fast ship she appears too. Let's have a look at her."

The two ships were tied together in the gently rolling ocean. David and Phillip jumped to the deck of the undamaged schooner and leapt back after a fast tour.

"Miss Connie," Phillip reported, "Thee've captured a fine fast vessel, likely a lot faster than little *Martha* here. Appears she is French built, and likely as a slaver."

"A slaver?" she queried.

"Aye. She 'as ringbolts for chains rigged through the 'tween decks, but she's no smell of slaves, that's something cannot be cleaned away. No, somehow those pirates got to her first."

David spoke up, "Connie, come on over for a look. I think you'll find the schooner a lot more comfortable than *Martha*. It's bigger. And, we've seem to have found quite a chest of gold, probably stolen by the pirates but seems it's ours now. Of course, we'll share it with our crew."

Connie quickly decided she liked the new ship, even though it really needed a thorough cleaning. Phil, Connie and David decided that Phil and eight of the crew would sail aboard the captured schooner, while David, Connie and the four other crew stayed aboard *Martha*. They would sail together back to Pensacola, hoping to find enough crew to sail both ships home to New England.

As the ships parted under the moonlight David and Connie looked at the lovely trim schooner.

"It is really a beautiful ship." Connie said.

"Well then," David hugged her, "we'll just re-name her *Constance Shaw*. We certainly don't want a ship named *Black Witch*"

Phillip in the schooner beat *Martha* back to Pensacola by a full twelve hours . Phil couldn't stop talking about how fast and weatherly she was.

Apparently the *Black Witch* was well known and feared in the little town; in fact whenever it had been sighted off the pass the fort had been manned and the town vacated. Phillip had to heave-to for three hours under a white flag until the young lieutenant in the same longboat had been rowed out through the pass. The British were surprised to find the former pirate ship had been captured by the little crew from *Martha*. The ship, under new ownership, was cleared him to enter the bay. Some hours later John and Mollie ventured from their barricaded store to the town pier, also finding the ship had changed hands.

And as the sun was setting, David and Connie appeared through the pass in *Martha*, tying up at the pier next to *Constance*. They and Phillip accepted an invitation to dinner with Colonel Scott who wanted to hear how the former pirate ship had been captured.

"Twas quite a feat," the Colonel said after hearing the tale. "Very clever to use ye'r deck cargo to slow her down, then to trick their boats under ye'r guns."

He continued, "But ye've lost ye'r deck cargo, and appears ye'r short of crew to sail both ships back to Halifax."

"Both true enough," David replied.

"But we captured a small purse with the ship, so perhaps Smoat will sell us another cargo for *Martha*. We can load what is in her hold into *Constance*.

Still, you're right. We've but seven hands per ship which is dangerously under manned for a long voyage."

"Well," the Colonel replied thoughtfully, "if I were to sail up river with thee I'd think I could pull out about a dozen of Smoat's men who've about served their sentences. Now, I know which of 'em I can trust, but Smoat will listen to me. The good ones will certainly wish to sail out of here, and I presume you'd pay 'em off in Halifax where they could take passage back to England."

"Thank you, Colonel," Phillip said. "We can split our trained sailors between our ships, and the new crew can learn enough from them."

He then addressed Connie and David offering, "Why don't we switch ships? Your new *Constance* is easier to handle with a simpler rig than *Martha*. She's faster too, just in case of more trouble.

Early the next morning David and Phil asked their first mate, Harold, to call all hands. Twelve youths, the cook, and the old sailing master assembled at the main mast.

"Crew of *Constance*," David started, "it's been a very busy voyage so far. And, I know you've seen some things, particularly in the fight for this ship that may leave you with questions."

Continuing, "My wife, Connie, and I come from a far place from here. We bring some rare and different weapons, and as you sail with us you may see other strange things. Indeed, some of our ways are strange. Still, you've all earned some fine prize money from the gold we recovered, and we'll pay you fair share for the capture of this fine ship"

"We first need to split you between these two ships. We'll be finding some raw hands to help us all get back home, after that we'll ask you to rejoin us all on this ship. I know not where this ship will take us all, but I offer you all a partnership in our voyages. You will all continue to share in half the profits we earn. It is only required that you keep totally silent about anything you may see that you may not understand."

"If you all agree you'll have to sign a paper binding you to *Constance*, and affirming your secrecy. Do I have your word?"

The reply was a throaty roar "Hooray for Captain Saunders"

Later Connie asked, "What was that all about?"

"Darling, I know that Stephen and Joe, the watch leaders, were full of speculation on our capture of this ship. We need a loyal crew, and one that won't talk too freely. Besides, they are all good guys and great sailors. We just got a permanent crew who will keep our secrets. I'm really happy that

Phillip will find the help we need, but we want to keep our original crew together. These are good lads."

Two days later on the morning ebb tide both ships cleared the pass into the Gulf of Mexico. Before nightfall *Constance* had dropped the handy, but slower, *Martha* over the horizon astern.

Twelve days later, having slipped through Plum Gut in a dense fog, *Constance Shaw* was moored to the new stone jetty on the Roank under a new sign in green letters on a cream painted backboard that read "SHAW SHIPYARD".

"My God !" exclaimed Connie, "this Yard is exactly where we left it, before ——."

Of course it didn't look like when she'd last seen the Yard. Corn was still sprouting where the large two story clapboard office building would be, and none of the shop buildings were there yet. There was only one small log cabin, an office/warehouse building of sorts, a large stack of cut lumber, and a huge squared-off tree lying across logs that was clearly the beginning of a keel for a ship. Instead of the long wide dock reaching almost halfway across the little river, there was only one narrow stone jetty close to the rickety wooden pier, seemingly too close together.

Still, it was the same jetty that she had left just a few months, and two centuries, past.

It was a lovely crisp October day as she and David stepped ashore to the unfinished pier. The trees in the distance were showing their full autumn glory. Thaddeus Jones himself caught their docking lines after David had skillfully jibed the black schooner into her berth.

"What be this fine fast schooner?" he bellowed across to David at the helm, "and I see thee've brought me a cargo of fine knees."

He turned to a young boy, "Fast as ye can, lad, dash ye off to Mr. Shaw's new house and tell 'em 'es family is back."

But, the boy had hardly turned to his task when a light wagon pulled by a galloping horse clattered into the shipyard. Jake leapt down and strode up the pier.

"Connie, David. Welcome home!" thundered Jake, giving a warm hug to Connie while vigorously shaking David's hand, "where did you get this fine new ship? And where's Captain Phil and *Martha?*"

They all started talking at once.

"Whoa," said Jake, his hands up, "let's have you all over to Anne's. We can talk there, and she'll feed you too. Then you two can come back here for the night."

"Oh David", Connie hugged her husband, "I am dying for a hot shower on *Anne Marie*, and we got here just in the nick of time for me to grab some personal stuff."

"Sure," replied Jake, "she's all repaired and snug in the cove. You two can say there for a few days, or until Stephen arrives. I'll tell you later what we've planned. It's important. Mr. Jones will have one of his boys row you around to the cove."

A skinny older man in a threadbare coat who was dropping stones onto the new pier took especial note of the new arrival. He stood up and slowed his work to overhear all he could.

"Yes," he smirked to himself, "I'll be having me a fine purse of British gold soon."

CHAPTER FOURTEEN

"She's really not a topsail schooner any more," Jake commented to David as they sat under an awning on the quarterdeck of *Constance*. "I'd now more correctly call her too a barkentine. In fact, her new rig is similar to *Martha*. A topsail schooner has only a single topsail on the foremast, perhaps a top and a sky, and the foremast is a lot shorter than the main. Here you have both masts almost the same height, and four squares on the foremast. You also have two foremast staysails."

"Whatever you call her, Jake, she was already faster than anything we've seen this century. Now, with the staysails she'll go to windward perhaps not quite as well as *Anne Marie*, but we sure will blast away from those British blockaders."

Jake replied, "Thaddeus thinks she's French built, and recently too. He also said she was likely built as a slaver. I wonder how those pirates got her away from the original owners? Anyway, I like the rig, but were I to rebuild her it'd be with a sharper forefoot, rounder bilges and steeper tumblehome. She could be a good eight feet wider. That'd give more stability and a great deal more cargo space with no loss of speed."

"Still," he continued, "what are you gonna do with her? She won't carry enough trading goods to pay her crew, and, I don't think Connie will let you go priveteering."

"Actually, Connie and I did discuss just that, and Stephen offered to send paperwork to the War Department for a Letter of Marque for us. Connie really wants us to move back to Escambia Bay in Florida, It would be a good base for us. *Martha* can profitably trade between New Orleans and Havana."

"Besides," he continued, "there is the property we bought there."

"I know about it," said Jake. "I've already agreed to allow Connie to take most of the amenities from *Anne Marie*. We can't have Thaddeus' men see the ketch, so you and I will need to strip what we can from her, and be quick about it. *Anne Marie* and I have a most urgent mission."

"I've got to get to France," he stated. "By the end of November, so I need sail by the end of next week."

David was surprised.

"France?" he asked, "Now? With the winter nor'easters coming? Who's going with you? You can't do that single handed in the winter. Why would you go dashing off to France?"

Jake continued as if he hadn't been interrupted, "Stephen sent a message with a young naval lieutenant name of Arnought. Speaks good French too. He's at the Crown & Coach in town now, and off in the big wagon tomorrow to buy us twelve barrels of whale oil."

"Whale Oil?" David queried

"Yes. You remember. We filter it slowly through cheesecloth and *Anne Marie*'s engine runs fine, not even a bit smoky. It also works in the generator. Connie will like that."

David interrupted again, "Jake, I guess I understand that Stephen and the General have you blasting across the Atlantic for some reason. And, that means you are stripping out *Anne Marie* for the trip."

"Oh, yes, David", Jake paused. "It is very important Stephen and I get information to Dr. Franklin in Paris."

"Ben Franklin?" asked David with an incredulous voice. "Like in Benjamin Franklin, father of electricity and all that?"

"Yes, David, but we can't speak of it. No choice. We'll be fine, and if my family history is correct, I'll be here again, at least by the end of the War. I'm really happy that you and Connie have found a safe place that she likes. Let's see how much of the stuff on *Anne Marie* we can salvage to make her transition to life here better."

Jake continued, "Now, you can have anything I won't need. You should start with the generator and all the 110 volt AC stuff; I can run the ship on 12 volt DC from the main engine. What else?"

He continued, muttering to himself, "Well, I need as much space as I can get for fuel. Let's start with the Onan, eight of the ten batteries, the water heaters, the refrigeration and the stoves, as well as all the galley equipment. Let's also take all the plumbing and strip out both forward heads. Leave me the radar and sonar. I'll also want one of the AK-47's, and one of the automatic .38's as well as two tubes of the plastique. You can also take all the tools except for one mechanic's set. You take the rest of the frozen stuff, I'll need the remaining cans and dehydrated supplies."

"Wow, Jake, we're leaving you with nothing!"

"I won't need much but rations for two for four months, which the cans and dry stuff will provide. And I'll need as much whale oil as we can safely ship."

"Again, Jake, what is so damned important that you've got to push 3,000 miles upwind in the winter, and with only one crew? Why ARE you going to France?"

"Again, son, I can't say, except that with success we should be back by the end of March. We must sail by the end of the week, so you and I, with only Connie's help, have a huge amount of work to do. Let's move *Constance* to the cove next to *Anne Marie* as soon as we can."

Jake then thought to share his plans with Arthur and Anne. He walked down through the orchard, along the road past the inlet, and up the lane to William's door. He found Anne sitting on the porch with her knitting needles flashing.

He sat in a chair next to her.

"Winter's coming, Jake. Making a sweater for father," she smiled at him.

"Aye," Jake replied, 'we'll be sailing out on another of Stephen's missions within the week. Thought to drop by and share thoughts with your Dad."

"He's gone into town with Tad. Just me here now. Are you taking your pretty little ship? I'd like to see it some time," she said.

Jake sat up shaking his head, He realized that Anne was right, she'd not seen his *Anne Marie*.

"Well, set that knitting down and let's take you out for a look. You'll find many things you've never seen. Come on," taking her hand, "let me show her to you before we take her apart."

As they walked across the yard to the path through the woods Anne asked, "Take her apart? Why ever for?"

"Well, as I said, I'm off on a voyage for awhile. When I get back I simply can't keep this boat in this time; you'll see why soon. It simply would raise too many questions. So, we're gong to hide many of her secrets in *Constance* for David and Connie"

Reaching the beach, Anne saw the rubber boat pulled up beyond the high tide line.

"Oh, should we go back and get a horse to pull your log raft into the water?" she asked.

He smiled and said, "Tad said almost the same when he first saw this boat. You're soon to see some strange and new things that came with us from our home in the future. I'll explain as I can."

She nodded, noticing that he lifted the apparently heavy boat made of great gray logs with just one hand, and easily dragged it to the water edge.

"Hop in" he said, holding the boat so she could step from the beach without wetting her leather shoes.

She raised her long skirt and stepped into the boat. Climbing over the center wooden seat she sat on the rear seat looking forward. Jake pushed off and sat facing her, sliding the aluminum oars onto their slots. She said nothing, just sat there looking very prim and proper, her hands folded in her lap and her hair wrapped up in the usual bun behind her head. Jake pushed off and rowed the short distance to *Anne Marie*. When the rubber boat bumped gently against the green hull Jake stood up, grabbing the toe rail. He took the painter to the little boat, and pulled himself up onto the large ketch.

"Wait just a minute while I get you a boarding ladder," he said.

"Don't be silly," she retorted as she too pulled herself from the little boat up the side of the yacht.

As David had done with her brother months ago, Jake started Anne with a tour of the upper deck, explaining the rig and telling her that the 'silver' metal wasn't silver at all, and showing her the electric winches. It looked odd to him to see this tall young lady dressed in a floor length cotton skirt with a white blouse buttoned to her neck and wrists climbing over the decks of *Anne Marie*.

He then slid the hatch open and dropped down into the salon. She followed.

"Aye, and it's so lovely in here," she blurted out, "and, there's that cushion I repaired for thee, I'm sorry that I couldn't exactly match the color."

She walked slowly through the salon, her eyes missing nothing. Then, she stepped into the galley.

"And, this is where ye cook," she said. "Where's thine fire?"

Jake walked to the propane stove and turned a knob. The flame popped up.

"Would you like a cold drink?" he asked.

She nodded, entranced by the immediate flame. He reached into the refrigerator and pulled out a can of Coke, which was all that was left of the canned drinks. He popped the top to her amazed eyes, and handed her the cold can. She sipped.

"On, that's so good! And, it bubbles in my mouth," she giggled.

Jake gently took the can from her and picked a glass from the rack. He poured the coke into the glass so she could se the bubbles rising up.

Passing it back to her he said, "I like it better out of a glass. Do you want some ice?"

"Ice?" she questioned.

"Sure," he said, reaching into the ice maker and dropping cubes into the glass full of Coke. "It's really best with ice."

She smiled at him.

"Do thee have any paintings or drawings of your former life?' she asked.

He thought for a moment, then said, "Sure, I almost forgot. Of course I've a bunch of pictures saved on my laptop. Here, have a seat at the table and I'll go and get it."

She wondered why he'd need to find the top to his lap. Still, he went to the nav station and picked up a small flat black box. He flipped a switch on the panel, and the cabin became filled with the piano notes of Chopin. He sat next to her, opened the 'box' and booted-up the PC.

"Why it's a miracle," she mouthed as the Windows icon faded.

Jake's PC Wallpaper, showing the Shaw Shipyard logo, appeared. He clicked into 'My Documents' then into 'My Pictures'. The screen filled with tiny thumbnails. Selecting one, he clicked on it. A photo of Connie sitting in her new red Miata filled the screen. Behind the Miata was Jake's house set in a green grassy lawn. Connie was smiling and waving towards the camera from the little sport scar.

Anne reached towards the screen and gently touched it. Running her fingers gently across the photo she said, "Why, it looks like we're looking through a window, actually at Connie, but her clothes are different, and what is that little red wagon? Oh, of course, this is from your future, er, where you came from, but how can that machine see into it?"

Jake said, "Let me show you."

He took a small silver box from a drawer and pointed it at Connie. It made a click. He then silently connected it with a wire to the small laptop and punched a few keys. Anne's face appeared on the screen.

"That's me!" she exclaimed. "How did that machine paint my picture? It was so fast, and it looks like, well, exactly as I see it?"

"Anne," he rested his hand on her shoulder and said softly, "There are so many things that will change in the next two centuries. In fact, more will change than have changed in the past thousand years. Still the only changes are inventions that will make life on this Earth perhaps easier, more pleasant, and perhaps more entertaining. Really, in the true important matters, relationships between people and beliefs in their God, well, nothing changes.."

That makes sense," she said. "And, of course you can't go back there, can you?"

"Nope," he grinned, "I'm stuck here with you. In fact, I think I like it better. Life is really much simpler. Still, Connie misses it a great deal, which is why I am taking all the future things off of this boat and giving it all to Connie."

"And, what of this little ship?" she asked.

"I'm going away for awhile, on a mission with Stephen. When it ends and I come back we'll just have to find a way to hide her permanently."

"Destroy it?"

"Perhaps," he said ruefully, "but it'll wait until I return."

"When will that be do you think?"

"Well, not before mid winter at best, maybe as late as early spring."

She snuggled closer to him and raised her face to look into his eyes. Without thinking about it he lowered his chin. Their lips came together.

"No," he whispered as he pulled away.

"It's too soon," he continued. "But, when I get back-"

"We'd better get up to the house," she said, standing with a small smile. "My stew will be cold if I don't feed the fire."

It took most of the following week to disassemble *Anne Marie.*

The small stores and spare tanks, tools and small pumps were easy. However the ONAN and the refrigeration were a special problem, particularly as there remained still a frozen pile of basics in the freezer. To uncouple the power for even a full day would cause it all to thaw.

Jake allowed the deck house over the reefer box to be cut away. The yardarm of the *Constance* was used as a boom crane, with *Anne Marie*'s electric winches on the ropes, to haul the reefer full of food from the bowels of the sleek green ketch and deposit it into the hold of the barkentine. Within less than six hours the Onan generator was likewise disconnected, hauled up from *Anne Marie*'s engine room, and bolted deep in the after hold of *Constance.* A line was run to a fixed barrel of whale oil, and they had power to the reefer plates before anything had had chance to thaw.

So followed the heating and A/C plant, the washer and dryer, the entertainment center and even Connie's hair dryer.

At the end of five days *Anne Marie* was a stripped-out hulk below decks. Only the Captain's cabin retained any comforts, and the two pipe berths had been left untouched in the fore peak. The full 40' length of the former salon, galley and center staterooms was gone, leaving an empty hold which Jake planned to fill with barrels of whale oil.

Anne Marie would be a floating bomb.

Meanwhile the rear third of *Constance* had been transformed into a modern yacht below decks. It was not yet all quite plugged in and working, but Jake and David had created a modern head (bathroom) for Connie, complete to a hot shower. There was also a functioning modern galley with under-deck access to the reefer of frozen foods. Connie was thrilled with it all, and with David's encouragement she envisioned having most of the modern equipment moved to a private rear upstairs apartment in their new home in Escambia.

Constance still had her twelve nine pounders on deck, and had not lost any storage in her powder magazine. She still carried the cannon balls, chain shot and bags of grape shot needed to fight the ship. She could ship a crew of forty in hammocks forward. The ship remained a trim and fast privateer.

On the last day, with all the work finally done in late afternoon, Jake planned to use the ketch to tow *Constance* back to the shipyard where the oil could be loaded. He'd arranged for all the workmen to have the afternoon off so nobody would see the green ketch. Both little ships planned to sail east up the Sound together on the next morning ebb.

Jake, Stephen and young Arnought would sail on *Anne Marie* in company with *Constance*, with David as Captain. Once past the blockade David planned to wait for *Martha* so he could re-assemble his former crew of the same fourteen sailors who had traveled south with them on the last voyage. *Constance* would turn south for a new home in Escambia and *Martha* could return her crew of Englishmen to Halifax. Of course, Jake, in *Anne Marie,* wouldn't stop. He planned to blast east towards France with news of Saratoga just as fast as he could cross the Atlantic.

At dusk, with the oil loaded below, Jake was preparing to cast off from jetty to take *Anne Marie* back to her hiding spot in the little cove.

He went to Connie and put his arm around her waist saying, "Connie, 'how bout you and your old man sail *Anne Marie* around the point. Just may be the last time we're both on this particular boat together; y'know we can't keep her."

"I'd like that, Dad"

Then to David she called out, "gonna sail around the point with Dad. We should be back in the cove in an hour. Will you meet us at William's when you're finished here?"

"OK", said David, watching as his crew loaded fresh water into casks on *Constance*.

Under a gentle westerly Jake simply used the large furling Genoa to coast *Anne Marie* out of the river and around to the hidden cove. He had become so familiar with the anchorage that he didn't even bother with the sonar.

As they made the first turn in the tricky channel, now pointing almost due west, Connie piped up, "This is the first time I've sailed into the cove since we got here. Hmmm, isn't that Griffish Rock?"

"Sure is. Certainly looks different now."

The last time Connie had seen that large rock at the shore it had a cute little gazebo on top of it, with Dr. Griffish's large white brick home on a rise behind acres of manicured lawns and gardens. Now the rock, unadorned, simply sat at the water's edge in a corn field.

"Are you and David gonna be all right?" Jake asked quietly as the ketch ghosted along in the evening breeze.

"I think so," then she smiled. "He's been so wonderful. It's been really tough to realize that life here is so different, and that I'll never see Mom again. I just wish she could know that we didn't just die at sea. She'll be so sad thinking we're both gone."

"I feel the same, sweetheart," Jake said quietly to his daughter. "Still I have a confession for you."

He held her hand and continued, "Your Mom and I were always so close, and here we've been apart for almost four months. It seems far longer since it's so different here. And, Connie, your Mom and I always agreed that if something happened to one of us the other could, uuh."

"Dad," Connie exclaimed, "you're going to tell me that you and Anne ~."

He looked at her, "Nothing has been said at all, and my aren't you the perceptive one? I just don't want to ~."

"Dad, I think Anne and you are a fantastic couple, and that's not saying anything bad or against Mom. Really, Dad, we are stuck here. There's no way you can ever get back to where Mom is. I just wish so much that we could tell her that we're not dead. I mean, she would go on with her life too if she knows you and I are alive, even if we can't be with her again."

"Dad, there's one more thing she needs to know," Connie blushed, "David doesn't know it yet, but we're going to have a baby in the spring."

"Oh Connie," Jake hugged his daughter, "that's wonderful!"

"Now, Dad, listen to me and don't let Anne get away," she kissed his cheek, "Mom would approve. Really."

"Darling, I promise I'll find some way to somehow get a message to your Mom. I do promise."

"Well, Dad, you need to ask Anne to marry you. How about an April wedding? The weather should be good here by then, and I should still be able to travel."

He replied, "Anne will have something to say about that, and I certainly can't ask until I am safely home. I'll get word to you before winter is over. We're back to communication through letters by sailing ships now, no more instant phone calls. On second thought, perhaps you should stay here from April until the baby comes. We've got to have better care here for you than you'll have in the wilds of Florida. Anyway, think about it."

As the moon was rising they were ghosting up-river to anchor in the cove.

David was waiting on the beach for them. As soon as the anchor was down, Connie and Jake inflated the small Zodiac, and Connie took Jake in to the beach.

"Dad, I can't go to Anne's house dressed like this. Come on, David, let's go back to the boat together. Dad, we'll be along shortly".

Jake nodded and walked up the path towards the farmhouse.

After Jake left the for Williams' house Connie took David by the hand and puttered the small Zodiac back aboard *Anne Marie*. She wanted just a little more time with David alone. She stepped aboard the stripped ketch and led him down into the untouched stern cabin. Flipping on the one remaining 12 volt light so well hidden in an old lantern body, she then sat him on the soft double bed and gave him a deep kiss.

"Wait here" she whispered, and vanished into the little head, returning in a moment in a sheer negligee carrying a small vial of liquid.

"WOW!" he exclaimed, already aroused by his beautiful wife's body visible through the sheer material.

"Come here," he purred.

"Not just yet. Look at this," she said softly.

"What is it?" he was distracted by the green stuff in the vial.

"It's green."

"So?"

"I had two of those kits, y'know, just in case. I mean, its green which means you're gonna be a daddy."

"Oh, my lovely wife," David crooned as he folded her in his arms.

An hour later David arose and dressed. He nudged Connie.

"Come on honey. We're already late for dinner."

"Go on ahead, I'll need a bit longer than you, you messy boy," she whispered a satisfied reply.

"I'll wait."

"No, go on ahead. Jake. Anne and Dad are waiting with Stephen and that young kid, what's his name?"

"Steve Arnought."

"Hmmm, but he seems young for an Officer. Anyway, tell them I'll be right along. I know my way up the path."

"Okay," he replied, "but take this, you'll need it," setting a five cell Maglight on the table, "and this too, no arguments," pulling his small chromed .38 automatic pistol from a pocket in his jacket.

"I don't want to carry a gun." she retorted.

"I know you're safe. It's not far up to Williams, but it is dark outside. Please humor me, or I'll just wait on deck for you."

"No, I'll take the damned gun. Go on, get out of here," and she jumped in his arms, naked, and gave him a deep kiss.

"Maybe we ought to— ," he started.

"No, you horny old man. Go tell the folks I'll be along soon. It is our last night here and we'll need to be there for Dad. I think he's going to ask Anne to marry him."

CHAPTER FIFTEEN

It had been a long wait, John Aaron exulted to himself with a smirk.

He had not heard from the farmer Stone for almost two months. Yet, just three days ago Stone had arrived on a small fishing smack hailing *Reliant*. He had appeared very surprised to find Aaron was the ship's captain, but he still delivered the long awaited message that Aaron had hoped for.

Stone had said that both the young blonde woman witch-doctor and her husband had been spied by Stone in the new shipyard where Stone had finally been hired on. And, Stone had found the green ketch in a hidden cove on William's property, on the east side of the Point, where the charts showed no such cove existed.

Aah, Aaron gloated, he could now follow the rest of his orders! He could grab the witch, and perhaps more parts from the damned mysterious ketch. He would then depart his station immediately and sail directly for Portsmouth to get her to Whitehall where her phony story would be disproven. He had orders for this eventuality, signed by Sir Wembly. All he had to do was send a message to Wembly as he departed these infernal shores.

Aah, he gloated, to bring the witch with such a healing power to the King could bring him a peerage!

Indeed, after she had escaped the second time he had felt the fool with Sir Wembly. Now he finally had orders to find the little bitch and drag her to Portsmouth. It was finally possible.

At long last this October evening he had the answer he'd been waiting for from that weasel of a spy, and he had arrived just in time. Captain Wembly had given up on finding her, and Aaron had just received Orders to immediately sail *Reliant* to Portsmouth with dispatches, and for a much needed refit.

God knows, Aaron thought, his ship needed the refit. Her copper had been pulled off her bottom in long strips, and she dragged long green trails of weeds. He and Captain Wembly were both aware that without the copper covering, worms could soon destroy *Reliant*, as she was far from new.

Now his Orders to sail for Portsmouth would have the added bonus of delivering Wembly's prize. He exulted again; he'd now have that vixen.

As soon as the spy, Stone, had been dropped back in the smack with his ten guineas Aaron wasted no time. He was on his quarterdeck yelling for all hands.

Reliant charged west towards Roank Point.

A day and a half later, an hour after dusk with a half-moon in the west, *Reliant* had silently dropped anchor off the west side of the point. Lt. Aaron was in the twelve-oar longboat ghosting along the shore towards the secret cove, a map of which his spy, the noxious Stone, had drawn for them.

Aaron was gloating to himself that he'd soon have that mystery ketch captured or sunk, and, with luck they would find the bitch in the self same farmhouse. The eight armed marines in the boat would indeed make short work of a handful of undefended Yankee farmers

The silently rowing cutter did find the cove using the crude map drawn by Stone, and just as had been advised, the ketch was silhouetted in the moonlight. Aaron had his crew row silently around it. Moonlight glistened off what appeared to be bright silver rigging, and there were no ratlines. How, he questioned to himself,, did they raise the sails?

"Give way quietly now, Men'" he commanded, "Bring us along her port side."

The longboat slid quietly along the side of the ketch until with a SLAM a hatch was flung open, and an incredibly bright stab of light shot straight upwards! There she was, dressed in full length dress, looking indeed like a proper lady. She stabbed the piercing light over the starboard side and jumped lightly into a small bobbing boat on the opposite side of the ship.

"Close with her," Aaron whispered roughly.

The twelve oared boat jumped forward, wheeling around the stern of *Anne Marie*. Aaron saw the girl pulling on something at the back of the boat.

As soon as Aaron noticed that they were aimed to collide with the little boat, he whispered, "Toss Oars."

Then he barked, "Grab her!"

As Connie heard the shout she reacted instinctively. She turned from trying to start the outboard motor, pulled the .38 caliber automatic pistol from a pocket in the billowing dress, and pointed it at the black boat looming from the moonlight. She closed her eyes and blasted off all eight shots in half as many seconds.

Two men screamed in pain.

Aaron slashed at her boat with his cutlass, trying to lodge the blade into the wood. His cutlass passed right through the boat causing a huge blast of air; the sword flying from his hand to land 30 feet away at the water edge.

Connie felt the sword swing by her and pierce the rubber boat as a dark figure in the rear of the black boat yelled out.

"Do not harm the lass! Grab her boat."

Still, momentarily distracted, she felt several strong arms pluck her from the shriveling small rubber boat and twist her into the large wooden boat. She threw the gun at the guy in the rear seat, seeing it bounce off his head and splash into the cove. She clobbered the giant who held her with the five cell Maglight in her other hand, screaming at the top of her voice.

It did no good.

The Maglight fell out of her hand on the rail of their boat, and sank into the cove. She was dragged over the side, roughly gagged with a rag that tasted like vomit, and felt herself thrown in the bilge. A huge boot was forced the air from her lungs.

"We've got her," a hoarse whisper.

"Grab her boat's line and back to the ship wid her and her boat."

"'Er boat's half sunk, but megods it's light," another voice remarked.

Connie was quickly tied ankle to wrist and left in the bilge of the boat as it was rowed for a very long time, her half-deflated Zodiac bobbing along behind. She felt the boat bump alongside a ship in the moonlight. The boat crew climbed up the side of the ship leaving Connie tied in the boat until it too had been hoisted aboard. She was then unceremoniously dumped on the deck and dragged down three ladders to the very bowels of the ship. She felt the ropes loosen around her legs only to immediately find her ankles were placed in solid hoops of iron which were bolted closed.

As they tore off her gag she screamed, "You damned bastards, why have you kidnapped me again".

The heavy door slammed closed and she heard the heavy bold sliding home.

Very soon later she heard the clanking of the pauls of the capstan as the anchor was hauled up, followed by the now familiar sounds of muffled shouts and the thunder of many booted feet as the crew was sent to the yards to make sail. With a creak of rigging the ship healed very lightly and Connie could hear the lap of moving water outside the hull above her head.

Just then she felt a furry rat scurry across her jeans, and another tug at her deck shoe !

"No," she yelled as she kicked at the rats in despair.

Then she forced herself to calm down. She stood up and leaned against the hull for what seemed a very long time, knowing the rats wouldn't bother her standing up.

"Clank, Thud," and the little door flew open. Lt. Williamswright was there with a lantern.

"Good evening, Miss," he began, "methinks we need —"

"What the hell do you think you're doing?" she screamed at him," who are you British thugs? This is the second damned time you've kidnapped me. What the hell is going on? Where are you taking me now? You simply must put me back ashore."

She stomped her foot on the deck, her chains rattling.

"Miss, ye'r a recaptured prisoner of the Crown," Williamswright continued firmly. "We can leave ye here, and re-bolt the door, or ye can help us revive the Captain, and help with the damage ye've done to Jones and Sherman, both gunshot and bleeding in the orlop, thanks t'ye. What'll it be? The surgeon's on his way to bleed the Captain, then 'e says Sherman's arm needs come off."

Connie was instantly mortified that she'd done such harm to people.

"Okay, I'll help," she said.

"Aye, thankee," the junior lieutenant responded.

He bent down and unlocked the chains. Then he led her upwards and aft to the Cabin.

"And, if ye'll give ye're parole that ye'll not do more damage or try to leap from the ship, we'll give ye ye'r old cabin back."

"I'll not give you any damned promise," she retorted. "I'll make every attempt to run as soon as you get close to the American shore".

"That'll be a very long time, if forever," he quipped, "Y'see we're bound for Portsmouth, and a cold and wet voyage it'll be at this time o'year."

"England?" she stopped, aghast.

"Aye, M'lady. Now will thee offer ye'r parole? It'll be a far better crossing for thee in the cabin than locked here."

She nodded, instantly aghast at the thought that she was lost to David. Then she quietly smiled to herself. No, David and Jake would find her gone, and they had to follow, didn't they? Dad was also crossing the Atlantic, wasn't he?

By then they had reached the door to the Captain's cabin. As soon as it was opened Connie saw the old sail maker/surgeon, Oakes, leaning over the unconscious Captain. The Captain's arm was bare and a dirty scalpel was poised to open a vein to drain blood into a stained little white porcelain bowl.

"Stop that man," cried Connie.

"What are you doing, Oakes," she demanded.

The sail maker/surgeon simply stared at her replying, "I'm bleeding 'em, can't yer see? Wot else ees ter do fer the unconsciousness but to take humors off the blood."

"Get him away from here," demanded Connie, "Let me see this man," referring to the unconscious Captain Aaron.

"Hmmm, he is out cold," she said to Wilright, "but seems no depression of the skull, just this nasty wound where my gun hit him when I threw it. Damn, but he's cut to the bone."

"Ian," she said to the Captain's servant with the wooden leg, "Bring me some fine brandy, and boil these bandages. Get me the sail maker's needles and some catgut."

"Canna, Miss," said the steward. 'Der galley fires be out fer the night. Canna boil nothing."

"For the love of god, Man, get the fires re-started. We need clean boiled bandages and catgut. While you're boiling I need to look at the injured men in the Orlop. The Captain will be fine for the moment."

With that she simply left the captain's cabin and took herself, Williamswright following, forward out of the cabin and down two levels to the smoky lantern-lit orlop deck where the Sail maker had preceded her.

As she entered the poorly lit little space in the bilges of the frigate she saw the bent frame of the old sail maker, who had arrived ahead of her, preparing to lop off an arm with a multiple fracture where her pistol's bullet had smashed through the forearm. The sailor, Saunder's, bone had pierced through the upper arm, and three sailors were holding him down on a wooden trestle, There was a knot of pine in his jaws, and his eyes were rolled back in his head.

"Stop there, Oakes," Connie demanded, stamping her foot. "We can save the arm. No need to amputate."

"Nay, missy," the old surgeon replied, "even if we can reset the bone, putrefaction will set in and he'll be gone in three days. Thar's no other way."

"Dammit, Oakes, leave it to me!" she insisted, pushing the older gent aside.

"Willright (using the nickname) we need more boiled cloths here, some more boiled catgut, and a strong oak barrel stave some four inches wide and three feet long. Move now so we can save this man's arm."

"Cookie's got his fire going, Miss", retorted Williamswright. There's one more over here. You know t'was you who injured the Captain and shot these two."

"Oh yes", she was aghast, "I'd not realized that until you so said, Lieutenant. I'll do my best to see these men recover, but you all still are nothing more than criminals."

"Miss Connie", Williamswright replied, "I must be about the ship. Y' know seaman Cory, ee's back with us, and I've assigned him to look after ye."

Connie was startled. Cory? Her first patient from, oh how long ago when she was first on this smelly tub? Yet there he was, smiling at her.

The third injured man, a simple topman, sat with his hand pressing a bandage to his leg.

"Tiz okay I am, Maam. Friend of Cory's too, aye, never thought 'ee'd ever come back aboard, but 'ere he is. I know ye'll get the damned bullet out of me so it won't putrefy, and so as the master won't take me leg." he said tentatively.

"And what's your name, sailor?" she asked him.

"Ned Cox, Maam," he replied, "and your doctoring is famous here so I won't worry none."

"Okay, Cory" she began, "the most urgent is the Captain. We'll work him first. I just hope the boiled bandages are ready soon. After he's settled we need set this arm, and last, get the bullet and splinter from Mr. Cox' leg."

Cox, overhearing, asked, "Wat's this 'bout a splinter, Maam? All I know is that splinters cause putrefaction, and that'll cost me leg."

"No, Sailor. Worry not. Yes, you've a splinter from the boat railing, and I'm sorry to keep you waiting behind more urgent cases, but all of you will be fine. Perhaps, Ian, you can find a double ration of rum for this sailor?"

She ascended to the Captain's Cabin, Cory, Oakes and Williamswright all following. Sitting by his head she took one of Oakes scalpels, now having soaked in brandy for a half hour, and cut off the dirty rag wrapped around Aaron's head. It was a nasty mess there; her gun butt had cut him deeply leaving a six inch gash all the way to the white bone in his forehead. First, she cleaned the wound thoroughly with the brandy. Next, she took a freshly boiled sail needle and a boiled string of cat gut. She gently made seven neat stitches to close the wound.

There, she nodded to herself, at least he'd not die, although the scar would always be visible on his forehead. Then she thought further, another scar on his face shouldn't matter. He deserved worse.

As soon as he was re-bandaged in clean boiled linen, Connie and Willright left for the orlop, leaving strict instructions with Ian to call her when the Captain awoke, or at dawn if he did not.

First she treated the unknown seaman with the compound fracture arm. It was easy enough, now with clean bandages, to get Oakes to hold his arms while Cory and Connie pulled the crenellated muscle back to a stretched position under the skin. The sailor screamed once with the pain and passed out. Connie set the compound fracture end-to-end so it could heal straight, doused the wound with more of the captain's brandy and wrapped the oak stave splint in the clean white linen bandage.

Last, she turned to seaman Cox who was all but passed-out from the rum. She asked Willright and Oakes to hold his leg down while she probed into the wound with the crude forceps from the sail maker's kit. She grabbed the bullet and pulled it out, followed by a small wooden splinter behind it. Again, more dousing in brandy as the red blood welled up out of the incision. She took two neat catgut stitches to close the wound and used the last of the boiled bandage.

"You'll be walking on that leg in a couple of days, Cox," she told him as she rose, realizing she was totally exhausted.

She climbed up the two ladders from the orlop deck to the main deck and back to her little cabin just off the gunroom. She asked Oakes over her shoulder if he would please get her a bucket of water to clean up, and find her a clean jersey and pair of ducks for the next day.

Ten minutes later she had climbed into the little hard bunk after bolting the door and washing her face. She did notice that at least the water she got in the bucket was reasonably clean. And, after all the activity of the previous hours, following such a wonderful day with David, Connie was simply too exhausted to cry herself to sleep. She passed out in the little cabin with no idea if it was day or night.

"Sail Ho," she heard a cry on deck over her head, waking her.

"Shall we put about to give chase?" a voice cried.

"Nay," came Willright's muted reply. "We'll not take action without the Captain."

Connie fell back asleep.

CHAPTER SIXTEEN

The eight shots from the pistol boomed across the peaceful point.

"What was that?" Anne startled.

"Pistol Shots!" David jumped up.

"Connie!" he yelled, worried.

He ran to the door with Jake and Stephen on his heels. They dashed through the woods to the little beach. They could see *Anne Marie* still anchored with the hatch open and a light glowing inside, but there was no Zodiac and no Connie.

David didn't hesitate. He dove into the water and swam quickly to the ship. He pulled himself hand over hand up the anchor chains and ran through the vessel.

He found no Connie.

"Connie!" he yelled.

And yelled again, "C O N N I E !".

It was dead quiet.

Jake yelled to David, "Come on ashore, David. I've found something."

David quickly swam to the beach.

"What's that?" he asked.

The moonlight glimmered against a long piece of dull metal sticking up from the stones at the edge of the water. It had a handle on it.

Jake pulled it up.

"This is a damned sword."

He turned it in his hand.

"British navy cutlass," corrected Stephen, "but from where?"

David put it together fast, "Jake, Stephen, the only answer is that the damned Redcoats have again grabbed her, just like the last time. Damn, but I should have paid her more attention when she said she was afraid they'd come back, I just didn't think it would happen. Who would go to all that effort for one escaped prisoner? Yes, it can only be that those British bastards have re-captured her."

"Seems they also got a Zodiac and a fifteen horse Evinrude too," Jake said. "Those things can't get away from us either. We'll be discovered if real authorities get that stuff."

"They can't be gone more than a quarter hour," stated Stephen. "It's been no more than that since the shots."

Jake replied, "Back to the house and let's find a way to get Connie and the Zodiac back."

Less than a half hour later they had the beginnings of a plan. They realized that the only way Connie could have been so neatly taken was by a ship, and any such ship could only sail east. And, the breeze was light.

Jake and David ran to *Anne Marie*, fully fueled and ready for sea back in the cove. They could run at a full 13 knots under engine alone along the rocky Connecticut lea shore, where the Frigate would never dare sail. They could get to Plum Gut before the Frigate, and would follow the damned ship by radar until they learned where she was headed.

Jake wondered briefly where they might be going? Was Connie being taken back to New York? To Halifax? To where? Certainly, if *Anne Marie* could catch the frigate, that ship's course outside Montauk would indicate the frigate's destination. Jake's plan was then to double back to meet *Constance*, just past the blockade line, south of Montauk.

Stephen, and Arnought would sail with Jake, immediately, as *Anne Marie* was ready for a morning departure anyway. David and his crew would follow *Anne Marie*, in *Constance,* several hours behind. They'd plan their recovery of Connie depending on the frigate's course from Montauk.

All night Jake squeezed the wheel of *Anne Marie* as the ketch pounded at full speed up the unlit Connecticut coastline. He watched the radar screen closely, but his mind was in a turmoil. What if they were taking her back to New York? How could they retake her from under the guns of the entire English fleet?

At dawn Jake was surprised to see a brig sailing west across the sound. The surprise was greater when the frigate he was just passing in the dark failed to wheel about and pursue the prize. *Anne Marie* slipped un-noticed past the enemy warship.

By afternoon *Anne Marie* was creeping along in a fog bank smack in the center of the Race at the exit of Long Island Sound. The engine was barely ticking over, keeping her in place against the three knot ebb.

"Stephen," Jake called out. "There's something moving east, inshore along Fisher's Island. Bear right, about ninety degrees."

Stephen turned the big wheel.

"Steady there, it should be 500 yards ahead. You ought to smell them soon."

"By the mark four," came a faint cry through the fog.

"Hear that, Jake ?" asked Stephen.

"Aye," replied Jake.

"They're creeping along in soundings. When they loose the bottom to the east of the island they'll know they can bear south to clear Montauk."

"Are you sure it's our Frigate?

"Who but them would be in enough of a hurry to risk sailing in this pea soup with nightfall coming? Let's give them some sea room in case it clears."

An hour later they had sailed out of the fog and into a moonlight sea. Their radar continued to show the British ship a few miles ahead. They soon had their answer as to the ship's course. The frigate did not bear west towards New York once clear of Montauk. It didn't veer north towards Halifax either. No. The larger ship simply continued due east, just barely visible in the moonlight, spreading more sail in the light northwest breeze.

"I fear they're headed home." Jake said.

"Home?"

"Yes, lad. Odds are that they're off to Portsmouth."

"England?" Stephen queried.

"Yes."

"Now, let's jibe back towards Montauk and have a war council with David."

"How far ahead is that frigate?" Stephen asked.

"I've been holding at 5 miles. They've certainly not seen us, but they surely might were we to hoist a sail or draw any closer."

"If we double back can we find it again?" Stephen queried.

"Yes. This time of year she'll bear due east as long as the weather holds. She'll not try for the North Atlantic, the storms are worse to the north in the winter. No, she'll cross the Gulf Stream and bear east north east just at the south edge of the Stream. The weather will worsen past Newfoundland. Anyway, as long as the wind doesn't pick up they'll be moving slowly. We should have time to find *Constance* and return before that damned ship has too much of a head start. It'll be easy to find them with the radar."

With that they doubled back, the big diesel pushing them at thirteen knots through the gentle swells.

A half hour later they could see *Constance* emerging from the east of Gardner's Island under full sail in the now ebbing current. There was no sight of any British blockade ships.

"David, this is Jake," he spoke into the VCR microphone.

"I hear you, David replied on the hand-held unit, "did you find her?"

"Yes. And, I've no doubt that she's aboard. Damned frigate passed-up an easy prize and that tells me it's on an important mission."

"David, he continued, "I read it that they're off to home, theirs I mean, Portsmouth."

"You think they're taking her to England?" David said through the radio.

"Not much doubt of that, son. 'Round up and drop an anchor, we need a plan to get her back."

Within minutes the two ships were anchored together close to Montauk Point. David, Stephen and Jake were huddled on *Anne* Marie. And, Jake was surprised to see Phillip Strong was with them.

"Phillip, how did you get there?" he asked.

"Damned strange, Sir. We were returning up sound in *Martha* with ye'r load of knees and a frigate passed not two miles from us. We thought we were gonners, but she sailed right on by. Then we see *Constance* just a few hours later going the same way. She saw our signals."

David interrupted, "Phil came aboard and offered to trade the rest of our original crew for the new Florida boys on *Constance*. We've our original crew back, and Phillip is with me as our sailing master."

"Okay, I guess that *Anne Marie,* can dog the frigate using my radar," Jake said, "and keep in touch with you on *Constance* by radio."

"Nay, Jake," came Stephen's reply. "I know it's ye'r daughter, but thee said urself, if we dinna get to France before end of November we'll not git Franklin's news to 'em."

Stephen continued, "Aye, it's ye'r daughter, Jake, but she's also David's wife. Really, Sir, I believe that only you and I together with Arnought could get safely to France in ye'r ketch, and it'll take all we can do to get an audience with Dr. Franklin. He'll then need to have something to convince the French Court."

Jake replied, "Perhaps, Stephen, but without the radar on *Anne Marie* we'd likely loose that frigate at sea. Then Connie would be lost. I'll not risk that. Worse, they have some really damning evidence on that ship that will really change History if it gets to London."

"Can the radar machine not be moved to *Constance*?" Stephen asked.

"Hmmm," Jake thought for awhile.

"Yes, I suppose we could do it, as long as it remains calm. It would take me several hours to take the sending unit off the mast of *Anne Marie*. See that box on the main mast?" Jake pointed upward.

"Then I'd need fish the power line and the coax cable down through he center of the mast. Meanwhile, David could remove the receiving unit. I suppose he could then get underway. He wouldn't need me to re-install the unit."

"Hmmm," Jake continued, "He'd have to install the sending unit at the top of the main mast and duct tape the power and coax wires to a jack stay."

"Yes, Stephen, we could do it."

"Then, Jake, t'would seem that *Constance* could shadow the frigate on her voyage? Won't *Constance* be much faster in any weather? More, will *Anne Marie* not make the crossing weeks faster than under sail? Was that not the plan?"

David spoke up, "Okay, Stephen. And yes, I need to get my wife back from those assholes worse than Jake needs that damned Zodiac. Still, I agree that the Zodiac and whatever of our stuff they have simply can't find its way to England. So, yes, you need to stay on this boat, and let me chase that damned Brit in *Constance*."

"What 'bout the Radar?" asked Jake. "I can get it off the mast and packaged for *Constance* in an hour. Y'all will need it to follow that frigate."

"I'll take it," replied David., "we'll even drape it in old canvas so nobody can really see it. You know my crew is a part of us, sworn to secrecy and all, so we're okay there. And, with the radar aboard, the damned Brit simply can't get away. We are much faster and more agile than he can possibly be. It'll be fun to drive him nuts."

Jake said thoughtfully, "All you can do is follow him. I can't see how you could get close enough to get Connie back without being blasted out of the water. Yes, I'll be sure to meet up with you before you reach England, and perhaps with two ships we can find a way to stop them. Anyway, it's probably better they aren't going to New York. It'd be really tough to recapture her there."

He continued thoughtfully," I'm guessing from looking at the wind charts for this time of year that he'll hold east almost directly for the Azores, then beat north to England once clear of the worst of the North Atlantic gales. It'll take them twenty-five days at best, and I'll have *Anne Marie* across to France in only nine or ten."

Within an hour of amazingly fast work Jake single-handedly removed the radar unit from his mizzen, pulled the wiring down through the mast, and lifted the repeater from its pedestal. David then swung it all across to *Constance*.

While David was busy installing and camouflaging the radar unit with Phil and old Howard's help, Thad Williams already had *Constance* under all plain sail, moving gently east towards the horizon over which the British had disappeared with Connie.

Jake pulled *Anne Marie* along side *Constance*.

He yelled, "David, how 'bout a tow until the wind picks up? I think we can get you to seven or eight knots. If the breeze stays light we can probably catch the frigate before dawn."

A half hour later, just after midnight, found *Anne Marie* straining against a one inch nylon anchor line with *Constance Shaw*, fully rigged, her sails barely pulling, in tow. Together they were making just over seven knots, or likely over twice the speed of the frigate, somewhere ahead of them over the horizon. Hopefully Jake's guess was right.

But,, but by dawn there was still nothing in sight. They kept pushing through the daylight. At 10:14 in the morning Jake's VHF crackled to life.

"Jake, we have them. Picked them up on radar awhile ago and we've just seen their sail on the port bow, hull down."

"Okay, David," Jake replied through his hand-held unit. "We're casting you off. Remember, no matter what, we will be waiting for you at the agreed coordinates, just 120 miles southwest of the Lizard. I'll be there ahead of you, no matter what. We'll have to figure out how to deal with that frigate before she makes landfall. We have an EBRIB sending unit. Use your receiver when you're positioned. We can then find each other."

"Okay, and safe voyage to you and Stephen."

Anne Marie retrieved her anchor (towing) line and veered northeast under full power in the still light breeze. She was out of sight to *Constance Shaw* within an hour.

David and Phillip with *Constance's* crew of fourteen were left to race after the frigate, then just barely in sight twenty miles ahead. No, David didn't want to get too close, but neither did they want to loose track of the ship with Connie aboard.

The next day at dawn they sighted the British ship again. Phillip had purposely sailed a full two points farther off the wind than *Constance* could, attempting to track a heading that the square rigged frigate should head.

And, indeed, just after dawn the next day Harold, from the foremast top had spotted square topsails poking over the horizon to leeward.

"Tad," hollered David from the main deck, "do you think it's her? Is she flying a commission pennant from the main?"

" Aye, a long narrow red one. Can only be the same frigate."

David and Phillip ran up the foremast ratlines.

"That'll be the British frigate then, I guess we have to assume it's the same one." David said as he slid down a back stay to the deck.

"Canna be more than one dispatch vessel for England this late in the year. And it'll be a rough passage when the storms hit," replied Phillip.

"Storms? Yes, I've heard a winter crossing is rough."

"Aye, Cap'n," Harold, the mate, replied, "The North Atlantic's no millpond this time o' year. We can plan for strong easterly gales all the way across. Hope thee can keep yonder ship close enough to follow, and still keep away from 'er teeth."

"Let's drop down on 'er?" David smiled. "We'll let 'em know we're here. And, knowing that Connie's aboard, perhaps a sight of our topsails will cheer her up."

"Aye, Sir, but don't get too close."

Harold, a natural sailor, simply kept *Constance* sheeted for a close reach and drove her head to a far reach, slowing the vessel down and giving her an unkempt appearance. They still crept up on the larger British ship.

When they had come to perhaps two miles from the frigate the aftermost gun port popped open and a squirt of fire and black smoke belched out. A cannonball splashed to the sea perhaps 500 yards from their leeward bow.

"Shall I run up our colors?" shouted Phillip with excitement in his voice.

"That'll be enough." David cautioned, "No need to let them know exactly who we are. Sharpen her up and let's away to windward. They'll not sail within two points of us into the wind."

The sheets were drawn in, the sails were all trimmed, and with Phillip at the helm, the speedy barkentine flew up into the wind. It took less than a half day; but by noon the frigate was a mere spec of white from the main top at the apex of each wave.

Still, the radar pegged their target, albeit a poor return, at over 16 miles.

They held their exact position, sixteen miles to windward of the frigate, for the next four days. All the time both ships were headed just north of east, with the frigate clearly on a close hauled tack headed for England. The frigate was slow, and it sagged off to leeward farther than Phillip thought she should. He thought her bottom must be really foul.

At 4:00 on the fifth morning, as he did at the end of each watch after nightfall, David lit off the tiny diesel generator and powered-up the radar set. He peered at the rotating strobe and found no frigate. It was gone!

"All Hands on Deck!" he yelled at the top of his voice as soon as he got to the poop, "Slack Sheets! Set forecourse, topsail and skysail."

David thought, recalling his long talks with Phillip, that the British frigate had probably slacked sheets in the dark, trying to slip away to the south and east. It was the only course open to them. In ten minutes the handy barkentine was also creaming away to the southeast at a lovely fifteen knots.

Fortunately, Phillip's counsel proved right. Just after noon the lookout at the masthead cried out, "Sail Ho, one point on the larboard bow."

By the next morning the North Atlantic had reverted to it's usual late fall weather. The wind had increased to a mild gale, consistently over 30 knots from the west North West. The track to England required the square rigged frigate to beat into the wind, taking many long tacks with small daily gains.

David, with the *Constance* sailing far easier than the heavy frigate, simply followed in the frigate's tracks. At the end of each tack the topsails of the larger ship could be barely seen on the windward quarter, yet after *Constance* would make her following tack the other ship would cross directly down wind, with her hull almost visible. Their courses would again diverge until they both tacked again.

Phillip commented one afternoon, "Got to be driving that red coat captain plum daft. 'E can never get the windward gage of us. We just keep sailing circles around him."

"To be to windward is important, is it?" asked David.

"Aye, Sir, especially for a fighting ship. All the advantage always lies with the windward vessel."

After four more days the wind veered to the southeast and almost died for a full day and a half. *Constance* merely stayed her usual sixteen miles behind the frigate.

David kept himself on four hour watches each night. Every four hours he fired up the generator and the radar; he would not let that ship get away again. Then, after the second full week, the north Easter came back along with freezing rain.

Still, the two ships plodded across the empty ocean averaging just under 80 miles forward progress each day.

CHAPTER SEVENTEEN

Jake had never driven *Anne Marie* this hard. The 250 horsepower Caterpillar diesel had been throbbing away at almost full speed for days.

He was taking the most direct route to LeHavre, circling north past Cape Breton Island then towards the tip of New Foundland. He'd then bear south of Greenland and east towards Iceland. He ignored the gentler more southern route favored by sailing ships in the winter, deliberately bearing the worst of the North Atlantic northers to get the shortest possible route to France.

The weather had been worsening for the past 24 hours. The wind had reached gale proportions. Still, *Anne Marie* was making her usual full twelve-plus knots, knocking down 240 miles each day, knifing through the huge swells. They carried only her working jib and reefed mizzen to keep her steady, and to add a bit of power to the throbbing big diesel..

It was a wild ride on deck, but worse in the cabins.

In this weather the auto-pilot could not be used. It took an experienced hand to walk the ketch over the crest of each swell and power her down into the next, the spray drenching into the cockpit in a solid green wall. Below decks, the wooden casks holding the whale oil fuel had worked and some of the seams were seeping. Everything in the cabin was slimy with the stuff, and nothing seemed to ever dry out. It stank.

Jake was in his element, He enjoyed this stuff. He knew his little ship was up to it. Stephen and he had been on 'watch and watch' for days and had settled into a routine, four hours driving the little ship and four hours off watch. Unfortunately, Arnought had been lashed into his bunk, too seasick to move.

Jake and Stephen had gotten used to sleeping in the small aft cabin where the stench of whale oil that permeated everything below. Having ripped out the galley, and having given the refrigeration and propane stove to *Constance* they were left with just a single burner sterno heater and canned food.

Still, Jake didn't mind, and Stephen had claimed that the canned hash, stew and vegetables were better than he could expect at sea. Arnought had so far only drank water to keep from dehydration; he couldn't even keep a soda cracker down. One way or another they'd have to get some chicken broth into him soon.

The long voyage gave Jake a great deal of time to reflect on the changes in his life the past four months.

He still didn't know how or why they had been displaced in time, but he was certain that the crew of *Anne Marie* had made a critical difference this event-filled year. More, they'd made a difference that was, to this point, undetected and still consistent with the history of the period. Yes, he knew they had in fact changed the course of history for without his intervention the American Revolution may well have been already lost either at Philadelphia or Saratoga

That would change, he knew, if the frigate got to England with the Zodiac and the Evinrude. Jake knew what effect the appearance of his twenty-first century equipment would have in London, if it got there. He knew the result to future history books.

On a personal note, Jake naturally found the customs and culture of the times very much different from that which he had left. Indeed, most of the social life in these times was centered around the church and/or around the family. There was very little external stimulus available except for expected rough drinking in the pubs.

Thinking about his relationship with his wife, guess former wife, Martha, Jake recognized now that their lives together had become somewhat empty, regardless of his talk with Connie. Simply, Martha had been actively wrapped-up in a number of charitable circles, everything from a church ministry in Pakistan to her bridge group. Meanwhile he had been totally involved in his business and his sailing. They did almost nothing together except for an occasional late evening movie on television or a social function at the Club.

Yes, he mused, they did sleep in the same bed, and they were cordial to each other, even deeply caring, but the passion had gone out of them for each other years ago. Yes, infrequently they would share a passionate moment, but lately that had almost vanished.

And, he remarked ruefully to himself, most of the marriages of his close colleagues were similar.

But with Anne, and in this time, it was wholly different. He had spent every evening the past summer while he was in Deerford at her hearthside, sitting in armchairs side by side, just talking. They talked about everything, anything, and sometimes nonsense. Often Arthur would join them, but he usually retired early. Jake found great delight in Anne's keen wit, her understanding of her world, and her fine education. She had not been to college, girls didn't do that, but she was a voracious reader. She'd encouraged Arthur over the past decade to fill three walls of their home with books. She could discuss anything.

It was she who remarked on the seemingly empty life he'd previously lived with Martha, a life filled with diversions and toys, as she called his ski trips, boats and cars. How much of substance had there been, she'd asked?

Anne, conversely, had been engaged at twenty-two to a young Deerford neighbor who had sailed off as first mate on a whaler eight years ago. He'd planned to earn enough on one three year voyage to buy a small ship for himself and start a trading career.

Yes, Anne had admitted, they'd planned to marry. She'd waited for him, reading everything from Aristotle and Plato to Copernicus.

After he'd been gone for thirteen months a letter arrived, passed to a home bound whaler from somewhere in the Pacific.

She waited two more years.

Still, no further word of her Joseph or his ship ever arrived.

Arthur had started to gently push her towards a marriage with Jason Lot, son of a hemp and tobacco grower with a large farm on the Connecticut River. She visited there and spent some time with Jason, but she found him a shallow young man with no real ambitions.

She'd just kept waiting for her Joseph.

But, when he failed to return after five years he had to be presumed lost at sea. Yes, his ship had been seen in the Pacific, and yes she'd received one letter thirteen months after he sailed, as had his parents, likewise Deerford landowners. Since then there had been no further word of the ship or the man.

That all left Anne well over twenty-seven then, and considered too old for marriage. Stephen had suggested to Jake one night after a couple of drinks that he believed she was still a virgin.

So, no. Jake was not mourning for Martha. He had left her very well situated. His business would run itself until Connie's older brother could take over. Indeed, over the past five months, while Jake was diving on the outer Bahamas reefs north of Walker's Cay seeking a lost Spanish armada, his Executive Vice President had virtually run Shaw Industries.

Jake realized that he should now consider himself a widower, as he was certain that Martha was a widow. Would she re-marry, he wondered? Perhaps, he was certain, in time.

He had actually planned to ask Anne to marry him the same night those scoundrels grabbed Connie, but he knew she'd wait.

"Morning, Jake", Stephen quipped, breaking Jake's thoughts, as he crawled out of the little access hatch to the cockpit from their little shared cabin.

"Coffee ? "

"Thanks," shouted Jake against the gale, taking the steaming mug and setting it in a cup holder behind the binnacle.

"How's our passenger?"

"Seems a bit improved. Got some crackers into him and a bit of broth. He's kept it down and he seems sleeping."

"Wind's freshening. We'll need shorten sail again soon."

"Coffee first, breakfast after?"

"Aye."

Stephen sat with his back to the cabin house sipping the brew watching Jake con the ketch over a series of huge combers. She would heal sharply at the top of each, dipping her starboard rail deeply into the swell, then blast down the back of the wave, loosing wind in the trough, then knife through the curling edge of the successive wave.

He finished his dregs and tossed the mug below.

Jake shouted against the gale, "Gotta get the working job down, then hoist the fore-stays'l. Want to take the helm?

"I'll do it," Stephen said.

He tugged the drawstring tight around the hood of the weatherproof collar of his foul weather jacket. Snapping his lifeline to the cable railing as Jake had shown him, he pulled himself along the weather rail, re-snapping this lifeline at every stanchion until he reached the foredeck. He then snapped the safety lanyard to the staysail stay and worked aft to the foremast.

He cupped his hands and shouted to Jake, "Slack sheet."

Which Jake did, causing the working jib at the end of the bowsprit to spill wind. Jake kept just enough tension on the sheet to keep the sail from tearing itself to pieces.

Stephen pulled himself forward and re-snapped his lanyard to the railing around the little catwalk that covered the six foot bowsprit. As *Anne Marie* plunged down the next wave and dug into the monster behind it, the bowsprit dove under the wave filling Stephen's soggy trousers with freezing water. He gasped and pulled down on the flapping jib. Little by little he yanked it in. When it was fully down he furled it into a tight ball and tied it to the bowsprit railing with the sheets.

He then waited for the little ship to rise on another wave, and took that moment to crab back to the club-footed staysail. He had only to hank on the proper halyard and toss off the stops; the wind pressure pulled the little sail almost all the way up. Three wraps around the winch, a quick pull on the winch handle and the sail was set. As Jake was sheeting in the job-boom Stephen crabbed back to the cockpit, out of breath.

"Anything dry left below," shouted Jake against the wind, noting the water slopping out the tops of Stephen's boots.

"Aye, Drier than this."

"Go change. She's riding a lot better."

"Shall I put on some breakfast before I relieve you?"

"Aye, I'm fine for awhile," Jake retorted, still delighting in the way *Anne Marie* was thrashing through the winter gale at full speed.

At noon the sun was just visible, peeking through clouds low on the horizon. Stephen was at the helm and Jake was braced against the main shrouds to weather, one arm looped around a heavy stainless wire. He was trying to get a sight on the Sun with his sextant. Stephen held a waterproof stopwatch.

"Mark." yelled Jake, "that's as close as I can tag it."

He took the watch from Stephen and crawled down into the cabin.

A half hour later he emerged with a steaming bowl of stew.

"I'll take her while you eat," he stated, placing his hand on the big wheel while handing the bowl to Stephen with his other hand.

"We can start sheets and bear off. My sun line showed us making good over 14 knots. We're just past the Grand Banks."

"How far?" Stephen asked.

"I'm guessing another ten days will do it." Jake yelled against the wind.

Stephen nodded and dug into the stew.

Six days later, with twenty-three of her barrels of whale oil exhausted and seventeen remaining full, *Anne Marie* made landfall on the Isle of Wight. They immediately bore away to the South to avoid any British shipping, or worse, their Navy. Later that day they were able to finally shut down the hammering diesel and enjoy two days of glorious sailing at *Anne Marie's* 16 knot hull speed. They sailed a swooping curve about 150 miles away from the British coast.

Arnought had recovered, and the young man was taking his turns at the helm.

On the third evening, just after his twilight celestial fix, Jake said, "Stephen, we've got about 180 miles to run up the Channel to LeHavre. I'm guessing that the Brits have it blockaded, and their Channel Fleet will be somewhere ahead too. I think we'll push along without sails from here so we can't be seen from any distance. But, we both need stay sharp and on watch. I'd hate to smash into a British ship in the dark."

"Aye"

They were lucky that evening. With the diesel throbbing under the deck, Jake followed his dead reckoning position forward. Just as the sun peeped over the eastern horizon they could see green coastline of France under their lea bow.

Jake put the helm down, pointing *Anne Marie* into the wind and engaged the electric winch that hoisted the mainsail. He was hoisting the mizzen as David cinched the Genoa halyard. In minutes they were sailing on a reach toward the shoreline.

Jake engaged the auto pilot and motioned Stephen to his side saying, "Let's have a look at that chart you have."

Stephen had purchased several charts of the French coast from a merchant before they'd left.

"Aah, here's our position," said Jake with his finger on a penciled X on the chart. "What we need to do, Stephen, is to find a way to get you and Arnought ashore while keeping this boat away from questioning eyes. She'll cause a stir if seen too closely."

"Aye," Stephen replied, "and ye'll need to get us ashore without being seen, and then ye'll need hide somewhere while we go and fetch Dr. Franklin, or convince him of our bona fides."

Jake said, "The city is on both sides of the river, and those stone jetties protect the entrance. Wow, look at all the spars in there! There must be dozens of ships, and we'll not be able to go anywhere near them."

After a few more minutes studying the chart Jake pointed, "This, on the other side of the point, looks to be a small fishing village. The name is Hosfleur, and it looks to be near the river mouth. Bet we could slip you in to shore here."

He was pointing at a spot several miles south of the village.

"Looks like an empty beach. Do you think these three little islands here are inhabited? Couldn't you walk from there to the city of LeHavre, and from there find a fast way to Paris?"

CHAPTER EIGHTEEN

Connie awoke from a sound sleep. She wondered where she was. She heard the ship's bell ring eight beats over her head, then she heard the pounding of many feet, the clank of the pumps and the scraping of the holystones across the deck. Then she inhaled. Wphew! It smelled the same. She knew instantly where she was. She remembered leaving *Constance* to meet David, and the brief struggle in the Zodiac. Then it all came back to her; the rats, the chains, and the following furious medical work.

"Oh, the God dammed bastards!" she said aloud raising from the narrow bunk.

Shitheads, she thought. Why again track me down? I can give those cretins nothing! But, then she remembered the Zodiac, the clothing they'd taken from her and the shiny blue Evinrude. Yes, she realized that she had again been nabbed, and by the same damned ship with the same damned Captain. And, she'd heard them say they were taking her to England this time.

"Oh why had I not gone with David?" she moaned to herself, her head throbbing.

Arising and wrapping the blanket about her, she staggered as the ship lurched over a wave. Then she remembered that she had worked on the captain's head, and on the two other sailors after she'd been forced aboard. She thought that she'd better see how they were doing.

Connie dressed in the clothing she'd been given, thinking she would need to take them in again to fit. She wrenched open the little doorway. A young midshipman, just really a boy, was studying at the far end of the gunroom. She remembered him.

"Good morning Mr. Clark," She said.

"'Mornin M'Lady," he replied shyly. "Working on me sighting from this morning."

As she made her way aft towards the captain's cabin she ran into the steward, Ian, hobbling along the passageway.

"Ian," she halted him, "can you find me a needle and thread, again?"

"Aye, Miss. And I'll be letting Captain Aaron know ye're about."

"Is he up this morning?" she asked.

"Take more than a knot on the 'ead to put him out o' action," the crippled steward replied.

"Please also get me something warm, and allow me an hour to take in these clothes. I'm in no hurry to see your Captain again."

"Aye, Miss," and with that Ian hobbled away.

Connie returned to the little smelly cabin. In a very short time Ian knocked and handed her the same needle and ball of thread she had used before. He also passed her a woolen cloak that was somewhat large but looked warm, plus woolen stockings, sea boots and a knit watch cap.

She braced herself against the swaying motion of the ship, pulled the coat around her and took off the too big trousers. The cotton duck pants and shirt were well worn but soft. It didn't take long to take in the waist and hem the legs. It felt good to be in dry clothes that almost fit.

As soon as the socks and the too big boots were pulled on, and with the cloak around her, Connie tucked her hair into the knit watch cap and again quietly opened the cabin door. She wanted to slip on deck. The ship was riding easily, but she could feel ocean swells.

She wondered if she could she still see land?

Slipping quietly up the scuttle onto the main gun deck just ahead of the quarterdeck she walked to the leeward side, then up to the quarterdeck. The ship was reaching in a light off shore breeze. In the distance, directly behind the ship, she could see a bare green tip of land.

Damn, she thought, they were heading out to sea. Oh yes, she remembered again with fresh dismay, they were taking her to England. Then again, she pondered, certainly David and her Dad would know she was gone, and they must do something?

But what, she mused, could anyone do to rescue her from such a heavily armed war ship in the middle of the ocean?

She watched the green land vanish over the horizon behind the frigate.

Connie's reverie was broken as she heard the Lieutenant on the quarterdeck call to the captain, "Sir, have 'er on course due east as ye laid out. Breeze is a mite light. Shall we rig the studding sails?"

Captain Aaron pulled himself up to the quarterdeck, looking haggard. The white bandage was still on his head. He seemed not to notice Connie at the leeward rail.

" Have we passed Montauk?"

"Aye, sir, about an hour and a half past."

"Ye'r new course is east a point north. Aye, and she ought bear windward studdingsails on the foremast topsail and t'gallant yards. No time to loose. We've dispatches and an important prisoner for Portsmouth."

Overhearing this, Connie's heart sank. She'd been kidnapped, and now they were dragging her off across an ocean. How would David find her?

They would find a way, she told herself. They just would.

She realized she was very hungry. She'd not eaten last night, and she'd slept through whatever edible may have passed for breakfast. She thought that perhaps Ian could find her something?

She went back to the gunroom and indeed Ian found her a hard piece of cheese, an equally hard biscuit and a mug of water. At least, she told herself, the water had improved since her last trip on this ship.

An hour later she heard Ian's querulous voice outside her cabin door, "Capt'n will see ye now, missy."

Just the thought of that kidnapping bastard made her angry. She tossed her head and stamped through the door to the captain's cabin.

"Just who the hell do you think you are!" she shrieked at Aaron, who was writing at this table. "You barbarians think you can just steal a pregnant married woman away from her home for your pleasure? You need to put about now and return me to Connecticut."

He curtly cut her off with a bark, "Quiet, Miss Shaw!"

"I thankee both for this," pointing to the bandage on his head, "and for ye'r doctoring last night. Me and me crew. Ye'll please remember ye gave ye'r parole, and we'll bring thee no harm."

"Ye've been apprehended as a spy against the Crown under Orders of Post Captain Wembly. Ye've escaped his prison just before ye'r transport arrived in July, and nothin' will keep thee from the Kings gaolers now."

"And," he dragged a cover off of the half-inflated Zodiac with the blue Evinrude attached, "what type devilment be this?"

He then picked up one of the aluminum oars, looked at it with awe and said, "Never seen the likes o'this. An oar, clearly, but weighs like a feather, and made of pewter too. How could ye have an oar made of heavy pewter, but weighs like a feather?"

Then he turned to her sharply and said, "Nae, lass. Ye'll not spirit these away from me this time. They're off to me private store room they are. Ye can explain all this," waving his arm at the pile on his cabin floor, "to their Lordships."

"And, me thinks your explanation will make me a peer."

"What's a peer? Connie asked.

"Aye, tiz a Noble of the Kings Court. Are ye daft not to know that?"

He continued, "Ye know too much and we're going to get the truth from thee, willing or not. Now, Miss Shaw, the last time ye were in *Reliant* ye gave ye'r parole, and we gave thee the run o'the ship. Ye promised the same last night. What's it t'be now?"

"I am now Mrs. Saunders, thank you," Connie replied sharply, "and I demand to be returned to my lawful husband right now."

"Sail Ho," came a cry from a masthead before Connie could continue.

"Keep thee here and ye'll not this time dispose of that," waving at the pile on his floor.

"Ian, get in here and watch this prisoner."

Aaron dashed out.

Moments later Connie heard Aaron yell to the maintop, "Whereaway and what d'ye see? Be she one o'ours?"

She couldn't hear the reply.

"Willright, my glass and quick with thee," she heard Aaron bellow.

The door crashed open and the Lieutenant ran to the Captain's desk withdrawing a brass telescope.

"What is it?" asked Connie, hoping for something that would return them to American shores, still so close.

"Dunnow miss. Cap'n said somethin 'bout a barkentine with an odd rig."

Connie's heart leapt.

"Which direction?" she queried.

Over his shoulder as Williamswright dashed out with the telescope he muttered, "Somat said starboard quarter."

She dashed to the large stern window on the starboard side and pressed her face against the glass. She could see nothing.

She then saw a clasp and flung the window open. Leaning way out over the stern she still could see nothing but tossing waves behind the creaming wake. Still, with the window open she could hear the orders from the quarterdeck, above her.

From far away she could hear Aaron, presumably up one of the masts, yelling, "Furl the studding sails. Man sheets and braces. Helmsman, bring 'er hard on the wind."

Feet pounded on the deck over her head. Blocks screeched, and *Reliant* healed sharply to port, rising to the swells.

"Damned Yankees," she heard Aaron curse sometime later, "That'un goes to weather like smoke and oakum. Then it vanished; sails and all in just a moment. We'll not catch 'er."

"Willright, take 'er back on course and re-set the studdingsails".

When Aaron re-entered the Cabin, Connie kept her eyes downcast, hoping he would not see the bright excitement in them. She wanted to believe that a 'barkentine with an odd rig' could only be *Constance*.

She said meekly, "Sir, you may have my parole as before. I assume you would like me in the orlop with ye'r surgeon? I've two sailors there I should see."

"Y' know something 'bout that barkentine?" Aaron demanded.

"Bark, what?"

"Aye", he replied, "damned Yankees have another odd rig. Tiz not as odd as the one with almost no bowsprit, and with sails with no gaffs and no ratlines. Still, this'un is a witch to wind'ard. How do ye Yankees find such odd rigged ships?"

"Sir, I know nothing of odd Yankee ships. I've not seen them. You've had me locked in here."

With that Connie simply left the cabin and descended down the scuttleway to the stinking orlop and her two patients. But,, she was secretly smiling and quite happy. She now knew that her *Constance* was near. Yes, she grinned to herself, Dad and David would find a way.

All day *Reliant* reached east in light winds at almost 4 knots under studding sails. There was no further sight of the any other ship.

Connie awoke the next morning to a hail from the lookout at the mast top, "Clear Horizon, no sight of shipping."

She started to worry again. It just had to have been *Constance* that Aaron had seen as they cleared Montauk, she questioned? But, perhaps David and her dad did not know she was aboard the frigate that they must have seen. She worried that she had mis-guessed yesterday and that she was still lost.

Meanwhile, over the next day, she found she was nearly starving. The boiled salt beef that Ian brought to her was inedible. It was actually green and slimy, and it stank like a cesspool. Along with the slimy bowl of salt beef she got nearly rock-hard ships biscuit, which was a brown lump of something that may have once resembled bread but that now actually crawled with insects. Lice, she wondered? No, she gagged, they were maggots.

But, she reflected, the nasty looking food appeared to keep the crew well nourished, as unappetizing as it was. Further she thought she would just have to eat as much of it as she could, if for no other reason than she did have a baby needing every bit of good nourishment she could stomach. She reminded herself to be sure to insist that Ian bring her a half-cup daily of the lime juice that the sailors mixed with their rum.

At the end of the first day she went to her little cabin at sunset, wrapped herself in her thin blanket, and tried to sleep. She was deathly worried. It took her a long to me to drift off.

She was awakened in the morning by another cry of, "Sail ho, one point on the larboard stern."

Her heart leapt. Could it be? She was on her feet in seconds. Still dressed, she dashed through the gunroom and up to the quarterdeck. Aaron was at the taffrail peering through his telescope.

There was just a flash of tan colored sail at the edge of the horizon in their wake.

Willright spoke up, "Looks to be a merchant vessel, perhaps same as we saw yesterday. Sir, should we beat to quarters? Might we make her a prize?"

"Nay," replied Aaron. "She's the weather gauge of us and we've not the time to chase prizes. Our orders are for dispatch."

The ship in their wake dropped back over the horizon..

Connie dropped back below. She was now sure she had seen her family yesterday, and again today. She told herself that they'd certainly find a way to rescue her. She took a deep breath, stuck out her chin, and told herself to simply make the best of it until she'd find a way out of this mess. She climbed down into the bilges to the orlop; at least she could change the bandages on the broken arm and the wounded leg.

Other than the food and the foul stench of the frigate below decks, which nobody noticed but Connie, the sailing was glorious. The ship was reaching along in a light breeze with every sail set on the three tall masts. The weather had cooled off. It was brisk on deck and quite cool at night. Connie especially enjoyed climbing to the mizzen top in her blue pea coat, watching and watching the horizon around her for any further sign of *Anne Marie* or *Constance*.

"Sail Ho", came a cry from the lookout at the main top on the second day.

"Whereaway?" Willwright replied.

Connie was standing on the quarterdeck watching the dolphins play at the bow.

"Broad on weather quarter."

Connie scrambled to the edge of the deck, grabbed the ratlines to the mizzen top and scrambled up. At the topmast she slid around the futtocks and clung to the slender topmast, looking to windward. She peered carefully at the sails she could barely make out in the far distance. Yes, saw that there were two square sails on the foremast, and two staysails between the masts. It was familiar, even to the over-sized jib. Yes it was, she hugged the mast with tears springing to her eyes. It could only be *Constance!*

"YES!" she wanted to shout aloud, "yes."

The barkentine was just hull-down on the horizon and there was no question in Connie's mind. She clearly remembered the unique and distinctive changes to the rig that her Dad had explained. Still, she wondered, what was that canvas ball on the main mast?

No matter, she gloated to herself, *Constance* was here.

Below her she heard drums and bugles as *Reliant* beat to quarters. The crew swarmed about the decks below her like a kicked-over hoard of ants. Covers were removed from all 32 cannons. As usual, all the cabins were gutted. Again, all the walls were removed and all the furniture was tossed below decks. The main gun deck was again emptied clean from bow to stern.

Within ten minutes from the first drum beat all the guns were manned and ready to be run out. The slow matches were lit and the decks were again covered in a coating of sand. The same red coated marine guarded each hatch. Even her quiet hideout on the mizzen top below her was manned with marines loading the little swivel popgun mounted on that tiny platform.

Yes, she'd seen all this before.

"Ranging shot, aft larboard," ordered Aaron.

CRASH, and one gun fired.

Aaron then spied Connie's form high in the mizzen rigging.

"Mizz Saunders," he yelled, "Get ye to ye'r station in the orlop."

She nodded and climbed down. Her heart was pounding; she had seen *Constance!* But, she couldn't allow anyone on this ship to know.

As she was climbing down the ratlines her *Constance* hauled sheets and scooted away at forty-five degrees to the wind; far closer than *Reliant* with her square sail rig could ever hope to point. An hour later *Reliant* was again on an empty sea. Aaron's curses could be heard throughout the 110 foot Frigate.

The next day, just at twilight, the lookout cried again, "Sail ho, broad on weather quarter."

The Frigate beat to quarters again. Connie descended to the orlop this time, as was required of her. Still, she had seen the topsail schooner again, and she knew who was on the horizon. The same thing happened 24 hours later, and again the schooner twisted away to windward where the Frigate could not go.

"Miss Shaw!" Aaron bellowed after the schooner vanished for the third night in a row, "Get thee to my cabin."

Connie entered the cabin with a somber expression.

"Yes Captain", she started, "and please, it is now Mrs. Saunders," looking at him with defiance.

"Damn, woman," he began.

She stopped him. "Please, sir, address me by my proper name. I am Mrs. David Saunders."

"Aye, Mrs. Saunders. I demand to know if ye know anything about that damned ship that has been dogging us these past several days."

"Sir, is it the same as you spoke of several days ago? The one you said had no bowsprit or ratlines?"

"Nae woman," he thundered, "this un's not a proper brig nor a true bark. She's in fact somewhat odd of rig, deuced fast and well sailed though. She's got what looks like jibs rigged 'tween her masts, another Yankee bastard rig for sure. Why would she play tacks with a Kings Frigate? We could blow her out of the water with one fast broadside. Why's she not playing the proper Yankee pirate, preying on honest British merchant ships?"

"I know not, Captain," replied Connie, "although sir, I would appreciate anything to eat that doesn't have crawley things inside."

"Crawley things?"

"Yes, Captain. It is unhealthy for me, or any of your crew, to have to eat the insects that inhabit the food we are served."

"Damn woman!" he exploded. "The English Navy has lived and fought for hundreds of years on salt beef, pease and ships biscuit. Believe me, Mrs. Saunders, you'll eat it happily or starve. Damned lucky y'are t'av limes too."

"Aye," he continued, "and we'll plan a surprise for that brig, should she come back. I'll fix that bastard. Now, leave me. Send Willright."

After dark that night, which happened to be particularly cloudy and moonless, *Reliant* wore ship ninety degrees to the left, heading due south. An hour before dawn she again hauled sheets, bearing back to the east.

Aaron was shocked to his soul to find, at the next twilight, the same Yankee rig appear on his weather quarter! And, each day thereafter, just after sunrise, the same ship appeared over the horizon to windward; then it would haul away before the ship-rigged frigate could give chase.

Aaron decided to try every twist and elusive tactic he had learned in his 15 year Navy career. He ran *Reliant* south with no lights. He doubled north three hours before dawn to elude the intruder. He then ran west with the swells, giving up a hard won twenty miles to windward. At dawn he ordered *Reliant* to point directly north, now certain that the damned Yankee had been lost well over the horizon.

Yet he was shocked to his soul at eight bells of each morning watch to hear, "Sail ho, larboard quarter," hailed from the masthead.

It was the same dammed ship.

For four more days Aaron tried every tactic he could devise. The crew became exhausted, having been at all hands almost without break. Still, every morning, those same odd sails taunted him, and always to windward. How, he puzzled, could they have found him again and again, day after day?

So, in the end, after days of futile chasing and attempts to elude the mysterious Yankee, Aaron called for braces and sheets to be bent around hard on the strong easterly, beating for Portsmouth to deliver his dispatches and his prisoner.

The renegade continued to follow, the tops of her sails just visible over the horizon. When *Reliant* would wear back to the starboard tack the bark would cross over her bow, almost hull up on the horizon. And after four hours on the larboard tack the brig would again cross hull down. It was maddening to Aaron, but he could do nothing. The other ship was simply too fast and agile.

The wind got stronger and colder each day, and with it *Reliant* kept taking in more sail. They had slowed to a forward advance of less than sixty miles a day, and still they were followed.

One morning the Yankee appeared crossing their stern. For the first time *Reliant* had the weather gage. Captain Aaron quickly called his three officers into the cabin and laid out a plan.

Reliant's helm was put to weather and every sail on all three masts instantly popped out and was sheeted home. She ship leapt instantly to life, bowling now down wind on her best point of sail, aimed right at the smaller bark.

"Aye, we'll 'av her now!" Aaron exulted. "We've the weather gage on 'er."

"Beat to quarters, sharply now!" he screamed.

The barkentine likewise spun away down wind. Her topsails flashed out and she heeled over under their press. For the first time, Aaron got a look at the hull under those sails. Damned ship looked like a French built slaver, narrow and flush decked. Shortly he realized that his prey was once again was pulling away. It was faster than the frigate, even on her best point of sail. Oh, John Aaron lamented, if only his ship had a clean bottom.

He secured the ship from quarters and rounded back on to the wind to resume their long beat towards home. As always, the strange rig still kept peeking over the horizon each day just after sunrise. Aaron had to admit to himself it was a damned fine show of seamanship on the part of that ship, however he was sure the Channel Fleet would clean them off his tail as soon as the Lizzard hove into view. Of course, at their present pace of advance into the easterly gales, it would be some weeks at best before they would see England.

Connie was secretly thrilled. She knew that was her ship that she saw every day. Still, she kept a quiet and demure attitude, helping in the orlop daily to minister to the few sailors who appeared at morning sick call.

And, she was always hungry.

It was not a fast crossing. The weather was as irregular and foul as usual for the early North Atlantic season, with expected gale force headwinds and squalls. Finally, after six weeks, Aaron was estimating Portsmouth but four days away.

"Mrs. Saunders," Aaron accosted Connie in the gunroom. "We'll raise the Lizzard off of Portsmouth in no more than four days. We'll have thee in London within a week."

Connie wondered what her family aboard *Constance* would do when she was landed in Portsmouth, in the heart of the British fleet. She presumed she'd then be carted off under guard to London for inquisition, over 200 miles across the country. How could she explain the Zodiac and all its parts still under her feet in the Captains locked store room?

CHAPTER NINETEEN

Yes, there was one last tiny little rubber inflatable boat on *Anne Marie,* but it was a very tiny little boat not over six feet long. There was no motor for it, and no gasoline were there a motor. It had to be rowed with tiny aluminum oars. It was bobbing in the dark water next to *Anne Marie* in the darkness, stopped just over a half mile off the beach. Arnought and Stephen's bundles of dry clothes were already in the boat, wrapped in a waterproof bag.

"Remember, Stephen, to hide that boat very well. We'll not need get it back but we can't leave any part of it there."

"Aye," Stephen replied, "but I wish we had that radio. T'would be much easier to get thee word of my return."

"Can't be helped. It's aboard *Constance* and they may have further need of it there. Now off with you. I'll return here in eight days, just after midnight, and for two days after that. You have the light to signal me from the beach."

He thought for a moment then added, "Hold on a minute, Stephen. I have an idea."

He re-appeared on deck in a few moments holding a small plastic gray tube with a clip on it.

"Almost forgot about this. It is a spare EPRIB, a radio beacon to find sailors lost at sea. I've a receiver here. This is our last transmitter, after the one I gave to David. When you get back to Hosfleurs simply push this switch to on, like this."

A little red light started to glow.

"I can get your bearing from us, but don't use it until you have to. You've only the one battery. Remember, you have only ten days. If you are not back by then I'll need to sail for the Lizard. I can't have the damned Brits take Connie ashore in Portsmouth."

Stephen nodded, slipped the EPRIB into his pocket and slid over the side into the tiny boat. He put the little aluminum oars into their slots and paddled towards the beach in the dark with Arnought perched on the bundles of clothing on rubber floorboard.

Jake turned *Anne Marie* back to sea. He knew that it could be tough to stay out of sight of the British Channel Fleet for ten days, but he believed he could manage.

Stephen reached the beach easily. The tiny boat slid through the surf, and the two of them dragged it to the base of a dune. He unscrewed the three plugs as Jake had shown him, and with a hiss the boat just went flat. He dug a hole with an oar and buried the boat with the oars, looking around carefully to be certain he could find it later.

Arnought watched this all, his mouth agape.

"Remember," Stephen said to his young companion, "this all is in strictest secrecy. Ye're along with us only because ye can locate Dr. Franklin and get me to him. Aye, ye speak French like a native and I've none of it. After that ye're to join our diplomatic group here. Any discussion on how ye got here must never be spoken. And, I'll promise thee that nobody will ever ask thee how ye got news of Saratoga here in but twenty-one days."

They then dressed themselves in their best clothes, amazed at how dry they were after traveling through the surf in the waterproof duffel that Jake had packed.

A drizzling dawn found them striding through Hosfleurs in their white lace shirts, red waistcoats and tail coats, all under greatcoats and plumed hats. They had ten days to get the 182 miles to Paris and back, and somehow convince Dr. Franklin that Saratoga had been won an impossible four weeks ago!

And Stephen, knowing that he could speak just a tiny bit of French, did not want to be taken for an English spy, which was a real possibility.

An hour later they entered a very elegant looking café in LeHavre and took a seat to one side where they could listen to the other customers.

A waiter appeared.

"Café noir, et un petite fromage, si vous plait," Arnought muttered.

Minutes later they both had breakfast, a large slice of cheese, half a loaf of bread and a two cups of black coffee loaded with milk and sugar. When Stephen placed a gold Spanish sovereign on the table the waiter's eyes popped wide at such a sum. Still, he brought back change in francs.

Breakfast completed and feeling stronger, Stephen and young Arnought set out to find the merchant who had been recommended by the same captain who had sold Stephen the chart. Mr. Gilhomme had been said to be a reliable businessman and well disposed to Americans. They set off along the waterfront looking for a sign reading 'Gilhomme et Freres'. Finding it on a side street as described, they entered and asked for Henri Guilomme. A clerk took them through an office with other clerks busy at ledgers, and knocked at a rear door.

"Entrez."

Stephen and Arnought were waved through the door.

Henri Guilomme was an unhealthy looking pear-shaped man. He did not appear to be over 40 and was almost totally bald. Still, he smiled at Stephen

He rose and started, "Monsieur –," and a fast jumble of French that Stephen did not understand.

Arnought replied in fast French. He then said to Stephen, "Monsoir Guilome has good English so we can all speak freely."

"Ah oui, yes, un American," waving at a chair, "Ave you a cargo here to sell? You've arrived from the Americas?"

"No cargo, sir, we are just travelers seeking passage to Paris."

"One can not be too careful these days," the Frenchman replied. "From whom did thee get my name?"

"Captain Pearson of the brig *Emily* advised ye may be willing to help. I can pay thee for fast passage to Paris. I am a colonel in the army of the American colonies," and with that Stephen handed over a document.

"Mr. Arnought is my business associate."

"Oui, I've 'eard of zees General Washington," he said, peering at the large signature on the Commission.

"Et eess a long two days by post chasse a' Paris," Guilomme replied, "Eets gone today, but another will leave early the morrow. Tomorrow morning, perhaps?"

"Can we not rent a horse and a guide? It is urgent we get a message to Paris."

With that Stephen slid two of the Spanish crown coins onto the merchant's desk.

The Frenchman smiled, stood, and waddled to his door.

"Philippe," he called.

He gave the boy fast instructions in French. The boy was back in a half hour and along with him was a grey haired older man, apparently quite fit.

"Mr. Downey, this ees Guillome Sen," introducing the older man. "Ees a what you would call farmer 'ere and maybe can have an idea for thee."

Sen spoke up, "Understand ye'r in a god-awful hurry t' get to Paris. Think I can get thee there by tomorrow night if'n it don't rain," he spoke in good, but rough English.

"Won't be cheap though. Cost ye four of those Spanish Crowns that Henri's mentioned."

"Done," said Stephen, slinging his bag over his shoulder.

"Thank ye, Henri."

Sen led Stephen and Arnought to a nearby stable yard and negotiated a week rental of the large dun colored stallion that Stephen was riding and a mare for the younger man. Stephen beast was magnificent. The horse was seventeen hands tall at the withers and able to trot or slow-canter all day, even carrying the heavy saddlebags that Stephen had brought along, and which he must protect with his very life. They cantered away, east towards Paris through the French countryside.

Stephen hadn't spent a day on horseback for months. By the time they'd found an inn, several hours after dark, his backside was rubbed quite raw.

"Allons-nous et bonjour," quipped Guillome Sen as Stephen appeared from the taproom with a hunk of fresh bread in hand the next morning, "Paris aujourd-hui so vous plait."

"Okay, Guillome, please speak English. And, let's go."

Stephen was not looking forward to another day in the hard French saddle, and from the look of him Arnought was not faring much better.

"Aye, we go now, then," stated Sen switching to English.

The three of them mounted and rode east from the yard.

By early afternoon they were entering the suburbs of Paris, and before nightfall they booked rooms at the fashionable Bristol Hotel near the Seine. While Stephen rested, Arnought was supposed to try to find Dr. Franklin and pass him a letter heavily sealed in red wax. Stephen knew the letter conveyed news about the capture of Burgoyne's army at Saratoga by Colonial General Gates. This news would be welcomed by the diplomat. Franklin was the Colonial Congress' Ambassador to the Government of France and he had been deeply involved in negotiations towards gaining official French support of the American Revolution.

Stephen was thrilled at the opportunity to actually meet Benjamin Franklin. He'd heard a lot about him from General Washington, and had read a number of Franklin's 'Poor Richard' flyers before the Declaration of Independence, over a year ago. Jake had said that he too had deeply studied Franklin and was fascinated by Franklin's histories. Actually, Jake had said that Franklin would be as well known as would be Washington two hundred years hence!

So, while Arnought was searching Paris for Franklin Stephen was nervously pacing the hotel room. He knew that the future that Jake had told truly depended on his ability to convince the Doctor of the very unlikely story he had to tell. At least, he told himself, he could make a quiet demonstration of some of the things that he had in the saddlebags.

But, Jake had insisted that Stephen could show them only to Dr. Franklin and, or, only to the French King, Louis 16th, in person. If that did not get results, Stephen knew would be permitted to bring not more than Dr. Franklin and one senior French person to *Anne Marie*, but that was to be avoided if at all possible.

He waited in the room until after midnight. Nobody appeared.

He undressed and tried to sleep.

Finally at breakfast the next morning David saw a wizened little man with a wispy beard hustle across the lobby and approach his table directly.

"Mr. Downey," he addressed Stephen directly, " good to make ye'r acquaintance."

The gentleman doffed his hat continuing, "A young man named Arnought advised me that thee've something of importance to impart?"

"Dr Franklin," Stephen replied, "Ye're exactly as the General described. Tiz good news we're bringing thee. I presume my companion, Stephen Arnought, shared the some if it with thee?"

Dr. Franklin looked over Stephen. His piercing blue eyes were a shock in Franklin's otherwise affable and smiling visage. Stephen felt as if he'd been examined to the soul in those first few moments.

"Aye, I've read the letter and ye'r friend Arnought brought from my good friend, General Washington." Franklin stated.

Stephen replied, "Please have a seat, Doctor."

As Franklin sat down Stephen continued, "We have some amazing and very secret things to share with thee. If necessary, only some of this may be advised to Louis 16th, some not. It'll be at ye'r discretion, of course."

Then, looking into Franklin's amazing and quizzical eyes, Stephen asked if the Doctor would accompany him to his private room for a discussion. They rose and climbed the stairs. Entering the room, Stephen locked the door behind him.

He continued, "Tiz hard to believe Doctor, but we've crossed from Connecticut to LeHavre in but twelve days."

Franklin interrupted, "Why sir, that's plain daft! Tiz simply not possible to make such a crossing in the winter. Why it's near three thousand miles."

"Aye, Sir, I swear it's true. We came in a new-fangled ketch powered by some contraption that never allows her to fall below eleven knots, even into the eye of the wind in a gale."

He continued, "The reason for the urgent passage was to bring thee news of the Rebellion. Ye know we lost the Capitol after our loss at Brandywine. Ye'll have learned too that Washington's retreated to Valley Forge in Pennsylvania."

"Aye," nodded Franklin, "that news arrived by packet last week, and Louis has been unavailable to us since. I am afraid for our cause to enlist France's aid for our new Nation here without some news of British defeats."

He continued, "Our good friend and supporter, Compte de Vergennes despairs of our cause. He's a close confident to the King."

"But," Franklin looked up, "Is the letter delivered by Mr. Arnought true?"

"Aye, that be the news, Doctor Franklin," Stephen grinned. "Gates whipped Burgoyne at Saratoga. The British effort to divide the Colonies, sorry Sir, States, has been thwarted. Burgoyne's army is in tatters and there are thousands of his surrendered soldiers moving on parole now to Boston to await return to England."

"Incredible!" mouthed the astonished Franklin, "I know that Gates had almost twice the force, but they were all untrained farm boys facing experienced English campaigners who were supported by Hessian cavalry. How did they do it? My, but this will help de'Vergennes to cause a stir at Louis' Court."

"Dr. Franklin, please understand that these things are true and they happened as I said, however, ye'll not receive a true courier with this news for some many weeks. Stephen Arnought came with me simply to establish my bonafides as we know ye trust him and his family. Simply, with the battle won in early October, the Congress at York will not dispatch Mr. Sommers with a formal message to you until nearly November first. Ye'll not get that message until the last week of December."

"Aye," the old man replied, "Compte de Vergennes has an audience with the Court on December 3d. Should he not bring news favoring our Cause it is feared the King will loose heart."

Then he looked sharply at Stephen and continued, "Mr., er you say it is Colonel, Downey, how can it be thee crossed the perilous ocean in what ye say, twelve days? Tiz simply impossible."

Stephen replied nervously, "Dr. Franklin, I think that God only has come to our relief, I know no other explanation. Yet, I believe that Mr. Arnought told thee the same tale. Here, sir is a full account of some strange gifts to our Cause since July."

Stephen then detailed an accurate account of his experiences since the green ketch appeared in early July.

He finished with, "these visitors from a future time know well of thee. 'Tiz said in their advanced time that ye're a leading scientist, philosopher and statesman from this era. They say ye've even experimented with electricity, unknowing it's end use."

He concluded, "These people accidentally learned that time travel is likewise possible. Their little ketch and all aboard left what we know as the Spanish Floridas in the year 2006, and sailed into Connecticut this past July."

"How can that be possible?" Franklin interjected with a loud whisper.

"I've not been privy to the message that Arnought brought thee under Washington's seal, but I must expect that it referenced something of assistance from people with strange powers, did it not?"

"Aye," Franklin replied, "there was a strange reference in that letter."

"Indeed, sir," Stephen interrupted, "Washington has seen just a bit of the marvels that have been visited upon us. Yet he knows of some surprising results these people have brought to our cause. We don't know why, Sir, and they've unwillingly left all their families and histories behind, but Jake Shaw, his daughter and his son in law somehow sailed two hundred and twenty-seven years into the past aboard *Anne Marie* which is a sixty-eight foot diesel powered ketch – . "

"Whoa there young man, what is diesel power?"

Stephen held up his hand and started on the speech that he and Jake had practiced.

"Sir, at this time in the history of mankind, thee, er, I guess we are on the brink of amazing discoveries that in the next two hundred years will change the way mankind lives more than the changes in the past two thousand years. Thee, sir, are to be credited with the first discovery of electrical power. Remember your kite and the key?"

"Aye," Franklin replied, rubbing his scraggly beard, "t'was a painful experiment."

"Well, sir, I believe Jake Shaw when he states that the American Revolution will succeed. We will manage to convince Louis 16th to ally with us. It is most interesting because Louis 16th will be known to secretly authorize Compte De Vergonnes to dispatch Marquis de Lafayette and materials to the Americans in but a month. The French Court will be advised on January 3d, which will actually be just a day before Mr. Sommers will arrive with official news of Saratoga."

Stephen concluded, "The December decision of the King is in the future history books. That is why we are here."

Franklin interjected again, "Tiz known that the English and French have be at each other for decades. It will flare again very soon. Both are simply waiting an incident."

Stephen resumed, Franklin enthralled, "Mr. Shaw has studied history; his history which is our future. He states that the coming wars in Europe will last off and on into the next Century. Regardless of that he says that the nineteenth century will become known as the industrial revolution wherein all sorts of machinery will be invented and put to the use of mankind. In but one hundred years from today huge iron machines powered by steam, with the force of hundreds of horses, will pull carloads of people and freight along iron rails at speeds over thirty miles per hour. In a hundred years ships powered by similar steam engines will replace sailing vessels."

"Your electricity, Dr. Franklin," Stephen continued, "will power messages that will be sent instantly for hundreds of miles along wires hung between poles. And guns that fire many rounds will replace single shot muskets."

"In the next hundred and fifty years your electricity, generated by steam engines, will replace candles and oil lamps in all civilized cities and towns across America and Europe. A new type of engine that works on internal combustion of oil and that drives large flywheels will be employed at a fraction of the weight and cost of steam engines. These engines will power motor cars that will replace horses and carriages and will run on smooth roadways."

Stephen went on noting Franklin's rapt attention, "Jake Shaw claims that even the poorest of laborers will be able to afford such motorcars, and they will be able to travel hundreds of miles on smooth roadways at speeds exceeding a mile a minute. Even more amazing, men will learn to build flying machines powered by the same engines, which machines will carry people and cargo from London to New York in less than eight hours."

"Nae, Son," Franklin shook his head, "Ye've gone too far not. Ye can not be telling the truth. Such is all quite the dreams of madmen and quite impossible to comprehend or believe. Why, such changes have not occurred since the time of Christ."

"Dr. Franklin," Stephen interrupted, "tiz true. Mr. Shaw has given me a small machine that can show thee of these things. It works on a battery and can be used but one time. Mr. Shaw said to show these wonders to thee, and only to thee. Ye're aware that at all costs the passage of Mr. Shaw and his wizardry can not be recorded in this time."

Franklin looked at Stephen, "Aye, Mr. Downey, may I see ye'r proof of this incredible tale ye're telling?"

"Yes sir, if ye please I will retrieve my bag."

Stephen fumbled a small leatherette bag open and followed the procedure as he and Jake had practiced.

"First, sir, here is a small piece of CRX Plastique explosive with a blasting cap inserted".

Stephen handed to Franklin a small grape sized chunk of blue material with a tiny red button inserted in one end. In his hand Stephen held a small black box with a button on it.

"What be this plastic material?" Franklin asked, holding a cool golf-ball sized cool piece of clay in his hand.

"That sir is one hundred times more powerful than a barrel of gunpowder. After we've finished here, and if thee can find me a secure place, I can show thee what this mere harmless looking ball can do."

"Next, sir", Stephen pulled a dis-assembled AK-47 from his saddlebag and quickly snapped it together.

Franklin's bushy eyebrows shot up at the appearance of the knobby weapon.

"This, sir, is a rifle that shoots twenty rounds per second, and can hold forty-eight rounds in this clip. It is loaded. All the shots can be fired at once by switching this lever, or they can be fired as fast as you can aim and pull the trigger by switching to manual fire."

"My God what a terrible weapon! It's inhumane. Why that will replace 48 soldiers!" exclaimed Franklin.

"Yes sir. Actually it replaces ten times more than 48 soldiers because we can change clips in a brief instant, whereas it takes the fastest soldier today a full half minute to re-load one shot in a Brown Bess. With these guns only two of us stopped the Hessian advance in New Hampshire in their attempt at horses before Saratoga. That's perhaps one reason why Burgoyne had no cavalry. We likewise convinced Howe's lieutenants that Washington's army was south of Philadelphia in July, instead of where it was. That ruse sent Howe back to sea."

"My God, without either of those incidents we'd have been lost." Franklin mused aloud.

"Last, sir, before I show you the effects of the plastique, Jake thought you might like to see a video of his business as he left it in May."

'Video?" Franklin mouthed the new and odd word.

The last item that Stephen pulled out of the bag was a little CD player with a small screen, He inserted a shiny disc. Franklin's eyes were wide open, transfixed on the small silver and black box in Stephen's hand which looked like a very ornate jewelry box.

"On his boat Mr. Shaw has a far larger screen that they usually use for these, but this will do for now."

Stephen pressed the 'on' button and set the little black and chrome machine on the table in front of Franklin, who was staring at it in total amazement. He was speechless as the color image of an eagle's crest swam into view on the flat grey screen. Below the eagle a golden name appeared reading, 'Shaw Marine Industries'. It was a ten-minute promotional video prepared for the House Armed Services Committee showing the newest of small naval warfare ships and boats being produced at the Shaw Shipyard in 2006.

After the opening slide faded, the announcer introduced Shaw Marine Industries while an American Flag was panned out to show the Capital Dome in Washington DC, taken from a helicopter's over-flight.

"Can you stop that?" Franklin spoke.

Stephen pushed a button. The scene froze on the city from the air. The capitol was visible, as was the White House, a mere spec on the little screen.

"What are thee showing me here?"

"This, sir, is Washington, in the District of Columbia, which will be the capitol city of the United States of America. It was taken shortly before Mr. Shaw set sail less than six months ago."

"My God," Franklin exclaimed, "how many stars are on the flag? Does each represent a Colony?"

"Why, I believe that Jake said were fifty states when he left in June, sir. The United States of America will be fifty States, or so Jake said. They'll no longer be called colonies"

"And the city?"

"That is Washington DC, located on the Potomac River between Maryland and Virginia. It is a one hundred square mile city where the United States government is located. This building," Stephen pointing to the Capitol Dome in the foreground, "is the Capitol Building where the Congress and Senate will meet to debate new laws. This little spec in the background is the White House where the President lives. Actually, General Washington will be the first President of the new Union. John Adams will be the second."

Franklin, clearly amazed, asked, "What are all those other white buildings, and that huge park with the rectangular lake? And, what is that huge white spire?"

Stephen replied, "All the buildings, Jake said, house most of the government agencies. These around the park, I think Jake called it the Washington Mall, is the nations largest museum. I think Jake called it Smith's or something like that. Oh, and the white spire is the Washington Monument, memorializing General Washington who will be our first president, of course.

"What's a president?"

"Jake said that we won't have a king. It's all a bit confusing, but I've learned only that our Revolution will win, and our new nation will still be strong in two hundred years."

"Did your friend Shaw talk of other presidents?"

"According to him, they govern only a few years. The only other one he mentioned was a man named Lincoln. Well, Sir, I don't remember a lot of what Jake said, but I think this Lincoln won't govern for another ninety years, so I guess he's not yet born. I've somewhat gotten used to this time thing," Stephen faltered.

"But, I remember that this Lincoln was President during a Civil War between the States which of course he won. Jake said he kept the Union together. Oh and yes, it was this Lincoln who will end slavery altogether. May I continue?"

Franklin retorted, "Tiz wonderful news that slavery will end. Me brother and I've been at odds over it for years. One more question, young man. These, " Franklin pointing a bony finger at the cars on the streets, "Are the horseless carriages of which thee spoke?"

"Yes sir," Stephen retorted, "and Jake said that most people own one. May I continue with the machine?"

Franklin nodded. Stephen again pushed the 'run' button. The announcer introduced Chairman Jake Shaw of Shaw Industries who was sitting on a corner of his desk dressed in a blue suit and usual red 'power tie'. Jake spoke while the rest of the eighteen minute video presentation ran on.

He introduced the newest Shaw miniature nuclear submarine, and showed it departing to the Persian Gulf on board the USS Ronald Regan. There was a shot of the Regan's F-18's taking off employing Shaw Industries electronic catapults, and another of the new Shaw fast motor gunboat, capable of carrying 100 troops over 300 miles at speeds that were undisclosed, but from the photo it was durned fast. In closing Jake touched on Shaw Industries' history starting with mention of design work on the earliest of Frigates, the

USS Constellation in 1794. He spoke of a unique design of mass produced gunboats during the War of 1812, and a number of other Company successes including the parts of the infamous USS Maine and the more famous PT boat and Fleet Submarine of WW II, and on to the modern day.

The presumed point of the film was to depict Shaw Industries as a Contractor who historically delivered cutting edge technology against federal contracts, always on time and within budget.

Stephen broke the silence as he folded-up the little, now dead, machine saying, "That gentleman, Dr. Franklin, is my friend Jake Shaw who is today on his personal diesel powered sailing vessel, the ketch *Anne Marie,* hiding out in the English Chanel off LeHavre awaiting my return."

While Franklin sat in silence Stephen excused himself and went into a little closet off the ornate room and urinated into a chamber pot. He then splashed water from a pitcher into a china bowl, washed his hands, and dumped the remaining water into the pot. He returned to his chair.

Sitting down beside the stunned and bemused Dr. Franklin he commented, "Y'know I think the best invention in the next two hundred years will be internal plumbing. These chamber pots stink, as do the streets where they're dumped."

"And how does this internal plumbing work?" asked Franklin.

"Well, I am told that all the houses and workplaces must by law have water piped into them, both hot and cold. The water goes to sinks with faucets one can simply turn to get water to run. Water also runs to toilets which are simply self-flushing chamber pots, and the sewage is carried off to city limits where Jake said it is treated to remove odors and bacteria, and returned to the earth. Indeed sir, even the little ship *Anne Marie* that brought us across in twelve days has such plumbing. I was able to bathe each day at sea in a bath they call a shower, as do all these people. They told me that that most people in their time bathe daily."

"Another amazing thing, Doctor Franklin, is that had a machine on the vessel that washes and dries clothing in a mere hour. Mr. Shaw's transferred it to another vessel now."

Franklin lurched to his feet and said, "Hide thine baggage away, son. We need a drink and we'll discuss how to use all this all to our advantage. Me Gods, though, but I am stunned."

"Dr. Franklin," Stephen replied rather sharply, "Mr. Shaw demands that ye give your solemn word that ye'll speak of these wonders only to the King, and that no records of these discussions ever become recorded."

"Aye, Son. Your Mr. Shaw is a wise man, for to have any of this broadcast would certainly tarnish the course of history. I am recharged to now know of our Cause' eventual success, and of General Washington's enduring fame. He's most worthy of it. Yet ye'll need to trust my judgment to share these wonders with the good Count. Ye see, it'd never do to take it to the King. I'd like only to keep this little gray ball for the Count's eyes when I'll see him the third. How is it used?"

Stephen nodded and explained, "Thee must be careful sir. First ye push this little stick into the clay. Than be certain ye'r well off, and then just push the red button on this little box. It'll make a fearsome explosion. Then ye must destroy and dispose of the black little box."

Franklin placed the gray ball in one coat pocket, and the black box in the other. With that he opened the door and thundered down the stairwell calling out, "Service mais amis, un boutelle de vin si'l vous plait, non, deux boutelles!"

A short time later Stephen Arnought arrived, and the three of them dispatched three bottles of fine red Madeira before dinner planning their approach to the Count, and another two during a quiet evening meal at a nearby café.

☆ ☆ ☆

Jake spent the days sailing the French coast. He was busy converting his little ship to an eighteenth century period appearance.

He ran his whisker pole up the mizzenmast to resemble a gaff, and made a similar rig for the spinnaker pole on the main mast. He then cracked the lid off a pail of black bottom paint. He used the electric winches to haul himself up each mast and coated all his lovely stainless rod standing rigging with flat black anti-fouling paint, hopefully to resemble the tar used in the 18th century.

He then dipped strands of dock lines into the paint and tied them across the lower shrouds to resemble ratlines. He even spray painted the large chrome wheel with some brown engine primer. He wrapped old t-shirts coated with bottom paint at the end of each spreader to resemble baggywrinkle, and made the former dingy cover into a paint-encased glob at the head of his fake 'gaffs' so the masts would not appear unusually tall and true.

"Well," he grunted to himself when finished, "she won't fool a true seaman, or anyone else very close, but at casual glance I should slip by."

And with that rig he sailed back and forth off the coast of France for six days. Every time he saw a ship in the distance he would turn the opposite direction until they were under the horizon. Some days he saw nothing, but one day he had to run from a line of four large lumbering warships, each with two decks of guns.

At midnight of the sixth day he was just out of sight of land, due east of Hofleur again. He turned the squelch and volume on the EPRIB receiver to the maximum.

An hour later the machine screeched. Damn, he exulted, but Stephen was back on time!

Anne Marie turned towards the shore and within an hour Jake saw a flash from a light dead ahead.

He flashed back.

Three flashes from the beach.

Jake stopped *Anne Marie* dead in the water and waited.

One more flash, much closer.

Jake pressed the trigger on his searchlight and there it was, his little rubber dingy with Stephen paddling towards him. In moments he was aboard.

"Success, Stephen?"

"Aye, Sir, but I must go back. Franklin does not believe that just the news of Saratoga will move the King to support us. The Court is most worried about renewed fighting with Spain if they should support the Colonies. No, Franklin says his council to the Court, Compte de Vergennes, will need more than just the words of himself. Seems he's viewed as just a bit erratic by the French".

"What does he need?"

If you, sir, can trust me, and only me, with the little machine and your moving pictures, than Franklin says that will convince the Compte."

"But how could you get it to him," Jake asked, "and could you totally be sure it would not be lost or compromised?"

"I am convinced of it. Franklin introduced me to an amazing young Marquis named Lafayette who is a favorite of the King and the Compte. He is trustworthy and can be sworn to secrecy. He can get me a private audience with Compte de Vergennes, and it will be on the third of December. Did thee not mention something about that date?"

Jake then broke in and finished, "and, of course, if you then destroy the machine, the Compte could never say anything to anyone for they would never believe him. Go then. But, Stephen, I need your word that that DVD Player will not leave your hands, and that it will be seen by no one except the

Compte and perhaps Layfayette. You must grind that machine to dust when you leave France. Your word and your life on it?"

"Aye, Jake," Stephen promised.

"Then, it will take an hour to recharge its batteries. It will be off with you before the sun is up. You'll have to book your own passage home. We'll hope to see you in Deerford by spring."

"But Sir," Stephen protested, "is it not more important to thee that I help thee get Connie back? How can ye go alone against a Frigate. Could thee not get me back after?"

"No, Stephen. Your Country needs you in Paris. I'll soon have *Constance* and her crew with me. God willing, we'll still find a way to stop them. In fact I think I've worked out a plan that may work. Now be off with you and bury that Zodiac very deeply."

CHAPTER TWENTY

For the next 24 hours *Anne Marie* surfed from wave to wave, topping 17 knots, carrying all sail she could across the English Channel towards the Lizard, just south of Portsmouth. She was truly flying, Jake thought, despite the rags and paint in the rigging.

Jake was grimly focusing on each passing wave like a man possessed. He was frantic with worry that they would miss their chance to find Connie and that damned frigate. He didn't think the frigate could possibly have made the crossing in the three plus weeks since he'd left *Constance* off Montauk, but his concern was increasing. His planned rendezvous with David and *Constance* was already a day passed.

As the next day ended Jake was able to engage the auto helm and grab three hours sleep. When he awoke, refreshed, he brought a fresh mug of steaming coffee to the cockpit. He'd been up for almost a day and a half, allowing himself just this 3 hours sleep while sailing on auto-helm. He passed under the heel of Brittan. The sea was smoother but the breeze was unabated. In the overcast dawn the town of Brighton could just be seen in the distance to starboard.

He dozed a lot that day, seeing no shipping, and cruising just over the horizon along the south coast of England.

That evening, as soon as he could pick out individual stars and still see the horizon, he stood up and aimed his sextant at six successive stars. He marked the exact time of each sighting and wrote the azimuth of each from the sextant dial onto a notebook. With that done, he opened his navigation calculator and reduced each star sight to a line on the chart. He had a perfect fix on his position, and he was just five miles from the coordinates agreed with David.

Jake dropped all sails, except only a reefed mainsail. *Anne Marie* was hove to; she'd stay in this spot. With that he turned his EPRIB and hand held radio unit on while he dozed off, hoping to hear from David in *Constance Shaw* soon.

He stayed hove to the next day. There was no sight of *Constance*.

At sundown on the second day he was forced to run forty miles to the west as three large ships appeared, clearly departing Portsmouth. It took him until the following morning to return to the empty sea at the rendezvous point. The waiting was hard

"BXBXBXBXB," the EPBRIB squawked briefly.

Jake popped awake the third morning, what was that?

"BXBXBXBXBX," more static, but the direction pointer said south. He was flooded with an overwhelming rush of relief. He had made it in time. Connie had not yet been landed in England. They still had a chance.

He shook out the reef in the mainsail, rolled out his big jib and headed south.

An hour later he heard static on the VHF, and very faintly he could hear what sounded like *Constance* calling for him. Certainly there were no other VHF set on the planet.

Jake fiddled with the squelch dial and tried to transmit, "*Constance, Constance*, this is *Anne Marie*." He then pressed the unit to his ear.

David's voice over the radio replied, "Jake, great to hear your voice. I see you on the scope. You're only seventeen miles to our north."

"Do you still have that frigate?" Jake queried into his hand held radio unit, holding his breath for a positive reply.

"Yes. They are eight miles to my northwest. He's moving Northeast at 5 knots."

"Okay, David. Please give me a compass bearing to you. If the wind holds from the north that guy will be a couple days getting in, but if it veers he could be there in no time. We need to plan on how to take him out and get Connie back."

An hour and forty minutes later *Anne Marie* and *Constance* were hove-to close to each other. David had a boat lowered and six of his crew rowed him across the choppy waves to *Anne Marie*.

"Hold fast, boys," David said as he jumped over the rail.

"Jake, you look dead beat!" he exclaimed, looking at Jake's gaunt frame, scruffy four day old beard and red rimmed eyes.

He continued, "And, I would not have recognized this mess," waving at the camouflaged little ship, "had I not known it was you."

"I'm okay. We've just got no time to loose." Jake continued, "Here's how I think we can take him."

And, he laid out the plan he'd developed.

Jake had spent the past month agonizing on how an almost unarmed brig and a small ketch could surprise and overcome a huge frigate at sea, armed to the teeth and manned with several hundred well trained hand-to-hand fighters.

"That's totally crazy! What do you think that frigate will do?" asked David when Jake had finished speaking and drawing.

Jake thought, then replied, "You gotta remember that they have only sun and star sights, when they can get them, to navigate by. And their instruments, time pieces and calculations are far behind ours. They probably know they are close to the Lizard, but they have no idea they are as close as they really are."

"Still," he continued, "on their present heading they'll be in the lea by this time tomorrow, and any good English skipper will know he's in the Channel. He'll only need to wear ship to duck 80 miles down the coast. If we don't stop him by daylight Connie'll be jailed in Portsmouth Harbor within two days."

David replied, "If that happens I don't know how we'll ever find her, let alone get her back. And, the Brits will then have a Zodiac."

"Okay, again. Listen. Let's go over my plan again." Jake then went over his notes and drawings.

"'That's the craziest damned thing I ever heard of." David retorted to Jake's plan later. "You'll never get away with it. No, not you, Me, Jake. If it's the only way, then I'm gonna do it myself," David solemnly stated.

"The hell you are!" thundered Jake.

'Look, goddammit," David fumed back, "if you do this, and you and Connie don't make it, you will have left me here stranded in the eighteenth century with nobody. I don't have a damned trade, and I don't really know anyone. I'd rather make this crazy effort and if the worst happens, and Connie and I both die, at least you have Anne. Even if I blow it, and Connie gets taken to England, then at least you'll have a chance to find her and the baby later."

"No, son," Jake replied, "You've sailed *Constance* for six weeks now dogging that damned frigate. You know best how she handles. I don't. And, I've sailed *Anne Marie* in every condition. The only way this has a chance is if we both skipper the vessel we know best. Any real risk is mine. Worst case they'll nail me, but Connie will be fine, although if I fail she'll then be taken to England. You'll then need to find your wife and child."

He took a breath and continued, "If they do get her there, there'll be a huge uproar and you will need to get to someone in England with enough sense to keep this entire event secret. You'll have to do just that if I fail."

"God Damn it anyway, Jake, David retorted, "have it your way."

Jake changed the subject and asked, "How fast does that frigate sail full and by anyway?"

David replied, "The boys on *Constance* tell me that a properly sailed ship like that should top fourteen knots full and by in a stiff breeze, however that one has not done over ten since we left. She gave is a good chase one night, and we ran clean away. I guess she's a really foul bottom. Since *Anne Marie* can do twelve knots easily under motor alone and I feel really certain that *Constance* can do her part your plan has something of a chance. We both can sail circles around them in any weather."

Jake replied, "I haven't pushed her over thirteen all the way across, but if I wind her all the way out she'll hit fifteen knots with the diesel for awhile. And, perhaps she'll make a knot better without the rig. That should do it. It'll have to."

"The engine is running well after your hard push across?? David quizzed.

"Well, Jake replied scratching at his chin, "Yesterday I used my last Racor fuel filter and the last of the whale oil seems a bit buggy, but it should be fine for what we need today."

He went on, "Now, we know the breeze should hold the rest of the day at between eight and twelve. Let's get out a plotting sheet and draw up our plan of action. We've got one chance to take out that frigate without killing Connie, but it'll take very careful timing."

As David turned away Jake muttered, "I hope Connie remembers her flags."

Twenty minutes later they had a scheme on paper.

Jake finished saying, "Remember, David, all you need to do is keep the damned ship focused on you, and stay out of range of her cannons. Your radar should help with that. It would be a lucky shot for them to hit you over about a mile."

David then asked, "How much fuel have you aboard?"

'Tanks are nearly dry. There's that one barrel of whale oil below. It'll take two of us to strain it into the tank."

David helped Jake to strain the last barrel of whale oil into the nearly dry fuel tank. It was dirtier than the former oil, but Jake was sure it would work for the task planned.

"Wphew, stinks in here," commented David as they finished.

"Wish we could use the acyletene torch for the next job," Jake said, "but I used the last of it fixing the hole that damned frigate blew through the hull. We'll need bolt cutters and careful timing for the next part."

"Are you sure you want to do this to your *Anne Marie?*"

"Of course. It's the only way we have a chance at the frigate. And, this damned boat is a liability in this century anyway. She's worthless after today in any case. Best we start with the mizzen."

They ran the mizzen staysail halyard to the main clew and tightened it securely.

"Up you go," Jake pulled David swiftly to the top of the mizzen mast in the boson's chair with a heavy bolt cutter.

Then, "thwang," the triatic stay yielded to the bolt cutter.

David dropped swiftly to the deck.

Jake turned the boat crosswise to the swells, *Anne Marie* was now rolling thirty degrees each way as David cut all the stays and knifed through all the sheets to the smaller rear mast.

Jake was watching him carefully.

"Next swell," Jake cried.

As the ketch leaned over to port David cut the last remaining starboard stay with the bolt cutter while Jake threw off the staysail halyard. With a huge crack the varnished spruce mast snapped at the deck and toppled over the port railing with a huge splash, taking the port lifelines down with it. As it had been cut free in advance, it simply sank out of sight under the weight of all its metal hardware. As a last cut, David made short work of the port upper stay after the mast had gone.

"She's a sloop now. Mainmast next," Jake said grimly.

This one was more difficult and dangerous since this mast was much larger and heavier. A mis-step could cause a snapping stainless steel stay to cut off a leg! But, as they had with the mizzen mast, the two men used the various halyards to 'sister' the primary stainless stays, first cutting the stainless wire mast supports that were less important. After twenty minutes of hard and careful work this mast too yielded to a roll to port, and crashed over the side taking all its sails and rigging with it. It too sank quickly.

Anne Marie rode higher in the water, having lost nearly a ton of rigging.

With a heavy heart and great worries David called for the boat and allowed himself to be rowed back to *Constance* where he briefed Phillip on Jake's crazy plan.

CHAPTER TWENTY-ONE

Anne woke to the sound of drums and fifes calling the ship again to quarters. She was exhausted.

She had to quickly throw on her now filthy duck trousers, which had been washed only in seawater for six weeks, and her scratchy rough cotton blouse. Her hair had grown; she shoved the stringy and matted mess under a knit cap and dashed for the ladder down to the ever stinking orlop deck. She'd learned to move fast when quarters were beat or the walls to her cabin would come crashing down before she was even dressed.

As her foot hit the top step down to the bilges she heard Aaron on the quarterdeck above yelling, "Damned if it ain't that same bloody Yankee topsail schooner again."

Connie's heart leapt as it did almost every day when she heard the same.

She didn't continue down the ladders to the stinking orlop, instead she slipped behind a 12 pounder cannon until the rushing team of sailors had torn down the cabin bulkheads to make a clear gun deck. Before the gunners appeared again she dashed into the captain's tiny sleeping cabin; the only place where the bulkheads were not dismantled. There she could look out through one narrow stern window on the starboard side of the frigate.

She was sure that Aaron would stay on deck, and not catch her here. He never came below when the ship was at quarters; she should be safe. Connie just wanted to see her ship again and to know again that David was near.

"Whereaway be that damned brig?" yelled Aaron to the mizzentop.

Connie couldn't hear the reply.

John Aaron was excited. He finally, for a second time, had the weather gauge of the Yankee brig that had bedeviled him across the ocean. The breeze had freshened with the dawn, and *Reliant* was full and by on a reach, sliding ever so gently down wind towards the hapless Yankee.

"Be we gaining on 'er?" Connie heard Aaron bellow ten minutes later.

She was nearly right under a small skylight from the captain's cabin to the quarterdeck so she could hear his every command. She heard nothing for awhile. It could only be that Aaron had gone up the mizzen with his telescope.

Then she heard Aaron command, "Bear off 2 points. Sheet home t'gallents and staysails."

Connie felt *Reliant* settle down to a reach and pick up speed.

"Damn, Willright!" she heard Aaron exclaim shortly later, "We're finally gaining on that cursed Brig! T'won't be long and we have 'em almost under our guns. Aye but I'll love to sail her into Portsmouth as our prize."

"Sail ho," came a cry from the mast head, "Looks a coastal fisherman."

"Willright!" thundered Aaron.

Moments later she heard the Lieutenant rely, "Aye, aye, sir."

"Look ye at the new sail and tell me ye'r thoughts. If it be a simple fishing smack we'll let 'em be."

Connie heard some minutes later Willright reporting, "Appears not a sail at all, sir. Looks to be a dismasted fisherman. It's barely on the horizon, p'rhps four miles. Shall we try for a rescue? Must mean we're close to Portsmouth."

"Aye," replied Aaron, "mark it on the chart. We'll see to it after we win our prize."

He then forgot the small wreck, focusing on the Yankee brig that had bedeviled him for six weeks.

"We'll sail them down, whichever way they turn. The wind is finally favoring us," Aaron exulted. "Tell ye'r gunners not to hole her, I'll not want her sunk. Save her for prize money, lads."

Connie heard Willright's voice again from above, "Captain, sir, she's making a signal."

"Can ye make it out?"

"Aye sir. Appears to be that damned Yankee yellow flag with the snake, and it has a signal below it. Flags read C 1 Q D K."

"Masthead," Aaron yelled, "see ye any other sail 'cept the brig?"

"Nae, sir," came the faint reply.

Connie, hearing this, was startled to realize that signal could only be meant for her. Certainly, her father's yellow Gazden flag followed by a C 1 could only be for herself. But, what the hell, she wracked her brain, did Q D K mean? She sat down on Aaron's gimbaled bed in the tiny cabin trying to puzzle it out.

Aboard *Constance*, Phillip was at the helm while David was in the cabin below watching the radar repeater. The ship was deliberately oversheeted so it would sail poorly, allowing the large frigate to slowly gain on them. *Reliant* was now just over three miles directly to windward; both ships were slicing along on a nearly parallel course at just over ten knots.

"Let her come closer," David called to Phillip. "Jake is almost in position."

"If ye time this wrong we'll be in for it," replied Phillip. "Hope ye'r father in law is right in his guess as to what that ship will do."

"Bring her just a little closer. I want to see when they fire on us," replied David.

Phillip headed up into the wind by a few degrees, both ships drawing imperceptibly closer. Suddenly, as the frigate rose up on a wave, there was a spurt of black smoke followed by a boom. A splash appeared about two hundred yards off the beam of *Constance*.

"Close enough," yelled Phillip.

"Hold your heading," David replied.

He was watching both the frigate and the *Anne Marie* on the radar repeater. Their next turn must be exactly timed.

"Aye, hold her steady here," he called to Phillip, "We need Jake to get in place. Damned frigate needs to pass less than a mile ahead of him. They need think they've got a chance at us, and not even notice him."

Philip was increasingly nervous. He had someone grab the helm and he popped into the aft cabin where David was plotting bearings on the radar.

"David, thee'll get us all killed," he started. "One broadside hits is from that stinking frigate and we'll be a pile of splinters."

David shot back sharply, "Damnit Phillip, get back on the helm. I'll not let them line-up for a broadside, but they need to think they can. We may take a hit or two, but only if we're unlucky, and then it'll be from long range."

"Come on, Man," he continued grimly, "follow my plan. My wife's over there. And, act sharp when I tell you."

Phillip nodded, climbing back to the wheel.

In a few minutes David called up, "Okay, Phil, loosen sheets and pick up a knot or two. She's come close enough."

As Phil's crew dashed to slack the staysails and trim the topsail and courser there were another two booms from their port quarter. A moment later there was a large splash just under their stern and a neat round hole round appeared in the spanker.

"They've got our range, David!" Phillip yelled.

"Hold ye'r course."

David allowed the frigate to continue to draw closer.

All eyes on the frigate were awaiting the moment when they could get the Yankee with the offensive yellow flag in range and cowered her under their guns. They knew their first shots at extreme range had done little. They needed to get 300 yards closer. All hands strained to pull the utmost from *Reliant's* rig.

Of course, nobody noticed that the dismasted fishing smack had vanished.

Jake was circling in behind the two racing ships under his own diesel power. With all masts gone, *Anne Marie* was barely visible from the frigate, and besides, nobody was looking back over the stern for a boat with no sails. Jake was counting on that.

On *Constance* David hollered "Now, Phillip, harden her up."

The handy little ship reacted immediately. The crew was standing at the sheets as the helm went down. The barkentine turned in her own length and pointed forty-five degrees into the wind. They would barely cross the bow of the thundering frigate, but the frigate had no guns directly in her bow anyway.

BOOM!

All sixteen cannons on the port side of *Reliant* fired at once. A sheet of water splashed up just yards from *Constance,* exactly where she would have been had she not turned! Two cannon balls bounced off the water and blew holes in the lower staysail.

"Timed that damned close," Phillip shouted.

David grinned back, "Worked just fine. Now, watch them sheet in and try to catch us. As soon as she's dead astern of us slack sheets. Match her course and sail at her speed. Jake said it would drive them nuts."

David then keyed the VHF and spoke into it, "Jake, are you in place?"

"Yes, David, but you've got to slow them down as much as you can. Just keep the frigate pointed as far upwind as you can. She's a poor sailor on that heading, and that's just what I need."

David then hollered up the hatch to Phillip, "Over trim up your sails, Phillip. We'll need your best to slow her down. Not too fast, now, just sail. Try to keep that Brit thinking they can maybe catch us, but keep 'em dead astern of us so they can't get a gun to bear."

On *Reliant* Aaron was pleased to see two holes appear on one of the sails on the fleeing Yankee after his broadside. Damned little barkentine had changed course the moment he'd fired his broadside or he'd have stopped them cold. And, double-damn, the Yankee had hardened up.

"Hands to braces," he yelled. "Hard on the wind boys and match her course. Don't let her get away again. We'll have her for supper, we will."

"Bow chasers," Aaron hollered forward, "train ye'r guns carefully. We'll yaw when ye'r ready and give thee a shot. First larboard then starboard. Gold Doubloons to the gun crew who hits her with a disabling shot."

"Watch her topsails, Phillip," David warned, carefully watching the large frigate closing behind *Constance*.

"When her foretop luffs you'll know the bastard will yaw upwind and fire her starboard chaser. So, when you see a luff, count to ten then put your helm down. And, if we see her begin to veer to port, put your helm up after a count of eight."

"Aye, David. With him havin' but two guns as bow chasers, and since he's got to change course twenty degrees to shoot them, or 'ee'l shoot off his own bowsprit, I can keep him dancing for awhile."

"Sheets and braces" he hollered, "bring her up two points."

The frigate followed, heeling more sharply over as her sails were drawn tighter, yet with the dirty bottom she made more leeway. Worse, as the fleeing Yankee was directly on their bow, Aaron now really could not get a gun to bear. He'd just have to trust to the skill of his bow chaser gunners. He was hoping that they could just knock down a spar, or sever a halyard. Any little damage would stall the fleeing Yankee and make her his.

Constance was heeled over to starboard with her lea rail buried in the foam. The mainsail was again drawn in too far, and the staysails were deliberately too loose, causing her to heel over and gripe at a weather helm. This trim kept her slowed down to match the frigate's speed, but the fast schooner was straining at the poor trim.

David had shut off his radar since it was now useless at this close range. He was at the windward rail looking for *Anne Marie* through his powerful binoculars. Aah, he saw her, just a spec on the horizon appearing over the stern of the frigate on a converging course.

He glanced up at his main mast and noted the signal flags still whipping in the breeze. C 1 Q D K. Oh, but he hoped that Connie had seen them and had received the critical message.

"Hold your heading, Phil" he hollered, "Jake will need awhile to get in position."

For another half hour the two sailing ships thrashed through the ocean on a following course, the fast schooner sailing deliberately slowly to match the straining frigate's speed with the larger ship's sixteen pound bow chaser cannons unable to reach the little brig. Every time the frigate tried to bear up to take a shot, Phillip counted to eight and did the same. The frigate tried two fruitless shots from both guns before they just gave up and chased.

THWACK. A furrow appeared in the deck by David's foot. Damn, he realized those Brits had sharpshooters with muskets in the fore-top.

""Slack sheets a bit, Phil. They're close enough for muskets."

Aboard *Reliant* Aaron had been fuming for an hour. No matter what he tried he could not gain on that damned Yankee pirate. It just stayed where it was just within gunshot range on his bow, matching his speed. It still appeared that the Yankee could not outrun *Reliant*. If the brig were to try to bear off downwind the frigate would quickly blast her out of the water with a full broadside. Aaron had no choice but to chase after the barkentine. It appeared a stalemate. Perhaps, Aaron thought, he could chase the Yankee all the way to England.

Glancing quickly over the rear of the frigate, Aaron saw a large splash on top of a wave. Whale, he thought, and focused again on his prey ahead.

But when he looked back at the Yankee he was shocked to see her suddenly pick up speed and charge ahead of his straining frigate. After an anxious ten minutes, the Yankee had pulled ahead of the frigate, almost out of cannon shot range. Then, amazingly, Aaron was shocked to see them trim sails and shoot closer to the wind, as if to finally give him a clean shot with his larboard bow chaser.

Aaron briefly wondered if that Yankee had hit something, or if they had simply made a huge mistake ? Did that fool not know that *Reliant* could simply head to the wind, bear off, and plaster him with a full broadside? If only *Reliant* were a just few yards closer.

Connie was still sitting on the little bunk listening to the details of the chase from the skylight above. She kept puzzling over the message that she was sure had been directed to her. Yes, the House Flag. And yes, C 1 would indicate her. But what could Q D K mean ?

Then, she noticed a flash of white spray out of the corner of her eye coming from the small rear window of the cabin. She looked again. She focused. Her jaw dropped in amazement! Not two hundred yards away she saw the green bow of *Anne Marie* rear up over a wave then descend in a cloud of spray! It was charging directly at the unprotected stern of the frigate at a huge rate of speed. And, there were no masts. The tallest thing on the mastless green ketch was her father, Jake, wearing his crazy old flop hat while he stood at the wheel.

Connie was sure he'd not been noticed from the Quarterdeck above her. No, they were all focused forward, to the fleeing *Constance*.

She watched transfixed as the ketch drew closer. She estimated it was crashing through the waves at twice the speed of the frigate. Yes, her Dad was going to ram *Anne Marie* directly into the stern of *Reliant*. It was less than 100 yards away and closing very fast.

She was frozen at the cabin window.

Then it was 50 yards; the chrome bowsprit railing on *Anne Marie* was pointed straight at her.

"QDK", it came to her in a flash. Quarterdeck! Of course, she instantly understood that she was told to get to the Quarterdeck, just above the captain's cabin, at the time of impact; that or she could be crushed!

She ran to the little door and yanked it open. She was about to dash out, then quickly realized that the rest of the cabin was gone. There were just grim faced sailors manning the huge guns all around her. And, they were craning their necks out of the open gun ports looking towards the front, hoarsely whispering news about the chase of the Yankee. Nobody was looking back through the windows, and *Anne* Marie was going to crash into this space in mere moments.

She dashed to the closest gun port, squeezed past a gunner unnoticed and pulled herself outside and up to a large double dead eye on the chain plates where the aftermost mizzen shrouds attached to the hull. She flattened herself to the hull and gripped the ships rigging.

David, staring transfixed over the taffrail of *Constance,* watched the frigate's bow pull ever closer. In mere moments he knew they would receive a direct impact from a well aimed cannon shot. If it hit a rudder, or even parted a critical part of his rigging the light brigantine might quickly thereafter become a dismasted hulk. Still, he did as Jake had planned, and had the ship pointed further into the wind.

He looked again through the binoculars at the wave crests just behind the laboring frigate. Yes, he saw *Anne Marie* crashing dead up-wind under full diesel power behind the unsuspecting frigate.

What a sight!

The mastless green hull was moving at top speed, seemingly over the sixteen knots that Jake had thought, creating huge clouds of spray as she crashed through each wave. He was amazed that nobody on the frigate had apparently noticed. Jake had been right; they were all focused on his *Constance* as their prey.

David's VHF, clipped in his pocket, squawked, "David, I'm in position. Impact in less than a minute. Make your move now. That will stop him fast just before he can get off a shot at you. And, if I miss, be sure to find Connie before you look for me."

David replied, "Helm's already down, Jake."

On *Reliant*, John Aaron was fuming and shaking with anger. The Yankee had again eluded the carefully aimed bow chaser with an incredibly fast dog leg turn. Before his sweating gun crew could reload the schooner would be out of range, again too far forward to hit them without shooting through their own rig.

"Back the jibs to starboard," he yelled, "shift helm."

But it was too late.

They had pointed too far into the wind to take the last shot, and the ship was thrown into irons. The square sails had caught the wind and were pushing back on the masts. *Reliant* was dead in the water, caught in 'stays'. She would have to now back around to fill her sails to resume pursuit of the Yankee.

It looked like the Yankee may have finally eluded them again.

Aaron heard a growing animal-like roar coming from behind his ship. He cast a worried glance over the taffrail; totally shocked to see what looked like a green sea monster blasting directly up-wind, with no sails, surfing over and under the waves. It was headed directly at the unprotected stern of his now immobile and wallowing ship!

"Mizzen top," screamed Aaron, "fire on that damned thing to our rear!"

The Marine Lieutenant at the mizzen top, who had been absorbed in the chase of the schooner, looked back at the captain's command, He dropped his jaw in total amazement. A green and white sea monster was crashing up-wind through the waves, aimed directly at the stern of *Reliant*! He instantly shoved his swivel carronade through 180 degrees and aimed at the green monster at point blank range. He couldn't miss, yanking the lanyard at the same moment that his fifteen troops likewise fired their muskets.

Jake was totally focused.

He had the throttle to the diesel all the way to the stops; the engine was howling and smoking at higher RPM's than it had ever been pushed. The ketch was light now with no cargo, all the barrels of fuel now gone, and no rig. She was making over seventeen knots into the Atlantic white-capped rollers, aimed directly at the stern of the frigate.

Connie was on that damned ship, and Jake would get her back. He had it all planned, right down to the life raft inflated on the stern of *Anne Marie*.

And, his elaborate plan was working.

At no more than fifty yards from the stern of the suddenly stopped and wallowing frigate he saw the gouts of gun smoke from the mizzen top. He dived to the deck as a hail of heavy bullets rang around into the decks him.

Then, with a huge crash, the cannon ball from the carronade thwaked into the front of the deckhouse. It ricocheted around the steel insides of the ketch with tremendous bangs.

Jake jumped back to his feet and straightened the helm. *Anne Marie* continued her mad dash towards the unprotected stern of the frigate; the gold gilt windows glistening above him. He braced himself against the wheel pedestal as the bow of *Anne Marie* smashed into the fragile stern of the back-winded frigate.

The green ketch didn't stop immediately. The screaming power of the 250 horse power engine at full throttle kept jamming *Anne* Marie deeper and deeper into the tortured bowels of the frigate as both ships rose, joined together, over the next wave.

John Aaron heard the carronade above him fire. He instantly recognized that he was being attacked not by a sea monster, but by the same green ketch he thought he'd left far behind in America. Shockingly, now, it had no masts and it was making a fearsome roaring sound. He saw the deckhouse on the ketch crumble as the carronade ball hit, but the terrifying green monster came charging on .

His mouth fell open. It just kept coming. He could hear the loud rumble growing to a roaring sound as the green mastless apparition charged directly into his unprotected stern at enormous speed. He pulled his two pistols from his belt and ran to the stern rail, not believing that *Reliant* was about to be rammed in her weakest spot.

CRASH!

Connie was momentarily stunned by the impact. She was almost shaken from her perch, clinging to the mizzen shrouds on the starboard side of the frigate just below the quarterdeck railing. Shaking her head she looked up, stretched and pulled herself up and over the railing, dropping through the nets of hammocks planked deck.

It was bedlam. Pieces of rigging were falling from the masts. Sails were flapping wildly above her, and men were running every direction, yelling meaningless orders. She dashed to the taffrail and saw her Dad, still standing at the wheel of *Anne Marie* less than forty feet from her. Their eyes locked.

"Jump," he yelled as he cut the life raft loose.

She started to climb over the taffrail.

Aaron picked himself up from the deck after the unbelievable crash. He looked about his ship. The force of the collision had knocked yards loose from the masts, crashing to the deck. Many of the guns had rolled over on their carriages. Many of his crew had been knocked off their feet, and others were running about to the shouts of confliction orders from bosons and gun captains.

He then looked over the stern of his ship and saw the rear two thirds of the green ketch below him. The madman who had rammed him was still standing at his large wheel. Then he saw the girl mounting the wooden rail at the rear of his ship, clasping on to the flagstaff.

"Dad," she yelled.

"Connie", the man hollered back, "Jump on down here and run to me as fast as you can. Now!"

Jake fired one shot from his .38 revolver at an officer who was reaching up to grab her by the waist.

Aaron raised one of his large pistols and aimed it at the man on the ketch. He pulled the trigger and the gun roared, but the shot went wild. He took his other pistol and aimed it at the back of the scrambling girl. As she jumped to the rail he grabbed her around her waist, pointed his second pistol at Jake and fired.

Jake fell.

"I've got thee now," Captain Aaron yelled to Jake. "I've still a loaded pistol and I'll shoot the lass unless ye drop ye'r empty gun. She's to come with us and if this ship is mortal hurt we'll get ye both to Portsmouth. I'll see thee on the gallows."

Jake let the man yell. He stood up, realizing he'd just been grazed by the bullet. Then he simply aimed the pistol and pulled his trigger again, firing another shot from his trusty revolver. The taffrail on the large ship splintered in the face of the officer.

Jake fired three more times while Connie dropped from *Reliant* and scrambled across the wrecked deck of the ketch to his side.

Aaron was shocked! How could that madman have fired man have four pistols? In any event, he knew that they had to be empty now, so he pulled his cutlass from its scabbard and leapt to the deck of the ketch, six feet below him. He landed ten feet behind the scrambling girl and ran behind her.

No, He'd not let them get away!

The second that Connie reached his side, Jake aimed carefully at the crazed officer, now just a dozen feet away brandishing a sword as he dashed through the wreckage on top of *Anne Marie*. Jake squeezed the trigger and the sword clattered away. The man stopped, holding his now bloody hand. Jake took aim at the now disarmed officer, ready to shoot his last bullet between the man's eyes.

Connie grabbed his arm saying, "Don't shoot him Dad. Captain Aaron isn't a bad guy. He's not harmed me, and he's just following his orders. Let him go, okay?"

"Get back to your ship," Jake said to the younger man who was standing on the wrecked cabin top of *Anne Marie*. Jake noticed the ripped blue coat with faded gold trim over white trousers, the livid scar on the man's face under long black hair blowing in the wind.

"Look to your crew," Jake continued in a lower voice. "I've no more quarrels with you. Look to your crew and get in your boats. You'll sink in less than five minutes. And, best you don't try to explain what happened here today; you'll never be believed."

As Aaron watched, with Willright and a score of Marines looking from the ship above him, Jake took Connie's hand and led her to the stern. He pushed her gently inside the inflated life raft and slid it into the sea, jumping aboard himself. As they drifted clear of the two jammed together ships Jake took a small plastic box from his pocket and pushed a red button.

"What's that, Dad?" Connie asked, amazed.

"Timer. The anchor locker of *Anne Marie* is packed with the last of the plastique. Both those ships need to totally vanish without a trace. They'll blow in five minutes. Here, take this paddle. And look, here comes David in *Constance*."

He continued, "I hope that Captain can get his crew into their boats and safely to Portsmouth, but with *Anne Marie* on the bottom they can't speak of her. They'd be laughed out of their Navy. I wonder what that Officer will tell his Court of Inquiry?" he smiled.

CHAPTER TWENTY-TWO

Jake was shaking the little switch. More than five minutes had passed, and David, aboard *Constance* was tossing Connie a line. They'd be aboard in moments.

Jake climbed out of the life raft, puncturing its rubber sides as he stepped to the deck of *Constance*. The raft sank.

"Hurry, Jake," David rushed to his side, hugging Connie, "Look."

He was pointing upwind at the horizon and, yes, three clouds of enormous sails had appeared over the horizon the distance, heading towards them and the joined wreck of *Reliant* and *Anne Marie,* which was just a half mile up-wind of where they were hove-to.

"We've got to get underway."

"Not so fast," Jake cautioned. "Look. Those wrecks aren't sinking. My transmitter didn't work, and they're afloat and they still look stuck together."

Aboard the wrecks Aaron had climbed back up to his own quarterdeck. He and a group of his crew were staring down at what appeared to be the same green ketch they'd been chasing for a half year, only she was dismasted and almost half her length was jammed inside their ship. The green wreck was making a fearsome growling howling sound, and water was boiling up under the wreck's stern. He shook his head wondering what was holding that wreck jammed inside *Reliant*. Why were they not sinking?

He then remembered that the crazy man, who'd claimed to be the girl's father, had said he only had five minutes. No, that couldn't be true. But, the crazed man had thrown Connie into that orange topped ball. He'd jumped in with her and it was drifting fast down wind away from Aaron. And, yes, the Yankee barkentine that he'd seen for the past weeks was 'rounding up to meet the orange ball.

He shook his head, still somewhat dazed. What was that loud roaring and heavy vibration coming from under his feet? What the devil? Why was the water behind the dismasted ketch boiling? In fact, it seemed the ketch was somehow pushing *Reliant* against the pressure of her backed sails into the wind. Indeed, the two ships were not moving at all with the green wreck jamming her nose ever deeper inside the stern of his frigate. That he'd been told they'd all sink in five minutes, and that was almost five minutes past

His ship, from his viewpoint, if he looked only forward, appeared mostly undamaged. The crew was standing in groups looking dazed and doing nothing. They could clearly hear the loud roaring of the ketch, and they could feel the joined vessels plow slowly over the waves, but no one seemed to know what to do.

Nor did Aaron.

He thought for a moment, then took the only action that seemed to make sense.

"All hands, slack sheets. Furl sails. Willright, jump down on that ketch and keep us pointed dead up-wind."

"But there's a growling dragon inside that ketch," Williamswright sputtered in terror.

"Sail Ho," came a cry from the masthead. "Three sails, hull up. Appears two frigates and a three decker."

Aaron shouted at Williamswright, "Hop to it man! If whatever pushes that ketch will keep pushing, we may keep from sinking. What a prize she'll be if we can bring that devil ship to the King!"

Williamswright reluctantly scrambled over the stern of the frigate and picked his way over the shattered cabin top of *Anne Marie*. He tentatively grabbed the cold silver wheel, pulling it over to the left. He found he was able to point the two wrecks more directly into the wind and waves. He ignored the thundering and shaking from the deck coming through the soles of his boots. He just steered as he was ordered, white faced and shaking, swallowing the terror he felt.

As the sails on the frigate were clewed up the two joined wrecks began to make headway. Willright was able to keep them headed into the wind and waves, pointed at the approaching three friendly ships.

Aboard *Constance* Jake was shaking the small transmitter box. He was trying to think why it had not worked? The explosives in *Anne Marie* should have blown. He wasn't paying any attention to Connie, hugging David, or to the schooner. He snapped off the back of the switch and peered inside.

"Damn!" he exclaimed. "Battery is probably dead. And, I gave the other one to Stephen."

"David, he yelled, "have you got any double A's aboard ? Blast, but there's a package on the shelf on *Anne Marie*."

David replied, "No, Jake. Of course we've nothing to use them for. Look, Jake, we've got to turn and run! There's three large ships coming right towards us. That wreck has got to founder shortly anyway."

Jake took a long look at the wreck.

"I don't think so, David. Look. They have a helmsman on *Anne Marie* and the engine is still running flat out. That's why it's not sinking. The engine is holding the ships jammed together. Probably has hours of fuel still left, so if the diesel doesn't blow itself up it could push the wrecks all the way to England. We've got to break them apart."

"What if we harden-up and ram them?" he asked. "They certainly can't get a full broadside shot at us, the rear guns on the Frigate are knocked all askew."

"Dad," Connie said, then louder, "DAD!"

"Yes, darling", Jake finally looked at her.

"You need an AA battery?"

"My God, yes! Have you got any?"

"Actually I've two new ones for my electric toothbrush, if my toilet kit is still where I left it."

"Run, Girl!"

"David," he continued to snap orders, "Harden us up. We'll need to get within a quarter mile to be sure the transmitter works. Then we'll need wait another five minutes for the timer. How far are those ships? They look to be less than an hour away."

David yelled orders to Phil to get *Constance* moving up-wind towards the wreck saying, "Take close tacks so you stay clear of the guns on that frigate. She still has teeth."

He then dashed to his radar repeater and re-emerged next to Jake at the wheel.

"Those three ships are just eight miles upwind. And, in this breeze they're moving at nearly twelve knots. They'll be in firing range in a half hour, and long before that they might fan out to keep us from escaping."

Connie dashed to Jake with her hand out saying, "Here Dad, two double A's."

Jake fumbled one into the box.

"David, I'm off to the bowsprit. Close the wreck until you see their musket balls splash just ahead of us, then turn and run like hell. I'm just going to have to trust that this damned thing will work now; wish it had an indicator light."

"How will we know if it worked?" asked Connie.

"We won't until exactly five minutes after we turn. If it hasn't blown, then we'll need to turn back and ram the wrecks where they join to make sure it all sinks."

He continued more quietly, "If they then capture us, that may make us all prisoners of the British, but that's better than giving them *Anne Marie* . Cross your fingers."

Jake dashed to the bow of *Constance* and climbed to the tip of the bowsprit. He started jamming on the red button as soon as the barkentine was pointed back towards the wrecks. Five minutes later, when the first musket shot appeared at the mizzen top of the frigate, Phillip turned *Constance* away again.

Jake changed batteries as they turned, and keep pushing the red button as they hauled down wind.

Aaron was focused on the three ships sailing towards him. He was smiling in full confidence that he could keep this double wreck afloat long enough to at least get senior witnesses to the green ketch, and maybe even salvage some of it. Who knows, he gloated to himself, perhaps we can even drive the wreck onto a beach. Still, just in case, he had his crew all on deck and his boats righted.

Then, he heard a yell from the mizzen top, "Captain, behind us."

He wheeled around and was shocked to see the brig hard on the wind slicing through the waves towards his barely creeping wreck.

"Mizzen top, muskets and carronade. Stop them!"

Yet, just as the bowsprit of the brigantine came into musket range, the ship turned tail and scooted away.

Aaron smiled broadly, visions of his upcoming fame danced into his head. He had driven them off and both rescue and validation was at hand..

Jake waited five minutes. Nothing happened. The wrecks, still joined, were still being pushed by the roaring diesel in *Anne Marie,* with a large cloud of blue engine smoke still blowing down wind.

"Bring her about again, David," Jake said grimly. "I'm gonna have to ram them."

He continued, "Get the boats launched, and get Connie and the crew ready to jump in as soon as the cannon balls get close. If those Brits don't kill me before I ram them, I'll probably see you in Portsmouth in a day or so. You can be sure they'll pick you up."

When Aaron looked back again he saw the black barkentine with the large yellow flag again come about, hard on the wind. And, again it pointed directly at his wallowing two ships. The black ship scooted upwind until it was directly abeam, then slacked sheets. It picked up speed, and charged directly at him.

"Larboard guns," he yelled, "Load and run out."

The gun crews ran to their cannons. They straightened the few that were knocked from their carriages and tamped in fresh balls.

"Wait until ye're certain of a full broadside hit," Aaron screamed. "We need to stop her."

The black ship tore closer. When Jake thought they were within cannon shot range he had the boats drawn close to the lea rail where they bobbed and crashed against the side of the fast moving ship.

"David, get Connie safely into one of those boats," Jake yelled.

David replied grimly, "I'd be happier if she were to slip overboard in a life jacket. She's had a rough time already, and we don't want to harm the baby."

'Okay. Be ready. You'll have to move fast as soon as they try a ranging shot."

With the small crew, David, Connie and Phillip all huddling under the lea rail, the black barkentine tore through the ocean drawing quickly closer to the frigate with *Anne Marie's* big diesel still pushing the wrecks through the waves. The scream of the tortured diesel grew louder as they closed in. Jake could see Williamswright, still holding the wheel on *Anne Marie* as clouds of black diesel smoke continued to gush from her stern.

Aaron watched the oncoming Yankee carefully. He was pleased to notice that the deck of his ship was more steady than usual, being pushed evenly forward by the thrust of the green wreck jammed into his stern. Twelve of his cannons on the larboard side had been righted. They were trained on the approaching ship. The gunners held their slow matches just above the touchholes.

"One shot for effect," Aaron commanded.

KABOOM. A cannon hole appeared through the Yankee's flying jib.

"Now, Jake shouted, "Overboard fast all of you."

He was holding the big wheel on *Constance,* keeping the brigantine aimed directly at the joint between the two stricken ships not two hundred yards ahead.

Suddenly, there was silence. The diesel had stopped.

At the same moment all eleven remaining loaded cannons on the frigate fired, but without the thrust of the engine in *Anne Marie* the frigate had lurched just backward enough to throw off the gunner's aim. The broadside crashed into the ocean with the closest ball smashing through the empty longboat next to *Constance*.

Jake reacted instantly. He spun the wheel, turning the barkentine directly down wind before another broadside could be loaded.

David ran to his side.

"What happened?" he asked.

Jake rubbed his jaw and replied, "Either the diesel filters clogged, or the engine threw a rod. Either way it simply stopped. Let's watch what happens now."

Reliant's bow fell off the top of the next swell, but without the thrust of the large engine, *Anne Marie* kept riding up the same wave. The motion loosened her hold into the stern of the frigate. Seconds later, as the frigate's bow rose up to the next swell, the mast less ketch kept going down the former wave. One more large wave did the trick; the two ships finally broke apart.

Anne Marie sank in less than a minute. Her entire bow was now wide open to the sea. She just kept pointed down; her large bronze propeller was slowly turning as she dove under the waves.

Reliant took longer, but with her transom ripped wide open she slid backwards into the deep ocean in minutes. Through binoculars it appeared to Jake that the crew had clamored clear of the wreck before it sank, and were climbing into the boats, waiting for the approaching ships to rescue them.

Constance fled east under full sail.

CHAPTER TWENTY-THREE

It was the best food Connie thought she'd had ever eaten. She'd been forcing herself to choke-down appalling garbage for weeks, and here she was just finishing the best baked cod she'd ever devoured. One of the crew had caught it crossing the banks, and it had been frozen. With it were roasted potatoes, yes canned but still terrific, and a string bean casserole. And, to top it off, a bottle of her favorite Fetzer Chardonnay.

She, her dad, David and Captain Phil were just finishing when Phil spoke up, "Didn't look like a huge blast to me, but it sure took 'em down quick."

David said, "Well, *Anne Marie* was gone in an instant. I'll never forget seeing her prop spinning in the air just before she drove under. Still, the frigate just kinda settled. Did you see that the crew got off?"

Jake leaned back and said thoughtfully, "Sure appeared that that they were all in boats just as we turned. I'd guess that Captain had them ready just in case."

"What will they tell the Admiralty?" Phillip asked, "Will the secret of our little ship get out?"

"Sure," Connie giggled, "John Aaron is going to tell the British Navy that a green sea dragon monster swam up the tail of his pretty frigate and ate it with a bolt of fire. Haah, no way. He'll swear his crew to secrecy and claim the seams parted or something like that."

"What about your crew, Phillip?" Jake queried. "They too need to keep this entire voyage a deep secret. Can I offer them all a large bounty, like a hundred gold pounds per man?"

Phil thought for a moment.

"What they'd really like, Jake, is for thee to sell us *Constance* and pay for her outfitting as a privateer. We'd need eight long nines per side, and that will come dear. Still, with that, this ship will earn ten times her value as long as the War lasts a year. I'm sure that Stephen can arrange a Letter of Marque."

" It's not my boat," replied Jake, "its Connie's."

David spoke up, "I'm sorry, Connie, but I've thought about it. We can't take this ship back to Pensacola. The Colonel and our friends know otherwise, but too many locals there know her as a feared pirate. We'll just have to move all your things to *Martha*."

"Whatever you say, David. *Martha* is lovely. I just want to get home to Pensacola. But now, I just can't keep my eyes open."

David and Connie walked back to their comfortable private cabin. They were climbing into the large double bed when they heard the crew yelling from the waist of the brig, "Hurray for Captain Phillip! Hurray for Commodore Jake!"

As Connie was just drifting off to sleep with David's head on her breast she felt a tiny flutter deep in her stomach.

"Yes" she whispered to her husband, "the baby will be just fine.

EPILOG

The mason was replacing the north and original chimney to the Shaw mansion. It was a work of restoration that had been ordered months ago by Mr. Shaw, before he had been lost at sea.

The two hundred year old mortar holding the chimney together had simply begun to fall to dust, and the insurers of the old colonial home had insisted on a rebuilt chimney from the ground up. Mr. Shaw had required that the original stones be dis-assembled, new mortar applied and the chimney re-assembled in exactly the same pattern. Such restorations by the area wealthy folks kept this master craftsman very handsomely employed.

Clank! The tip of the mason's cole chisel bounced back at him. He was truly surprised; he'd never found any metal in an antique chimney.

He got out a smaller stone chisel and carefully chipped at the stubborn stone. He loosened it and finally he worked it out. Surprisingly he found an empty hole behind the stone. He dug deeper to see if something else was in there. Working more carefully he chipped the mortar from the surrounding stones and dropped them carefully from the ladder to the soft grassy earth below him.

He saw a faint glint of metal.

An hour later he slid his trowel around more loosened stones and carefully extracted a metal box that had been completely encased in the stones and mortar of the chimney. It was located right where the stonework sloped in at the second floor level.

He shook his head at finding such an oddity, knowing it could only have been placed when the chimney was originally built. He shrugged, telling himself that he'd seen other strange things from disassembled houses. Whatever this box contained, yes, he quickly realized that he should take it to Mrs. Shaw right away.

He descended the ladder and walked around the screened porch, past the heated swimming pool and across the circular driveway, kicking through the fall leaves. He knocked on the large oak double door, metal box in hand, and asked the maid for Mrs. Shaw.

Martha came to the door.

Jake had been gone now for almost six months and she had reconciled herself to his and Connie's loss. She caught her breath whenever something brought one or the other to mind, but the initial shock had worn off.

Today she looked quite elegant, short and trim in a woolen skirt and sweater.

"Mrs. Shaw," the mason said, "this is very strange, but I found this box encased in the chimney well behind all the surface stones. I can't imagine what it would be."

"Thank you, John," she said, "Let's have a look."

Martha took the sooty and amazingly heavy black iron box in her two hands, examining it closely from all sides. It must have weighed over ten pounds. Indeed, it had no opening, appearing to be welded closed on all sides and it offered no opening.

"John, can you carefully open this up? I'm curious, and I doubt that it could be harmful, do you think? Perhaps there's something of value inside. Certainly is strange to find a sealed box buried in our chimney, but some of the Shaw ancestors did strange things, and some were in questionable businesses."

"Just a minute. Maam. I have a hacksaw."

It took the mason over a half hour to carefully cut one end off the iron box. As he finally bent it open, he could see a large package sealed in some sort of wax tied together in string wedged inside the box.

He re-approached the front door and again knocked.

"Mrs. Shaw, here's the box. It's open and look, there's a package inside."

Martha Shaw took the box to her kitchen. She wiped off the dirt and soot with a dish towel, then pointed the open end of the box into her large sink and shook. The waxed and wrapped package slid into the dry stainless steel sink with a thud. The covering was a heavy paper sealed with wax or tar, and it was almost as hard as cement. It took Martha quite awhile to carefully pry an end flap open with a butter knife. Then the rest came away easily.

It was a manuscript, and clearly very old.

Opening it further she was shocked to tears! It was a hand-written manuscript in Jake's own crabbed hand writing. There could be no mistake, could there?

She remembered the funeral services they had had for Jake and Connie just five months ago. Over five hundred people had attended, and she still had the last live preserver from *Anne Marie* locked in a chest.

What, she was stunned, was this?

She sank to her tiled kitchen floor and simply stared at the package, not yet even reading the words. Then she scooped it all up and carried it to her favorite spot, her screened porch overlooking a few knurled old apple trees with Long Island Sound in the background. She unfolded the top sheet and read.

It started:

My Dearest Martha,

The year is 1802. I am sixty- seven years old, and in fair health for an old guy with no teeth, and suffering arthritis with no aspirin. Connie and David are also doing fine, and they have five grown children. Yes, I am a grandfather too.

I know you will receive this some months after I've gone, for certainly the mason will find it in the chimney. We're just finishing that same chimney for the first time now, and I know its restoration was ordered before I left for Ft. Lauderdale.

Many years ago I promised Connie, to get word of our survival to you, and I hit upon this as the best way. It's likely the only way.

Martha, I still do not know how we got lost; for lost indeed we were, but in time not place. Yes, I am gone from you and from all we had together, but Connie, David and I did not perish in that storm so many years ago. No, we got displaced in time.

I know you'll have to think about that for a little bit, but somehow it did happen. We did not perish, and, I have lived a full life here in this time. I may even live awhile longer. Still, I will be long gone by the time you read this, albeit you can find me under the oldest stone in the family plot.

The enclosed package is the Log of the first voyage of my last "Anne Marie". Nobody will believe it, so it's just for you, and I know you'll keep it just for yourself. It's best that way.

Indeed, if you read the archives of the Shaw Family that we've kept so well preserved in the 'relic trunk' you can read of the life I've lived, and of the Shaw Family descendants. No, there's none of that in the enclosed document, this is simply the tale of how we got here and what we did while the last "Anne Marie" was still afloat.

You have the only record of this amazing history. You'll know now from the histories of our family that we've shared together that I've indeed become my own ancestor.

With Love, and Regret for all that we did not share together. As we've discussed, you too need go onward and enjoy a full life.

Now, here's the 'rest of the story'.

Jake

Made in the USA
Charleston, SC
14 April 2012